SIGN OF THE DRAGON

SIGN OF THE DRAGON

A Tigress Publishing Book

ISBN: 978-0-9801510-5-3
0-9801510-5-8
Library of Congress Control Number: 2009932916
Printed in the United States of America

Book Design & Original Cover Illustration: Steve Montiglio
Editor: Amelia Boldaji

10 9 8 7 6 5 4 3 2 1

For my wife, Lesley, whose encouragement and unwavering support has made this dream possible.

The Navy sailor and the government agent made

an unlikely pair as they cautiously worked their way through Seattle's Interbay railway yard, crawling over grease-caked train couplings, and sliding through open boxcars. The agent's haphazard raingear and galoshes contrasted sharply with the sailor's wool pea coat, dress blues, and spit-shined shoes. The night's rainfall, which the Northwest seemed to get more than its share of, turned out to be a blessing for them. The heavy drops chattered on the metal rooftops of queued-up boxcars and helped cover the sound of their footsteps as they crunched through the graveled rail beds. Bone-breaking danger lay ahead if the yard's heavy hitting railroad watchmen mistook them for hobos and chased them with ax handles, eager to inflict a beating. But those risks were insignificant compared to the punishments the White Dragon would dispense if her spies found the pair snooping through the cargo destined for Japan.

Because it was a small island nation with no ore deposits of its own, Japan was forced to import what it could, often in the form of scrap metal. Its approach to re-cycling provided welcome work in cities like Seattle. Japan's hunger for munitions grade brass made it the most sought after of all

1

metals. Chinese-Americans with a vested interest in China's welfare tried to thwart the exportation of metal bound for Japan. They were often seen picketing Japanese ships in American harbors.

As the war between the U.S. and Japan grew more imminent, President Roosevelt embargoed the exportation of scrap steel to Japan, but an oversight failed to cover metal that had been reduced to ingots. The White Dragon was passionate that her cargo make it onto the Hiye Maru. In addition to the steel there would be three railcars chock full of navy shell casings—invaluable brass. But if brass were discovered under the steel ingots, Port authorities would impound the entire shipment.

Despite the heavy rain, Kenny Jessup took off his Cracker Jack hat and hid it inside his navy coat, afraid its brightness might draw attention that could be deadly. He stepped over a coupling next to the last set of boxcars and eased himself down to the gravel. He pressed his back against the end of one car while he waited for Jamie Chan to slide down next to him.

Jessup and Chan had met for the first time a few hours earlier, after Jessup contacted Navy Intelligence to tip them to something he thought was more dangerous than the usual graft and petty theft at the Navy piers. A few days earlier, Jessup had noticed three large gondola cars full of brass being towed by a locomotive out the north gate toward the Interbay rail yards. He had come to expect a certain amount of larceny, but this went thousands of dollars beyond the norm. He sought out the Division's lead NCO, and reported that there was no paperwork authorizing disposal to a private vendor, but he was told to mind his own business. The following morning the section chief's scolding was even more severe. Was Jessup trying to create trouble for a man taking care of a few loose ends before retirement?

Angry and disgusted Jessup took his lunch break early and wandered across the street to Ship's Restaurant to call Naval Intelligence on the payphone.

Jamie Chan was about the same age as Jessup. They didn't discuss his motivations or Naval Intelligence contacts, but it was clear he had no love for Japan and what it had done to his people, the Chinese. Chan swore Jessup to secrecy and then briefed him on what would likely happen to the brass. It was far more serious than grand theft of Navy property; Naval Intelligence had evidence that someone was shipping large quantities of brass from Seattle to Japan, helping arm its war machine.

The men quickly conceived a plan to find the missing rail cars, check for a waybill or manifest, document what they found as best they could, and report back to Chan's handler. Naval Intelligence would then contact Port authorities to sidetrack this dangerous sham.

Jessup had never heard of the White Dragon or her network of spies until Chan suggested she was behind the operation, but if she really existed and was as terrible as claimed, he didn't want any trouble with her or her little army. The railroad watchmen were scary enough. Still, when Jessup joined the Navy he'd sworn to protect his home and country, and he knew that might mean personal risk. More was at stake than just their two lives: the fate of three nations could turn on what they might find in the forty-foot railcars that were stashed in the back of the immense rail yard.

Chan lowered himself next to Jessup, pressing his backside against the opposite railcar. He stuck his head out to survey the line of open gondola cars on the side spur, and turned back to face Jessup.

"There's about a dozen coupled together. They all look pretty much the same," Chan said.

Jessup considered this for a moment, and then peeked out at the queue of cars, squinting up and down the line. "We'll have to check the card racks on the end of them, see if they'll tell us anything," he replied. A thundering clang pierced the night several tracks behind where they were. It was immediately followed by the high-pitched screech of wheels being pushed against their will along the rails. Chan grabbed Jessup's arm. Jessup forced a grin. "Relax. It's just a yard locomotive coupling boxcars," the sailor said. Chan released his grip but continued his hyper vigilance.

After a moment Jessup placed his hand on Chan's back and nodded toward the far line of cars. The men darted across the open ground and wedged their bodies in between two of the gondolas. Jessup pulled out his navy issued flashlight, cupped his hand around the lens, and held it over the waybill card. Chan acted as lookout, while Jessup read out loud. "*Destination: Pier Six. Cargo: steel ingots.* This is it. Our brass is somewhere in this queue."

Jessup stepped to the side, put his toe in the steel stirrup, and pulled himself up so he could peer inside the car. "This one's got large ingots—too heavy to lift," he reported. He dropped down and repeated his climb on the next boxcar to the north. "These are the size of Idaho spuds." Playing his hunch, Jessup threw his leg over the edge of the car and sidled out on top of the load.

Chan clambered up the side of the car behind him. "What are you doing?"

"I'm going to find out if the brass is in here."

"But you can be seen!"

Jessup quickly squatted and then knelt on the pile of ingots. "All right, my uniform's so filthy now, a little more grime ain't going to hurt." He sighed with a sense of relief. "I'm new at this spying stuff, but it'll go faster if you help."

Chan joined Jessup and motioned for the sailor to lie flat on top of the ingots. Between the two of them they quickly worked out a plan: Jessup would pass the steel to Chan, who would stack it out of their way in the corner of the gondola as best he could. It took a little more than a minute for them to find what they were looking for. Jessup cupped his flashlight lens as before, and directed the light's beam into the small depression he had made. Clearly visible, the open mouth of a five-inch brass shell jutted upward, like a salmon spawning in an Alaska river. Jessup tried to lift it out of the pile, but the hole had already filled with the small ingots, making it impossible to move. He dug a little deeper and unearthed an empty forty mm shell, which was only about a foot long and weighed as much as a good hammer. Jessup tugged it free and handed it to Chan. "Jamie, we have a 'Blackout Bingo.' Our card's a winner."

Behind Chan a dark silhouette popped up over the side of the gondola and was quickly joined by another. The silent specters directed bright flashlights at the two trespassers, piercing the night as they illuminated their prey. In a heavy Asian accent a voice spoke out, "You wrong, Sailor. No Bingo for you."

Before the era of asphalt the city's downtown streets were constructed of multilayered kiln-fired bricks, a welcome replacement for the original mud and coarsely cut wooden planks that had once proclaimed to the rest of the nation the city's meager pedigree. But even with the upgrade, Seattle was a rough-cut mill and shipping town that owed its existence to lumber and prostitution. In the case of Yesler Way, one of the infant city's most infamous arterials, the bricks replaced the embedded logs that served as a skid for the virgin timber that teams of oxen pulled down the steep hill to Henry Yesler's saw mill. This timber dragging process earned the route down the steep grade its more famous nickname, Skid Row, a term that later came to symbolize hard men and hard times across all of America.

Similar were the origins of the arterial one block to the north, James Street. Unlike Yesler Way, James sprang from First Avenue—like a cedar sapling with stunted roots. It struggled up Seattle's First Hill, away from plugged sewers and the salt flats, as if competing with Yesler Way for a splash of sunlight or a breath of fresh air. The fact that James deadheaded on First Avenue gave the impression it was afraid to get too close to the foul salt water and the detritus near the mill.

Between Yesler and James sat one of the city's oldest financial institutions, the Great Pioneer Safe Deposit Bank, known regionally as the Vault. The bank proudly proclaimed that it had survived the Great Fire of 1889, a testament to its resoluteness, security, and the safety it provided to its customers and their precious valuables deposited within.

George, the elderly security guard, liked to remind customers that the bank's vault had once been at street level, but after the Great Fire the city's fathers rebuilt the town on top of the rubble, raising the streets and sidewalk levels a whole story. Subsequent visionaries looked forward to laying asphalt on top of the streets' original brick pavers, removing the old trolley rails and homogenizing the roads for smoother automobile and bus travel—feats that they had already been accomplished on Eastlake Avenue and a few other arterials.

George looked over the top of his cheaters, snapped a fold into the newspaper he'd been holding at arm's length, and greeted Alan Stewart with a smile and a nod. "You been following all this about the shootings with those Canadian bastards, Mr. Stewart?"

"I haven't read today's news, but I'm trying to stay up."

"Damn shame is what it is. That's...how many now? Four cops killed in one week—two retirees and two still on the job, plus their lieutenant's been clipped twice—both times head wounds."

"So I heard. Lieutenant Harry Frantz, wasn't it? Too bad about that. He must lead a charmed life. An inch closer and he'd have been a goner."

"Papers say he's got a hole in his jaw, lost some teeth and a piece of his tongue in that last shooting, so he can't talk yet. All he can tell is what he writes down. When he recovers poor guy'll be scarred for life, and that's too bad. He was quite the lady's man."

"You know him?"

"Oh, sure. He's got a box down here, just like all the other police."

Alan nodded thoughtfully.

George continued his musing. "We haven't had trouble like this since the Repeal, and as I recall, almost all of that involved smuggling hooch. A lot of the shooting involved Canadians, even then. People got greedy and wanted a bigger slice of the pie."

"My mother and a best friend are from the Great North. There not all bad, George."

"I didn't mean to offend."

"No offense taken, but I'm in a bit of a hurry and—"

"You don't need me to show you the way down there, do you?"

"Course not, but I'd like a private room for viewing if the one across the hall is open."

"It's unlocked, and no one's down there. It'll latch shut when you pull it closed. On your way out, just leave the door open for the next person."

"Got it."

"And don't wander off and leave your key in your box because—"

"It's not security if no one practices security."

"You catch on, Mr. Stewart."

After signing in Alan stopped on the stairs midway to the vault room and thought about what George had said. This was the second time in a week that Lieutenant Frantz had told the newspapers it was Canadians who'd shot him, killing a total of four men in two separate incidents. Outside of the force, few were aware that the two pensioners were on Frantz's private payroll, a situation the police department chose to overlook.

Alan wondered if Frantz told the same story to Chief

8

of Detectives Mike Ketchum. No matter what Frantz had said, Alan was pretty sure Frantz had left his and Vic's names out of his statements, like he had after the shooting at the Kasbah. Even if Frantz wasn't absolutely sure it was Alan who'd killed Hoff and Schneider, he was bound to be suspicious and figure it out soon enough, especially given the strong resemblance Alan had to his late father, whom Frantz had known all too well.

Alan grasped the key to Vic's safe deposit box, which the big man had entrusted to his care. Before going into hiding somewhere in China, Vic left vague instructions for Alan to check his box. Alan tossed Vic's key in the air and caught it before unlocking the door, and pulling the drawer free. Despite its larger size it wasn't all that heavy. He carried the box across to the room George said was available and pulled the door shut behind him. He made sure it latched before sliding Vic's box onto the viewing table. Then he sat down, leaned backward with a deep breath, and exhaled loudly with his fingers pinching at the bridge of his nose. He grabbed the box firmly and cautiously began lifting the lid, as if he were expecting a jack-in-the box to spring madly at him.

There was no terror, no trap. Inside the box was in disarray, an eclectic assortment of scraps and souvenirs, like a squirrel's nest or a boy's junk drawer long ignored. But on top of the clutter, Alan found the "instructions" Vic said he'd left for him, neatly folded. Alan pulled it out and thumbed it open.

Champ,

It's been swell working with you. You not only look like Mackie, you got his smarts, too. You're a natural detective.

Besides me telling you enough so you could even the score against those who killed your daddy, you need to know about a few other things I left for you. Inside the Crown Royal pouch is the most beautiful medal you're ever going to see. It's the Verdienstkreuz Deutscher Adier, the German Service Cross of the Eagle (second class). It's the same as Lindy's, but this one is mine. Guard it with your life and don't show or tell NO ONE about it. If anyone should ask, you know nothing, and you should be damned worried about those who do the asking. If certain people find out I have one, they might come after me, even if I do make it all the way to Lilly's little island that ain't got a name. Believe me, they can reach that far.

Now I'm going to tell you what I never told Mackie—I had a job moonlighting with Navy Intelligence. The times when Mackie was home with you and his family, I was checking on who was scouting the warplanes the Boeings were building for Britain and who these folks were telling what they saw. I also kept track of goings-on down at the shipyards. More than just the Germans want to know about what we're building and for who. The Japanese are also interested in this coast and what's going on here. That should tell you something's in the winds, and they've been trying to recruit people to help them sabotage the works. Figure their agents won't all be Orientals or Ruskies.

If you want to help some other real fine people put a stop to this, Navy Intelligence would welcome you. My contact knows about your talents—in general terms—and that you can be counted on in a pinch. I trust these people, but don't never give anyone something to hold over your head.

Mr. B is fine with what I was doing off the clock. He didn't want to know the particulars. I recommend only telling him you need to do a favor for old Vic. He'll be fine with that, won't ask for details. You already know how patriotic he is and what he's always willing to do for God and country.

If you're agreeable to this, call ME-8119 from a payphone. Use one in the lobby of the Sorrento Hotel. Just give your phone number to the woman when she answers, and then wait a few minutes for a call back. The caller will send you to a safe place where you can meet your contact and finalize your arrangement. Only deal with one person, nobody else. Don't ask to meet the next one up the ladder or ask who else is helping Uncle Sam, because that will only give you more secrets you'll have to protect.

Don't talk about this to anyone ever, not even Alice, because that would mean there's one more pair of lips that would have to guard your secrets. See how this works?

As far as the rest of the stuff in the box, if I'm not back in seven years, keep it—it's all yours. Until then, borrow what you want and snoop to your heart's content.

Best of luck to you, Champ! Your daddy would've been proud how you turned out.

Vic

Alan studied the phone number, refolded the letter, and tucked it deep into his pant's pocket. Below the letter sat a purple *Crown Royal* pouch and Alan lifted it from the box. The soft velvet protected the firm angles of a large irregularly shaped medal. "So this is it," he whispered. He set the pouch gently on the table, loosened the draw strings to reach inside, and slid his hand over the prize. He carefully tugged the medal out and blew a soft whistle. "Ahhh! This is a beauty," he said to himself.

A large silver cross trimmed with black hung from a red ribbon. Four golden eagles were placed around the axis of the cross. The great birds' wings were spread wide, each pair touching a vertical and a horizontal beam of the cross, and each eagle clutched a Nazi swastika in its talons. The swastikas were positioned so they nestled closest to the heart of the cross. Alan admired the bold design of the cross and its eagles. It was striking, but he wasn't so sure about the other symbols. At least Vic's service had really been as a double agent—and his allegiance to the Allies.

Alan stirred to the sounds of footsteps outside on the stairs. He slid Vic's medal back into the pouch, put it back in the box, and closed the lid. He stepped over to the door and listened to George prattle on with a customer about the vault and the Great Fire. Alan waited until the other customer entered a separate viewing room, and then he scooped up Vic's box and returned it to where it belonged. He had what he needed for now. He would examine the remaining contents another time.

From its prominent perch above Seattle's downtown, the Sorrento Hotel had a commanding view of the city below, as well as the waterfront and mountains beyond. Although it offered valet service as a courtesy, Alan parked the family's Hudson just off Madison Street on Terry Avenue and walked to the entrance in the damp twilight.

Despite his handsome salary as a driver and private detective for George Brinkman—Mr. B to his most loyal employees—the Washington Federation Union's president, there was no need to act flashy and draw attention. Those were neither Alan's ways nor his father's. Flashy wasn't a Stewart attribute.

McAlister Stewart hadn't been Alan's only male influence and Alan realized that when he needed an answer on how best to handle a problem, he often asked himself, "How would Vic handle this?" His father had taken him close to manhood, but it was Vic Morrison who was there for him when bones needed breaking and bullets started flying, and it was Vic who'd helped him find a full measure of retribution against those who had killed his father. Towards the end it was also Vic who let him know when enough was enough, gentling the wide swings of his emotional pendulum, which

13

had been driven to extremes in his need for revenge.

Alice Mahoney was the only other person who understood Alan's need for righting a wrong that everyone else felt helpless to challenge, and she had stood by him through the deep lows of those difficult times. She was the only one he trusted enough to confess that his gratification had been tinged with a bitter taste when the score was finally settled. Revenge wasn't always sweet, as he had imagined it would be. He had opened the gate and let his inner beast escape, and he worried he wouldn't be able to cage the creature again, or control his skill at wielding death.

Inside the mahogany paneled lobby of the hotel Alan found a bank of empty telephone booths, side-by-side. Before entering the one furthest from the front doors he scanned the Fireside Lobby for idle eyes that might be paying him too much attention. The concierge and front desk staff were helping late check-ins, and the only other people in the lobby were a couple on their way to the Hunt Club.

Alan squeezed into a booth and closed the door. He lifted the receiver, dropped a nickel in the slot, and dialed the number Vic had left for him: The ME prefix was for MELROSE, a north-end exchange he recognized for the area near Greenlake, a predominantly residential neighborhood, which couldn't be a hotbed of spies and counter-spies, Alan figured.

A woman who was probably in her sixties answered curtly, "ME-8119."

Alan hesitated for a moment, but nothing more was forthcoming from the other end. He cleared his throat and said, "I was told you were expecting my call. I'm at MA-6400. This is Alan—"

"Code name only, please."

"Sorry...I don't have one, yet."

"Very well. Wait for your call back," she said before hanging up.

Alan stared at his heavy handset before replacing the phone in its receiver, as if expecting something else to emanate from it. While waiting for the phone to ring he leaned against the rear of the booth and scanned the lobby. The staff was still busy and no one seemed to be aware he was even in the room. Like a chameleon he seemed to blend into the woodwork. His heroes from the *Black Mask* detective magazines his father had given him, Dashiell Hammett and Raymond Chandler, would be proud.

Before a minute had passed the phone rang loudly in the small enclosure, startling him even though he was expecting the call. Alan jerked away from the large box as if zapped by a strong charge of static electricity and picked up the receiver before the phone completed its first ring. He forced himself to pause before speaking. "Yes?"

A woman's voice responded in a forced monotone. "Alan?"

"Yes."

"You wish to meet?"

"Yes."

"The Observation Deck on the brick water tower at Volunteer Park. Can you be there in fifteen minutes?"

"Yes, but...doesn't it close at dark?"

"Not for us. Use the north entrance."

"How will you know it's me?"

"I will," the woman said as she hung up.

Alan smacked his receiver against his left hand nervously before hanging it in its cradle. He took off his fedora and ran his fingers through his hair, needless grooming as he tried to catch his thoughts. *What am I getting myself into?*

🐉 ⊕ 🐉

Alan parked his Ford Coupe in the only available space across from the Volunteer Park Museum. This gave him a picture perfect view of the open water reservoir, the north end of downtown, the Puget Sound, and Queen Anne Hill in the distance. It was similar to the view from his family's home, only higher and more sweeping. While Alan got out of his car, the two young men parked next to him sat up and watched his every move. Their smiles were inviting, not suspicious. Alan glanced away to be polite, but they didn't budge or nod a greeting—they only smiled. When he turned back to them they were still watching him appreciatively as though he was a performer on a stage. Alan shook his head, more so for himself than for them, and walked away.

"First, the girls and now the boys. It must be this coat and hat," he muttered. He was in a hurry to put some distance between himself and his new admirers, but he slowed down to scan the area around him, taking in as much as he could. There were other males walking alone in the park—cruising, he guessed, but no one was following him toward the tower. Would his contact already be there? Behind him, the two in the parked car seemed to have already forgotten him as they returned their attention to each other.

Alan veered from the drive and wound his way up the path to the north entrance of the huge tower. Constructed of dark brick, the tower encased a massive, steel water tank. On top of the tank was an observation platform, and its rustic architecture fit well with the area's large manor homes and carriage houses that belonged to Seattle's gentry. All of the large hills in Seattle had water tanks, but this was the only one girded in brick. It featured small windows that traced a path of steps on either side of the huge tank. The thick encasement of bricks and the small size of the windows gave the tower the appearance of a castle turret, ready for battle. Carved in stone above both entrances were the inscriptions, *Aqua Pura MCMVI.*

The winding gravel path was partially obscured by junipers, ferns, and mature rhododendrons, but Alan followed it easily. The tower was just as he remembered.

A wrought iron gate blocked the entrance, and there was just enough light for him to make out a new sign that said, *Closed at Dusk.* He approached the grill and took hold of it firmly enough to verify it was latched securely. From just inside the darkness, at the foot of the nearby steps to the right, a woman's voice broke the silence. "Is that you, Alan?"

Before he could answer, she stepped forward and lightly clasped his fingers with her gloved hand. "No matter how many times I've seen you," she said, "I can't get over it. Wearing that hat and coat you look so much like your father."

Alan flinched and almost withdrew his hand, but after recognizing the undisguised voice, he relaxed. "So, it's you," he said.

The woman released her grip on Alan's hand. She took a step away and turned a key in the gate's lock behind her, pulling the door open far enough for Alan to squeeze in sideways. As soon as they were both inside, she quietly closed the gate, took him by the arm, and steered him toward the shadows at the foot of the steps. She reached out and put her arm across his chest, holding him back while she took another peek behind them. Satisfied he hadn't been followed she lowered her arm, letting it drop so that it brushed down his abdomen to his upper thigh. He knew she wouldn't apologize, she never had before.

"Vera," he said.

She quickly put her gloved hand over his mouth. "No names. I swept this place and no one's in here, but we don't take chances."

"Understood, ma'am."

She cupped her hand around the back of his neck and knocked his hat forward, tousling his hair. "I told you that makes me feel old."

"You don't need to worry about your age."

A glint of light revealed her ready smile. "I could kiss

17

you," she said, "but then you'd never want to stop. So I won't."

She leaned close, took his arm to wrap her fingers in his, and pulled his hand close to her bosom. She spoke softly, letting her breath dance across his neck and into his ear. "Walk softly and slowly up the steps. We'll stop along the way if you need to catch your breath."

"I can't believe it's you. You and Vic—"

She put her hand softly over his mouth. "Wait till we get to the top."

Vera led the way up the steel steps, which narrowed so that they were forced to walk in single file. Alan stayed close behind and downwind from the hint of perfume that wafted his way. It was her trademark scent, something expensive, but he didn't remember the name. It was a subtle feminine charm he didn't think she needed given her God-given assets. But of course it only added to her complete package, a detail she wouldn't overlook. Age-wise, he guessed she had to be near forty, but she could still cast her nets and pull in all the young fish—even those half her age, just like him—and they'd be glad for the lessons she could teach. Now that he knew who she was he could relax a little.

Alan had worked with Vera in the union office, and depending on her sales pitch tonight, would be willing to work for her in this new endeavor, if she was the one who'd be his boss. His chief concern was whether or not she would be straight with him. He wasn't about to let her play him for a sap.

Alan suspected she'd had a thing for his father, there didn't seem to be much doubt about that, especially given that bright spark in her eyes the very first time she saw Alan enter the union's offices a few weeks back. Yet he could find no one who would confirm it—not even Vic. Every time he'd seen her since, she was almost too friendly with him, and he wondered how much of that might be a longing for

18

something she once had.

They continued up the long spiral staircase. Through the faint light that stole its way through the windows Alan watched the fabric of her coat wrestle against the curves of her firm posterior. Two-thirds of the way up the tower they stopped on a landing to rest. She leaned close, breathing heavy. "You okay, Champ?"

He caught his breath. "I'm fine."

She motioned for him to continue the climb behind her. When they reached the top of the stairs and entered the observation deck both stopped to catch their breath and take in the view. To the southwest the bright lights of the city, against the water's edge, made for a spectacular scene. As if an artist had designed their vista, two large ferryboats crossed each other's paths a little farther west in the middle of Puget Sound, one coming from, and the other going to, Bremerton.

"Takes your breath away, doesn't it?" Vera said.

"That's quite the climb."

"I meant the view, silly."

"Yeah...that too."

The top of the observation deck was capped by a pitched roof, which protected visitors from the elements but not the cold. Vera grabbed Alan's arm again and escorted him over to a bench that faced the large open windows with their chain-link screens. She sat next to him and drew his hand onto her leg. From past experience around the office Alan was familiar with her need for touching, so he didn't resist, and to his surprise he felt remarkably at ease with her.

"How much do you know, Champ?"

"Some that I pried out of Vic when we got to Canada, and more of it I'm still putting together."

"Like what?"

"Vic says you had a hunch about the second kidnapper of the Lindbergh baby, and so it must have been you who put Vic and Dad on his trail."

"Why do you think that?"

"The handwriting on the Lindbergh articles I found in the vault looks the same as what I found on envelopes in Dad's suit coat, the one's with all the money, which had to have come from you."

Vera stared down at the floor a moment and then glanced off into the distance before answering. "That's right."

"That's about all I got, and then Vic left me a note to contact the phone number I called. Said Uncle Sam might need more help catching people spying on the shipyards, rail yards, and the Boeing plant. There was also something about most of the spies around here being Japanese, not Germans."

"I wouldn't be so quick to count them out, but was there anything else?"

"No."

"Did he say what to do with the Verdienstkreuz Deutscher Adler?"

Alan's eyes bulged wide and his mouth fell open.

"Relax, Champ. I'm the one who presented it to him, but we won't discuss that." She smiled and stared quietly at him for a moment, apparently evaluating him and the way he might fit with her needs. "We're going to have to work on your poker face. You're an easy read," she said as she patted his hand. "If I was a Black Jack dealer, I'd have a pretty good idea what's in your hand."

Alan shook his head, embarrassed.

"So do you want to help?" Vera asked.

"I'm barely old enough to vote and order a drink in a bar, would I be any good?"

"I wouldn't ask if I didn't think so. You don't have the proper training, and we don't have time to put you through it—but you do have raw talent. Experience is the best

20

teacher, and controlling how you display your emotions comes with experience. You just have to adjust your mind to expect the unexpected. It's not like you've had a lot of practice or need for that in your life. You grew up in a nice home, not in a world of cheats."

"What about my dad, was he in on this?"

"No," Vera said and turned away for a moment. "Mackie had a family, and maybe because of that he spent time doing other jobs for Mr. B."

"Bootlegging?"

"You could say he was working outside the law, maybe even doing things the FBI might have been interested in, but not Navy Intelligence. As for Vic, he was already on our payroll. What he did was part of his undercover role, so the top boss looked the other way when things got sticky, as long as they didn't involve national security."

"There's a difference when the law is really the law?"

"I'm afraid so, but different times allow for different exceptions."

"Exceptions...like now, with me and the police?"

"Given that Lieutenant Frantz was making up his own rules as he went along, that qualifies as an exception in my book. Besides, I'll put in a good word to the top for you."

"What kind of assignment would I be working?"

Vera turned fully on the bench to face him and rested her hand on his upper thigh, overly familiar but confident he wouldn't object. It served to distract him, and Alan wondered again about her power over men and her attraction to his father. Was her flirting only because of his resemblance to Mackie, or could it be something she felt for him? Or did she just do this kind of thing with all the men in her life?

Vera unpinned her hat, shook her hair out, and set the hat and pin next to her. "We are in possession of a letter that had been sent to a mail drop in South America. There was something wrong with the address or postage—I'm not exactly sure—but when it was returned to the originating address, the woman there didn't recognize it as hers. She brought it to the police department and claims she knows no one in Brazil and didn't send it. The police didn't know what to do with it, so they forwarded it to us. We had our cryptographers examine it, and it appears to be in code."

Alan nodded for her to continue.

"We alerted the postal service, and they intercepted six other letters sent to the same address, supposedly from different parts of the country, but their postmarks all bore a Seattle stamping. When we contacted each of these people, none of them sent the letters or knew the others involved, and we haven't yet found a connection that makes sense. We used the FBI laboratories to test the typing, and all the letters appear to be written by the same person on two different typewriters. While we're looking for the person or persons behind the letters, the FBI is taking samples from typewriters available to the public in libraries and hotels around Seattle, figuring that since two different ones were used they wouldn't be privately owned, but that's not a foolproof theory."

"Can I ask what was in the letters?"

"I can tell you this much: they're about ships' movements on the West Coast."

"Navy ships?"

"Precisely. From San Diego to San Francisco, Los Angeles, Seattle, and Bremerton. The messages were cleverly coded into innocuous drivel about collectible antiques, saying this one needed restoring and would be in the shop for six weeks, which just happened to coincide with a destroyer undergoing an overhaul in the Navy Shipyards. Another spoke of a mother hawk tending her chicks that the writer could almost reach out and touch while she was in San

Francisco, which would tell someone where the battleship and her squadron were—that kind of thing. I can't tell you anymore about it until I have your commitment that you're working with us. And before that, there's one more thing you need to know. This work is dangerous."

"I figured that much."

"Another of my agents has gone missing, and so has his contact. The FBI's approach to this case is a slow, tedious process. I don't have time to wait, and neither does my missing agent. Our job is to see if we can find him and the spy first."

"Another? So you mean another—besides Vic, or—"

"Besides Vic I lost an operative yesterday, and the Navy's missing a sailor. I need your help finding what happened to them."

"Are they dead?"

"Let's hope not, but there doesn't seem to be any other explanation. It was a routine assignment—if there is such a thing in this business—but I think they must've stumbled onto something bigger. We should have gotten back a report by now either way."

"Are the police looking for them?"

"It's not that easy. Sailors go AWOL all the time, and my operative is Chinese. The police have shown no interest in helping the Chinese, unless it's to carry their rucksacks across the plank of the next boat out of town."

Alan leaned backward and stretched. "Vic told me those stories while we were holed up...something about unemployment back in the 1880s, particularly in lumber after San Francisco hadn't burned down in a while. Said the police stood by on the docks while the mobs gathered up the Chinese to send back to China. But Vic also said the mobs missed the Chinese who hid in the smugglers' passage, the catacombs underneath Chinatown."

Vera stroked Alan's thigh, a touch too slowly and softly for it to be a gesture of encouragement; instead it crossed the border to arousal. She tossed her hair to the side as only women can do, a movement that captured his eyes and drew them into hers. "That was long before my time, but you still haven't answered me, Champ. I could use a man with a strong backbone, who's good with his hands, and can be counted on when things get rough." Vera lowered her chin and somehow managed to make it so she was looking up to him. "If you're with me," she said, "I'd be grateful for your help, but I need your word as a man on it."

Alan took in a deep breath and exhaled noisily, pondering her question. Vera continued to rub the top of his thigh encouragingly and he glanced down at her hand for a moment before meeting her gaze. "You've got my word. What do I do now?"

"Since this is the government, you're going to have to swear a solemn oath of allegiance and sign paperwork."

"Paperwork? When do I do that?"

"Right now."

Before he could ask, how, Vera pulled her coat open and hiked her skirt above mid-thigh, exposing the top of her hosiery where it was clipped to a garter belt. Inside the band of her stocking was what appeared to be a legal document, folded into thirds. As she pulled it out, she glanced at him and smiled. "I'm sure you've seen these before."

"Legs?"

"No, silly. Stockings, garter straps."

"Oh sure," he said, trying to sound convincing.

"Maybe we need to work on your worldly education some?"

Alan smiled wryly and turned away, embarrassed for a moment. Then he inclined his head toward Vera. "Miss Deward, it would appear you're flirting with me."

"You like it, don't you?" she said with a grin, as she smoothed her skirt back over her thighs.

"Perhaps I do, but you know I'm seeing Alice."

"Yes, I've heard talk about that around the office, but I don't see a ring on either of your fingers."

"As Vic would say, my problem is that I'm monogamous, or something like that."

"Vic and his big words."

"It means—"

"I know what it means."

"—that I like to keep my romantic life simple."

"And why would you want to do that? I could teach you things you've only read about in under-the-counter books."

Alan laughed. Realizing he was getting over the awkwardness of the moment, he began to enjoy their bizarre rapport. Still, it was all so new, given his proper background and his recent loss of virginity. He imagined that if the light were better, Vera would see he was nearly as red as her lipstick "Maybe that's not all I'm looking for in—"

"Oh, don't think for a minute Alice is all that innocent."

"I know what she did up in Canada."

Vera sat back and stared at him. For the first time there was surprise on her face.

"I found her publicity photo from her fan-dancing days," Alan said. "And while we're at it, I saw yours too."

Vera's pouty lips slowly creased into a smile. "The one with tassles?"

"Tassles twirling...impressively, Miss Deward." He glanced at her covered breasts without thinking, caught himself, and looked away.

Vera's smile was confident again. "I bet you'd like to see how that's done?"

Alan sat forward with his hands on his knees and stared down at the floor, collecting his thoughts. Of course

25

he wanted to see that, but he couldn't let her know. He also didn't want her so see that the crotch in his pants had become misshapen by his erection. "No, Vera, that's something I'm going to take a pass on."

"Too bad, I think you'd really enjoy the show. Others have. But no matter, we've work to do. Besides, I talk a good game, but I really don't mix business with pleasure."

Alan peeked sideways at her and nodded hoping his erection would subside and not embarrass him. Vera fussed with the paperwork and somehow magically produced a fountain pen for him to sign the agreement. While uncapping the pen she suddenly dropped both pieces, and the barrel and the cap rolled away from her. Alan got up quickly and retrieved the pen, while she picked up the cap. As he offered her the pen she reached past his proffered hand and groped his crotch squarely. "Ohhh Champ, your mouth's saying one thing but your body's saying another!"

Alan reached for her hand but hesitated at dislodging it. Her grip was firm and commanding. He'd wanted her to do this from the first moment he laid eyes on her in Brinkman's office, when she greeted him so warmly, fussing over his resemblance to his father. She was the kind of woman who was confident in her power, which only added to her allure. Still, even as she massaged and kneaded his scrotum, he knew she was dangerous. Finally he tugged her hand away, holding it by the wrist.

She stepped forward and pressed against him. "Pull it out, I want to taste it."

His eyelids drooped to half-mast as he rolled his eyes skyward, dreamily. "Damn it, Vera. This isn't going to work." He threw her hand free and walked over to the window to inhale a deep breath of cold night air.

After a moment, Vera walked up behind him, and gently rubbed his shoulder. "Your resolve is either very good, or

I'm losing my touch," she said.

"You're not losing your touch—not by a long stretch."

"When I used to perform in burlesque, I'd pluck the youngest sailor out of the audience and drag him up on stage. Then I'd run a string of gags on him, making him the butt of a few jokes. His shipmates would whistle and tease him mercilessly—they call what I did *striptease* for a reason. When we were done, I'd turn my back to the others and give him a sight the rest of the audience couldn't see—a treat for being a good sport. The other sailors would all stay for the next show, all of them wanting to be the next guy I'd call up on stage." Vera shook her head at the memory. "I'm sorry, I shouldn't have tried that on you."

Alan rubbed his face with both hands and peeked out between his spread fingers. "No need to apologize," he said.

"I think you're going to work out even better than I'd planned. There're going to be wicked temptations out there, maybe even more alluring than what I have to offer. It could come when your defenses are low, because you've had too much wine, or someone slipped a Mickey in your drink. Losing your focus could cost you your life. No matter what you run across, you'll have to keep your mind on business and the final goal—not just the quick release when you ejaculate in some girl's mouth."

Alan dropped his head and glanced back at her. "Vera, if our working together is going to happen, you can't go on teasing me. Like I told you—I've got Alice."

"You mentioned that, but does she have you?"

"I don't get what you're asking."

Vera tugged her coat closed and flipped the collar up. She walked back past the bench without looking behind her. "I'd forgotten how cold it is up here in the breeze," she called over her shoulder. No matter what else she'd been about to say, Alan knew the conversation was over.

On the way out of the tower Vera walked down the path ahead of Alan, and he watched her slip out the park's side entrance to the tree-shrouded streets that provided a buffer to the old money homes. He wondered where exactly she lived.

As Alan reached his vehicle he saw that the car parked next to his was still there, and it seemed to be rocking rhythmically. The two men's faces were no longer visible and the windows were completely steamed over. Alan decided he wouldn't check any further, and he hoped they wouldn't notice him again. He backed his car out and was soon on the street where he'd last seen Vera, but she was no longer in view.

Alan worked his way to Broadway Avenue, but instead of heading home he steered south on Capitol Hill's main arterial, past the Kasbah. He couldn't help but shiver as he drove by the scene of one of Seattle's worst shootings, which had happened less than two weeks ago. It still drew a nauseous reaction out of him because he'd been the trigger man, firing all the shots as he saved Vic from a bloody beating—the same kind of beating as the one that killed his father, Mackie.

Part of Alan was still glad that his father's killers had met their maker, while a lot of him ached at the thought of what he'd done, what he had been capable of doing. If he didn't count Frantz, Mr. B was the only one left on this continent that knew the full story. As far as Alan knew, Vera had only heard pieces of it, circumspectly at that, while Alice had been told a little more.

Within another couple of minutes, Alan had worked his way through Japan Town to Chinatown. He drove by Maynard and King Street and then past the nondescript door that led to the brothel where he and Vic had hidden while Vic was patched-up by Little Papa after the shooting.

Alan parked at the curb, up the street in a position where he could watch the brothel's street-level door. There were no formal notices of closure or abatement nailed to the door, and the floors above it seemed to have lights on, indicting there was life in the portion of the hotel where Big Mama held the lease.

Alan had hoped that Big Mama and Little Papa would have managed to keep their brothel running, despite Lieutenant Frantz's threats to shut the business down. Frantz had angrily bullied the brothel owners after he chased their working girls into the smugglers passage. Some of the girls eventually fled to Canada and beyond with Vic. And because of the raid, the brothel might only have two young women left in the stable. Mama would have to recruit more talent from China.

Alan kept a short vigil, staring at their door, eager for the female companionship that the business offered without attachments. He craved a hot bath he would share with a Chinese beauty, undoubtedly named after a delicate flower. And after he had taken care of his sexual cravings, he'd eat a meal Little Papa would magically conjure from his gas-heated woks.

Within ten minutes, Alan's patience was rewarded. An elderly Chinese male walking alone, slowed to a stop in front of the brothel entrance. The man checked around him before knocking on the door. A moment later a large Chinese woman clad in a bright silk kimono opened the unmarked door, stuck her head out, and whisked the visitor inside. *Open for business*, Alan decided.

Alan drove around the corner and down a block. He parked at the curb and returned to the brothel, making his way up the slight grade of the main street on foot. The sidewalk on this street was busier than the one near the brothel entrance. It was filled with people entering and leaving restaurants with brightly colored signs. Other shops still open late displayed pork loins and poultry in their front windows on hooks. Alan stopped at one, pretending to examine the freshly barbecued meat while he scanned the area behind him, using the reflection in the glass to see if anyone was following him or paying too much attention to what he was doing. He repeated this process again as he neared the end of the block. From there it was a straight shot to Big Mama's brothel.

After Alan reached the establishment's door, he knocked and waited. Although Vic trusted him with his life, he had never shared the password to the front entrance. Big Mama's voice spoke in Chinese, but Alan only recognized one of the words. He took a chance and said, "It's Alan—Vic's friend."

Big Mama repeated what he'd said in broken English, and then she excitedly opened the door. She stuck a fleshy arm out of her bright kimono and clasped hold of his lapel, pulling him quickly inside, reminiscent of what Vera had done to him earlier that evening at the water tower. She closed the door and clasped both hands around his shoulders, smiling broadly.

"Alan, so good to see you. How is Vic and my girls?"

"They made it to Canada, and I put them on a ship headed to the South Seas."

Mama nodded along with what Alan was saying, but it wasn't clear how many of the words she understood. She got the gist, Alan thought. He used his hands, somewhat in pantomime, to clarify his story as he repeated and added words. "They're on their way to China."

"Ahh," Big Mama said, smiling. She clasped his shoulders again and sized him up, head to toe. "You skinny. You need to eat." It was a maternal statement that was not open for discussion.

Alan was a welcome guest in Vic's adopted home. He grinned and blushed while nodding, feeling a little guilty about his real purpose for the visit. Big Mama spun him around by the arm and began pushing him up the wooden stairs. "You like girl, too?"

Alan glanced back with a smile, relieved that she'd brought it up. She prodded him to the landing at the top of the stairs, and he waited for her to catch up. "You like bath?" she asked.

"A bath, a girl, plum wine, and food. Yes, ma'am."

"You like two girls, like first time?" she asked. Alan remembered Vic proclaiming that nothing happened here unless you wanted it to—and that their secrets stayed within the walls. Later, Vic also told Alan that although the people didn't spread stories, the walls were thin and not discreet.

"One girl is fine."

"That good, because I only have two girls now, and one is busy—unless you want me?" Big Mama asked. She slapped him on the back as she rolled forward with raucous laughter.

Alan chuckled along with her. "One girl will be fine."

They passed a door Alan remembered. It appeared the

same as all of the others on the floor, including a room number screwed to the middle of the door, though it's only purpose was to access a secret hallway that led to other parts of the building and the smuggler's passage. The original door had been destroyed during Frantz's police raid, but it had been replaced and repainted, not a bit worse for the wear.

When Vic was there he had regaled Alan with stories of the hidden passages in buildings nearby that once sported Chinese names, like the Goon Dip Young down the block and around the corner. Another building, across from the Young building, had a room with a potbelly stove and a small family to sit in front of it. The family's job was to serve as decoys and spotters for the police or Immigration authorities. The stove was never lit, the pots and pans on top of it only props. Instead of providing heat, it rotated away from the wall on discreet castor wheels, chimneystack and all, to reveal a secret doorway. Other numbered doors in that building opened to brick walls and voids. The passages deterred robberies from rival Tongs and renegade gangsters, but their main purpose was to confound police and Federal pursuers enforcing the Chinese Exclusion Act.

Mama called out orders and a young woman hurried out of a room to dash into the bath ahead of them, her Chinese sandals slapping softly on the wooden floor. She was young and fresh, an exotic Asian beauty dressed in a silk robe that wasn't as brightly colored or elegant as the one that covered Big Mama. Hopefully this new girl would take Alan's mind off Vera—but that could take all night. Damn, Vera had made him hot. He didn't know what would explode first, his head or his loins.

The young woman was filling the large bathtub when he entered the room, adding scented oils from a brown bottle kept under a small cabinet piled with bright white towels.

Alan took off his overcoat and hat and then plopped his rear on a bench while he watched her delicate hands at work. When she seemed satisfied that the water was the right temperature, she knelt in front of him and began to take off his shoes. Her black hair cascaded down and danced below her face as she tugged at the laces. "Name is Violet," she said without looking up.

Her English was difficult, her pronunciations off the mark, but he got it. *Of course, another flower.* "My name is Alan."

She pulled off his other shoe and sock and set them aside. Still without looking up, she said, "Take pants off, please."

Four blocks from where Alan soaked away his frustrations in a hot bath, a woman of mixed ancestry stood next to a powerful telescope in a window shrouded by lace curtains on the top floor of the Panama Hotel. Instead of gazing at the stars or counting craters on the moon, Mischa Ohara stared across Elliot Bay toward the shipyards and Harbor Island. Although it was night, the yard lights were ablaze as a night crew worked furiously to complete a new Navy destroyer. Mischa's concern for the moment was the front of the ship, draped in canvas. When they finished painting the hull designation, would it reveal what country the warship was destined for? she wondered. Her sources told her the Americans were in negotiations on a lend-lease proposal that would send U.S. built destroyers to Britain in exchange for long-term leases on military bases. But then there was also talk that the U.S. was covertly preparing to send warships to Russia, if Stalin promised to engage Germany in battle. This created complications for Japan, because if Russia were to receive warships it would thwart Japan's ability to rule East Asia unchallenged.

Even though a courier was present, Mischa would need to send more letters to Brazil, alerting Japan to the possibilities unfolding in front of her. Redundancy was sometimes a necessary evil, but it also ensured that proper credit was given to the message sender, not the messenger. Sending a coded message through established channels would also convey to those who had been skeptical that she could be counted on to deliver helpful news. Her value to Japan was deep on many levels.

Mischa's mother was of Irish-American descent, her father a Japanese immigrant. They met while picking vegetables as migratory workers in California. Displeased with their marriage, her mother's family disowned her, but the Oharas took in the new bride and groom. Ironically, years later as a college student at UCLA, a sorority mistakenly invited Mischa to visit them. Her reception was tepid, and she was surprised to find she was the only non-Caucasian at the social. Finally, one of the co-eds told her that Asians were not allowed into the Panhellenic Sorority system. They'd thought Ohara was an Irish surname, confusing it with O'Hara. The sorority regrettably had no choice on the matter; it was written in the rules of their constitution. Her presence was also an embarrassment for her hosts.

Compounding her mortification, finding a place to live near campus was difficult because Asian prejudice was deep-rooted in L.A., where Japanese were not allowed to own property. The hurt lingered years after she finished her schooling. Her comfort came from within her Japanese culture.

Mischa glanced away from the telescope, lightly inhaled through a long cigarette holder and exhaled. "There are other possibilities to consider," she said to the diplomat on the couch. "The Americans aren't stupid. They could sail with the designation covered, which of course means the ship is definitely going abroad, but no one would know where. Or they could always paint on a false designation and change the name and hull number later, but many sailors think this practice brings bad luck. Either way I'll have my people keep track of hull numbers to make sure the ones they use are real and actually new. The U.S. government can only pull this ruse for so long before they duplicate numbers."

"We need that information, it's important for us," said her handsome guest.

"It's important for me too. I'm confident I can get it for you."

Hideki Hasakawa set down his brandy snifter and started for the door. Mischa's manservant Riki waited to the side, holding Hideki's coat. Hideki turned around and slid into his coat without acknowledging or thanking the large hulking servant for his assistance.

"This could be the last time I see you for awhile, unless you want to return to Japan with me," Hideki continued with a wink. "With tensions growing the way they are, there is always the danger I'm being followed." He retrieved a handwritten note from inside his jacket pocket. "I fear the old address in Brazil has been compromised. My secretary has written the new one for you. Keep it in a safe place."

"Of course, and do you have something else for me?"

Hideki reached into the same coat pocket, retrieved a thick envelope, and slapped it against his other hand before handing it to her. Mischa knew he meant to convey his contempt for the business part of their dealings, implying that she should be doing this solely for the love of Japan's Imperial Highness and the country they held so dear.

"This should tide you over for several months," Hideki said, "including your operatives. I trust the White Dragon will advise if her canaries need more bird seed?"

"Of course," Mischa replied.

Hideki pulled leather gloves from his coat pocket and slapped them against his other hand, as he had the money

36

envelope. "I must say that your obsession with money is disconcerting. Before my country's struggles you were a penniless college student, and now look at your suite. It has become a 'safe harbor,' as you like to call it, for ancient treasures from old dynasties and—"

"Japan is my country, too."

"Indeed, but you've done so very well exporting scrap metal and cotton that you could underwrite the country's economy for an entire decade."

"I understand your family benefits also."

"Old money can't help but have connections to several lines of business. Shipping just happens to be one of our endeavors—"

"As well as building ships and planes with the iron and steel I send home."

"But the new U.S. trade embargo will soon stop the sale of scrap, and then Japan will counter with an embargo on cotton, a product we also need, just so that we can leverage the Americans. And that means Japan loses twice. We'll have to find a new source. China, Russia, or South America. Who knows? Perhaps we'll have to send in our own laborers and dig it from the ground ourselves."

"The trade embargo only stops the sale of scrap—not what has been recycled through a smelter."

Hideki raised a hand and rubbed his chin. "Please explain."

"This word comes straight from the Senator's office. The new law leaves out ore and ingots. We will begin loading the Hiye Maru with ten rail cars full of ingots melted from surplus trolley lines—from these very streets. She is one of your ships, isn't she?"

Her guest rolled his eyes and finally nodded, almost apologetically. "My family owns the shipping line, but how about brass? Obviously we need it for shell casings. Can your sources find more, preferably something that can be reloaded?"

"You are surprisingly prescient. That was to be my little surprise. I will gladly provide it as a bonus, and perhaps you will show your gratitude by sending more treasures."

"When the Hiye Maru arrives it will have a shipment of the bishop's treasures," Hideki said. "I will see that certain choice figurines are diverted your way."

Mischa inhaled again, and her Eurasian eyes lit up dreamily.

"So you do have brass?" Hideki asked.

"The American Navy has been saving shells from their test firing, collecting it in rail cars behind their pier. Three carloads have worked their way into my collection. I imagine their contents amount to several tons. The brass will be hidden under steel ingots and loaded on the Hiye Maru."

Hideki finally smiled.

"The brass came at a cost. One of our men was badly injured, but they lost two," Mischa said.

Hideki nodded. "It seems we will have more business to discuss during the next week after all, and I will have preparations to make," he said. "No need to show me to the door."

Mischa's eyes followed him as he made his exit. Hideki paused and checked the hallway before leaving, as a man might do if he were worried about being caught with his lover. She didn't call after him, asking him to stay this time, which she was sure he wanted. Hideki's background of privilege allowed him to be contemptuous of others less fortunate. He was handsome, charming, educated, and... spoiled. He was used to getting what he wanted, and he pouted when he didn't. She didn't mind disappointing him once in awhile. There would be no romp in the pillows tonight.

Riki entered the room with a tray to gather Hideki's empty brandy glass. "Are you sure their bodies won't be found?" Mischa asked Riki without looking up from her telescope.

"They're being stored in a freezer car," Riki replied. "We'll thaw them out later and scatter pieces so it will appear they were run over by a train while scavenging the rail yard. The railroad detectives will argue with the ignorant police, who will dismiss it as an unfortunate accident."

Mischa took another drag from her cigarette and exhaled. "I want you to double our security the next two nights," she said. "Someone might show up searching for them. We might even draw out the infamous Tiger Lee. Then she'll finally get her chance to meet the White Dragon."

Following his meeting with Vera, Alan spent the next day hanging around Mr. Brinkman's office. With little to do, Alan busied himself packing much of Vic's hastily abandoned desk items, keeping out some of it—like the chess board that still held Vic and Mackie's last game, the one Vic might have won, if not...some memories couldn't help being bittersweet. Alan would hold onto this one as long as he could.

Around lunchtime, Vera stuck her head in the office and held her index finger to her mouth to signal secrecy. "Call the number tonight," she whispered.

Instead of telling her he had a dinner date that might run late, Alan lowered his eyes and nodded. Vera could wait until after he'd said goodnight to Alice. It would serve her right. As she walked away, he put his hand over his face and rubbed his eyes, trying to wipe Vera's image from his mind. The more he tried to steel himself against her allure, the more he thought about her and the more she aroused him—a contradiction he didn't understand.

That night at the Sorrento Hotel Alan used the same

bank of phones as before to call the Melrose Exchange. He forgot to ask Vera about code names, so he only relayed his phone number. Moments after the call, the phone rang. This time Vera didn't disguise her voice. "You're late."

"Sorry, I had dinner plans and didn't have—"

"Meet me at the University Bridge."

"Outside again? Won't that be cold?"

"We'll use the shack for the bridge tender, the one on the eastside. I have the key."

"Twenty minutes?"

"It's downhill from where you are. Fifteen would be better."

"I'll do my best."

Seventeen minutes later, Alan walked out onto the University Bridge, heading for the bridge tender's shack as directed. He slowed and approached the door, though he doubted that Vera could have possibly gotten there before him. He reached for the handle, just as the door opened before him to reveal Vera's face. "Come in," she said.

"How'd you get here so fast? You have wings or a cape?"

"Maybe. Come upstairs."

She led the way, climbing the steep steel ladder to the observation level, which spanned across a shoulder lane of traffic. He was right behind her and fully aware there would be an opportunity to look straight up her skirt, but he fought the urge and waited for her to get to the top, forcing himself to be a gentleman. She wasn't going to have the upper hand tonight.

"Where's the bridge tender?" he asked.

"There's only one at night, and he's working the west side. He's a college student at the university, doing his homework. If he gets lost in his studies and doesn't see a ship coming, it'll slow and toot its whistle to get his attention.

41

If we don't turn on the lights, he won't see us."

"So we don't have to whisper?"

"Not at all."

She sat down in a chair and patted the one next to her with the palm of her hand. He grabbed the chair, pulled it a little ways from her, and sat facing her. The ambient light from the street below revealed the consternation on her face and he suddenly felt the need to apologize. "I had plans, and you didn't give me a chance to ex—"

"You could have called the safe number and left a message," she said.

"I didn't know you were using it for that purp—"

"This is more important than canoodling with Alice— its' important that we meet. I have an agent who's gone missing, and I need your help finding out what happened. You have to be inventive, Alan. At the moment I don't have anyone else I can send."

Alan apologized again, hanging his head. Vera kicked off her shoes, crossed her legs, and nudged his pant leg with her toe. "We don't have time for you to mope."

He started to apologize again but stopped himself. "What is it you need me to do? Where was this agent when he disappeared?"

"There's two of them actually. One's our agent and the other's a sailor who's now listed as AWOL. We were working a tip, three missing rail cars full of spent brass the Japanese are hungry to get. My agent was supposed to find out what this sailor knew. They were to meet outside of Ship's Restaurant on 15th Avenue West, near the Navy gates."

"That's not a lot to go on."

Vera began rubbing Alan's calf with the instep of her foot, and Alan had to admit he liked it. Maybe he was being too tough on her. Vera cocked her head slightly and stared

42

out at the University District's lights, as if looking for an answer. "The rail cars can only go so far," she said. "It's not like a stolen auto some kid can drive up any alley and stash behind a building or hide in a garage. These cars have to stay on the rails.

"We could check between the Navy piers and the main waterfront," Vera continued, "but I don't think they would take that kind of chance. I'm betting they would hide them in the Interbay yards, where most of the rail cars get queued up."

Alan nodded quietly, following her line of thinking.

"The problem is," she said, "that Interbay is so large—it's maybe twenty tracks wide and runs from Galer Street up past Dravus, all the way up to Emerson where there's a round house."

Vera took her foot that was nudging Alan's leg and swung it up onto his lap, settling it down gently. "Do me a favor and massage my foot just under the arch, would you, Champ?"

Alan stared down at the well-shaped calf and ankle, its beauty enhanced by silk hose, and then he glanced up to find the owner with her eyes closed, lost in thought. He grabbed Vera's foot with one hand, ready to throw it off his lap but he stopped and held it with both hands. There was nothing erogenous about rubbing feet, was there? he wondered. After a moment he began kneading her high instep. What was the harm?

Vera let out a soft pleasurable coo and squirmed in her seat. "You have nice strong hands."

"Sure, but you were saying." Alan paused to let her continue.

"We'll have to take a look for ourselves. I would guess the cars would be on a side spur or rail, whatever they're calling them, and it wouldn't be very far from the Navy gates."

43

"When do we—"

"Time's a wasting. I could just sit here and let you massage my foot for hours, but we've got work to do. We're both overdressed for this, so come up to my place. I'll have something you can change into."

🐉 ☉ 🐉

Alan followed Vera's car, a Darrin Victoria Packard convertible, up the north end of Capitol Hill to Roanoke Street, over to Tenth East, and then further up the avenue to an apartment building a few blocks west of Volunteer Park. This explained her ability to get to the meeting spots so quickly. Her unit was on the top floor in a well-established brick building. Once inside, Vera casually set down her purse and dropped her keys on a hallway table. She pointed him in the direction of the second bedroom, across the hall from hers, and told him to look through the closets for something warm and dark. He could leave his clothes on the bed. "I'd offer you a drink, but we don't have the time. I also want you alert."

Alan opened the closet and found an assortment of men's clothing, ranging in size from large to double X. There were sweaters stacked on top of dress shirts, sport coats, and pants folded on hangers. Alan's mind raced with the possibilities, not just of what to wear, but why Vera had all these men's clothes in the first place. Had his father been one of those men? Alan found a suitable sweater, heavy pants, and a pair of work shoes. He tossed the sweater and pants onto the bed and sat down to take his pants off. Maybe when they returned he would get a chance to search through the other items there.

Vera tapped and pushed the bedroom door open. "I'm sorry, I didn't think you'd be this far ahead of me. You'll find socks, underwear, and a wool hat in the dresser."

Vera crossed the hall to her room but left the door to his room ajar. He was about to say something but decided not to bother. After all, this was her apartment. He stood up to finish dressing, sliding the pants over his hips. While pulling the sweater on he wandered back around the bed. She called out from across the hall. "Have you found everything you need?"

He turned in the direction of the voice and had a clear shot into her bedroom. She was sliding into her trousers, pulling the pants over the silk underwear that covered her taut rump. He averted his eyes for a second but then quickly glanced back at her. She's the one who left the doors open, Alan thought. Suddenly Vera spun around to face him with a smile, pulled her sweater over her head, and shook her hair out. "There's no time to drool, Champ."

Alan chuckled quietly as he sauntered back to the dresser in search of a wool hat. When he turned back around she was gone and her door was closed halfway. He moved cautiously into the hallway, but she wasn't there either. To his side there was a light visible under the bathroom door. "Just give me a minute," Vera called out.

"Sure," he said, stepping away to give her some privacy. Her bedroom door was ajar, so he stepped farther back and stuck his head inside for a quick peek. Her evening clothes were tossed on top of her large bed, which had a number of decorative pillows gathered at the top. Across from the bed, near the window, was a vanity that housed a collection of make-up and featured a large, tiltable mirror. Tucked into the frame of the mirror were a number of pictures, and from a distance one looked to be his—

Behind him Vera's shadow loomed near the bathroom door. Alan stepped back into the hallway as she came out to meet him, smiling in her ever-confident way. "Are you ready, Champ?"

$\diamond$

Vera let Alan drive her car so she could think on the way to Interbay. She told him about the dangers in the rail yard and the sort of people they might encounter: hobos, vagrants, robbers, yard bulls, and worst of all, the Dragon Lady's spies, who would most likely be Japanese—but there was some risk in this assumption.

"Did you say the 'Dragon Lady'?"

"Yes, the White Dragon actually. We don't know her real name or who she is—only the rumors that she's the one directing Japanese spying throughout the Puget Sound region."

"So the White Dragon's her cover name?"

"Seems that way."

"The lady who answers the safe phone asked me not to use real names. Will I have a cover—"

"We'll talk about that later. For now we have to focus on this mission. If we get too close to Navy property we might have to deal with Marines, which could get dicey. Our goal is to avoid everyone and every encounter. We only shoot if we have no alternative—and hope to God it's nobody in our military."

"You have a gun?"

46

Vera frowned. "Of course. The enemy doesn't play fair, but neither do we. This is not a game. It's for keeps."

"What kind of gun?"

"You mean how big? Same as yours. Government issue .45."

Alan started to make a comment about her gun's size, but thought better of it. Vera would be able to handle the kick of a .45.

When they reached the foot of the Garfield Street Bridge, Vera directed him up the ramp that would bypass the Navy Base's entrance and take them onto Magnolia. "You know how to change a flat, Champ?"

"Sure, but it doesn't feel like we have one."

Vera had him slow down near the middle of the bridge span, just past the fuel tank farm and in front of the Navy warehouses below them. "No flat, but we need to go through the motions in case someone asks us what we're doing. While you play with the jack and tire, I'll scout the rails for our missing brass."

Alan retrieved the jack and carried it to the right front bumper while Vera sauntered over to the thick cement bulkhead that served as the bridge's railing. Alan quickly snapped the jack in place and connected it to the bumper before Vera could stop him. "Easy, Champ. I don't want any scratches. Just leave it like that until someone comes along."

Alan stopped his chore and joined Vera at the wall. Below them in the yard, rail spurs stretched past the Navy warehouses all the way to the piers on the south end. "I'm betting that the brass came this way and went north, taking the cars east toward the main rail yard. Our brass is probably there," Vera said, pointing to an area that wasn't lit up like the rest of the yard.

She leaned in close to Alan and pointed again. "How's your eyesight?"

"Better than 20-20. I think they call it 20-10."

"Great, now look along the outside spur and tell me what you see."

"There's a string of open cars on the end—probably a dozen or so," he said.

"That'll be them," Vera said. "I don't see any other open cars in the yard."

"That'll make it easier."

"Oh sure. Just a walk in the park from here," Vera said. "What I meant was at least we know where to look."

"And how do you propose we get there, detective?"

"I'd come in from the west, down off Magnolia, but that means we'd have to cross a lot of open military property, which they might object to."

Vera nodded, indicating for Alan to continue.

"I say we come in from the other side, use that angle street off of 15th to get as close as we can."

"Good plan. Only problem is that's the National Guard Armory, which really might not be such a big risk. Since they're Reserves, they're probably all at home in bed. There shouldn't be anyone inside to care about what we're doing outside their little playland, but let's be careful and not put that theory to the test if we don't have to."

"Understood, ma'am."

Vera grabbed his arm to pull him close, and ran her hand up under his hat, mussing his hair. "I hate it when you call me that," she said with faux rage.

"I know." He grinned wolfishly.

"You rascal." She released his hair. "Put the jack away, Champ. We've got work to do."

◇◇

Alan parked behind a warehouse off of Fifteenth Avenue West near Armory, and from the trunk Vera retrieved her .45 caliber pistol and its custom built shoulder holster, which she strapped in place. Next, she grabbed flashlights for both of them. "By the time we get where it matters, our eyes should be better adapted to the darkness. We don't want to use these," she said, holding up the flashlights, "unless we have to."

They walked down Armory to the dead-end at the fence bordering the rail yards. Vera immediately crouched down and began to search for a soft spot under the fence. The Great Depression had taken its toll on the railroads, and many hobos used the rails as "affordable" transportation, traveling from city to city looking for seasonal work. The sheer numbers of men and women who tunneled under and pulled up the otherwise secure fence made it an easy passage. Alan noticed worn paths in several places where there normally should have been uninterrupted weeds and blackberry bushes.

Fifty feet from the dead-end's turnaround Alan tapped Vera's shoulder and pointed to where the chain link was curled up and the ground was worn bare underneath it.

"What about this one?" he asked.

"Too much light here...and too much traffic," she replied.

They moved another hundred yards down the fence to a spot more to Vera's liking. The light from the rail yards and bordering warehouses was dimmer and a thicket of blackberries protected their location from prying eyes. No more than thirty feet inside the fence a boxcar offered them immediate protection. If we make it that far, Alan thought.

Vera gave Alan the quiet sign and nodded her assent. Alan bent over and pulled up the fence, while Vera dropped to the ground and slid on her back underneath the wire. Once on the other side, Vera held the fence, allowing Alan to slide under and join her.

They scanned the area around them and ran toward the boxcar, Vera in the lead. When they reached the car they pressed their backs against the large wheels, and again surveyed the vicinity for movement. Deeper into the yard behind them a diesel engine roared as it pushed and pulled other boxcars, assembling lines of cars for a train.

"Let's work our way around the main clutch of boxcars and over to the far rail," Vera whispered.

Within a few minutes they had traversed two hundred feet of empty boxcars, climbing over couplings and sliding through empty boxcars until they came to the spur closest to the Navy's base. Ten yards away from their final goal, they reached the last line of boxcars and pressed themselves between two of the cars near the middle of the line. Alan checked one direction and Vera the other. They both signaled that their direction was clear. Just as they started to make their dash, a nearby voice said, "Have you got a light?"

Alan and Vera both froze mid-stride and stepped back into their place of safety. The voice had been muffled, and they scanned the area around them frantically but still found nothing. Inside the car behind Vera, another voice said, "Sure. Roll one for me while you're at it."

Vera leaned over and pressed her mouth close to Alan's ear. "Hobos."

Her breath blew softly on Alan's neck, and then she pressed her fingers against the center of his back before leaning away. Alan's eyebrows pinched together as he tried to stay focused on their mission. He shrugged and shook his head as if such action would drive away any thoughts of lust. Vera moved close again and placed her hand gently on his upper chest. This time her chin rubbed against his. "Let's move up the line a couple of cars where there's more cover. We'll cross there." Vera stared into his eyes a moment, before leaning back again. She let her hand drop, raking her fingers gently across his chest and abdomen.

Alan's nose flared wide as he inhaled her scent, a wonderful combination of perfume and pheromones. She knew what she was doing, no doubt about it. He vowed he wouldn't let her get to him. Damn, she could be annoying— every voluptuous ounce of her, but at the same time, she sure seemed to know her business. Her eyes bespoke calm and calculation, as if she'd risked her life hundreds of times before.

Vera pulled his arm as she darted into the open, and he followed closely. Together they raced alongside two boxcars, step for step, and then climbed into an empty one, five cars ahead of the caboose. There they pressed themselves against the wall on either side of the door. When they were sure they were safe they quietly lowered themselves down to the gravel rail bed, and then dashed across to the open gondolas. Immediately they wedged themselves between two cars at a coupling, pressing their backs against opposite sides. Vera drew close to his ear again. "We'll need to check the waybill."

"There's one next to me, but it's too dark to read. Do we

51

want to risk a flashlight?"

Vera inched back far enough so he could see her face fully, and she shook her head, minimizing the need for conversation. Her eyes were alive, hinting impishly at mischievousness. She was clever and didn't mind showing it. Maybe it was that kind of confidence, he wondered, that allowed her to be a headliner in a burlesque show in her early years.

"We have to mute the light," she said. "I'll show you how."

She took her flashlight, unzipped her coat, tugged her sweater up, and slid the light behind the fabric. "Get in close to me so none of the light escapes. You ready?"

Alan nodded.

Vera fumbled with the stubborn switch, and the light came on inside her sweater. Both pair of eyes focused on the card slot. "*Destination: Pier Six. Cargo: steel ingots,*" Vera read.

"That's it," they said in unison.

Vera again struggled briefly with the switch, before getting the flashlight to shut off. "Now all we need is to verify the brass is here."

"May as well check this car," Alan said. He put his foot in the steel stirrup and pulled himself up, peering over the top of the car. A second later, he glanced back and nodded towards Vera. Then he threw his leg over the side and climbed in partway, only to return seconds later with a trophy. He climbed back down and handed her an empty forty mm brass shell. "This was sitting by itself on top of a load of ingots. Careful, it feels oily."

Vera abruptly handed it back to Alan. "This is the proof we need," she said. "Hold it close. I want to see it in the light."

They huddled together, with Alan cupping the brass shell in both hands as though it was a fresh caught Rainbow trout he was afraid of dropping back into a stream. Vera slid the flashlight under her sweater and turned on the switch to examine their prize. The light flickered through the wool sweater for only an instant, before she gasped and quickly tried to cut the light as if it was a timing device on a ticking bomb. As she struggled with the switch, the muted beam illuminated a bold red smear across the back of the rail car before she finally pointed it angrily toward the ground. There was something wrong. This wasn't the Vera Alan knew. For a brief instant the light's beam slipped clear of her sweater, but she finally managed to shut it off and clipped it to a belt loop on her side. She took the brass shell from Alan, sighed nervously, and sat back against the opposite car, raising her free hand to her brow.

Something was wrong, but Alan didn't know what it could be. The normally unflappable Vera was off her game. He moved close to reassure her. "Let's move to the other side of the coupling, down a car or two," he whispered. "Whatever it is, it'll be alright."

Vera shook her head, as if she were trying to shake out a haunting image. She pressed her mouth hard against his ear lobe. "It's not oil on the shell, it's blood, and there's more on the side of the car."

Alan anxiously stepped over the coupling to the side closest the Navy base and tugged on Vera's arm. "We need to move."

Vera clutched the military shell to her bosom and slid one leg over the coupling, but with her hands full, her back leg slipped and caught on the hydraulic hose coupling. Alan leaned into her, one hand pressing on her lower back where her sweater had pulled up, while the other hand grabbed her lower leg and helped guide it over the coupling. When she slid over, he quickly followed, and as he passed her, he gently grabbed her arm to help guide her and the brass shell toward safety.

As Vera and Alan passed the end of the next car, a dark specter raced past them in the opposite direction on the other side of the open cars. A second figure and then a third soon followed. An angry voice barked orders in a dialect Alan didn't immediately recognize but thought sounded vaguely like some of the Asian dialects he'd heard in Big Mama's brothel.

Alan and Vera neared the end of the second car, only eighty feet away from where they had turned on the light. They tucked into the next opening and crouched low. As they hid behind the coupling, their knees banged together roughly. Vera's eyes smoldered with anger as she continued to clutch the bloody shell close to her.

Alan rolled forward on his knees, clasped Vera by the arms, and pressed his lips to her ear. "I saw at least three operatives. They may split up and send a scout this way."

A hundred yards away a diesel engine roared to life, startling them. The behemoth's loud growl was soon followed by the sound of couplings clanging together, their huge knuckles groaning with metal on metal scraping, as a queue of cars was pushed together. As soon as the noises subsided, they were replaced by more angry commands in Japanese, followed by several feet running on gravel. Alan reached for his gun, and then hesitated. "There's too many of them. We've stepped into a beehive."

Alan released Vera and peeked around the edge of the car, exposing as little of himself as he could. A man carrying a flashlight in one hand and a revolver in the other was rapidly working his way toward their position. Vera was right about flashlights: it was not only easy to see the man as he approached, but his reliance on the light's beam showed where his attention was focused. Alan watched the light shine under the cars on one side and then across the path into some weeds and a ditch toward the Navy's chain-link fence. The sound of the man's feet on crushed rock drew nearer. Alan nodded to Vera and took the military shell from her, gripping the tapered end like a beat cop would a billy club in a bar fight. "Cover me," he whispered.

Deep in the yard behind them, the diesel engine roared again and couplings creaked defiantly, just as a pair of feet slid to a halt nearby. Alan sprang from his hiding spot with a boxer's timing. He swung his left arm down and knocked the startled searcher's flashlight to the side, while at the same time he unloaded a powerful swing with the heavy end of the brass shell, crashing it down on the bridge of the nose of his opponent. Action beat reaction. There was a sickening crunch as the man's facial bones broke and collapsed inward. The Japanese agent dropped his gun, and his knees immediately buckled. His lifeless body fell flat on the gravel railroad bed.

Alan lowered and dropped his improvised weapon. He squatted and grabbed the man by his coat's lapels, pausing to stare at the agent's crushed face for a long moment, committing it to memory. Alan grimaced and shook his head, then tugged the dead body up the rail and shoved it under the gondola. Alan tried pushing the man's hand in with the rest of him, but it flopped back over the rail. Alan tossed the agent's flashlight in next to his body, but he stuffed the dropped revolver into his own coat pocket. After the scene was tidied, Alan returned for the brass shell, but it had rolled away from the railway bed, and all Alan saw was a shallow ditch filled with muddy water.

Alan raced back to their hiding place. Vera was holding her .45 automatic in a high-ready position. He squatted next to her. "Won't be long before they come looking for him. I say we move while we can."

Alan extended his hand, and Vera grabbed it, pulling herself up. "Where's my brass?" she asked.

"In the ditch. It's too risky to search for it."

Alan tugged Vera along next to him, pulling her by the hand to ensure they would stay close while they raced along at a fast clip, passing one gondola car after another. Behind them the commotion continued to get louder as the angry Japanese voices multiplied. Alan's immediate plan was to put as much distance between them and their pursuers as they possibly could. Soon they would reach the end of the cars and have to hope for the best. From there they'd have to try and make it deeper into the yard, where it would be harder for searchers to find them.

Passing the last car in the line, Alan scanned ahead to plan their next move. At the end of the next train over was a caboose they could cross behind, if the way was clear. Rounding the last gondola he glanced back to see how close the enemy was to them. Vera's eyes followed Alan's. About two hundred feet away, murky silhouettes raced about, but it was unclear where their attention was focused. Alan turned back, prepared for their dash across the open ground to the caboose, and immediately froze. Their escape route had been blocked.

On the caboose's rear platform stood the imposing figure of Riki Yamamoto, nattily attired in a three-piece suit, tie, and white shirt—a Japanese version of Teddy Roosevelt campaigning for President. On the ground below two angry Japanese raced toward Alan and Vera, both of the men pointing double-barreled shotguns directly at each of them. They yelled something in a dialect Alan and Vera didn't comprehend, but they understood its intent all the same. They raised their hands.

A few hours before, Riki Yamamoto, Mischa Ohara's manservant, had spoken sternly to the team of Japanese operatives he had assembled. He towered over them all, both in height and body mass. He had encouraged vigilance and threatened that he would settle for nothing less. Much was at stake for their country with this upcoming shipment. This was not the time for them to relax and let up. Japan was starving for what was in the nearby gondola cars, particularly the three with the brass shells. A two hundred dollar bonus, in U.S. currency, was promised to the first man who spotted a spy near their railcars, and the sum would jump to an astounding one thousand dollars should one of the spies turn out to be the notorious Tiger Lee.

The Japanese agents roughly shoved Alan and Vera toward the caboose, prodding them with the business end of their shotguns, while two more men emerged from behind a stack of railroad ties and quickly bound the prisoners' hands with lanyards.

"Remove their weapons and bring them both inside," Riki said. "I wish to speak with them."

One of the Japanese men roughly opened Alan's jacket and pulled it off his shoulders and down his arms toward his bound hands, where it bunched into a large knot of fabric. The frisk revealed Alan's semi-automatic. The other man unsnapped the holster and removed the exposed .45 pistol, holding it up as a trophy. The agents repeated the process on Vera, taking her weapon from her shoulder holster and similarly displaying it. The men shoved the confiscated pistols into their own clothing and roughly forced the pair up the steps and inside the caboose.

Riki took a lantern from one of his men and held it close to Vera's face. He smiled broadly and then moved the light down her body. "Ahhh," he sighed. He lowered the lantern and shouted something to his companions, which was quickly followed by excited cheers. Pushing Alan back into a chair, Riki positioned his face to within inches of Vera's, and switched back to English. "It appears," he said, "that standing before us is the infamous *Tiger Lee.*"

Unblinking, Vera met Riki's gaze and held it. "And you are?"

"Riki Yamamoto," he said, rolling his head on his powerful neck like a Sumo wrestler preparing to engage his opponent. "You don't deny it?" he asked.

"Why should I?"

Riki raised a clenched fist and shook it under Vera's nose. "Finally, we have flushed you out. You have caused my country great consternation and are responsible for the disappearance of many men. You shall pay!" he shouted. He contemptuously placed the palm of his hand in the middle of Vera's chest and pushed her into a chair next to Alan.

Strutting confidently through the close quarters of the caboose, Riki spoke to one of his agents in Japanese. The man looked over at Alan, and then quickly left the caboose. Riki glanced back to his prisoners. "We are going to take a ride. There is someone who has longed to meet you, and she will not be disappointed."

"I look forward to our meeting," Vera snapped.

"Not for long, you won't," Riki growled.

Riki's men led Alan and Vera out to a black Cadillac
that was idling near the rear steps of the caboose. One of
the Japanese agents climbed into the Imperial limousine
first and pulled Vera inside, forcing her to sit next to him.
Riki climbed in next, bracketing her between them. Alan
found himself in the same position between two men on
the rear seat facing Vera. He sat back, which was awkward
because his coat was still pulled behind him into a large
ball that had a hard lump inside. Alan almost dismissed the
strangeness of the lump, but then he remembered. To be
sure it was what he thought, he squeezed and prodded at
the lump with his fingers. He was right, and the knowledge
of it sent butterflies flying throughout his system. It was
the dead agent's revolver that Alan had picked up from the
railroad bed and slipped into his coat. When they'd frisked
him for his .45 they'd stopped at his shoulder holster
without bothering to search his coat.

The driver motored through the rail yard and across
embedded timbers that enabled the heavily laden car to
cross the tracks where the Wheeler Street Bridge once
traversed Interbay. When they reached an unguarded gate
that the rail company used for its service vehicles, the front

seat passenger got out and unlocked it.

Alan slouched down in his seat, which gave him room to explore the knots in the lanyard tied around his wrist. He also probed the revolver again with his fingers. He hadn't got a good look at it when he recovered it, but he was sure it was a .38 caliber, probably a Smith and Wesson, not a Colt. He rubbed the gun again, like a talisman, hoping it would bring him luck, but there was no way he could get a solid grip on it and bring it into play.

Alan glanced across at Vera. Despite the circumstance she exuded inner confidence and strength. It was infectious, giving him hope. With a sly smile she blew him a kiss. The gapped-tooth guard next to Alan saw the gesture. He scowled, and without warning swung his elbow sharply, striking Alan hard just above his right eye. The force of the blow rocked Alan's head and almost knocked him unconscious.

Alan had been dealt worse in the boxing ring a few years back when he'd won the Golden Gloves. He'd taken the worst his opponent could give in the first few rounds, but he didn't give up the fight. Somehow he'd found it in him to storm back and win by a knockout in the seventh. To keep from blacking out Alan thought about that pair of Golden Gloves, now hanging in his bedroom, and how proud his dad had been when he won them. It helped to block out the pain while he feigned a stupor, hoping it would get his abuser to relax and lower his defenses. That tactic was another boxing strategy Alan had seen used effectively— but he knew it only worked the first time.

Their chauffer took Elliot Avenue up the regrade to Denny Way and then south on First Avenue. Alan figured the driver was unfamiliar with Seattle because if they were going to Japan Town there were faster routes. Alan watched out the window as they slowly approached First Avenue,

Seattle's original Front Street, which featured shops and bars—fine for sailors and dockworkers, but too many liquor establishments for his mother's liking. South of Yesler had been the worst part of town in its heyday. It was once called the Tenderloin and was at its height of debauchery during the Alaska Gold Rush when Seattle merchants outfitted the Alaska miners on their way north, only to fleece them again when they returned from the fields with gold dust in their pockets. This part of town had never fully recovered from that wide-open image, when it featured box houses with prostitutes behind velvet curtains, gambling, and opium dens that catered to the sailors, lumberjacks, and miners. Alan's family avoided this end of town.

They drove by the main entrance to the Farmer's Market, south past Cherry, continuing until they passed the Great Pioneer Safe Deposit Bank near Yesler. The driver worked his way east and then turned off near Sixth Avenue, looping down a few blocks before stopping on a steep incline near the basement entrance to a hotel. Either the driver had trouble finding where he was going, or he was trying to confuse everyone else, Alan thought.

The driver remained seated and kept the motor running, while the front seat passenger got out and opened the rear door behind him. Riki was the first to exit. He barked orders to the others, and the man beside Alan jabbed him sharply in the ribs and pushed him towards the door. As Alan got out of the limo he saw that the name of the hotel was painted in faded Japanese characters, with a sub-heading in English. Alan recognized the word *Baths* but nothing else.

With a glance over his shoulder, Alan saw them usher Vera in behind him. The men hurrying her along didn't seem to be as rough with her as they were with him. She maintained her regal bearing and the ever-present hint of a smile.

They had called her Tiger Lee, like she was Matta Hari, a master spy, and she didn't deny it. What was that all about? Alan wondered.

Riki and his men led them through a dimly lit entryway past wooden lockers into the large room with tiled floors and a large bath in one corner. Damp towels hung from hooks, and there was a mop and an empty bucket in the corner near a wooden wall that didn't rise all the way to the ceiling. Separated by a privacy screen with a flimsy door, the woman's tub was on the other side. The bathtub in the room they entered had a step for bathers to rest on. The men led Vera to a far bench and allowed her to take a seat. As Alan turned to sit next to her, his tormenter struck again with a kick that caught Alan near his left ear, painfully knocking him off balance. Alan fell back on his bunched up coat with the metal lump inside it, and his head landed near Vera's lap. He glanced up defiantly for a split second, and his attacker assumed a fighting stance, with his fists held in a strange defensive way, as if somehow Alan could attack with hands tied behind his back. Alan laid his head against Vera's leg and resumed his fake stupor. Comforted by her scent, the sharp pain passed quickly.

Alan had no experience with the Oriental form of Martial Arts. Other than hearing names like Jujitsu, Judo, Karate, Aikido, and Kung Fu, he didn't know one from the other. He wondered how he would fare as a boxer against this coward who struck a bound opponent. There was something the man had done to foreshadow his attack, indicating where he was aiming his blow, but Alan couldn't quite sort it out yet. He didn't have enough information. If he fought the man in a ring—or a back alley for that matter—he was sure he'd pick up the cheap-shot tendencies before the sneak could inflict much damage. But first he'd have to remember to watch the man's feet; they generated a lot of power.

Riki brushed roughly past the other men, approaching Vera directly. His voice was deep and staccato like. "You will please wait here. I will be back shortly," he said. Then he faced Alan's chief tormentor and scolded him in Japanese. Alan opened one eye partially to watch, taking a measure of pleasure in his foe's chastisement. The response Riki received to his tongue lashing must not have been to his liking, because he flexed his arms, hunched his shoulders, and dropped his clinched fists to his side while swiftly moving toward the smaller man, who slowly backed down, lowering his eyes as he did. Riki yelled something the other man didn't seem to appreciate. It included the word Kutsu, as if it were an epithet. Two of the uninvolved agents, one with a buzz cut and the other with small round glasses and the thin whiskers of a Disney rodent, reacted more quickly, jumping out of Riki's way. It was as if they were keeping out of range of a pit bull on a leash that was too long. Riki was the one to reckon with.

As soon as Riki left the room, the sentries immediately sat down on the benches, while the one who had been berated remained standing. Vera leaned her head back against the wall and glanced up at the steam pipes that ran along the ceiling and down toward the floor, one feeding a hissing radiator that heated the room, and the other leading directly to a spout above the empty bath. After a moment she lowered her head and leaned forward, as if examining the pattern of tiles on the floor. "You all right?" she whispered.

Alan took a deep breath rich with her scent, and then exhaled, nodding slightly.

Alan carefully watched the guard standing ten feet away, and wondered what Riki had shouted at him. He hoped it was a string of vile Japanese epithets but the fact that the cheap-shot artist didn't like it was good enough for Alan.

Alan tried to whisper, using just the side of his mouth. "Tiger Lee?"

"Stage name," Vera said in a tone that was barely audible. "I kept it as a cover. It's not connected—yet—to *Vera*. Keep it that way."

"Understood."

The standing guard rocked forward on the balls of his feet and strutted closer to Vera and Alan, first staring closely at her and then Alan. From the back of the room one of the sentries spoke up.

"Kutsu," the man scolded. And then he said something in Japanese that included Riki's name.

The guard sneered contemptuously at the admonishment, not liking the Kutsu reference, and then he slowly turned around, exposing his vulnerable backside to Vera and Alan. He placed his hands on his hips with his feet spread, and stood still for a moment before walking away without a word. It must have been a show of bravado to himself or the others, Alan couldn't be sure. After a few moments, Kutsu walked to a bench several feet away and sat down, making a production of it. The other guards did not appear impressed.

While the steam radiator continued creaking and groaning, Alan asked Vera for more information. "How many guns have you seen?"

"None," she replied.

"Me neither." After a pause Alan added, "Kutsu has my .45 in his belt. The guy in back with the buzz cut has yours."

Vera exhaled and the warm air from her nostrils rolled across Alan, which somehow offered a measure of solace. "Without opening your eyes, tell me how many of their agents are in the room right now?" she said.

"Is this a test?"

"Call it practice."

After a moment, Alan said, "Kutsu is closest to us, while the other two are in the back, but there's one more—with a gap tooth and swollen lips. I'm not sure—"

"He's sitting on the lip of the tub by himself, rubbing his jaw." Vera sat up for a moment and shifted her weight. "Now that wasn't bad for a beginner," she offered, "but you've only counted two weapons; that doesn't mean the others are not armed,"

"I know, just like me."

"You?"

"Coat pocket. I'm sitting on the .38 I took from the guy in the rail yard."

Vera leaned forward, purposely pushing her breasts firmly against Alan's face. "I could kiss you."

"Vera! Stop!"

"What?"

"I'm supposed to be passed out cold, but you're getting me excited."

Vera tried to suppress a giggle but it snuck out. She peeked at Kutsu, who had jumped off the bench and was staring at the both of them. Vera faked a cough, while Alan lay still. She shook her head and tried to cough again. Then she cleared her throat. After a moment, the man sat down. The other three never moved.

She leaned within inches of Alan's face. "Can you work your hands free?"

"I'm trying. Not getting—"

Outside the room there was commotion in the hallway. Someone was coming, but the four men around the room did not appear concerned. "I think our host is returning with someone special for us to meet," Vera said.

"Who?"

"The White Dragon."

"I hope you're not dying to meet her."

Vera snorted and smiled. "Curious? Yes. Dying? No."

"The men stay away from you. Why?"

"Because I'm a *savateuse.*"

"What? You're smart?"

"Not savant—I'm a French boxer," Vera said.

"I see," Alan said, knitting his brows. "Anything else?"

"Master of la canne and le baton."

"You fight with a cane?"

"Like the epee—fencing."

"So...you could beat me up, then?"

"If you want, but you'd have to pay me in advance, just like the girls downtown."

It was Alan's turn to snort and smile. While doing so, he opened an eye and watched Kutsu rise from the bench again. Alan rolled his head drunkenly, feigning delirium, and laid back down. While standing alert, his opponent puffed out his chest and strolled leisurely across the room to peek around the corner into the hallway.

"You smell good," Alan whispered.

"Thank you."

"What's going on?"

"I believe we're going to have a perform—"

Around the corner, Riki shouted something that caused Kutsu to hurry into the hallway and out of their sight. A moment later, out of the darkness, a strange figure came into focus. The other guards jumped to their feet, and they all bowed to the garish specter as she graced the room. Stunningly attired in a geisha robe, with her jet-black hair shaped into an elegant shimada on top of her head, Alan noticed that the woman wore a tiara made of carved ivory. The demure beauty gracefully glided across the ceramic tiles on okobo clogs. Her face was painted porcelain white, like an antique doll's, and her eyes were rimmed with red

67

and black mascara, drawn at a severe angle to accent her Asian features. It was the Kabuki theater style—but she was no geisha. Although she fluttered a bamboo and silk fan demurely, tucked into her sash were two swords that proclaimed the social rank of warrior. She was a samurai.

Alan rolled away from Vera, and without realizing he was doing so, he stood up along with the others. He didn't know whether it was out of curiosity, fear, respect, or old-fashioned manners—or maybe a combination of them all. Vera defiantly remained seated and exhaled contemptuously.

"Well," Vera said. "What have we here?"

Alan hesitated for a moment and then slowly sat down next to Vera. Without taking her eyes off the woman samurai, Vera whispered to him. "This has to be the White Dragon. I'm not waiting for her introduction. It's me she wants. Kill who you can, when you can. Our lives depend on it."

"Understood."

Raising her voice, not caring who heard, Vera spoke to Alan again. "Stay out of the way, follow my lead, and don't move until I do."

Alan nodded.

The group with the woman samurai neared within fifteen feet of the cornered prisoners. Riki stepped ahead of the others, protectively, and snarled at Vera and Alan. "You will be silent and wait until the White Dragon says otherwise!"

"If you wish to talk, that's close enough," Vera said.

The group hesitated, as if they had lost their momentum. Kutsu, who had trailed the procession as it came in, pulled out the pistol he'd stuffed in his waistband. The White Dragon quickly unsheathed her short sword and swiped it across the gunman's ear, nicking off a sliver of it and drawing blood. She snapped something in Japanese to him, and he carefully put the gun away, while clutching his ear. Without changing expression she addressed Vera in flawless English, ignoring Alan. "I have cautioned him that if he wants to keep the rest of his ear, he will learn to listen."

"What do you want?" Vera asked.

"Answers, for starters."

"Answers to what?"

The White Dragon smoothly returned her short sword to its sheath, flaunting her skill with the blade. She addressed her gap-toothed henchmen and he moved back to the large tub which he began to fill directly from a steam pipe, not bothering to mix in cool water. The White Dragon returned her attention to her captives. "Answers as to why your country is trying to stop my country's expansion—while it has done nothing to stop European Imperialism."

"I don't know what you mean."

"As committed as you are to espionage, I am surprised you would need a history lesson." The White Dragon closed her eyes and sighed impatiently. "During the past two-hundred years, Europe and the U.S. have carved up Asia for their own purposes. From India to China, Indochina, the Pacific Islands, and the Philippines, it's been the same story. The United States sent Commodore Perry to Japan with warships to size up our peaceful land for conquest—to see how strong we were and what resources we had that your country could suck from our soil or our people. We knew we would be the next country to fall if we didn't grow strong."

Vera's brow knitted into a scowl. She sat up and leaned forward. "She's already giving me a headache," she whispered to Alan.

The White Dragon's men stood by her pensively. "You treat civilized Asians as if their lands were yours to carve up," she continued, "like a pie to share among you friends—the ones who look the same as you—just as Spain and Portugal did to South America. You have done this to the Native Americans you call Indians. In the rare times you praise them, you refer to them as noble savages—not worthy to rule themselves—so it is okay for you to take their lands away. Caucasians claim *Manifest Destiny* and the right to rule coast to coast. We fear you have only begun your imperialistic expansion. Americans have no regard for red, yellow, black, or brown—only white. And so when my country reaches for what it desperately needs, your country, and you in particular, thwart our efforts."

"In what way?"

"When Japan entered China, America defended what Britain could no longer because of the war in Europe. Instead of staying out of what shouldn't be your concern, your President embargoed steel and gasoline—things we need for our campaigns. Since your bankrupt economy desperately needs the money these sales would generate, your motives have to be more than monetary—like perhaps a pact to help Britain continue its stranglehold on the East."

Vera exhaled deeply and shook her head in contempt. "My country will not sit by while yours kills thousands of innocent—"

"Lies! No one is innocent during war," the White Dragon proclaimed. "There are unfortunate casualties, no doubt, but it is the price a nation must pay when its people resist—"

"These are issues that should be discussed by leaders, not by us. I have no control—"

"But it is for these very issues that *you* intervene, stopping our efforts, killing our *innocent* men! I will send your head to Japan in a box." With that, the White Dragon clutched at the hilt of her long sword.

"I intervene for my country, because I protect *her.* My fear is the brass you smuggle will someday be used against her," Vera said. She turned away to watch the soaking tub as it filled with water, waiting out the White Dragon. The woman glared at her for several moments, but Vera ignored her. Finally, the White Dragon snorted in contempt. "We will ship the brass."

"I can't let you."

"You are not in a position to bargain."

"Don't be so sure."

The White Dragon's nostrils flared as she let out a Japanese curse, unsheathing her sword. Instantaneously, Vera pulled her knees up toward her shoulders, bounced off the bench high enough to whip her tied hands under her feet, bringing them in front of her body. Just as quickly she sprang to a standing position, her hands extended slightly beyond her jacket's cuffs. The White Dragon and her entourage hesitated momentarily, as Riki stepped forward, a pace ahead of the others.

"She's mine!" the White Dragon snapped. "Give me room to work."

Riki bowed slightly and stepped to the side, giving the samurai the room she needed to swing her long sword. The White Dragon's blade sang as it whipped through the air and she took an attacking position. Riki's backward step was all Vera needed to seize the momentum. She sprinted past Alan to the corner where a mop handle stuck out of an empty bucket. She grabbed the wooden shaft and flipped it in the air, along with the galvanized bucket, assuming her own defensive position with the bucket resembling an oversized helmet on the mop's knotted head.

Despite the poor traction of clogs on the tiled floor, the White Dragon was almost as quick as Vera. The White Dragon raced to meet her opponent, and then suddenly slowed to take a defensive, martial art's stance.

With everyone focused on the two women, Alan made the most of his own agility, pulling his legs up, and sliding his hands under his feet as Vera had done. But unlike with her, his coat caught behind his heels as he struggled to get them in front where they would do the most good. There would be no forgiveness, no second chances. He flexed his abdominal muscles fiercely, pulling his knees as tightly to his chest as he could, and then he stretched his arms, dragging them roughly under his feet and out in front. Alan stood up and frantically dug at his coat pockets until his hand finally wrapped around the revolver's grip. It was now possible to squeeze the trigger, he thought, even though he didn't have the necessary leverage to free the revolver from the tangled coat.

The man with the buzz cut who had Vera's gun tucked behind his belt, took his eyes off the fighting women long enough to notice Alan's struggle. He raced toward Alan, grabbing for the pistol in his waistband. A few feet away, he slid to a stop and began to raise the .45 to eye level.

Alan didn't have time to evaluate whether the man was actually going to shoot or merely menace him with the pistol. Neither choice was acceptable. Instead, Alan thrust his cloaked hands outward and lined up a shot, just as his father had taught him. Unable to see the pistol sights, Alan relied on his instincts alone. Inside the coat pocket he cocked the .38 with his thumb, exhaled, and squeezed the pad of his finger down softly on the trigger. There would be no warning given.

POP!

The coat sprang to life as if possessed by a small demon. The dark material suddenly fluffed outward from the cartridge's expanding gases, making a muffled roar as it did. The bullet tore through the fabric and smashed into his would-be-assailant's left nostril, snapping his head back. The man's eyes rolled up into his head, and he stumbled backward, tripping over the edge of the tub and falling into the steaming water, which sizzled like a deep fat fryer. The pistol disappeared into the tub along with the man's body, as the water boiled over him.

The White Dragon and her friends hesitated momentarily at the sound of Alan's shot, their attention drawn from Vera to the enigmatic threat, but the revolver in Alan's coat pocket was still hidden from view. While the White Dragon continued her battle with Vera, Kutsu glared wild-eyed at Alan. He withdrew the pistol from his waistband and brought it up, focusing on Alan as his intended target as he dangerously placed the White Dragon and Riki in the crossfire.

Vera quickly changed her focus from the White Dragon and snapped the mop bucket down swiftly, crashing it solidly into Kutsu's gun hand. The .45 dropped to the floor with a loud clang and slid to rest beside Riki. The sharp noise of the pistol's crash was followed by the bucket's noisy clatter as it bounced across the room. On her backswing, Vera thrust the mop's tangled head at Riki's face, catching him full-on and knocking him off balance. Riki's back foot came down on the pistol, which skidded out from under his foot, causing him to crash solidly to the floor, his head slamming into the tiled pier.

The White Dragon instantly responded to Vera's movements, chopping her sword instinctively at the mop head and severing it cleanly from the end of the handle. With a freshly blunted stick, Vera focused on Kutsu and jabbed him hard on the side of his Adam's apple. As Kutsu grabbed at his neck, Vera spun her staff around and cracked him on the back of the head, sending him reeling forward into the White Dragon's path.

Closer to the boiling water, the last two guards squared off with Alan, who held his arms extended in a shooter's stance, indicating to the wise and cautious that there was a weapon at the end of his hands inside the wadded coat.

Both thugs' arms were raised partially, somewhere between surrender and the ready position for judo wrestlers. Each time Alan took his eyes off one man to check on the second, the first would sneak forward and lower his arms, only to retreat the same distance and raise them when Alan gestured at him with the ball of clothing hiding the revolver. Expediency demanded that Alan simply shoot them and get it over with, but at the same time he struggled with this idea. Wasn't there some way to get them to surrender, he wondered? Something in his soul wanted to stop this body count from climbing any higher.

On Alan's left, Kutsu continued his blind stumble, tripping over the outstretched legs of Riki and tumbling in front of the White Dragon, which sent him sprawling to the floor in front of Alan. Within an instant, Kutsu lurched and tried to push himself up, while the guard who reminded Alan of a rodent stepped forward to help him.

Alan decided that divine providence had intervened. His tormentor had been delivered to him. Alan sprang from his boxer's crouch and kicked hard like a football punter, catching Kutsu heavily in the side of his face. "Try some of your own tricks, asshole," he growled with a wolf-like grin.

The man's head wrenched to the side and he froze for a moment in a half-standing position. Alan dropped his foot to the floor just long enough to catch his balance, and then he struck with a side kick, catching Kutsu at the base of his ribs, sending him sprawling over the lip of the tub, face first into the steaming water.

Alan glanced quickly to check on the men he'd been holding at bay, but instead of lunging at Alan, who was off-balance at the moment, the last two guards froze in place and stared behind Alan's shoulder.

Alan peeked sideways in time to see the White Dragon flying across the tiles toward him, her samurai sword poised to strike. Instinctively, he spun as fast as he could, clutching his revolver and diving the opposite way. At that moment Vera caught up with her nemesis and landed catlike on the tiles in front of the White Dragon, facing her squarely. With a blinding flick of Vera's makeshift cudgel, she cracked the White Dragon's right elbow sharply.

The White Dragon screeched in anguish, her arms caving together with pain. She stepped back to refocus her energy, her eyes still on Alan, and as she raised her sword again Vera moved in like a cat pouncing on her prey. She followed the White Dragon's arm motion upward with narrowed eyes and sent a sharp kick to the White Dragon's painted face, catching her squarely below the base of her nose.

Sprawled on the tiled floor behind the two women, Riki pawed for the .45 on the floor by his thigh. Reaching it, he snapped it around in front of him, tracing Vera's movement. Catching sight of Riki's actions, Alan stretched and pointed his bound hands at the source of the threat and pulled the trigger again.

POP!

The bullet tore through the fabric as the tangled coat jumped to life again. The bullet found its mark in Riki's right shoulder, setting in motion a spasmodic recoil. Riki's suddenly useless arm flopped on top of his leg. When Alan turned back to face the other two guards, they both stepped back a pace and raised their hands higher than they had before.

With blood flowing from her nose down her white painted face, the White Dragon shook her head and lowered the sword to waist level, holding it with both hands. She kept the tip pointed at Vera, ready to thrust when the opportunity presented itself. Vera, however, held her ground, backing only slightly toward Alan. Her movement was more protective than a retreat. It also brought her closer to Riki who lay immobilized on the floor, pressing his left hand to the bloody hole in his shoulder while the semi-automatic still dangled at the end of his fingers.

Vera whipped her cudgel around and slammed it down fiercely on Riki's extended hand, cracking bones, and causing him to drop the pistol entirely. She flipped her stick again, catching the pistol on its side and sent it spinning to the far corner of the room past Alan.

The White Dragon moved parallel to Vera, and let out a battle cry, thrusting her sword desperately at her intended victim. Vera stepped quickly to the side, dodging the blow and allowing the wooden baton to slide down the flat side of the steel blade, avoiding the keen edge before slapping the danger away. Vera was quick to seize the offensive, and she moved in close to the White Dragon, removing any chance for the razor-sharp sword to get closer. She pressed her body against the White Dragon, chest to chest, pinning the samurai's sword hand so that it lay immobile against her side. Their faces came within inches of each other.

Having better traction on the slick tile floor, Vera used this to her advantage, improving her leverage to hold the White Dragon back. As she pressed her cheek against the White Dragon's painted face, she slammed the broadside of her staff sharply against the warrior's armored breastplate, catching her under the armpit. At the same time Vera released her stick and snatched two-handedly at the samurai's short sword, swiping it cleanly, sheath and all, from the White Dragon's wide belt.

While clasping the stolen sword tightly, Vera attempted to push herself away from the White Dragon to allow room to unsheathe the short sword, but the White Dragon was in for the fight and was quick as a snake's strike. She swung down hammer like with the long sword, and the solid hilt caught Vera's jaw, delivering a teeth-rattling blow before she could jump out of range.

Alan dashed from the bench to the corner where he could see the .45 on the floor. As he sped across the tiles he kept the .38 extended, pointing it at the other two henchmen who continued to play cat and mouse with him. One jumped out and then ducked back behind the pillar, while the other attempted to help Riki. Alan watched briefly as the short rat-like guard squatted to reach under Riki's armpits, struggling to lift the big man to his feet.

Figuring this was his only chance, Alan let go of the .38 and tugged his hand out of the coat's pocket. As he bent over to pick up the .45, the gap-toothed guard dove at Alan with a blocking tackle, knocking Alan's head into the wall and pinning his body against it. The assailant dug his fingernails into Alan's right arm, which was the only hand holding the pistol. Alan's left hand was still trapped inside the coat pocket, and now somewhat dazed, he couldn't shake his hand free so it could help hold the weapon away from his enemy.

Alan flexed his abdominals and wrenched his body to the side, trying to pull the smaller man off balance. The man continued to hang onto Alan's arm with one hand, while reaching for the automatic's barrel with his other, wrapping his fingers around the pistol in front of Alan's grip. He pushed up and backwards on the barrel, as he tried to peel the gun out of Alan's hand.

Just as Alan was about to lose the pistol to his foe, he heard a sword slash through the air. The slicing whistle was followed by a soft thud and the sickening sound of a cleaver slicing through raw cartilage. Instantaneously, warm blood spewed forth from the carotid artery of Alan's opponent, spraying a red mist over Alan's cheek and clothing. A split-second later Vera was in front of Alan, roughly pulling the guard away by his nearly severed head. The man's body slackened and dropped leadenly to the floor, leaving the desperately sought pistol in Alan's hand.

Alan teetered, nearly falling on top of his assailant. Vera leaned in to steady him. "Are you alright?" she asked. Before he answered, she spun around and took a protective stance, bracing for another onslaught from Riki or the White Dragon. The White Dragon, Riki, and the remaining guard were gone, but Alan still caught the lingering scent of an expensive perfume made of lilacs and roses.

Vera walked over to the wooden bench, stabbed the short sword into it, and used the blade to cut the bindings from her hands. Once freed, she helped Alan sit down and very carefully pulled his coat back to cut him free. Without asking again how he was, she gently probed the bleeding gash on his head. The skin at the edge of his hairline had split when he smashed into the tiled wall and the injury was beginning to swell. Before long, he would have a nasty goose egg above the knot he'd received earlier.

Vera grabbed him by the jaw and held his face steady. "I need to see the pupils of your eyes. Look at my brow for a moment." After a few seconds, Vera nodded. "I think you're fine for now, but we'll need to monitor you."

"What? Why?"

"You may have a concussion. I can't say for sure. Right now we need to get out of here."

The tub was spilling over with boiling water. Vera took the short sword, picked up her mop handle, and shut off the steam pipe. Then she stuck the staff in the water and worked the submerged .45 away from the two steaming bodies. Once the pistol was in the corner of the tub she caught the trigger with the sword's blade and slid the weapon out of the water.

Alan watched as Vera used pieces of her jacket as oven mitts to retrieve the pistol. Once she had wiped down the pistol she ejected the magazine and the round from the chamber. Then she emptied the other six rounds from the magazine onto the bench.

"What are you doing?" Alan asked.

"I can't leave the pistol here. It's untraceable, but you never know. The metal's very hot, and so are the shells. I don't want the primers cooking off and igniting—not while I'm carrying them around, though the powder is probably ruined."

Vera wrapped the .45 in the shreds of her coat and carried it with the short sword to Alan. She reached under his arm and lifted him up, helping to steady him. "Alright, Champ, we need to get out before the Japanese cavalry arrives. Keep your pistol handy until we're clear."

"What about the police?"

"When we get to a safe spot, I'll have someone call this in. But by the time the police find this place, the White Dragon's army will have dragged off their dead."

"Why would they do that?" Alan asked.

"I'm not really sure. I think it's to keep their spy ring invisible, but then again it might be for religious purposes. They might even have a temple where they clean them up before burial."

Alan nodded, but he was no longer listening. He held a towel to his head that Vera handed him to contain the bleeding. His head throbbed horribly, alternating between a dull, thick ache and sharp spikes of pain, while his stomach twisted nauseously. He leaned heavily on Vera as they retraced their steps past the lockers to the front entrance. When they exited to the street the limousine was gone and the sidewalks nearby were empty of foot traffic. The brick street they had arrived on earlier dropped steeply to South Jackson. Going the opposite way would require a precipitous climb to South Main and then up toward Yesler Way. Vera looked around them for foot traffic or people sitting in cars. There were none on Sixth Avenue South, which turned out to be the street they had entered the bath on, but there were several people below them on Jackson. "Alright, I know where we're at, now," she said. "Fleeing people often run down hill and bear to the right when they can, but I don't think the White Dragon would have done that."

"Why not?" groaned Alan.

"There are too many people down there, and she was wearing that costume and those horrible clogs. Even in Japan Town her samurai get-up would draw a crowd. She either took the limousine or walked up the hill and ducked around the corner."

"That makes sense, and with Riki being wounded that would have slowed her down even more."

"Just in case, I want to see what's up around the corner. We might even find Riki plopped down on his fat rump waiting for someone to rescue him. Maybe there's even a clue that gives them away."

"What if that clue leads to the catacombs?"

"You know about them?" Vera asked as she lugged him up toward the corner.

"Vic and I used the smuggler's passage to get out of one of the hotels we were in once, and we saw an old Chinese friend disappear into another one after he shot a Japanese punk who'd been tormenting him."

They soon reached the corner, which was two blocks shy of Yesler. Vera quickly surveyed the streets. The only other person she saw was an older man a block farther east. Beyond him was the core of Nihonmachi—Japan Town. "Now, that wasn't so bad," she said. "There's no one on this side of the street."

"So are we done?"

"Maybe half a block farther should be enough, no more than a full one. I just can't picture her running very far in that outfit, dragging Riki along."

81

They walked past a closed restaurant and another shop, before Vera spun him toward the steps that led inside the Panama Hotel. "This is far enough."

"What now?"

Vera stepped back to the edge of the sidewalk and put her hands on her hips as she glanced up the side of the hotel, taking it all in. She scrunched her brow into a thoughtful scowl and nodded. "We get some ice for your head, four to six aspirin to go with it, and then we get us patched up."

"You're injured, too?" Alan stopped to examine Vera's face, touching her chin and turning her head slightly to the side.

"My teeth are sore and I'm going to nurse a bruise, but the White Dragon fared worse."

"You've got white greasepaint on your cheek and in your hair." Alan dabbed at it with a finger and then shook his head. "There's too much to wipe away."

"I've got some on the ball of my foot, too" Vera said with a smile.

"You're a savateuse? So do I call you Tiger now?"

"Only if you're pulling my hair while I'm digging my fingernails into your back."

Alan stopped and bent over to laugh out loud, catching his weight on his knees. He grimaced as he chuckled. "Ow! God, that hurts, but...you're one amazing woman."

"So you're finally noticing?" Vera smirked.

They continued to the end of the block at a more leisurely pace as Alan regained his strength, and then dropped down to Jackson Street. They stopped at a late-night market where Vera used the light inside the store to check Alan's pupils again. Then she bought them each a bottle of soda from the red and white Coca-Cola floor case. The Mae West shape of the green bottles worked well as cold compresses, and she pressed one against the goose egg on Alan's head while she held another to her aching jaw. The clerk didn't understand when the battered couple refused his offer to open the drinks for them, but when he saw the sheathed sword Vera was carrying, he stepped back to give her room and remained silent.

Outside, they approached a cab parked in front of the Bush Hotel. The Japanese cab driver was not eager to accept the battle weary team as his next fare, especially with Alan holding a bloody towel over his wound and Vera's sword in plain sight. The cabbie changed his mind when Vera pulled out a twenty-dollar bill and waved it in front of him. She promised not to ask for change for the two dollar fifty cab ride to Interbay if he could make the drive snappy. The cabbie took the twenty and stashed it in his shirt pocket.

Alan held the door for Vera as she climbed in the cab. The driver dropped down Jackson to Railroad Avenue and zipped north along the waterfront, a return route to Interbay that Alan hadn't considered. The driver made good time while Vera and Alan sat in silence. Vera rested her head on Alan's shoulder, and they both held the cola bottles against their aches. Alan rolled his head over and leaned it against hers, silently inhaling her scent. Her perfume wasn't as strong as the White Dragon's had been, and so it meshed with her own essence, which he found pleasant.

Alan's eyes roamed down her figure as he took in her curves. When his eyes reached the short sword clutched in her left hand, he cleared his throat. "What are you going to do with her sword?" he asked.

"Put it in my collection. I won it fair and square. It's mine now."

The taxi ride ended sooner than Alan hoped it would. Despite the throbbing pain and head wound, he was enjoying the intimacy with Vera. Alan gave a couple of hurried directions and had the cabbie pull over on West Armory, stopping short of the warehouse they'd parked behind. At the side of the road the cabbie opened the rear door and held it for Vera, while he glanced around the street. "Are you walking from here?" the cabbie asked, taking another glance at Alan's head wound.

"We're fine," said Vera. "We haven't very far to go."

The cabbie arched his brows, surprised, and climbed back into his car. He drove down to the end of the street and made a u-turn. On his way back up to Fifteenth West he passed Vera and Alan's silhouettes lumbering toward a Packard convertible, the only car left in the warehouse parking lot.

It was well after midnight before Alan and Vera made it to her apartment. She led him into the bathroom where she had him take off his blood-soaked sweater and t-shirt and sit down on the toilet seat. Lathering soap on a clean washcloth she turned his head to the side so she could gently wash out his wound. After it was cleaned and patted dry, she persuaded him to let her dab a cotton ball with diluted hydrogen peroxide into the wound to kill the germs. He held the sterilized cotton against his wound while she went to the kitchen for an ice bag. She returned with the bag, water, and a bottle of aspirin.

Inserting her fingers past his lips, she tucked a number of aspirin in his mouth, and handed him the water. When he finished washing down the pills, she gave him the ice bag and a cloth to put over the wound. "You really should have that closed with a couple of stitches, so it won't leave a scar."

"Does that mean going to the hospital tonight?" Alan asked.

"If we did, the White Dragon or the police might find the records and connect us to what happened in the bathhouse."

"We don't want that," Alan said.

"Of course we could always take you where Vic got his treatment—" Vera's voice trailed off, leaving the question hanging in the air.

Alan recalled his first visit to the Chinatown bordello, where Vic covered all his expenses as a way of saying thanks. Vic didn't scrimp on costs, paying for two young women to join Alan in his bath and relieve him of his virginity. "That might not be such a good idea," Alan finally said.

"Why not? I could drive."

Alan's mouth sagged open and he rolled his eyes. "It would be difficult introducing you to the people there— Mama San and Little Papa—because their English isn't very good," he said with more certainty than he felt.

"It all worked out well for Vic, and he had a gunshot wound," Vera said with a pleading frown that Alan saw right through. "In fact, they patched him up very well indeed," Vera added impishly.

"That's because he speaks enough Chinese to get by, and he has Rose to help him when he gets stuck—but they're gone now."

"I think the gentleman doth protest too much," Vera said, laughing. "Okay, if that's what you want, but that means I'll do the stitching."

"You can do that?" Alan asked.

"Of course. Sterilize the needle and thread, pull the skin together, tie little knots, and snip off loose ends when it's done."

Alan groaned and shook his head. "Doesn't sound like fun."

"You'll survive."

"Should I brace myself with a stiff one first?" he asked.

"You don't want me to answer that, do you?"

"What?" Alan asked.

Alan then glanced down at his lap, where Vera's gaze rested. Suddenly he got it. He rolled his eyes and shook his head, embarrassed he'd walked into that one. Vera smiled but didn't abuse her advantage in the play on words.

"Not a good idea to mix alcohol with head trauma," Vera said. "I read that somewhere. You'll have to tough it out for now."

"Let's get it done then," Alan sighed.

"Hold the ice in place while I get a sewing kit. We'll want the swelling to go down more."

Alan squinted up at her. "You still have grease paint on your face."

Vera touched her face and glanced in the mirror. "Well I've also got blood from at least three different people on me. What's a girl to do?" She unceremoniously grabbed the base of her sweater, pulled it over her head, and dropped it on top of his clothing. Then she unsnapped her trousers, shook her hips while tugging them down, and let them drop to the floor as well before she casually walked out of the room in her bra and panties. "I should probably burn those," she called back over her shoulder. Through the pain Alan managed a smile.

Three minutes later Vera returned dressed just as she had left the room, carrying a needle, thread, scissors, and a kitchen bowl. She mixed hydrogen peroxide with water and let the sewing kit soak in the solution. While the sterilizing solution did its work, Vera took a clean washcloth, immersed it in warm water and dabbed at the White Dragon's greasepaint that had transferred to her face during their battle. "Did you notice how good her English was?" Vera asked.

"What do you mean?"

"By most standards you would say it was flawless. She didn't have an accent or pause at all while she searched for the appropriate American word."

Alan had been examining the wallpaper pattern in the bathroom, then counting stitches on the towel in his hand, as he avoided looking at Vera's nearly naked body. While he held the sterile pad to his wound she stood casually at the sink, either oblivious to the effect she had on him or exploiting it. Was she teasing him again? This time, however, seemed more innocent. Alan glanced up at her face and tried to rest his gaze on her eyes, skipping her magnificent torso in the process. It wasn't working for him. She had too nice of a body to ignore it for very long, so he returned to staring at the wall. Meanwhile, Vera had worked a special soap into a lather and was busy dabbing it into the crevices around her eyes, not paying attention to him. But then why should she focus on him, Alan wondered. It's her bathroom.

Vera filled the sink with water. "I don't know why I'm doing this now. I'm just going to take a bath after I get you sewed up."

She leaned over the sink and splashed water on her face, rinsing away the lather. Without looking up she reached her hand toward him and bumped his shoulder. "Would you hand me a towel? I've got soap in my eyes!"

Alan reached behind him and picked a plush towel from the rack. He twisted back to hand it to her. Vera's eyes were scrunched shut and sudsy water ran down her neck and across her full breasts. She took the towel, clutched it in her hand, and dabbed at her face and throat. "It's not so much that she didn't have an accent," Vera said, "it's more like she had a west coast accent—an educated one at that."

"She sounded like everyone I know," Alan said.

"That's my point. You're from the west coast—Seattle. She sounded a lot like you, but a little different—like California different."

"You can tell where people are from, even American accents?"

"Not always, but quite a lot. You, for instance," she said, "could probably spot an east coast one, like Boston, Brooklyn, or Maine, and you would definitely know the southern ones. Of course they vary depending on region, education, and social class. Hers, I'm going to say, was Californian—probably south of San Francisco."

"Wow. I had no idea."

Vera set the towel aside, and suddenly Alan was eye level with her bosoms as her cleavage spilled over her brassiere. He dropped his head and turned back to stare at the floor. Vera continued talking as if she were having a dialogue with herself. "Her sword technique is adequate, but she would have posed a lot greater risk without those clunky clogs, which looked the part but gave her very little traction. It's almost as if she were trying her best to assume a role, one she wasn't born to."

Alan glanced over his shoulder and found he could do this safely. With his view of her partially blocked, he could keep her breasts out of his mind, thereby focusing on what she was saying. He tried to hold up his end of the conversation, forcing himself to concentrate. "What do you make of that?"

"I'm wondering if she's *not* Japanese."

"I'm not following you."

"Alright...maybe she's ethnically Japanese—but not actually from Japan."

Alan started to nod but stopped, not sure where this was headed.

"There was something peculiar about her, when we were face to face. Maybe she's called the White Dragon for a reason—because she's Caucasian."

"White?" Alan asked.

89

"Or partly white. That would fit. Her bone structure was slightly different, perhaps a combination of both races. Under the paint, she's very beautiful. The men she knows must fall all over themselves when they're around her."

"Like they do with you?" Alan asked.

Vera reached out to muss his hair, but went gentle around his head wound. "You're an awfully sweet darling."

"I wasn't trying to be. I'm just telling you what I see."

"Well, thank you anyways, but there was something else in her eyes."

After a moment of waiting, Alan asked, "Are you going to tell me?"

"No. I'm not sure. Besides, they always say this about strong women."

"What?"

"It's not important."

"But you brought it up," Alan said.

"It may be nothing, but when our faces met... it's almost like she reached out—let's just forget it."

Alan leaned against the toilet tank and chewed his lower lip while he thought. A moment later, Vera set the needle and thread on a dry washcloth at the end of the counter next to him. "Are you ready?" she asked.

"If I said no, then what would—"

"Don't be a baby. It's only going to hurt a little, and if your pupils look normal afterwards, then I'll give you that stiff one, mister."

Alan grinned sheepishly, and Vera smirked. She stepped in close, wedging her left leg between his legs to get near enough to do her work. He forced his attention past her brassiere, down to stop at her navel. There wasn't any other place on her where he could fix his gaze and be safe from arousal. He didn't think there was anything sexy about a bellybutton, but as he studied the area of her skin just a few inches from his face, he began to notice small, fine hairs gathered around this curious ornament of nature, forming a delicate swirl. The hairs were tinged with the color that proceeded south to her panty line, increasing in volume and color, hinting at the full pubic bush he knew would be there. She could torture him even when she wasn't trying. Why couldn't this be Alice? If it were, Alice would have to yank him by the hair to keep his face from smothering her body with hungry kisses.

Vera's knee was now mere inches from rubbing up against his erection, which had crawled down his leg. Alan sighed heavily and inhaled her perfumed flesh.

"It's the anticipation you're dreading," Vera said. "It won't hurt that much. Sorry, I can't numb it for you. When I pull the thread through you'll feel a little—"

"It's not... I'll be fine."

"You know what? Maybe you should have something to chew on, like a moistened cloth."

How about a nipple? Alan almost blurted out but didn't. He watched in awe as she stretched past him to grab a washcloth from the rack behind, and as she did her lacy brassiere brushed his cheek and earlobe. She had to know.

He squeezed his eyes painfully tight. "Vera?"

"Do you want me to soak this in scotch for you?" She withdrew her leg from between his and started for the door.

"Yes, please, and..."

"And what, dear?"

"Would you put on a sweatshirt or a robe while you're at it?"

"Alan Stewart, you're such a prude. You can't imagine how many men have tried to get me out of my clothes, and here you are trying to cover me up. You don't like what you see?"

Alan grinned, embarrassed. "I like it too much." He glanced

at his crotch and shook his head. "My skivvies are stretched out so far I don't think I'll be able to wear them again."

Vera laughed and shook her head, returning a few moments later clad in a soft pink robe and carrying a glass of scotch in each hand, at least three-fingers worth over ice. She set her drink down and handed him his. Then she twisted a clean flannel cloth until it formed a tight wedge, dipped it in his drink, and pushed the soaked edge into his mouth. "Here. Suck on this for awhile."

The scotch was smooth and Alan was sure it was expensive. He savored the flavor and closed his eyes, awaiting the stick of the needle to his skin. Before she could begin he pulled the flavored rag out of his mouth for a moment. "How many stitches will it take?" he asked.

"I'm thinking three if you're lucky, maybe four."

Vera extended a bare leg from the robe and wedged it between his legs again. This time it didn't bother him as much, but he tensed as she worked the needle through the flap of torn skin on his head. He clamped his teeth down on the cloth soaked in scotch. The thread tugged gently on his skin as she pulled the length of line through. The pain wasn't as intense as he feared, but the whole idea of what she was doing was unsettling. His mind turned to other things and he released his firm bite on the rag to speak again. "Does it bother you?" he asked.

"What? This isn't so bad." she said.

"I was thinking about killing the White Dragon's spies."

Vera finished drawing the thread through the opposite side of the wound and tugged the two pieces together. Alan squirmed and squeezed his legs tight, trapping Vera closer to him for a moment. "That's one down, and it wasn't so bad," she said.

Alan laughed nervously. "You should try it from down here."

"Hold steady or you're going to have a scar like the seam on a baseball."

"If you can handle that needle and thread half as well as you do a sword, I'm in good hands."

Vera kept working, intent on her sewing. Alan dipped the rag into the scotch again and sucked out more of the flavor before he withdrew it for a third time. "That's three more I've killed, and from what they were saying, this wasn't your first."

"Unfortunately not."

"Does it upset you?"

"Of course, but I sort that kind of thing out later, like when I'm soaking in the tub—which I'll be doing very soon. And knowing I did it for my country makes it a lot easier. There was nothing personal about it."

"Maybe that's the difference. I caved in one man's nose, shot another in the face, and pushed a third into a tub, boiling him like a lobster, and I'm not the least bit...who am I kidding?" Alan sighed heavily. "I feel awful, Vera. My body count just continues to grow. St. Peter must be pacing back and forth in front of the pearly gates, wringing his hands, wondering what he's going to tell the Big Boss about me."

Vera tied off a second stitch. "I meant to tell you earlier, but you handled yourself really well, Champ. You did more than just carry your weight—you saved both our lives. You heard what the White Dragon said. It was going to be an execution. She wanted to send my head to Japan in a box. They were deadly serious. Without you, I wouldn't have made it out alive."

Alan smiled and glanced up at her, a glint of admiration in his eye. "You're like the second coming of Joan of Arc," he said.

"But I don't want to end up like her, roasted on an English barbecue."

"I'm glad I could help, but...I'm worried about what I'm becoming," he said.

"Don't get lost in the gore. Instead, think of the good you're doing. You're fighting for your country, and they are the enemy. This whole conflict is going to end in a war. What we did tonight may slow the inevitable and hopefully block their ability to lay waste to China or attack us.... Which reminds me. In the morning we still need to show the Port Authorities what we found and where we found it—so they can place an embargo on the brass. Our work's not done yet, Champ."

Alan groaned. "I imagine morning comes earlier on your clock than it does mine."

"You can sleep in the spare room. It'll cut down on the time wasted coming and going."

"What will your neighbors say?"

"There's not a lot they can say. I own the building."

"There must be thirty rooms here."

"That's about right. There's actually twenty-nine because I converted the floor space for a separate unit into mine. I wanted the extra bath, bedrooms, and a second entrance."

"Why the extra door?"

"Privacy, emergency exit...that kind of thing. I take precautions and haven't had anyone like the White Dragon follow me home yet, but it helps to be prepared."

"And you own the whole building?"

"I had to have some place to put my money when I sold my share of the show, and I'm not ready to get back in the stock market. My timing was nearly perfect. I got out of burlesque before the movies took over, and prime real estate seemed like the perfect option. Besides, I get to live here too."

Vera tugged at the third stitch. "I think this should do it," she said. Vera snipped the threads near the last knot and leaned back to inspect her work. "We'll put a bandage over it in the morning if we have to, but I wouldn't cover it tonight. And don't forget not to get it wet."

"Extra bedrooms?"

"Champ, there's a line between being a good detective and prying."

"Sorry, I didn't mean to—"

Vera blinked thoughtfully. "Actually, it's me that should be sorry. You don't need to apologize, I was being rude." She wrapped her arms around his head, cradled it, and pulled him gently to her abdomen. "You're just curious, that's understandable, but there's a part of my life I don't take to the office. It's just like Mackie not taking his work home—or ever bringing his family to work."

"You have a family?"

Vera paused for a long second, her movements frozen in air. "That's not what I was saying...or where I was going with this. I was talking about keeping certain things private."

"You don't have to tell me anything you don't want to."

Vera released her hold on him. "I'll give you a tour another time. For now, just stay on this end of the floor. Now get some sleep. We have to get up early."

The room to the bedroom was ajar, and Alan woke to the smell of sausage and eggs. He checked his pocket watch on the nightstand and calculated he'd gotten a little less than six hours sleep. He rolled on his back and stared through the faint light at the ceiling, hoping that breakfast would include several more aspirin. Other than breakfast, he didn't want to think about what this day had in store for him.

Vera was either a saint or a devil woman to keep such inhuman hours. What happened to waking up slowly? he wondered. What was wrong with that? Not fully awake, his dreams beckoned to tie up the loose ends he'd only end up forgetting. He did nothing to drive away their yearning, because their pleasure lingered. He was still aroused and could feel his morning erection. His subconscious had tried to put Alice's face on Vera's figure, but it was Vera he had taken in his dreams in every possible way imaginable, using every possible part of his body to explore and taste hers.

Vera's voice shook him from his sleepy reverie. "I see your toes moving. You must be awake."

Alan rolled to his side, so she wouldn't see the pup tent his erection was making under the covers in the bed. "I'll be right there, but I need another minute or two," he said.

"We don't want to risk losing that brass, so don't take long."

Alan pulled the covers down and sat up with the sheets bunched at his lap.

Vera turned to walk away. "I've made a thermos of coffee and some breakfast we can eat on the way," she called back to him.

"Now you're talking. Throw in a quartet of aspirin too, please" Alan said. The day was starting, whether he liked it or not.

🐉 ⊕ 🐉

Vera drove and Alan rode shotgun. She steered the Packard down the brick pavers of Denny Way to Lower Queen Anne Hill and toward the waterfront. Alan poured a cup of coffee, filling the thermos cap half full so it wouldn't slop and spill. The coffee was softened with cream and sugar, the way both he and his father liked it. Alan wondered if it was a lucky guess on her part, or if she liked hers that way too.

Vera was an active driver, using all her mirrors and constantly checking her surroundings. "I called my contact," she said, "and we'll meet two Deputy U.S. Marshals and the Port Authority in the parking lot of Ship's Restaurant. We'll ride with them out to the rail yards, show them the brass, and they'll slap an injunction on the whole shipment. Then we can focus on finding Jamie and the sailor."

Alan withdrew half his egg and sausage sandwich from the waxed paper and took a bite. "Wow! This is good."

"Health-wise it's probably a train wreck, but it should keep the wolves from your door. When we're done we can stop for a proper breakfast. Get you some cereal or oatmeal and more aspirin. I could use a couple more myself."

97

Nearing West Galer Street, just south of where Elliott Avenue became 15th, they heard the wail of a siren growing louder as it came up behind them. Vera pushed her lips out into a thoughtful pout, pulled to the edge of road, and used the rear-view mirror to track the squad car as it sailed past. Ahead of them the police car slowed at Garfield Street and took a sharp turn onto the ramp leading to the bridge.

"Did you think they were coming for us?" Alan teased.

"No. They had their siren on the whole way. They're not sneaking up on anyone."

Vera drove under the overpass to Magnolia and turned into Ship's Restaurant's parking lot. As she pulled into a stall facing the street, the high-pitched wail of a fire engine screamed its way up the street, as if chasing the squad car and losing the race. The big diesel roared as it downshifted, and then the bright red rig made a sharp turn and headed up the same ramp as the police car. Alan stared with a furrowed brow, watching the truck disappear from view as its siren faded in the distance.

"Could be a house fire on Magnolia or a car accident on the bridge," Vera said.

A moment later the siren abruptly stopped.

"If it's an accident, it's either mid-bridge, or they've stopped at the Navy gates," Alan said.

Vera's scowl matched Alan's. "The marshals know not to bring a crowd. With all the sirens you can bet there'll be reporters and photographers showing up. In this line of work you don't want publicity. You get your picture in the newspaper, then you and your career both end up dead. By morning every foreign agency in the land will have your picture in a spy dossier. Even if the White Dragon doesn't send a crew to knock you off, your days as a counter-spy are over."

"So what do we do now?" asked Alan as he leaned back

in his seat and folded his arms.

Vera shook her head and squeezed the steering wheel tightly with both hands until her knuckles glowed white. "We see this through," she said. "We've got too much invested to do otherwise. I can't let the brass disappear to Japan."

"Do we go ahead and take the risk of being recognized?" Alan asked.

"Being recognized is always a risk, but we minimize it as best we can. Follow me," Vera said as she reached for the door handle.

Alan climbed out of the car and joined Vera at the trunk, where she opened an innocuous suitcase to reveal a catchall of accessories she might need for spying. Alan's thoughts quickly flashed back to the two suitcases his father had kept in the garage at home.

Vera took out a knit watch cap and traded it for Alan's fedora. He pushed the cap down on his head, while she pinned her hair up and quickly covered it with his fedora, pulling the brim low. She snapped up the collar on her trench coat, and suddenly she evinced the handsome beauty of Katherine Hepburn, only more fully-figured. She wrapped a bright silk scarf around her neck and covered her lower face before she handed him a pair of horned-rimmed glasses with clear lenses, selecting a pair of Foster Grants for herself.

"If you've got a large handkerchief," she said, "you might want to tie it around your neck. We'll ride in the back of the marshals' car, and I recommend you conceal your face if anyone comes close—even if we don't get out of the car."

"But I'll look like a stagecoach robber."

"There's something terribly ironic about that, but the marshals will understand," Vera said.

The marshals arrived in the parking lot in a late model Plymouth. The driver smiled when he spotted Vera. He climbed out and motioned with his head for his partner to join him. Walking over to meet them he stopped dramatically, raised his palms upward as if he'd made a tremendous discovery, and glowed at Vera and her Darrin convertible. "This is a thing of beauty!" he proclaimed.

Vera tilted her head to the side as she shrugged, indicating the need to play this low key. The driver tipped his hat slightly and leaned lower to give Alan a friendly nod. He spoke in a soft voice to Vera, shaking his head. "There must be a reason for the sunglasses and chapeaux. I should have picked up on that sooner."

Vera slid the sunglasses halfway down the bridge of her nose and smiled. "Nice to see you, Larry."

Larry grinned back at her and then looked to Alan. "I'm Larry Dosch, and this here is Jack Quilliam," he said with a nod indicating his partner behind him. "Jack, this is Tiger Lee and...I didn't catch your name," he said, grinning at Alan.

Vera quickly dropped her hand to Alan's knee and squeezed it lightly. "The Champ," she said. Dosch knew the rules and nodded. They were satisfied with monikers.

Vera explained that they had found the Navy's missing artillery brass on the far Interbay side spur, just north of the Navy's gate in a queue of a dozen gondola cars. "The waybill said they were destined for Pier Six, and one of the cars loaded with brass should be easy to spot. There's blood smeared on its side."

Their briefing was interrupted by more sirens, as three more police cars made the turn and raced up the ramp toward the Navy piers. The marshals spun around to watch the show, and when the cars disappeared up the ramp, Dosch slowly turned back to Vera with a puzzled look. "What do you make of that?" he asked.

"It appears they're following a fire rig and a squad car

that went that way just before you got here," Vera said.

"I don't like the looks of that," said Dosch.

They all listened silently for another moment, as the sirens all stopped at once, as if someone had suddenly yanked their wires loose.

Marshal Quilliam lit his pipe and wandered closer to the intersection. He took the pipe out of his mouth and called back to the others. "They've stopped at the Navy gates."

Dosch leaned closer to Vera. "They can access the rail yards from there. I say it's time we pay them a little visit."

Vera and Alan took a seat in the back of the marshals' car to minimize their public view while they waited. It wasn't much longer until the men from the Port Authority rolled into the parking lot and stopped abruptly, not bothering to park. They rolled down a window and motioned Dosch over. A moment later Dosch returned at a quick clip, climbed in the driver's seat, and put the car in gear. "The railroad bulls found a couple of bodies by the tracks this morning," he said over his shoulder.

Vera squinted sideways at Alan, and he leaned close to her to whisper. "I just dropped one guy," Alan said.

Vera nodded and addressed Larry. "Did you say a *couple* of bodies?"

"Well that's what they think, so far. But it's hard to tell—they've been dismembered. The detectives are busy counting parts to see if they all fit together."

"Do you suppose they were run over by a train?" Vera asked.

"That would be my first guess," Larry replied, "But then you have to wonder, how *would* a train sneak up on two men?"

After working his car through the Navy base, Marshal Dosch followed the Port Authorities through the railroad egress to the Interbay rail yard, where the police cars and the fire engine were parked. The Port Authorities waited until Dosch pulled up next to them, and then the two men got out. Uniformed policemen stood around while dower-faced detectives in overcoats slowly combed the area around the tracks. A tall, angular man stood alone with his foot up on the front bumper of his detective car, grimly surveying the scene in front of him. He was paying particular attention to a clutch of detectives about thirty yards away, some of whom were squatting down, fixated on a spot between the rails. Two of the detectives spread out a tarp, while another one stood back from the group and took a photograph of a dark blue object.

Vera leaned forward in the seat and peeked between the two marshals. "There's Chief Ketchum. You'll have to keep us apart. Mike would recognize me, even in this."

Alan leaned next to her and checked to see where she was looking. "He's seen me too, driving Mr. B around."

"So he knows you're a private detective for Mr. B?" asked Vera.

"That's right," said Alan.

Marshal Dosch twisted the mirror so he could better observe Vera. "This is your show. How do you want us to handle it?"

"I'm more interested in that queue of open gondola cars just beyond them—which looks...," Vera began to raise her voice, "...like it's suddenly gotten smaller since last night!"

Alan started to curse, but bit it off, and shook his head, disgusted. "I don't believe this."

Vera patted his knee, calming herself as well as him. "Actually, I do. The Dragon isn't a fool. Even though she was battered, she probably stayed up all night finding just the right people to move her freight. I should have done something to stop her."

Alan grabbed Vera's hand and squeezed it. Trying to keep their conversation private he leaned over and whispered in her ear, "We took out four of her men permanently, wounded a fifth, and you kicked her in the nose pretty good. Who would've thought she had anymore fight in her?"

Vera raised her voice so the marshals could hear. "In order to stop the shipment from getting to Japan we've got to find that brass, is that right?" she asked.

"We need proof before we can slap an injunction on it," Dosch said.

"Where could they have moved it? Couldn't it be somewhere else in the yards?" Alan asked.

"It's more likely that it's somewhere down the waterfront or out the north end, maybe even all the way over on Lake Union," Dosch said. "Hell, she might even have hid it on an empty spur behind an old warehouse on Eastlake—that's what I'd do."

Vera took in a deep breath and sighed. "Alright then. How much proof do you need to stop the steel ingots?"

Dosch spun in his seat to face her. "Give me anything

and our attorneys will get right on it."

"How about brass artillery shells hidden in the load? Would just one do?" Alan asked.

Dosch glanced at his partner, and then turned back to Vera with a wry smile. "If you find one shell in the mix of ingots, that whole line of cars ain't going nowhere—and that Japanese ship ain't going to load anything but potatoes and wheat."

Vera squeezed Alan's hand tightly before letting it go. He nodded back to her and gazed out the side window, grinning wolfishly. "We may have to wait for the detectives to leave first," Vera said.

"Did you have any part in this?" Dosch asked, waving his hand out in front of them. "Or do I not want to know?"

Vera held a hand out to keep Alan silent. "I can tell you this much: I had a man in this area the other night, and he was following up a lead with a sailor."

Dosch resumed looking out the window while Vera spoke. Suddenly, he winced and shook his head. "Ahh, jeez! Don't look now, but the detectives are sliding a torso onto their tarp, and I'd wager it belonged to a Cracker Jack."

Vera and Alan almost bumped heads as they tried to catch a peek between the two marshals. It was even grizzlier than Dosch had described. The torso had been decapitated, but the distinctive navy blue jumper still maintained its bright white piping around the back flap. It wasn't even blood stained.

Vera slumped back in her seat, pulled down her Foster Grants, and pinched the bridge of her nose as if trying to squeeze an image out of her mind. "Larry, I've got to stay in the car," she said. "Would you find out from Chief Ketchum what they have, please? You can tell him the United States Government is missing one of its agents. If there's someone who looks Chinese in that mess, it's probably Jamie Chan."

Vera's voice cracked. She grabbed Alan's hand again and squeezed it tight.

"Do I tell the Chief what this Chan fellow was doing out here?"

"Not at this point," Vera sighed.

Chief Ketchum chewed on the end of an unlit cigar. His head moved just a quarter turn to watch Marshal Dosch's direct approach. Introductions were made, and the Chief stood tall to shake the federal agent's hand without smiling. During their conversation the senior detective folded his arms, raised his head, and glanced past Dosch to the car he had arrived in. A moment later he nodded at something Dosch said, unwrapped his arms, and used his cigar to point to where the detectives were working. Eventually Chief Ketchum pointed to three or four different places where detectives had left inverted cardboard boxes.

Dosch nodded and returned to the car. He climbed in quietly and exhaled a sigh before saying anything. When he finally spoke, he faced away from Vera and Alan with an unfocused thousand-yard stare. "I'm sorry to say it, Tiger Lee, but it seems your man is there."

Vera leaned her head against the window and raised her hand to her brow.

Dosch continued. "It was no accident. They were decapitated cleanly—too cleanly for train wheels. Ketchum said this was an execution with some kind of sharp instrument. The bodies were frozen solid, probably kept somewhere else, at least for awhile. Hasn't been cold enough here for all that. And there's very little blood here—just frozen body parts."

Alan pivoted in his seat to rub Vera's shoulder and upper back.

Dosch took off his hat to run his fingers through his hair, and put it back on. "Everything's frozen, except for a fifth hand. They've got one right hand too many, and no body to go with it. They found it a little farther away from the rest, and that's about the only place the police found any blood." Dosch pointed through the windshield to where two detectives were scooping something into a cardboard box.

Just below where the men were standing on the railroad bed was a ditch that held several inches of water. Alan leaned forward for a better view of the rail yard and fixed the location in his mind. When he sat back against the seat, Vera turned away from the window and leaned heavily into his shoulder, bending back the brim of the fedora she was still wearing. He put his arm around her and squeezed her close. She nestled her head below his chin, and the brimmed hat tumbled to the seat next to her.

Dosch caught Alan's eye in the mirror. "You folks want to call it a day?"

"No, sir. There's spent military brass here, I promise you that," said Alan. "But we have to wait until the police are done before I can get it."

"The chief says they'll be here a couple more hours. In the meantime, I vote we get coffee and pie up on Magnolia. We can come back later."

"Sure. Why not?" said Alan.

"I'll square it with the Port Authority," said Dosch.

"That'd be great, but why don't they give us an extra half hour before they come back and join us," said Alan.

"Sure," Dosch agreed. "No sense wasting their time."

🐉 ⊕ 🐉

It was nearly two hours later when Alan, Vera, and the deputy marshals returned to the now abandoned crime scene. A solitary police officer sat in a patrol car, its engine idling as he tried to stay warm. Dosch parked the marshals' car forty feet away and walked with Quilliam over to the policeman, who rolled down his window to greet them. Alan trailed a few feet behind and Vera waited outside, near the marshals' car. Dosch made his introductions to the patrolman as he and Quilliam gathered around the car window, and struck up a conversation about his discussion of the crime scene with Chief Ketchum. About a minute into the conversation, Dosch indicated with a discreet nod that Alan could run his errand. The marshals returned their attention to the police officer, chatting up the morbid details of the gruesome discovery in the yards. The policeman seemed glad for the company. Knowledge was power, and he didn't mind sharing some of his.

Alan wasted no time crossing the rails to the spot where the detectives found the severed hand. After that it didn't take long for him to find the darkened blood on the rails. Alan scampered down to the ditch and squatted close to the brown water. Using his bare hand to sweep back and forth through the muddy soup, he found what he was looking for: the artillery shell he'd used to smash the Japanese agent's face. Alan dumped the foul water out of the shell. When he was sure the others weren't looking his way, he grasped the shell by its narrow end and let it hang by his side next to his leg, carrying it like bootleg whiskey he didn't want to share with others.

Alan hurried the hundred or so feet to the queue of gondola cars and disappeared down their far side. A short time later he returned to the end of the line, stopped abruptly, and put his fingers to his lips to blow a high-pitched whistle. The two marshals spun around and eyed Alan as he waved at them to join him.

The marshals excused themselves and hurried off in Alan's direction. Meanwhile, Vera slowly walked over to the police officer, who'd climbed out of his squad car to watch what was going on. As soon as he saw Vera he stopped abruptly and tipped his hat. She lowered her sunglass and met his smile, as if he was the most charming man she'd met all day. "I'm with those gentlemen," she said, "but I just couldn't bear the sight of what they found over there earlier. You must be so brave to do what you do. Do you run into that kind of thing very often, officer?"

The two marshals followed Alan around the back of the gondola cars. "You'll want to see what's inside the second one here," Alan said. The marshals exchanged knowing glances and followed Alan to the spot where the coupling's big knuckles connected the last two cars. Alan stopped near the steel stirrup and inclined his head toward the car. "There's a brass shell casing wedged in the steel ingots. You can probably figure there're plenty more of those stashed in the mix."

Dosch used the stirrup and pulled himself up to check. He leaned over the load, and a moment later he returned with a brass trophy. "This here looks to be a military shell. Forty mm I'd guess. The Navy uses these for anti-aircraft fire, at least so I've heard. We definitely don't want these getting shipped to Japan. I'm afraid we're going to have to ask the Port Authorities to embargo this cargo."

Marshal Dosch carried the brass shell like Alan had, wrapping his fist around the tapered opening. While they walked, Dosch slapped the heavier end with the indented primer against the flat of his open hand, gauging its heft. Before they reached the last gondola car, the wheels from the Port Authorities' auto clomped noisily across the rail crossing, right on cue. When the marshals and Alan stepped into the opening, Dosch proudly held up the trophy for everyone to see.

The marshals dropped Alan and Vera at Ship's Restaurant in time for a late lunch. Vera was uncharacteristically tired, checked her watch frequently, and offered little in the way of conversation. Alan was ready to listen, if she was willing to talk, but he decided not to force any topics. She barely touched the food, and finally pushed her plate away. "Would you be a doll and drive?" she asked Alan. "I've got a hundred things to do today, and I need to close my eyes a few minutes."

"I'd be glad to."

"Do you mind if we make a stop along the way?"

"Of course not."

"I have to meet someone at the train depot in about thirty minutes. There's no sense in making her catch a cab."

"Which station? Union or King Street?"

"She's arriving on the Great Northern, which I think would be King Street. I'm so tired I'm having trouble focusing on anything." Vera slid over on the bench seat of the Darrin and leaned into Alan's shoulder. "I hope you don't mind, Champ, but I need to rest my eyes."

"Not a problem." He was beginning to relax more around her and enjoy the physical contact. Times like this didn't come with the hormone driven tension, which so often defined their relationship. This was pleasant, less threatening, like being good friends. While driving Alan stretched up and flipped the mirror down to sneak a peek at her, admiring what he saw. It was little wonder his dad had trouble giving her up, but why hadn't someone as wonderful as her found another guy at some point and settled down, raised a family? It wasn't because she couldn't, so it had to be her own decision. Vera didn't react to what life tossed her way; she lived it on her own terms. Maybe that was difficult for men to accept.

109

Alan worked Vera's car up Elliott Avenue to where it wound easily into Denny Way and then turned south on Second Avenue. Vera stirred while he shifted gears, arched her back like a cat and then relaxed, keeping her eyes closed. "She's my daughter," she murmured.

Alan heard her, but what she said didn't register. It didn't fit with anything he expected to hear. "Excuse me?"

"Jennifer's my daughter. She's coming home for Christmas break from Whitman College."

"Really?" he asked.

"Really."

"I didn't know."

Vera's breathing grew softer, more rhythmic, like she'd sorted something out and was now at peace with it. She dozed for the next ten minutes as Alan carefully drove through town, feathering the clutch and avoiding jerky starts and stops. Slowly they headed in the direction of the Smith Tower, the white edifice that was visible from miles around.

When they reached Jackson and the Second South Extension, Alan stopped for a red light and uneasily eyed the Panama Hotel, which was up the hill just to their left. He wanted to be able to glance at it and know if and when something was amiss, like a cemetery gate that was dangerous to pass. He etched the building in his mind, memorizing the entrance to the Japanese bath, the scene of their battle with the White Dragon. Alan worked the layout of the area through his head, finding places to file his memories so he could retrieve them at the first sign of danger.

After the light turned in his favor, Alan directed the sporty Packard toward the brick tower at King Street Station. He nosed into a stall by the south entrance, just down from a taxi stand where several regional taxis queued up, waiting for train passengers. Some of the cabbies at the end of the line stood outside their empty cars, smoking cigarettes and visiting with each other.

Vera stirred awake on her own accord. She stretched, took a deep breath and moaned wearily as she exhaled. "I needed that," she said.

"Daughter from college?"

Vera sat up straight, returned Alan's fedora, and reached for the door handle. "Were we in the middle of a conversation?"

Alan hurried around the front of the car and met her on the sidewalk. "Yes, we were."

"Remember what I said about there being a line not to cross?"

"Sure, but you've brought me in this far. I figured there was more you wanted to tell me."

"Jennifer's a senior, maybe a few months older than you."

"Whitman? That's the rich kid's school, across the mountains in Walla Walla."

"It's not cheap, but it's a great institution—and it keeps her away from Seattle in a place that's safe."

They ambled past the group of drivers, who nodded respectfully to Vera. One Asian man, however, stood apart from the others, lost in another world. He was pre-occupied, holding his hand against his brow to shield out the sun, which was nearly a novelty during Northwest winters. Alan followed the man's gaze upward toward the clock tower. Funny thing to be staring at, Alan thought before he returned his attention to Vera. But it wasn't his business after all.

🦅 ⊕ 🦅

The Japanese cab driver went simply by Eddie. He'd

111

given up attempting to help people pronounce his given name, Shinyei Watada. He inhaled deeply from his cigarette and squinted at the familiar couple who walked past him as they moved toward the station's entrance. It was them all right, the people with the fancy car, only they weren't holding Coca-Cola bottles to the cuts and bruises on their heads this time. The woman was unmistakable, no matter what she was wearing. They were the big tippers from last night, only cleaned up and dressed much nicer.

The White Dragon's men that met Eddie when he returned to the Bush Hotel asked him what the white couple had discussed in the back of his cab, where he'd taken them, and what their car looked like. The men got angry when Eddie said he hadn't paid that much attention, but their car was a Packard convertible of some type—that much he knew, maybe even a Darrin. There couldn't be that many in all of Seattle. The men left a phone number for Eddie to call. If his memory improved, there'd be a handsome reward.

The gods must be smiling my way, Eddie thought. He stubbed out his cigarette and told the other drivers he had to go inside to pee—but he would be back in a minute. An angular white driver scolded him. "You'll lose your turn if you're not quick, Eddie."

Eddie almost laughed. This was his turn, and this time he had nothing to lose and much to gain.

🐉 ⊕ 🐉

Alan held the main door for Vera as they entered the terminal. "I guess I don't picture you as being—"

"It's not polite to discuss a woman's age, Alan."

Alan awkwardly bit off what he was going to say, and merely nodded instead. Being addressed by his given name set the tone for the moment—she didn't want to be teased.

They walked across the oversized compass inlaid in

112

the white tile floor, and turned south. Just past the men's room, not far from the busy main entrance, was a bank of telephone booths. Vera stopped in front and dug in her purse for nickels while people walked past them. "Do me a favor, Champ. Call Kurtzer's Flying Service. It's on Lake Union. It's too late for a flight today, so I want you to book a seaplane—actually, a flying boat would be better—for tomorrow morning, say 7:30 or 8:00 o'clock. Tell them the pilot I used before would be perfect. Bill it to the union office and use my name. We have an account. If they ask what our flight plan is, tell them we want to take a tour of the waterfront, Interbay, and Lake Union, to get a better picture of our holdings. There'll be three passengers. Two hours should do it."

Alan furrowed his brow as he puzzled over her instructions.

She leaned close to whisper, resting her hand on his lapel. "We need to find the gondola cars with the brass. Jennifer can come along for the sightseeing. But...don't discuss with her what we're doing. I don't want her to be involved in this."

"Yes, ma'am," he said, purposely exaggerating the vowels.

She reached behind his head and playfully flipped his hat forward, down his nose. "You rascal."

Alan grinned impishly.

"If you finish first, join me on the loading platform." Vera spun around and walked past the tall wooden benches toward gate number one, the spring returning to her step.

Eddie dug the phone number out of his coat pocket.
The young men he'd talked to last night had either been
visitors or new immigrants. Their language skills and dress
were old country. They had been very excited to hear about
the Anglo taxi fare but disappointed that Eddie didn't have
more information for someone they worked for. They had
been particularly interested in the woman passenger.

The Japanese man who answered the phone spoke
little English, and as with the men last night his accent was
almost too heavy for Eddy to understand. Eddie's Japanese
skills had withered over the years from lack of use, but
Eddie managed to convince the man he had important
information. "Is there a reward for leading their employer
to the lady called Tiger Lee?" he asked, hoping that the
promise wouldn't be forgotten.

A woman who spoke perfect English came on the line.
"You will please deliver this information yourself to the White
Dragon. She will be most pleased." The woman explained
that for security purposes, the White Dragon would send a
car to pick him up. He was to leave his cab parked in front
of the Bush Hotel, and then they would return him there
later, a far wealthier man than when he started his day.

Twenty minutes later, a shiny black limousine double-parked in front of the Bush Hotel. The big Cadillac was no stranger to this part of town, but Eddie had never been able to determine who owned or drove it. A young Japanese man dressed entirely in black exited the front passenger seat, opened the back door, and nodded. Eddie took a deep breath and cautiously approached to peek inside the open limo. A muscular, thickset man wearing a black suit and crisp white shirt sat stiffly on the far side of the back seat. He beckoned impatiently with his left hand for Eddie to join him. His right arm was wrapped in a black sling that lay across his expansive torso.

Eddie stepped into the car, wondering what he was getting himself into. He sat next to the oversized Asian, who might have once had aspirations to be a Sumo wrestler. He had the weight and strength, but he may have lacked the necessary height for proper leverage.

Adjusting his weight in his seat the large man withdrew a long, black scarf from his coat pocket and dropped it on the seat between them. "Please put this around your eyes, Eddie, and tie it snuggly. Leave it in place until I say you can take it off. Where we are going is not for you to remember."

"You know my name?"

"Of course, and you may know mine. I am called Riki."

Eddie stared at the scarf a moment, and then did as he was instructed, tying it around his face with the knot in back. "Is it far?" he asked.

"Not that far, and from this point forward your personal safety depends on the scarf staying in place—unless you are instructed otherwise. Am I clear?"

Eddie nervously nodded his assent and hastily adjusted the soft cloth, pushing it into place around his eyes and over the bridge of his nose. He double-checked the knot in back and cinched it even tighter. There was no sense risking the anger of these people.

After ten minutes of driving a circuitous course through the city streets, the limo slowed to a crawl and made a right turn, climbing up a hill before parking on level ground. Riki cleared his throat and paused a moment, gathering his thoughts. "We will soon proceed. You will have no need to remove the scarf just yet. We will lead you to where you must go, and you will be safe."

After walking across what he believed was pavement, Eddie's escorts opened a door that blew a musty scent directly into his face. Oddly, there was a hint of a waterfront smell to the air. After a short pause, Eddie heard the squeak of metal sliding against metal, followed by two clicks, and then he sensed the brightness of a kerosene lantern passing in front of his face. The group proceeded across ground that suddenly became uneven in places. The people with him jostled and bumped into him repeatedly as they walked, but it appeared inadvertent, indicating that their passage had become too narrow to walk three abreast.

Eddie relied on his hearing to help understand what his covered eyes couldn't tell him, and he was almost certain they were in the catacombs. He knew the catacombs existed underneath the roadhouses that bordered the city limits, which had allowed patrons to escape police raids during Prohibition days, and that there were other such tunnels in Chinatown. He heard they were located under the gambling houses, brothels, and opium dens, but the rumors said they didn't cross underneath King Street because the trolleys above ground were too heavy. Still, the tunnels ran as far west as Pioneer Square, where they connected with the twenty blocks of the underground sidewalks that had been the city's street level before the Great Fire.

Eddie counted the steps he took from the moment he entered, hoping they would end on a lucky number—a gambling and social trait he'd picked up living so close to Chinatown. He was at one-hundred thirty-two when their little group made a sharp left turn and started walking up well-carved stone steps. They stopped after six steps at a landing. Eddie heard the soft squeak of hinges and the sound of someone blowing out a candle or a wick. One of the men held his arm while the other men went ahead. The door squeaked again as it closed. A few seconds later Eddie was led inside behind them. After crossing a floor of uneven stone, he was guided over to a bench and encouraged to sit.

Finally, Riki spoke the first words Eddie had heard in several minutes. "You may remove your blindfold, but only look directly ahead. Do not look around."

"Hai," Eddie said in Japanese, hoping to please his hosts. He loosened the knot and let the cloth sag unceremoniously around his neck. He found the room was very dark, with only enough candlelight to reveal that his hosts were standing on either side of him. The room had the feel of dankness, as though it had been carved deep into a hill that had underground springs. Eddie thought he heard gurgling, like water running in a fountain. One of his escorts lit more candles to reveal a large Japanese goddess high up on a podium in front of him. The statue was strangely beautiful, with a face painted porcelain white, contrasting sharply with eyes rimmed in bright red and outlined in black mascara, drawn at severe angles. The figure was brightly attired in a golden geisha-like robe, and the black hair on the idol's head was shaped into a formal shimada. A carved, ivory tiara completed the image and indicated the demure beauty was indeed a woman. Thrust into the broad sash that covered her midsection were two swords, a short one and a longer one, indicating her rank as a samurai warrior.

Suddenly, something on the idol moved—just one arm. It dropped, and then her hand shifted as the idol came to life. Slowly she fluttered a bamboo and silk fan in front of her face as she gazed at him with an eerie expression of stillness. Startled by it all, a bubble of acid surged in Eddie's stomach, and he fought to maintain his composure. It was anything but warm in this chamber, so the fan she fluttered was for show, a formality of some kind. He felt the need to bow and show respect.

As though she had been waiting for his show of humility, when Eddie rose the woman snapped her fan closed and lowered it to her waist. His eyes followed her hand movement and stopped at the sash, where the two hilts protruded. The samurai rank was a rarity for women, but given the respect and distance the men next to him kept, she undoubtedly knew how to wield her weapons. Then the rumors *were* all true—there was indeed a White Dragon who provided a link to Japan's glorious past. The fear he felt a moment ago was now supplanted by pride.

The White Dragon cocked her head slightly to the side, as if trying to understand what she was seeing. "I am told you have news for me," she said in English.

Eddie leaned forward, cleared his throat, and adjusted his weight on the bench. "Yes."

After a moment she frowned impatiently. "Go on."

"It's about the lady, Tiger Lee. I saw her...maybe forty minutes ago at the train station."

"Are you sure it was her?"

"Very sure," Eddy said and then gazed at the floor in embarrassment. "She has a look that men remember."

"Go on," said the White Dragon.

"She was dressed very nicely and drove a fancy convertible that the three of them rode in. I saw the car in the distance last night when I dropped the couple off."

The White Dragon leaned back and touched the fan to her chin. "'Three of them?'"

"Yes. The man she was with last night and a young woman they picked up at the train station."

"Tell me about the young woman."

"Very beautiful. Strawberry-blonde. Dressed like a girl in private school."

The White Dragon sat forward and a trace of a smile emerged through the thick makeup.

Emboldened and eager to please, Eddie continued. "I followed the car through town and toward Capitol Hill, but I lost it in traffic."

The White Dragon's smile disappeared and she sat back disappointed. "And the license number...," The White Dragon sat forward and her eyes flared wide. "You wrote it down?" It was more of a doubting accusation than a question.

"Yes, of course—for you. I wrote it on the page I tore from the telephone book."

"Explain."

"They are chartering an airplane for a ride over Seattle tomorrow. I heard the young man book the flight, and I took the page he used from the phone book. That's what I wrote their license plate number on."

The White Dragon snapped the fan open, spread it wide, and held it in front of her face. After a long moment she lowered it. The smile had returned. It also seemed that there was a tear in her eye. "Eddie, is it?"

"Yes, Lady. I was born Shinyei Watada, but the people here won't trouble to learn to pronounce it correctly. I've gone by Eddie ever since I came to America as a boy."

"You have been most helpful today. I am very pleased and feeling generous. It would seem that the gods are smiling favorably on you, on Japan, and on our future. Wouldn't you agree, Shinyei?"

The closed glass door of the wooden phone booth muffled much of the public address system's announcement of the Great Northern arriving from various points in Eastern Washington. Among the cities were Spokane, Ritzville, and Walla Walla. Alan opened the door so he could hear the message better. After it was over Alan found the flight service number in the phone book and booked the airplane tour exactly as Vera had requested. As he waited for confirmation he nervously glanced in the direction he had last seen her, feeling a need to make sure she was safe. Finally, the flight service assured him they would have a flying boat available. Alan hung up the phone, opened the door, and walked away from the yellow pages he'd left open on the booth's triangular shelf. He fell in line with the crowd and followed a dark-skinned porter pushing an empty hand truck through the double doors and toward the loading platform.

A minute later Eddie stepped from the booth he'd been using and watched as Alan disappeared into the crowd on the loading platform. Eddie figured it was not likely the couple would recognize him from last night—after all his experiences had taught him that most Americans believed Asians all looked alike, no matter if they were Chinese, Japanese, or Filipino. Still, it was to his advantage to be cautious. Eddie took another drag from his cigarette, tugged his snap-brim hat low and entered the booth that Alan had abandoned. He compared the names of the flying companies in the yellow pages to what he thought he'd heard the white couple discussing while they were rummaging through the lady's purse. Eddie's eyes locked on the ad for Kurtzer's Flying Service. Just to be sure he tore out the whole page, folded it, and tucked it into his pocket. It would be his insurance policy and certainly worth a lot of currency, or so the men said last night when they referred to the woman as Tiger Lee. And wouldn't there be more of a reward if he followed the huntress to her lair? Perhaps there'd even be enough to retire and return to the home of his ancestors. *Who could this tiger be meeting?* Eddie wondered. After only a moment's hesitation, Eddie headed toward the loading dock after Alan.

🐉 ✸ 🐉

Vera was easy to spot in the crowd, and so was her daughter. The porter Alan followed headed straight toward the women, ignoring others who tried to wave him down for assistance. Alan strolled up behind the pair of women and stopped a polite distance back, just as Vera reached to hug the striking beauty, who was bouncing excitedly between two suitcases. Under a dark green hat with a black veil, Jennifer wore her reddish-blonde hair in a Veronica Lake peek-a-boo style. A dusting of freckles graced her pink nose and cheeks and her lips naturally protruded forward in an exaggerated cupid's bow shape, as if they had been pulled apart by the mischievous archer, while he launched an amorous dart. The young woman apparently didn't bother with make-up, preferring a natural look.

When the hug ended Jennifer opened pale blue eyes that sparkled with intelligence. She kissed her mother on the cheek, but Vera winced awkwardly, embarrassed. "Are you alright?" Jennifer asked.

"I'm sorry, honey, but I need to see a dentist about a tooth."

The young lady's face radiated delicate beauty, even in a frown. There was little wonder why Vera had sent her away to school, Alan thought. She probably would have preferred to send her daughter to a local nunnery if she could, but then the good sisters would have had to construct higher walls and post eunuchs with scimitars at all the windows and doors. Alan grinned at the thought.

The porter lifted the two grips onto his hand truck without waiting to be asked. Alan was about to tell the man not to bother, but it looked as though he might have a fight on his hands with the eager-to-please attendant. Instead, Alan smiled and took another step backward, anticipating Vera's next move.

Vera tucked Jennifer's arm close and turned to leave the platform, stopping as soon as she saw Alan. "Oh, good you're here. Alan, this is my daughter, Jennifer. Darling, this is Alan from work. He was nice enough to drive me today."

From under the brim of her hat, Jennifer's eyes flicked open wide as she met his. She smiled confidently and familiarly while offering her hand. Alan eagerly took it in his, careful not to squeeze too hard, like an oaf would do. Before he released her fingers, Vera had moved in close and began a stream of questions a worried mother would need answered: Was the train ride exhausting? Was this all her luggage? How was school?

The two women breezed ahead, and Alan fell behind, walking alone with the porter who beamed proudly. That was an amazing thing about beautiful women—most didn't comprehend how much joy their presence brought to men during the ordinary course of their lives. As living art their beauty inspired others with the promise of what life could be like in an ideal world. These two were a sight to behold. They traversed the crowded station, full of holiday travelers, and exited onto the sidewalk. Alan explained to the porter that they were parked just past the line of taxis and pointed toward the Packard. While they passed the cabbies, drivers crushed out their cigarettes, anticipating fares and Christmas tips. A number of the drivers stood taller, smiled, and touched the brim of their hats to greet the ladies. Eddie stood quietly behind the others and rubbed his eyes, avoiding eye contact while Alan and the women passed in front.

Some in the Capitol Hill community complained about the loud drone the floatplanes made as they roared for takeoff across Lake Union, but that wasn't so for the Stewarts. Although none of them had ever flown, Alan often sat on the front porch with his sister Margaret and watched the planes, wondering where the people riding in them might be going. Alan and Margaret also wondered how the newer planes that only had one wing managed to stay in the air. They seemed so impossibly heavy. Alan's guess was that the newer planes had better lift because the one wing made them resemble birds more, or in the case of floatplanes, ducks, with pontoons instead of webbed feet. In less than an hour, Alan would put his theories to the test.

Alan steered his Ford Coupe down the steep cobblestone streets toward Lake Union and turned south on Eastlake Avenue. He cruised past the tall chimneystacks at the coal burning electric plant near the southeast corner of the lake. As they had agreed last night, Alan would meet Vera and her daughter at Kurtzer's, about fifteen minutes before their flight. The flying service was located at the south end of the lake, only five minutes from his home and the commercial laundries that dotted the area.

It was a part of Seattle that was home to many of the city's light-commercial industries and a smattering of heavy industry like dry docks, which were replacing the houseboats that hugged the south and eastern shore of the lake. Alan pulled into a parking space at Kurtzer's, and when he didn't see Vera's car, he walked onto the dock to nose around. He slowly wandered past the two floatplanes tied to the dock and stopped down at the end. Next to him was a sleek flying boat with the name *Grey Goose* painted on the side. The man tending the plane wore a brown leather coat and a Royal Flying Corps helmet. Strapped over his forehead was a pair of flight goggles that loomed like a pair of gigantic eyes. The man had the weathered complexion of a sea captain, sporting fine lines around his soft, dark eyes, permanent marks etched by a ready smile. He was intently inspecting his flying machine, but as Alan approached the man paused long enough to greet his audience.

"Name's Gunter. Gunter Manheim, but you can call me Gunny."

"I'm Alan Stewart."

Gunny gave Alan a sideways glance, sizing him up. "You ever flown in a Grumman Goose?"

Alan shook his head. "I've never flown in anything before. I watch the planes here take off and land all the time—is that the right word? Land?"

Gunny chuckled. "It's a water *landing*, alright—even if the *land* is fifty feet under the surface and covered by a deep layer of silt. I do my best to keep the water below the pontoons and the plane above it. Otherwise, it's known as a crash-*landing*. Whether good or bad, it's a landing either way. Gravity rules nature. She'll have her way."

"You're the pilot?"

"Pilot, tour guide, instructor, owner of this tub, and mechanic—at your service. Are you my charter today?"

"I'm with the Deward party. Should be Miss Deward, her daughter, and me."

"I know a Miss Deward, but I don't believe the one I know has a daughter."

Alan laughed. "Neither did I, so she just might be the same one."

Gunny paused a minute to think that over. "Well then...you came early to make sure I did the pre-flight correctly?"

Alan grinned. "Not really."

"But you have questions, am I right?"

Alan glanced around as if he were about to share a confidence. "Well...yeah...like, what happened to the other wing? Wouldn't a bi-plane be safer?"

"Oh sure, I see what you're getting at. People ask about that all the time, but more often they just want to know what holds this bird up in the air in the first place."

"Yeah...that too."

"It's called aerodynamics. It's basically about the shape of the wing when it's combined with airspeed, and how the two create lift to overcome gravity. Guys were studying this in water long before the first flight. Since then, engineers have improved the designs of wings and propellers so now there's no real need for the second wing. This here in front of you is the Grey Goose, one of the best examples of man's using science to triumph over nature. Or imitate it. That's essentially what we're doing here after all—copying the big birds, and in the case of this puddle jumper—a giant goose."

Gunny leaned back to look past Alan down the dock toward the main office. Vera and Jennifer had spotted the men and were headed their way, chatting like best friends as they strolled along. They both wore pants and radiated casual elegance, like Katherine Hepburn and Loretta

Young on their way to a picnic. Gunny lowered his voice, conspiratorially. "You said mother and daughter, didn't you?"

"Yes sir."

"That's the Miss Deward I know, but that can't be her daughter."

"Trust me, it is."

"My but the years have been kind to that woman. She is a treat for the eyes, and it would figure that her daughter would be a real looker, too. You look about the same age as her. Are you seeing her?"

Alan shook his head. "No, she just got into town from school. I've only just met her."

"What a pity. Her hair's got some red in it—but not that of an Irish girl. I'd say she's more of a Scottish lass. It's almost like you two could be related."

Alan's brow knitted while Gunny went on without waiting for a reply. He leaned close to Alan and dropped his voice to a whisper. "When they get here, would you do the honors with the introductions? I'd love an excuse to shake Vera's hand again."

"Of course."

When the ladies reached them Gunny's eyes jumped back and forth between the two women before he locked on Vera's. He grinned widely and then saluted with the casual confidence of a fighter pilot who'd flown scores of missions, shot down a dozen enemy planes, and always come out on top. He tugged off one leather glove and reached for Vera's hand. "Miss Deward, it's always a pleasure."

So much for needing an introduction, Alan thought.

Vera met Gunny's hand with her own and held it for an overly long greeting. She too had a twinkle in her eye. "I'm glad to see you're still with Kurtzer's," she said. "I was afraid a man of your skills might move on, start his own company."

Gunny opened the oval hatch on the port side and again offered his hand, this time to help steady the women as they climbed inside the plane. "I'm a contract pilot, and I don't want to do all the bookkeeping and advertising. They call when they need my plane."

"That was very nice of you to come on short notice."

"Nice didn't figure into it much. It was more a case of needing to pay the bills."

Jennifer climbed into the small passenger compartment first and Vera followed. Vera perfunctorily clasped the pilot's arm to help with her balance and smiled as she stepped past him. "We all have bills to pay—or debts to collect," she said.

"That's right, Miss Deward, we do. Now if you'd take a seat in the forward cabin in the co-pilot's chair, you can help me with the navigation. Just tell me where you'd like to go and what you'd like to see."

Alan climbed in behind Gunny, who secured the door for flight. Before ducking into the front cabin Gunny made sure Alan and Jennifer wore their seat-belts snugly. "You'll want to cinch 'em tight, because every so often I like to put this through a barrel roll or a loop-de-loop—give the customers their money's worth."

When Gunny stepped into the forward cabin, Alan and Jennifer turned to face each other and spoke at the same moment.

"He isn't serious...," they said in unison.

Catching the expressions on each other's faces, they laughed. Alan rolled his tongue across his upper teeth, a habit he had when he was thinking, and grabbed his seat belt to pull it as snug as he could. "Somehow I don't think it would be wise to bet against him. He's liable to do anything to impress your mother."

Jennifer smiled and craned her neck to peek through the

window into the front cabin. "Would it bother you if he did?"

"What? I'm fine if he does a barrel role."

"I meant—impress my mother."

Alan shifted in his seat and turned his head so he'd have a better view of Jennifer. He didn't know her well enough to have a feel for her sense of humor, or know if she shared the kind of penetrating insight his sister Margaret had.

"Sure," he said. "I'm fine with that." He hoped he sounded more convincing than he felt because all of a sudden, he wasn't so sure. After he'd left the two women last night, it was still Vera's image that haunted him when it should have been Alice's face. He thought about all he and Vera had been through the last two days. They made a great team. She was smart, tough, confident, and so amazingly sexy. Even the sound of her voice made him feel good, especially her laughter. Even now he ached to grab her and run his hands over her body, touching every part of her.

Gunny waited to start his powerful twin engines until a young attendant cast off the holding lines and grasped the monoplane's wing to guide the Grumman towards the center of the lake. Once adrift, Gunny took his time letting the four hundred and fifty-horsepower engines warm up as he taxied into deeper water.

Suddenly there was a light touch on Alan's forearm, startling him from his reverie. Jennifer slid her hand forward and placed it on his. "I've never flown before. I hope you don't mind."

"Not at all. This is my first time, too."

Jennifer winked a reassuring smile.

The plane's take-off was a little bumpier than Alan would have imagined, but no blame could be laid to the pilot. The flying boat resembled a speedboat pushed to the limit and the small waves in the lake smacked at the plane's hull roughly, adding to his and Jennifer's apprehension. They braced themselves, but once they cleared the water it became the adventure of a lifetime.

Gunny banked the *Grey Goose* to the right and headed east toward Lake Washington, trying to increase their altitude before heading back to the heart of the city. His first priority was to get the plane above five hundred feet, which would be higher than Capitol Hill and Queen Anne, the two hills that bordered Lake Union. Both Alan and Jennifer were busy staring out the plane's windows, first one side and then the other.

Jennifer let go of Alan's hand but leaned closer so she could be heard over the roar of the engines without shouting. "Mother says you're looking for some type of railroad car."

Alan frowned thoughtfully and sized Jennifer up through hooded eyes.

"It's okay, she tells me everything," Jennifer added.

Alan had played this game before. He wasn't about to cave into the charms of a woman who was assuring him it was okay to blab. "Explain what you mean by everything," he said.

"It's always just been me and her, you know?"

Alan pointed past her, out her window. "We must be flying over Pill Hill. There's Smith Tower and King Street Station coming up on our right."

Jennifer leaned closer to his ear. "Tiger Lee," she whispered.

Alan leaned back and stared into her eyes. She didn't blink. "You know, you look familiar, like we've—" Alan began.

"We haven't exactly met before, but you've seen me."

"When?"

"At your father's funeral."

130

"I don't remember that—seeing you that is."

"Well, you had a lot on your mind that day. Mother and I were over with the Washington Federation Union people, Mr. Brinkman and Vic. You were busy with your own family."

Alan rested his chin on his hand and scratched at the closely shaven stubble. "What do you know about the Tiger?"

"You mean, like she was a stripper before I was born?" Jennifer asked.

Alan blinked and covered his eyes in embarrassment. He slowly shook his head.

"Or are you asking what's been going on in the Interbay Rail Yards?"

Alan stared at her. "Yeah. That."

Jennifer grabbed his upper arm and pulled him toward her. "Spying," she whispered softly.

Alan chewed on his lower lip and nodded thoughtfully.

Jennifer sat back in her seat. "You're looking for missing rail cars full of spent brass shells."

"Gondola rail cars."

"What? Do they have guys in striped shirts standing in the back with oars, singing Italian songs?"

Alan grinned. "No, they're open rail cars, rather than boxcars which would have tops and doors." He checked out the window on his side to get his bearings. "Looks like we're starting out over the Industrial Area. I'd forgotten about the switching yard down here. It's massive...and full of freight cars."

Jennifer leaned against the window and peered downward as they made a couple of passes over the area before working their way north along the waterfront. "I've got nothing on my side," she reported, "what about you?"

"Nothing so far," Alan said. "I'm hoping that all three cars are still coupled together, but they might be split up. If

I was going to hide them, I'd put them behind a warehouse on a side spur."

"Good point. This won't be as easy as I thought," Jennifer said."

"When we found it, the brass was hidden under a load of steel ingots, which were freshly cast, very silvery looking. If we can get the sun to pop out, that would help us."

"Sun in Seattle? In the winter?" Jennifer teased.

"It could happen."

"You're an optimist. No wonder mother likes you."

Gunny steered the plane over the waters of Elliott Bay and brought it back in for a closer inspection of the rail lines that ran beyond the new cement seawall all the way past Broad Street. Alan spotted several boxcars in loading positions alongside the many warehouses, but no open gondola cars.

When they reached the Interbay Rail Yard, Gunny circled the *Grey Goose* over the west side of Queen Anne Hill and across to Magnolia, giving his passengers ample opportunity to inspect the rails below. They found strings of gondola cars here and there, including the seven on the west end of the yard that the U.S. Marshals and the Port Authority had already embargoed. From what they could tell, the rest of the cars were loaded with coal.

Gunny swooped the plane low between the two hills, crossing over Interbay on his way north over the Ballard neighborhood. The sun finally made an appearance, making its way through the northwest clouds that so often bullied it into seclusion. Rather than providing relief, the thin sunlight hit the buildings below and cast inky shadows on the rail lines that paralleled them. Gunny veered left, taking them out toward Shilshole Bay and past the Hiram Chittendum Locks, which allowed boats to transit from the salt waters of Puget Sound through the ship canal to Lake Union. Still there was no sign of the missing gondola cars.

Gunny banked sharply to his left and circled back toward the north end of Magnolia and Commodore Way. As they approached the Fremont Bridge, Gunny veered slightly to the right, following the rail lines parallel to Westlake Avenue, which led back to Kurtzer's. The change in course put Alan's side of the plane at a diagonal to the upcoming bridge and the tracks below it. There in the shadows of the bridge was a silhouette of rail cars that demanded another look. Alan squinted at the area as they passed to the south, but Gunny banked the plane a few degrees, and the bridge dropped out of sight.

Alan unsnapped his seatbelt and opened the cabin door. He leaned in and spoke to Vera. "There's something under the Fremont Bridge that might be worth a closer look."

As Alan sidled backward through the aisle toward his seat, Gunny banked the plane sharply to the left and Alan pitched forward. Jennifer reached out quickly and grabbed his hand. Her grip was stronger than Alan had imagined, but before he could use her strength to catch himself, Gunny banked into the turn and the plane leveled out again. The upward momentum of the maneuver, along with Jennifer tugging on his arm, caused Alan to stumble across the aisle, unceremoniously landing on Jennifer's lap.

"Pardon me, ma'am, but I seem to have misplaced my seat," Alan said with a chuckle.

Jennifer smiled. "Really? It seems to be here in my lap, and I'm about to pinch it if you don't move it," she said playfully.

Alan shook his head apologetically. "Gunny wasn't kidding about the barrel roll and stunt flying."

"I've got the feeling he's more used to that than shuttling passengers around town," Jennifer said. Alan quickly moved back to his seat, cinched the seatbelt tight and hastily re-buckled the clasp. Gunny took the *Grey Goose* up the east side of Lake Union and banked the plane again, steering her back toward the Fremont Bridge.

Before they reached the bridge, they saw what they were looking for. Loosening his seatbelt, but not leaving his perch, Alan leaned over as far as he could for a better view out the starboard window on Jennifer's side of the plane. The late morning sun reflected off the steel ingots loaded into a gondola car protruding from the east side of the bridge. Still linked together, the three cars were too long to fit entirely underneath the bridge. Alan squeezed Jennifer's hand. "That's what we're after," he said. "As soon as we land, your mother can let Marshal Dosch and the Port know where it's hidden."

"Could the Japanese move it again before we let the authorities know?" Jennifer asked.

"There's always that possibility."

"So shouldn't we have Gunny radio in its location?"

Alan paused for a moment, then shook his head. "I'm not sure how much your mother wants anyone who can listen to the radio to know."

Gunny took the plane north across the Wallingford neighborhood and then banked it right, lining up his approach toward the lake. Alan cocked his head sideways and frowned. Now that they had found the steel, there were other things still nagging at him. "With us being so close in age it seems like I should have bumped into you at school," he began slowly. "Did you graduate from Broadway?"

"No. Holy Names. Mother sent me to private schools, preferring ones that were girls only."

"Did you like it that way?"

"Yes and no. I got a great education and have a lot of dear friends, but there were no boys. At times it felt like I was forced to live in cloister."

"In what?" Alan asked.

"Cloister. It's where monks or nuns have no contact with the outside world."

"Doesn't sound like a whole lot of fun, but Margie almost went there."

"Is she your sister?"

"Oh, of course, you wouldn't know. Her real name's Margaret, and she's a year younger than me. She's the smart one that gets the good grades. She could end up becoming an attorney, but dad said no."

"No to her becoming an attorney?" Jennifer said with a smirk.

Alan caught the tease and returned the grin. "No to private school I guess. But then he could have had an argument with a priest. He was a Catholic once, but I don't know where he stood at the end. There were a lot of things he never explained, which was just his way. When he made up his mind on something, that was it."

"Too bad. It would have been nice to meet her. With Holy Names being so small, we could have been friends."

As Gunny adjusted the wing flaps to slow their airspeed, Jennifer reached for Alan's hand and pulled it toward her. "It's my first landing, too."

Alan grinned, trying to send encouragement her way. "Even on water they call it a landing. Gunny said the important thing for the pilot is to keep the pontoons above the water."

"Oh! That's *very* reassuring," Jennifer said sarcastically.

Alan laughed. Even with the landing, this day was turning out better than he ever could have imagined.

🐉 ◈ 🐉

Once the *Grey Goose* landed Alan opened the smallish oval hatch on the port side and helped Jennifer out first, while the dockhand finished tying up the craft. Jennifer started down the dock toward the office, stopped, and called back to Alan. "I'm dying for a soda. They have a Coca-Cola machine in the office, would you like one?" she asked.

"That would be great, thanks."

"Tell mother I'll meet her there."

"Certainly," he said.

Alan waited pensively on the dock for Vera, who seemed to be taking her time with Gunny. The dockhand had already finished his chores and disappeared. After a few minutes, Alan leaned back inside the plane and found that Vera and Gunny still hadn't left the pilot's cabin. With the motors off, Alan could hear her laughter through the closed door between the cabins.

Jealousy was an emotion Alan hadn't had any experience with, and he had no idea how to keep it at bay. It angered him that he was getting upset over a woman he wasn't supposed to be interested in. After all, he had spurned her advances—how many times? If it wasn't for Alice though, he was sure he would have already given into Vera. He didn't want to think about that anymore, but he couldn't stop himself. God, she could drive him nuts, even when... she wasn't trying to *now*, was she?

The cabin door opened, and Vera was the first to step into the passenger compartment. Alan moved away from the plane, trying to assume an air of detachment. When Vera poked her head through the exit, he stepped forward and offered her a hand.

She took his arm and smiled appreciatively. "Why thank you, Champ."

Alan assisted her onto the dock, but before he could walk away Gunny called after them. "Would you give me a hand with my flight bag, son?"

Alan stopped short, rolled his tongue over his teeth, as if he were trying to get a bitter taste out, and forced himself to smile. He stepped back toward the plane and Gunny tossed him a canvas grip, which Alan caught.

Vera had taken a few steps away from the flying boat and was waiting for Alan and Gunny when the rear door on a white van slammed shut down by the office. Alan turned around in time to catch sight of the vehicle as it sped out of the lot to Westlake, slowing but not stopping as it cut into the southbound traffic.

"Alan, where's Jennifer?" Vera called over her shoulder.

"She went ahead to get a couple of sodas from the office."

Without saying anything, Vera hurried down the dock. Gunny joined Alan outside the plane as they watched her disappear into the office.

"What's going on?" Gunny asked.

"Jennifer went for sodas, and I'd say Vera's worried about her."

"What just tore out of the parking lot?"

"A white van from Troy Laundry."

"Really? What business would they have here? Lana usually waits until his overalls are ready to stand up by themselves, and then he washes them himself."

A moment later, Vera came back outside. "She didn't make it to the office," Vera shouted down the dock.

Gunny grabbed Alan's upper arm. "No time to explain, just tell me where they would take her."

Alan met his stare and decided this was a man he could trust. "Japan Town."

"Push the *Goose* away from the dock, and I'll take a look from above," Gunny said.

Gunny threw his flight bag back inside the plane and quickly jumped in after it. Alan grabbed the edge of the wing to spin the away from the docks, and he gave it a push. In a matter of seconds, one engine sprang to life, and then the other. Gunny revved the motors and raced across the taxi route he had taken earlier. As Alan reached Vera, Gunny already had the plane airborne, looping it perilously low over the Capitol Hill neighborhood before turning it south toward First Hill and Downtown.

Vera's arms were folded tightly in front of her chest, pulling her shoulders forward. Alan carefully rested his arm across her upper back, waiting to see what her response was going to be. Vera fought back tears and when she spoke her voice was tight. "She didn't make it to the office. I checked the bathroom to be sure and she's not here."

"You think she might be in the laundry van?"

"Of course. Where'd Gunny go?" she asked with urgency in her voice.

"He guessed that right away, and he's going to look for the truck from the air."

"There must be a half-dozen commercial laundries at this end of town, all of them with trucks running about."

"I think he's already figured that out, too. He asked me where I thought they'd be headed."

"What'd you say?"

"Japan Town."

Vera stared down at the dock and leaned into Alan for a hug. "Gunny is such a dear—and you are too."

"Is there anything I should know about him?"

Vera met his eyes and rolled her lip forward as she thought. "Let's just say he can be trusted," she said after a moment.

"Understood."

"Okay now, Detective Stewart, this is the time where I need you to help me. I'm far too upset to think straight."

"I'll check with the office about the laundry," Alan said. "Wait here."

Vera walked farther out on the dock, trying to follow the *Grey Goose's* path as Gunny gained altitude and criss-crossed over First Hill. A moment later, Alan returned.

"They don't have a laundry service, and there weren't any deliveries today."

Vera closed her eyes, shook her head, and frowned. "The White Dragon has my Jennifer."

Within twenty minutes, Chief Ketchum was on scene with two radio cars and a handful of detectives that took over the front office of the flying service. It didn't take long for the police to find out that Troy Laundry had reported the theft of one of their step-vans. The keys were left in the ignition while the driver was picking up a load. When he came back to the truck with his hands full the van was gone. Nobody had seen a thing.

Vera repeated the details of what they had seen, first to the chief and then to one of his detectives. When the detective taking notes asked about possible motives and suspects, Vera said they didn't see anyone, and there had been no ransom note or demands of any kind.

While Vera rattled off Jennifer's date of birth, height, weight, complexion, hair, and eye color, the drone of the *Grey Goose* grew louder as the plane passed overhead. Alan got up from his seat and went to the door. Heading across the lake, the flying boat cruised north and dipped its wing once to port and then to starboard. Was Gunny sending a message or just adjusting his course? Alan went outside to watch Gunny fly up the lake toward the north end of Seattle, where he circled and lined up the plane for its final approach on the water. Alan squeezed his fists tightly and shoved them deep in his pockets, hoping that Gunny would have some useful information—though he'd have to be careful giving any news to Vera with the police hovering nearby.

While he waited for Gunny's landing, Alan quietly slid back into the crowded office. One of the detectives was addressing Vera, trying to draw out more information for his report. "It's important that we know who the father is— in case he was the one who snatched her. It's one of the things we got to rule out, because a lot of the time, thank goodness, that's what it turns out to be: a family thing."

"It wouldn't be her father. Besides, she's almost twenty-two."

"Still could be if he was sore about something."

Chief Ketchum stepped into the scene and put up his hand, waving the detective off that line of questioning.

Vera pushed Ketchum's hand aside. "It couldn't be the father. He was killed two years ago." There was a sharp edge to her voice.

Ketchum raised his hand again, as if refereeing a boxing match. "I think you've got enough, lad. Let her be."

Ketchum stood up straight and arched his back. "And as for the rest of you men, I want you to go out and find who did this. Do whatever it takes, and spare no expense. Am I clear?"

🐉 ⊕ 🐉

Alan left the office ahead of the others and went to the end of the dock to help tie up the *Grey Goose*. He replayed in his mind what he'd just heard. If Jennifer's father was killed two years ago, then it matched up exactly with the time Alan lost his dad. Was it just an improbable coincidence? His mentor Vic had told him detectives didn't believe in coincidence. They happened so rarely they weren't a factor in investigations. He said it just meant he hadn't dug deep enough. Now, however, wasn't the time for a deep excavation.

As Gunny tossed the flight bag to Alan and hopped out of the plane, the dockhand secured the foreword line. "Would you like me to refuel your plane, sir?" the boy called out to Gunny.

"Would you, please?"

Gunny took his flight bag from Alan and draped an arm over his shoulder, leaning in conspiratorially. "You were right about Japan Town. I picked up the van scooting south on Boren, bee-lining across uptown, all the way to Little Tokyo. Once I had them locked in I increased my altitude so they wouldn't hear me circling. Three of them took one of those big laundry carts out the back and wheeled it into a theater up the street from the Panama Hotel."

"Was she in the cart?"

"If she was, she was covered with sheets and towels. The three of them had plenty of trouble pushing that cart around, so I know it wasn't just full of linen. Besides, you don't see Anglo laundries servicing that area of town. Asians do their own laundry."

When they reached the office, Chief Ketchum was the last officer out the door. He waited for Gunny and Alan as they approached, and then he focused his attention on Alan. "We've met before, haven't we, lad?"

"Yes, sir, I'm Mr. Brinkman's driver, from the union."

Ketchum stared down through hooded eyes and nodded slowly. "George's driver? Oh yes, that you are. Well then, I want you to take good care of Vera for me, Mister Stewart. You are a Stewart, aren't you?"

"I'm Alan Stewart, and I aim to take care of her, sir."

"Good man," Ketchum said, pausing for a moment. "Speaking of 'aiming,' would your daddy have taught you how to shoot, lad?"

Alan hesitated for a moment and swallowed. "We did a little plinking at cans and such."

"'And such' wouldn't include living creatures, would it?"

"Dad wasn't a hunter. Said he'd seen enough killing during the war."

"I imagine he did. George tells me you've got yourself a detective license, badge, and gun permit—'everything's in order' is how he put it."

"Yes, sir."

"George speaks highly of you. Says you've got moral fiber. If that's so it's a pity you're not working for the new team I'm putting together. I'm trying to build one for the times ahead and could use a good man, but the City doesn't pay as well as George, I'm sure of that. And I imagine that's important to you."

"Not so much the money, but I'm happy where I am."

Well then, you just need to remember that your P.I. badge has its limitations, and if you scrape together the *who*, as in *who* did *what* and *why* with Vera's daughter, I want you to contact me or my detectives. You're not to take justice into your own hands. There's been too much of that around town lately. I don't want Vera's little Jennifer getting hurt because you got yourself in over your head. There'll be hell to pay if you're the cause of any of it. That goes for the both of you."

"Understood, sir," Alan said, while Gunny merely nodded, keeping distance between himself and the Chief.

"I left the necessary phone numbers with Vera. Be sure to use them."

Ketchum turned to lope away, but then called back to Alan. "Send my best to George."

Alan touched the brim of his hat with a polite salute and nodded, inwardly breathing a sigh of relief.

Vera paused at the door, inhaled deeply, and then she joined the two men outside on the dock. Gunny repeated what he'd told Alan about the van and ended his report with a slight bow. "How may I assist you, Miss Deward? You name it, you've got it."

"Alan's in the same line of work we are, Gunny. We can drop the pretenses," Vera replied.

Gunny flashed a grin. "That'll make conversation much easier."

Alan nodded. "Unless you start speaking German, like—"

"Ist das ein problem? Sprechen sie Deutsch?" asked Gunny.

"Nein, aber ein freund von uns uberrashcte ihn," said Vera.

Alan's brow knitted in a quick frown.

Vera made an effort to smile, but it didn't work. "I'm sorry to risk exposing your cover Gunny, but this is my daughter's life that's at stake."

"I understand and agree," Gunny said. "Has there been any contact? Do you know what they want with her?"

"I'm sure it's to punish me—or lure me into a trap."

"So do you want me to tell the police where the van is?"

"Not just yet. If they go storming into the theater with that crazy samurai woman there, it could be Jennifer's head she sends to Japan, not mine."

Gunny winced and shook his head. "That's a terrible thought."

"It scares me to death," Vera said, "but the only thing I can think of is to stay here. Chief Ketchum invited me to wait in his office, but...I don't know. This is the last place I saw her."

"I don't think that even the White Dragon would be brazen enough to call demands into the police station," Gunny said. "They'd trace her call."

"Gunny, while I'm thinking, would you call Marshal Dosch

and the Port Authorities and tell them where the rest of the brass is hidden? At least we can remove that from the equation."

Alan frowned and shook his head thoughtfully. "Maybe it's not revenge. What if the Dragon wants to bargain? If we tell the authorities where they can find the brass, we can't use that as trade bait any longer."

Behind them the clerk from the office opened the door and called out, "Miss Deward, there's a phone call. Think it's for you."

Vera shared a worried glance with the two men and then hurried into the office. As she brought the receiver to her ear, a male voice with a strong Japanese accent spoke.

"Tiger Lee?"

Vera inhaled deeply and sighed, her shoulders sagging as she did. "Yes." She said.

"Your daughter is missing?"

"Yes," Vera said, dragging out the word into a long hiss.

"If you wish to see her alive, you will do as I say."

"And...you are?"

"My name is not important, but the person I work with is. She is who you call the White Dragon."

"Among other things," snapped Vera.

"This is not the time to be humorous, Tiger Lee. I remind you that your daughter's welfare is at risk."

"What is it you want?"

"Let's start with your airplane excursion today. Did you find what you were looking for?"

"If you mean a beautiful tour of Seattle, we did."

"You will find that we are not stupid, Tiger Lee. Since they were invented, airplanes have been used to find what is not always visible from the ground. You were searching for something that is already ours."

Vera pulled the receiver down from her ear and

motioned with her head toward the clerk. Gunny leaned over the counter and got the clerk's attention. The young woman smiled up at Gunny, eager to be helpful. "This is an important call," Gunny said softly. "Would you mind grabbing your coat, darling, and we can catch a bit of fresh air?"

The woman rose quickly, smiled with wide eyes, and walked around the counter. She grabbed her coat from a hook and met Gunny at the door.

Vera brought the handset back to her ear. "It's stolen property," she said flatly.

"That would be a matter of dispute," said the male voice. "We purchased it for a fair price from a government agent authorized to dispose of surplus government property."

Vera cupped the telephone's mouth piece with her hand and rolled her eyes in disgust. "Sometimes we're our own worst enemy," she hissed at Alan. Then she repositioned the receiver and snarled at the White Dragon's agent. "And who would that be?"

"That name is also unimportant. The point is that he offered the metal as scrap for sale to the highest bidder, which we were once again."

"He's not authorized to sell to Japan."

"How can you be so sure? Perhaps he greased the palms of those in higher positions so they would overlook his accounting errors. That is not our problem. We have made a purchase, and we want that property to reach its intended destination."

"So that Japan can wage war on other countries whose only sin is that they have the natural resources you crave," Vera said. "Look at the war you're waging to get it and the people you've killed along the way."

"We are not discussing our countries' political futures, Tiger Lee. That will get us nowhere," the man said.

"But we're talking about Japan's illegal acquisition of

brass for its military purposes—what's not political about that?" Vera asked.

"Let me make this easy for you. All we want is for the steel and brass to make it onto the Hiye Maru. When both are safely at sea, you may have your daughter back unharmed."

"The Port Authorities are in the process of embargoing your scrap steel, if they haven't already—"

"What?" the man's voice rose.

"The Port Authorities have—"

"I heard you. Why have they done this?" he shouted into the phone.

"You'll have to check with them. Have your attorneys challenge the embargo in court. That's how it's done. They work separately from me. I can't speak for them."

"You speak so casually about this when so much is at stake for you. Doesn't your daughter's safety matter?"

"My daughter's safety means everything to me, but I have no control over the steel."

"But you do have control over the brass."

Vera sighed heavy into the phone. "I do for the moment, only because I know where it is, but that doesn't mean the U.S. Marshals or the Port Authorities won't find it on their own—like they found the steel. Maybe they'll rent an airplane, or maybe the train engineer who pulled the cars to where they're hidden will have a change of heart and tell the Port. Believe it or not, there are things that happen in this city that I simply do not control."

"Still it seems we both have something the other wants. Since we are reasonable and civilized people, we are prepared to be generous with you."

"So it's my daughter for the brass?" Vera asked.

"That is correct."

"I am not in the position to make that decision," Vera said.

"Of course you are."

"First, it's not my brass to give, and second, if I let you have it I only save one life: my daughter's. Your country might end up using the brass to shoot at our planes, ships, and soldiers, which will cost countless lives. It's one life versus the many."

"It doesn't necessarily have to happen that way. Having brass affords Japan the opportunity to make a show of force, much like your country has done. It is only fair that when Japan flexes its muscles the rest of the world should take us seriously and realize how futile it would be to attack us."

"The picture you paint makes it an even more dangerous decision. I get my daughter back and Japan is on its way to world domination."

"Japan merely wants East Asia. Other than China, most Americans have no idea what is happening in the Orient anyway. You don't even have maps of the South Seas that are accurate. All your government knows about the South Pacific is what they read in travel magazines. We are only asking you to turn your back on this one little transaction, like the rest of your country is doing."

"I can't do that."

"Is that your decision? What kind of mother turns her back on her own daughter?"

"How do I know you still have her or that she's safe?"

"She is safe."

"Put her on the phone so I can talk to her."

"She is not available at this moment."

"I'm not agreeing to anything until I've heard from my daughter."

"Very well. We will make arrangements. It could take an hour or more. Will you still be there?"

"No. We can't stay here. Call ME-8119 and you'll be referred to another number to call. I'll need an hour to get to it."

"And our brass will be safe during that time?"

"As long as you don't move it where others might see it."

Vera hung up the phone, leaned on the counter, and rubbed her forehead as if she were erasing a chalkboard. She closed her eyes and sighed deeply. After a moment she turned to face Alan, who wore a serious scowl.

"My country or my daughter?" she asked. "I can't make that decision."

Alan moved in close and stroked her arm reassuringly. "Whatever you decide, Vera, I'm behind you."

"You're such a sweet darling, but we're talking about the future of the country," she said as she moved toward the door. Before she reached it, Gunny opened the door from the outside, and the clerk returned with a smile. As she passed by Vera and Alan she lowered her gaze and assumed a more somber expression. Gunny tucked a slip of paper in his coat.

Alan and Vera joined Gunny outside. Vera stroked her hair with one hand, brushing it back over her ear nervously. "If I finagle this so I get my daughter back, countless other lives may be lost. What about the greater good?"

Gunny squinted thoughtfully at her, pulled off his leather hat and goggles, and ran his fingers through his hair, pushing it into place. "That utilitarian bilge works well in a classroom—no offense, Vera—but out in the real world, I say family comes first. If it comes down to swapping your daughter for spent brass the Navy was too sloppy to keep track of, and if it gives Japan the upper hand, then the people of this country'll have to hike up their britches, get their heads out of their fannies, and carry their weight. I doubt this is the first shipment of brass to leave Seattle either. Isolationism's got us into this fix, and it's going to come at a cost you shouldn't have to pay. With the country's sitting on its hands, ignoring the rest of the world, Germany's been re-arming itself and creating an air force, and Japan's been building a naval fleet and airplanes out of scrap metal we send them. There's only so much sacrificing one person can do for those who don't appreciate it."

Alan stroked Vera's shoulder and rubbed her upper back. "I agree with Gunny completely. You've got to look out for Jen."

"But what you're suggesting goes against my life's beliefs."

Gunny folded his arms and leaned against the building. "Better they go than your daughter, Miss Deward."

"He's right, Vera," Alan whispered.

Vera inhaled deeply and glanced around her, as if getting her bearings. "Let's get out of here before they call back with a change of plans. I'd rather make them wonder where Tiger Lee is and what she's up to. But if anything happens to my cub, I'll eat their young. There won't be a door left on its hinges in Japan Town, above or below ground."

‹‹

Gunny had left his car on Orcas Island in order to fly down to Kurtzer's, so he hitched a ride with Vera. Alan planned to catch up with them at the Sorrento Hotel, right after he stopped at the union hall and picked up the Packard Super-Eight, the car he used to chauffer Mr. B and his entourage to important meetings. Because of the high level bootlegging the Mr. B had been involved in during Prohibition, his drivers kept a rifle and a Thompson submachine gun in the car's trunk for emergencies. Alan had proven himself an expert with both weapons, skills his father and Vic had taught him. Unlike Vera's sportier vehicle, the big Packard would provide enough room for all of them, including Jennifer after they located her.

Alan nosed his coupe into a parking space in front of the hall, right off Denny Way. Racing up to the front door he wondered what he would tell Alice, who was filling in as Mr. B's receptionist during Vera's time off. Of course she'd want to know why he was there and what had been going on the past few days.

Alice Mahoney's green eyes lit up as soon as Alan turned the corner and came toward her desk. Before he covered the twenty feet it took to get there, her brow furrowed with concern, sensing trouble was casting a shadow over his face. She stepped forward to greet him and gently gripped his arm. "What's the matter?"

Alan hadn't lied to her yet and didn't know where to start. "Vera's in trouble," he said. "My...her daughter's been taken."

Alice grabbed both of his forearms and made him look in her eyes. "Kidnapped?"

"Yes. I need the keys to the Packard."

Alice held her ground and stood firmly in front of him. "I want to help."

"I can't let you do that."

"Why? Because it's dangerous and I'm a girl?"

"Because you're *my* girl, and I couldn't bear to lose you."

Alice leaned in close and folded her arms over her chest. "Has this got something to do with what you two've been doing at night?"

Alan leaned back to get a better view of Alice's face. "What do you mean?"

"I know that you can't come over to my apartment because you're banged up and sore. And she can't come to work because she's been banged around and needs to see a dentist. So it's obvious. You two are either involved in something secret and dangerous, or you're having very rough sex."

"Alice Mahoney!"

Alice didn't back down or apologize, and he didn't really want her to. He liked that she had been around enough to survive her share of hard knocks and could cut to the heart of tough issues. Now that he was away from Vera's charms and the spell she cast, he felt a sense of relief that came with making the right decision. What he wanted in life was here in front of him, challenging him when he needed it. Alice was the tough but gentle equal, the one who wouldn't let him stray from the straight and narrow. Vic was right: he had it bad for Alice. It took all his strength not to grab her and kiss her like he had the day they'd first met.

"So do I get to come?" Alice asked impatiently.

"Grab your coat and tell Mr. B we'll call as soon as we can."

Vera set up their base of operations in the lobby of the Sorrento Hotel, only a stone's throw from Japan Town and close to the police department should they need the extra help Chief Ketchum might provide. Even Alan understood that while they played on the same team as the police, it wasn't easy for the city cops to explain away the mysterious deaths and disappearances that went with the spy business. Despite Lieutenant Harry Frantz and his crew of thugs with badges, the police were sticklers for accountability—especially when it came to dead bodies and how they'd gotten that way.

As Alan predicted Vera seemed aggravated by Alice's presence, which added yet another set of eyes and a pair of lips to the mix. Alan quickly explained that Alice had volunteered to coordinate phone calls, while the rest of them scouted ahead. The Melrose phone number would transfer the White Dragon's phone calls to the Sorrento, and Alice could take them from there. Grudgingly, Vera agreed.

After making sure Alice was settled, Alan climbed behind the wheel of the big Packard. Gunny stood with the car door open while he racked a round into a .45 semi-automatic. He attached a leather holster to his belt and cinched the weapon to his waist. He grinned at Alan and Vera, patted his coat pocket, and climbed inside the back of the car. "I've got a spare if either of you need one."

Alan shook his head. "We've got our own, and I have heavy artillery in the trunk."

Gunny grinned devilishly, like a man who enjoyed a

fight or a dare. "What sort of artillery?"

"A Thompson and M-1 Garand," Alan said.

"The Garand is that new rifle for the military, isn't it? You any good with either of them?"

Alan glanced sideway at Vera for a cue how to respond, but she was preoccupied with her own worries. He shifted his gaze back to the road. "They've both proven effective. I'd go with the Thompson in close quarters."

Gunny nodded and then turned to check a street sign as they passed it. "This all looks so different on the ground."

"I have a pretty good feel for this area," said Alan. "You said you saw them going into a theater, east from the Panama a block or so?"

"That's right."

"The Panama's just one block down to the west from here, and the theater is at the top of this one. I say this is close enough to park. We'll have to hike up the hill, but if we have to leave in a hurry, it's all downhill. I'll pack the Thompson, if that's okay with you Vera?"

Vera chewed on her lower lip, still distracted. "Sure. Fine."

"We're going to stick out like three raisins in a bowl of rice," Gunny said. He looked out the window and grimaced, preparing for the worst.

Alan skewed his lips to the side as he thought. "I've spent a lot of time in Chinatown the past few months, and I found if you don't act like a tourist they pretty well ignore you."

"But still, they see us coming and they might alert others, spread the word that intruders are present."

"You got anything in your flight bag that'll help us pass for Japanese?" Alan asked jokingly.

"Nah. Just a couple of fedoras, all a bit beat up compared to yours."

Vera spun in her seat and reached out a hand. "I'll take one of those hats. We can wear them low—just don't snap your collars up like they always do in the movies. We want to look like we're visitors passing through town, not gangsters coming to settle a score."

Gunny handed Vera a gray fedora with a black band. She leaned forward in the seat and tucked her hair inside the hat before squeezing it on her head. Alan couldn't help but watch. She was stunning, even when dressed like a man.

As Alan parked the car, Vera turned in her seat to face both of them. "Gunny, I know the Champ was a boxer and he's a first rate shooter. He's aces with the tommy-gun. Besides flying, what are your strengths?"

"The military calls them Defensive Tactics, which I taught after I was wounded in France: hand-to-hand combat, knife, and pistol."

"Those'll be helpful." Vera nodded thoughtfully. "Alright then, we head straight in, stay to the sides, and hopefully catch them by surprise."

Alan reached for the door handle and stopped. "What about shooting?"

"I want my daughter back—whatever it takes. Well, almost. I don't want to kill a bunch of innocents. In fact I don't want to kill anyone unless we have to."

Gunny cleared his throat. "I don't know how to tell you this gorgeous, but the White Dragon's responsible for the death of a number of our agents. She'll likely kill your daughter too, if it helps her get what she wants. Me? I call that evil, and I say we won't be running into a lot of innocents around here. What about you, Champ?"

Alan squeezed the car keys in his hand and stared out the window. "Personally, I'm sick of killing, but that's not what you need to hear. Machiavelli said that sometimes it's just plain necessary."

Vera and Gunny stared at Alan silently, evaluating what he said.

"But then, not exactly a recommendation." Alan sighed and thought for a moment. "My vote is we do whatever it takes to get Jennifer back, but no more than that," he said.

Gunny shook his head and puffed out his cheeks. "Champ, you're a regular scholar. For now I'll settle on doing what's necessary." He smiled at Vera. "I'll follow your lead, ma'am."

The glass-incased box office stood away from the theater's main entrance doors. Its red curtains were pulled shut, and a sign written in English and Japanese announced it was closed. Gunny and Alan tried each of the locked doors until they came to the employees' entrance on the side, which swung open easily. Gunny slid past Alan and went in first, drawing his pistol to a high-ready position as he did. Alan followed close behind, pulling off the blanket from the trunk that he'd draped over the tommy-gun. Vera went in last and eased the door shut carefully.

Together they moved silently to a corner of the lobby, which was empty and unlit. It's only source of illumination came from a popcorn machine that sat on top of the refreshment counter. On the other end of the lobby was a payphone mounted on the wall next to the balcony stairs. Alan got Vera's attention and pointed quietly toward the phone. She nodded. She had seen it too.

Vera motioned for them to stand still. She inclined her head toward the heavy curtain that separated the lobby from the theatre's seating area and tiptoed cautiously toward it. Deep inside the theater a male voice spoke in Japanese, which was followed by laughter. Vera slid her finger between the curtain and the door's frame, pulling the red velvet back far enough to peek inside. A second later she turned back and shook her head. Beyond the curtain there was more laughter, louder this time. The laughter was suddenly interrupted by Jennifer's voice.

"Stop!" she cried out.

Alan sprang from his haunches, like a sprinter from starting blocks and headed for the aisle. Vera put her hand straight out, ready to push him back and shook her head again. Alan's brow knitted with puzzlement as Vera mouthed the words, *Not yet.*

"What are they doing to her?" Alan whispered as quietly as he could.

Gunny had now joined the pair, and Vera leaned toward them. She blinked for a long moment, as if exerting maximum effort to maintain her composure. "It seems the boys are throwing dice to see who gets to remove the next piece of her clothing," Vera whispered. "She's down to her bra, and her slacks are probably next."

Alan sucked in air with a low growl and again edged toward the curtain, as if he would push by Vera. "What the hell!" he muttered.

Vera put her hand firmly on his chest and held him back. "There are about a dozen agents in there who are supposed to be standing guard, but they're busy watching her, not the doors. She will survive this, and it will give us an opportunity to get closer before they realize we're here."

Gunny put a hand on Alan's shoulder to steady him. "We'll go on your signal, Vera."

Inside the theater Jennifer shouted another protest amid the men's jeers. Vera peeked around the curtain again, and then looked over at Alan, who squatted next to her with his back to the wall. His eyes were blazing red, like a wild animal ready to rip out a throat.

From her coat pocket Vera pulled out a pocketknife and opened it to reveal a long, sharp blade. "Gunny, I need you to slip down the far aisle. There's a man standing halfway down the aisle by himself. "Use your knife, and hold your fire as long as you can. Alan, you follow me. The closer we get the better."

157

Gunny scurried across the lobby in a low crouch. Just as Vera motioned for Alan to follow her, a large gong sounded at the back of the stage. Vera shook her head and motioned for him to stop while she took another peek around the curtain.

"Imi wa nan desu ka?" From down on the stage, Riki's voice boomed angrily over his footsteps.

Alan joined Vera and peeked through the curtain just over her head. Riki, whose right arm was still in a sling looped around his neck, stormed across the stage like a bull set loose on a Pamplona street. The White Dragon was right behind him wearing a different samurai outfit with two swords and a look of outrage on her face.

Ten feet in front of the new arrivals stood Jennifer, held by two young men in laundry service uniforms. Jennifer's sweater had been pulled up to her shoulders and her pants were tugged down to her knees. Alan winced in pain at the sight, unsure why. He wanted to close his eyes, but if he did he knew he couldn't help her. He felt shame and overwhelming embarrassment for her, and beyond that he felt rage at the men surrounding her. He wanted to scream out loud for them to cover her up.

Besides the two agents on the stage, there were another two standing close by and five or so lounging in the first row. As Vera had described, there were two more standing halfway down each aisle, holding rifles. The entire dozen were focused on the drama on the stage.

"Signal to Gunny," Vera whispered. "Now is the time to go."

Alan caught Gunny's eye across the aisle and gave him the signal as Vera dropped into a low crouch and slipped past the curtain, keeping her head just above the height of the seats. Alan followed and mimicked Vera's movements as best he could with the Thompson submachine gun in front and above his knees. In seconds they were within

158

ten feet of the first sentry, who had his back toward them. Swiftly, like the tiger she had chosen for her stage name, Vera sprang on her prey. She grabbed the man's hair with one hand and stuck her long bladed knife upward into his throat like an oversized fang, ripping across his juggler. There was no sound, only torrents of gushing blood.

Vera pulled the man backward and down, throwing him over her knee as she pulled the knife out and dropped the dead body in front of Alan. The man still had his hand locked in a death grip around the twin barrels of his shotgun, though the strength of his fingers loosened as the blood ceased pumping to his extremities. Alan grabbed the shotgun by the barrels with one hand and twisted it free. He offered the blood-coated weapon to Vera, and she took it.

Up on stage the White Dragon advanced toward the men holding Jennifer and drew her long sword. One of the men in front moved quickly out of the way, as if he anticipated a lethal assault. The two men on either side promptly let go of Jennifer's arms and stepped back, careful to stay out of reach of the samurai sword.

The White Dragon gazed up and down Jennifer slowly. "Cover yourself. You have a phone call to make," she said.

Vera tapped Alan's shoulder and leaned close enough to whisper. "The White Dragon is mine. You and Gunny can have all the rest."

Vera sprang from her crouch and raced toward the stairs, taking them two at a time. The White Dragon whirled around at the sudden movement to bring her sword up into a defensive position.

Alan followed Vera down the aisle until he was within arm's reach of the Japanese agent closest to him. The man spun around with terror in his eyes, and reached for the revolver in his pocket. Alan rose to his full height and seemed much larger than he really was. He leaned forward with the tommy-gun's stock squeezed tight against his hip as his father had taught him, and took aim on the first man. The machine gun broke the silence with a deafening roar. BANG! BANG! BANG! The first two bullets crashed into the man's thigh, the third broke the wrist reaching for the pistol before it slammed into the man's pelvis.

Alan adjusted his point-and-shoot aim over the top of the barrel, and went after the second man in line. Again the gun roared. BANG! BANG! BANG! He shot in bursts of three, another lesson he'd learned from his father. The rounds tore into the man at mid-torso, causing him to jerk spasmodically, like a puppet missing half its strings.

BANG! BANG! BANG! Down went the one with the long-barreled gun. BANG! BANG! BANG! Down went the next... and the next...until they were all down, arms and legs akimbo, blood leaking everywhere.

Vera trained the sights of her twin-barreled shotgun on the White Dragon. Despite her clogs, the White Dragon moved with blurring speed as she drew her smaller sword and jumped behind Jennifer to wrap her arms around her captive's chest and cross both samurai swords threatenly. Vera hesitated. She couldn't fire the scattergun without the risk of pellets striking her daughter.

Vera inched forward on the stage as she lowered the shotgun stock and pointed the business end toward the rafters. She paused a moment and then spoke in a chilling, controlled manner. "Let my daughter go."

The Dragon sneered. "Stop where you are, or I'll chop her up for the hibachi grill next door."

Vera paused, holding her ground. Ten feet in front of her stood the two women, her daughter and her enemy locked together as one, like a lioness with fangs poised to crush the neck of a small deer. Her daughter's eyes were wide and pleading. "Jennifer," Vera said soothingly, "Stay calm and do as she says. Mother will take care of you. If she hurts you in any way there won't be enough left of her to cremate with her friends."

The White Dragon's eyes glowed red with rage. "You

did not keep our agreement!"

"What agreement was that? The brass is exactly where we found it."

"You didn't wait for the trade."

"Well it was good I didn't, considering what *your* men have been doing to *my* daughter!"

"I cannot make excuses for them. They are men."

"And you wouldn't think to hold them accountable either, just like Japan doesn't hold anyone responsible for raping Nanking."

"Newspaper propaganda!"

"If you doubt the news accounts, then talk to the people in Chinatown who have relatives there. They'll tell you what family newspapers cannot print: that it was worse than anyone could imagine."

"Lies!"

"It is pointless arguing with one whose passion blinds her to the truth."

The White Dragon stepped sideways and back, inching her prisoner along as she did. "Passionate? Yes. Blind? No. I am aware that my country is not perfect and makes mistakes. There is always collateral damage when great powers collide—feathers are ruffled and teeth are knocked out. Is your mouth still sore, Tiger Lee?"

"Probably the same as yours, but you aren't concerned with my mouth. Let go of my daughter."

Vera continued sliding sideways toward the front part of the stage, allowing Alan room to slip in behind her and block the exit doors. On the other side of the orchestra pit Gunny climbed the stairs. The White Dragon's eyes darted back and forth between the two men as she paused. "Unlike you, I am a woman of my word. You will get your daughter back when the brass is safely at sea."

"But you have failed to protect her. How can I be sure

she will be unharmed? Why should I trust you after this?"

The White Dragon stopped in the middle of the stage, as if she were considering the question. "Because...you have no choice." As soon as the words left her mouth she struck her swords together and tossed them so they dropped harmlessly to the floor.

Vera instinctively started to swing the shotgun's stock up to her shoulder, anticipating a clean shot. At that same moment the floor beneath the White Dragon and Jennifer gave way. The stage shuddered, and Jennifer screamed as both women fell through a trapdoor into the darkness below. Before Vera or Alan could respond, the trapdoor snapped closed with a thud, silencing the screams below.

Alan rushed to the foot of the stage, while at the same time scanning the auditorium for signs of movement. As he climbed the steps, he caught sight of a man disappearing behind the curtains. The two men who had been holding Jennifer had escaped, and Riki was nowhere to be found. Alan directed the nose of his Thompson backstage, but everything was eerily still. The smell of burnt gunpowder filled his nose, and his ears rang with echoes.

Gunny joined Alan and together they raced to the back of stage. Vera followed slowly as if she hoped this was a cruel magic trick and Jennifer would reappear through a stage door nearby. After some searching, Alan found a fire door sheathed in metal. He leaned against it and felt a faint flow of cool air coming around the edges. The door had a simple metal lever that Alan pressed down to pull the door open. There was a faint light below, revealing wooden steps that led to a landing underneath the stage. Off to the left was another door, and to the right was a series of pulleys and counterweights that ran toward the middle of the stage. As Alan descended the steps, he saw that the room was filled with shipping crates, wooden boxes, and wire-screened cages holding scenery and stage props. There were a thousand places someone could hide.

Gunny followed Alan down to the landing, with Vera close behind. Gunny turned around to face Vera. "Do you think they're still in here?" he asked.

Vera shook her head and Alan answered for her. "We can't afford not to look."

Vera rubbed her forehead with the heel of her hand and nodded. "Let's spread out and make it quick."

Gunny drew his pistol and moved to the right, while Vera followed Alan to the left. She held her pistol high and then lightly grabbed Alan by the shoulder. "Why don't you let me take the lead? I know you're aces with the Thompson, but we have to be careful here."

As Vera moved forward to slide past him in the narrow passage, Alan grabbed her arm. "She's my sister, isn't she?" he whispered.

Vera froze. She met his gaze and then glanced away. After a moment she took a deep breath and sighed slowly. "She knows so I suppose it's only fair you do too."

"Vera, this is great!"

"You're not angry?"

"Of course not. I'm scared for her but not angry."

"We'll talk about it later, but in the meantime you can't tell anyone. Now help me get her back."

They worked their way to the middle of the stage following the cable lines. Below what had to be the trapdoor they found another wired cage. The door to this one was open, and its inside was piled high with goose-down mattresses and cushions. Alan grabbed a pillow with a smear of white greasepaint on it just as Gunny came around from the backside and joined them.

Alan held the pillow in angry disbelief. "Do you think they had their getaway planned?"

Gunny nodded. "Planned and rehearsed. The Japanese

are very careful and leave nothing to chance."

Alan shook his head. "But who plans this far ahead, anticipating failures?"

"Smart people," Vera and Gunny said together.

Vera lightly backhanded Gunny on his upper arm and almost smiled. "My bet is they're no longer here, and we're wasting precious time," she said, growing somber again.

"Let's check that other door at the foot of the landing," Alan suggested.

They made their way back to the stairs and found the door unlocked.

Gunny stepped forward, holding out his cigarette lighter, and Alan let him go first. With his pistol in his left hand and the lighter in his right, Gunny inched down the stairs into the darkness. Alan descended the steps close behind and joined Gunny on the brick pavers at the landing. "So, they're real," Alan said.

"You'd heard about them before?" asked Gunny.

"I've been through a smugglers' passage in Chinatown, but we didn't make it down to the catacombs. I wonder if the Chinese ones are connected to these?"

"In Edinburgh, Scotland, they have a whole city under their Old Town," Gunny said. "They call them 'the vaults.' The poor used to live in them, but they're abandoned now."

"You've been there?"

"I've been to lots of places."

They stood at the crossroads of three arched brick tunnels that each led in opposite directions. Above each entrance were wooden boards painted with Japanese characters. Kerosene lanterns also hung on posts to the entries, and at the foot of one was a large red container marked *Flammable* in English.

Alan removed one lantern from its nail and shook it so he could hear the fuel slosh around. He slid up the glass and rolled the wick out another eighth of an inch so Gunny could light it. As the lantern came to life, Alan lowered the glass and let the light fill the area around the steps.

Alan guessed that the steepest of the three catacombs went south, down toward Jackson Street and Chinatown, maybe further. It probably ran parallel to the street above it, but how much deeper would it be? If he was correct, that meant that the right passage probably headed east, which would take it in the direction of Harborview Hospital, deeper into Japan Town. The last one most likely headed west toward the Panama Hotel and the Japanese baths. It was also the only entry way that was missing its lanterns.

Vera came down the stairs and Alan told her what they'd found. He pointed to the catacomb leading west. "So do we go after them?"

"We could," she said, "but we'd have to go slow. We'd be wasting a lot of time."

"Why so?" Alan asked.

Gunny cleared his throat. "These aren't our tunnels. Whoever made them might have installed booby traps. I've seen dirt tunnels in French Indochina, and those had piano wire strung across the ground, tied to explosives. There could be a dozen spur passages, any of which they might use—or hide in, waiting to ambush us. Since it's our first time through here, there's no way of knowing. It could take forever."

Alan sighed heavily, his frustration showing. "What other choice do we have?"

Vera rubbed his shoulder soothingly. "The Panama Hotel. Remember? They led us there before. Let's try that first, unless the police are already upstairs."

Alan frowned and scratched the back of his neck. "You think there's a chance of that?"

Gunny nodded. "The people are used to hearing fireworks in this area of town, but this was a bit loud, and it's more than a month to their New Year."

Alan nodded reluctantly. He doused the lantern, hung it back on its hook, and followed Vera closely up the steps. Gunny put up his hand indicating for them to stop so he could scout ahead.

A moment later Gunny returned. "There's a side exit across the stage we should use. It's probably safer that way. You never know who might be watching."

Gunny cautiously pushed the side door of the theater open and led Vera onto South Main Street. Alan was about to follow but stopped suddenly at the door. "Wait. I need to cover this," Alan said, indicating the Thompson.

"We can't risk taking anymore time," Vera said.

Gunny nodded in agreement. "Open your jacket and stuff it under your arm like it's a pirate's crutch," Gunny said. "If you grab it as far down as you can you should be able to keep the barrel from falling out."

Alan did as Gunny suggested, but the big spool of ammunition distorted his coat out of shape and banged against his side as they scampered across the pavement to follow the far sidewalk westward. Reaching the intersection where they had a clear view of the front of the theater, Alan snuck a casual peek at the entrance. Standing close to the ticket box, a Japanese boy spoke to a woman wearing a shop dress and an apron. They must have come outside from a nearby business Alan thought. The boy pointed at the theater, and the woman appeared to be listening intently to whatever the boy was telling her.

Vera tucked her hand under Gunny's left arm. "Walk ahead a little bit," she said loud enough for Alan to hear. "I want people to focus on the happy couple, rather than what you're carrying."

Alan passed the other two, hitching the Thompson up farther under his jacket. He forced a smile of confidence and an aura of nonchalance, but inside he struggled with a flood of conflicting emotions. He couldn't shake off images of the carnage he'd created—the sight of the men's grotesque faces with expressions of pain etched into dead eyes. It was a stark contrast to the romantic paintings of battles he'd seen before, where dying soldiers lay as though they were at peace, happy to have died in the service of their country. There was never any blood in the paintings either, not even with a head wound. Nothing in those paintings ever depicted the savagery of death—at least not as Alan had experienced it.

Alan also battled with the images of beautiful Jennifer. It angered him that all those men had seen her exposed and lusted after her, but she had handled it well, like her mother would've—and those moments of carnal craving had cost the men their lives. But before then every eye in the theater had been on Jennifer, even his own. He struggled with where in his mind he would file those images.

And now there was Vera with her arm wrapped around Gunny's.

Alan suddenly felt very weary. He didn't have the energy to fight the jealousy, which felt wrong. Alice was his girl, not Vera. Vera was old enough to be his mother—and she was the mother of Jennifer, his half-sister. This was not the time to think about it, but he couldn't help feeling the same overwhelming desire for Vera.

Directly across from the Panama, Alan stopped and shook his head, forcing himself to focus on the present danger they might encounter. Jennifer could be in the hotel somewhere. First things first. Vera and Gunny stopped next to him, and they all stared across the street at the hotel.

"Shouldn't one of us stay outside and watch the doors?" Alan asked.

Gunny shook his head. "We can't be sure what we'll run into inside there. There were about a dozen agents in the theater, but this could be the hive where the queen keeps the rest of her drones. Count the windows—should be a room for each set of them. Means there could be a lot of bees in there, and they could all be working for her. We don't even know which room would be hers."

"She'd have one on the top floor—at least I would," Vera said. "And I'll bet it's on the west side with a view of Puget Sound."

Alan nodded quietly, while Gunny grinned.

"Naturally she would," Gunny said.

"There's one more problem," Alan said. "If this place is anything like the one Vic and I stayed at, some of those inside doors could be false. We could run into a smuggler's passage that would lead us into a maze."

Vera closed her eyes as though she was saying an inner prayer. When she opened them she forced out a half-hearted smile and led the two men across the street, heading straight for the front door. "Let's tell the clerk we're interested in a couple of rooms. Gunny, you keep him busy and off the switchboard while Alan and I'll check the halls. We'll start at the top and work back down. If it starts getting noisy up there, come give us a hand."

"Of course," Gunny said.

🐲 ⊕ 🐲

Reaching the top step that led them to the fourth floor, Alan lowered the Thompson by his side. Vera put her index finger to her lips for quiet. Alan nodded once and motioned toward the hallway that led to the west end of the hotel.

171

Sliding silently across the floor they moved toward the fire escape window with a westerly view fifty feet above the street level, pausing briefly near each door to listen for any sounds. After passing several rooms they came to a hallway juncture which led south. Vera gestured that she would explore the south hallway, while Alan continued checking the row of rooms near to the hall window.

At the room closest to the window, Alan heard male voices speaking softly in Japanese. There didn't seem to be any urgency or excitement in their tone, but he peeked out the hallway window to get a better idea of their location. His gaze quickly scanned across the bay to the naval shipyards and then he peered down at the street below them. Immediately he caught sight of a laundry truck double-parked on the hill next to the building. An Asian male in an ill-fitting uniform sat in the driver's seat, patting the steering wheel like a nervous drummer.

Alan dashed back to the south wing and blew a low whistle at Vera, who was crouched with her ear pressed to a door. She lowered her .45 to her side, ran softly his way and followed him to the window.

Alan motioned with the muzzle of the Thompson at the laundry truck below. "Like Gunny said, Orientals don't send their laundry to Caucasian cleaners."

"Is that the same truck?"

"I'd wager it is."

They heard a door clang loudly against the side of the building, followed by voices and small wheels scraping across pavement, but their view of the commotion was mostly obstructed by the wrought iron fire escape just outside the window. A few seconds later, another Asian male in a laundry uniform leapt into full view and moved rapidly to open the rear doors of the van. Three similarly clad men wrestled a large laundry cart into the street behind him.

A handful of white linen lay crumpled on top of the cart's load, but Alan knew immediately what they were seeing.

"Jennifer!" he said.

Alan grasped the Thompson by its pistol-like grip and reached for the latch on the window. Vera stayed his hand and shook her head. "Too risky. Let's see if we can catch them on the street."

The duo raced back toward the central staircase and noisily sped down the wooden steps. By the time they reached the main landing Gunny was waiting to join them. "They're loading her into the laundry truck." Alan yelled as he raced by.

"Circle wide, out into the street, and come around their far side," Vera called out as the threesome hit the last stretch of stairs.

Alan slammed through the front doors onto South Main Street and veered sharply toward Sixth Avenue. Gunny did as Vera directed and ran into the middle of the street to catch the van from the other side. Before any of them reached the corner, the big laundry truck revved its motor, lurched through the stop sign, and turned west on South Main Street toward Elliot Bay. Alan slowed so he could raise the muzzle of the Thompson to track the fleeing laundry wagon, but then he thought better of it and lowered his weapon.

Vera caught up with him at the corner and placed her hand on his shoulder, reassuringly. "Thank you for not risking her life."

Down the hill to their left, a movement caught Alan's eye and he turned in time to see a snappily dressed figure disappear down the steps toward the bath. A door banged shut immediately afterward, and without waiting for instructions, Alan ran after Riki. Vera called something to Gunny before she joined Alan at the locked door to the baths. After a moment's hesitation, Alan trotted toward the rear of an unfamiliar Buick sedan parked at the curb. He tried the latch and the unlocked trunk popped open easily. Alan rummaged past the spare tire and removed a loose lug wrench. He skipped over the curb and passed the Thompson to Vera.

She shook her head and grinned in amazement. "How'd you know it would be unlocked?"

"Vic always said this was a safe neighborhood. I figured people might be relaxed about locking things up."

Alan squeezed the wrench end tightly in his fist, while he aimed the pointed end at the lock. He reared back for momentum and slammed the bladed tip in between the door and the jamb, smashing the feeble locking mechanism to bits. With the wrench firmly wedged in place, Alan leveraged his weight against the bar, and pried the door open.

Alan dropped the wrench into his pocket, and he reached back for the Thompson. As Vera handed it to him, she met his eyes with that confident smile he'd missed seeing the past few hours. He had impressed her again, even with Gunny nearby, and he felt a moment of unexpected relief. He quickly returned her smile and led the way into the darkened hall that would take them to the baths. He slid his index finger alongside the trigger guard and pressed his body close to the wall on his left, nodding for Vera to fall in behind him. No matter what, he'd be her shield.

As they reached the inside corner that opened onto the baths, the door behind them opened and Gunny joined them. With a nod in Gunny's direction, Alan swung the Thompson out and pivoted around the corner, ready to spray the men's tub with bullets. But there was nothing there.

Across the room was the inner door to the partition that separated the women's bath from the men's. Vera pressed close to Alan and whispered, "It's not likely he'd go back there, unless there was a way out, and I don't think there is."

"I agree," Alan said. "So where could he have gone?"

"Remember when they brought us in they had us sit against the far wall?" Vera asked. "That kept us from seeing what they were doing out here in the hall—where we're standing now. Just before the White Dragon came to meet us, there was some kind of fuss out here in the hallway."

Alan leaned against a locker. After a moment he nodded his head enthusiastically. "You're right. I'd just assumed she came in from the street, but she couldn't have walked very far dressed in that outfit—not in public. She'd have left a trail of curious people."

Alan stepped away from the lockers and glanced around him. "We might just be standing in front of the entrance right now," he said.

Vera stepped back, joining him, and re-assessed the lockers that lined the hallway. "But where could it be?"

"There's got to be a smuggler's entrance to the catacombs—and it's probably inside one of these lockers."

Vera beamed and leaned forward to kiss him on the cheek. "Now you're thinking, Champ."

"Well we've got to think fast. Riki's our only lead. If we can't find him and make him talk, we've got nothing. I may not have Vic's persuasive smile, but I did learn a few of his tricks. I might as well tell you now though—it won't be a pretty thing."

"I've seen my share of rough play, but we need to remember the White Dragon. She might be down there too, and we don't know what other reinforcements they have."

Alan shook his head. "I don't see what other choice we have, and I'm not just going to walk away. If we go back to the car and drive around looking for the laundry truck, where would we start? They could be anywhere. Right now,

Riki's our best chance."

"So you're willing to face whatever's down there?"

"In spades."

"You don't know how much that means to me," Vera said, rubbing his shoulder.

From behind them, Gunny cleared his throat. "What's your plan?"

Alan squatted down and encouraged the other two to join him. "The sidewalks around here are cement and the streets have brick pavers, but the catacombs are cut into the hill. Vic told me it was done by miners and people working to pay off their passage—like indentured servants. If they were coming in here from the catacombs I'm hoping the White Dragon or one of her crew dragged some dirt in around the entrance. 'Matter out of place' is what Vic called it."

Gunny managed a thoughtful grin, flicked on his lighter, and held it up so he could see better. "Let's try the left side lockers first," Alan said. "That should put us level with the hill."

Gunny started by the farthest locker and swept his lighter along the floor as he worked his way back toward the street entrance. After a few feet he slowed and inspected the tiles on the floor more carefully. He looked up and nodded at Alan and Vera, who gathered in close to him. Alan glanced downward but remained alert. He kept a firm grip on the Thompson, ready if Riki decided to suddenly reappear.

"What have you got?" Alan asked Gunny.

"Matter out of place: red brick dust that shouldn't be here—just like you said."

Gunny raised his lighter and pressed it near the inside edge of the locker. The tall flame flickered and blew towards him from the draft. "That's it alright," Gunny said. He eyed the solid padlock on the locker and gave it a tug with his free hand, but it didn't budge.

Gunny moved the flame toward the outer edge of the

locker while Alan inspected the surrounding lockers. As he suspected, the next two lockers were the only ones with matching padlocks. Before he could say anything, Gunny snapped his lighter closed.

"Did you notice that these three padlocks are all the same brand?" Gunny asked.

"I was just about to say that," Alan said, nodding.

"They're connected, and this is your entrance, but I don't see an easy way in." Gunny turned to Alan. "You've done great getting us this far, Detective, but time's a wasting. We need a solution here—and fast."

Alan handed Vera his Thompson again, pushed the brim of the fedora up on his head, and squatted so he was eye-level with one of the locks. "Can I borrow your lighter?" he asked Gunny.

Gunny passed Alan the lighter with some reluctance. "Be careful with Windy, Champ. I've had her ten years now."

Alan flicked on the flame, and ran the soft glow along each of the padlocks. After a minute he focused on the center lock. He lifted the bottom of it upwards so he could check the backside of the lock before he stood. "This one's got the feel of oil and a caked-on smudge on the back—probably kerosene and some dirt."

Alan held the lock until it was pointing directly toward him, and then he twisted it the same way he would a door handle. The internal mechanism inside the locker spun and gave way. Alan felt the rods click into place and heard a soft metallic clang. The locker swung open, driven by a gush of breeze from behind it, and dank musty air with a hint of salt water greeted them. They peered inside to find a dark brick lined tunnel.

Vera wrapped an arm around Alan's shoulders and gave him a proud squeeze, while Gunny stepped forward and patted him on the back.

"How'd you know to do that?" Gunny asked.

Alan shook his head and grinned. "I might've read it somewhere...I've read a load of detective magazines, but I don't remember this. I just knew it would work somehow."

Gunny stuck out his hand, indicating he wanted his lighter back. "I'll take Windy—she's my good luck piece and I keep her close. As for you, Mister...keep up with the reading."

Vera handed Alan the Thompson and Gunny grinned confidently at him. "Cover me with that, Champ, but don't shoot until I'm out of your way. And if you see me drop— for any reason at all—that's my signal you might want to cut loose with it."

"Got it."

Vera raised her pistol high. "And you know I've got you covered from behind."

Alan nodded. "Okay. I've got that too."

A few feet in they came to a simple wooden door. Gunny pushed down on the lever and tugged it open. Their passage joined a larger tunnel, very similar to the ones underneath the theater. A trio of lanterns hung on dowels nearby, and below them was a red and yellow kerosene container. Gunny shook one of the lanterns closest to him. Not satisfied with its fuel level he picked up another lantern and repeated the process. Once he was satisfied with his choice, he adjusted the cotton wick and used his lighter to set the lantern aglow. He held the lantern out at arm's length in the direction of the Japanese Theater, but Vera grabbed his shoulder to stop him. "Before we head off, why are we going that way and not the other?"

"You know, you're absolutely right. Riki could've gone either way," Gunny answered thoughtfully. "Before we get started, let's see if there's a trail."

Inside the large, dark cavern, carved deep into the rock base beneath Japan Town, Riki set his lantern on top of an altar cabinet under a raised podium. Behind him was a stone statue of Buddha, sitting cross-legged and holding a stringed instrument. The large but delicate figure was situated on a rock ledge in a shallow pool of water that had been diverted from an underground stream. Riki braced his right shoulder with his other hand as he lowered himself into a padded chair. He grimaced in pain.

Slightly above him on the podium, the White Dragon snapped her fan open and fluttered it in front of her painted face. There were a few other men on the edges of the room, and she spoke in English so only Riki could understand her. "Your wounds are slowing you down. I waited—alone—for several minutes before re-enforcements showed up!"

"My apologies, Honorable Dragon. We had to use chloroform again, to calm the young lady before I could alert others to your needs. You know how dangerous that chemical can be."

The White Dragon snapped her fan against the palm of her hand, indicating she was done with that line of questioning and changing topics. "Your shoulder and your hand, they still pain you?"

Riki closed his eyes and nodded.

"Perhaps you should see a doctor. There's a Chinese man with great skill only a few blocks below here. He made his reputation assisting those who choose not to have children but have nowhere else to turn. He works out of an upstairs brothel."

"A whore monger and an abortionist? Do the Chinese not have scruples? I don't want an abortion done to my shoulder."

The White Dragon opened and quickly snapped her fan closed again as she leaned forward. "Civil tongue, Riki."

"I meant no disrespect, Honorable Dragon. The pain obscures my judgment and my speech."

"The reports say that he has ancient remedies for pain, appreciates the value of gold ducats, and his discretion can be trusted."

Riki took off his bowler hat and set it to the side while he rubbed his face. "Ancient remedies mean opium, and we know what that did to his country. I am afraid of their drugs."

"They can be controlled. There once were countless opium dens in this area, but most are gone now. People have learned to temper their hunger for the drug."

Riki nodded, attentively. "The pain is affecting my ability to serve you, so I shall have it tended to—just as soon as the brass and the American girl are—"

"I don't want her hurt. I gave my word on that."

"She will be safe on the ship, and we can decide what to do with her once our cargo is loaded—"

The White Dragon held her fan up to stop him, but instantly lowered it, changing her mind. She glanced away to stare past him at the two oversized statues of warriors that stood menacingly next to the orange and black inner doors of the temple.

Riki cleared his throat. "We will, of course, follow your wishes with respect to the young woman."

The White Dragon slowly spread her fan open and held it in front of her face. "Very well then," she said. "I think it is time for Miss Ohara to take a cruise through Puget Sound, where she will meet a charming young lady in need of a benefactor."

Riki closed his eyes and partially smiled.

"Give me a few minutes to change my clothing," the White Dragon said. "But wait to put out the candles. You know how I hate the dark. While I'm gone, have the men clean up the mess in the theater. Add the fallen bodies to our burial chamber and while I'm away I want you to begin digging a new one. Our losses have been heavy, and we are filling American soil with the bodies of our dear countrymen faster than we can dig new tombs. No one should ever know how many we've lost."

The White Dragon turned away, covering her face with her fan while she composed herself. "This killing has got to stop."

Riki barked an order at the men sitting behind him in the temple and they all stood for the White Dragon while she departed through an arched passageway of stones.

Gunny raised the lantern slightly and swept it towards
the eastern tunnel where tracks were immediately visible.
After taking a couple of steps he paused abruptly and
squatted down. "These scuffs are from smaller shoes—
women's feet. This is where they were forcing your daughter
along."

Vera closed her eyes and nodded thoughtfully, as if
trying to compress the pain into a manageable size that she
could store away for later review.

Gunny rose and led them down the eastern passage.
After several minutes the tunnel widened at a place where
a new route seemed to be in progress. Bricks had been
pulled from the wall and were stacked in a pile near a large
mound of unused ones. Gunny examined the masonry and
tools that had been left propped up against the hole near
two wheelbarrows. "These diggers are like moles under your
lawn. This must be another escape passage," he said as he
sorted through the picks and shovels and latched onto a
garden hoe with a gooseneck bend near the heart-shaped
tip. "Don't know why they're using this down here—maybe
to mix mortar—but it's just what we need to hold the lantern.
Right now it's just a beacon that tells them where to shoot."

Gunny held the hoe at an angle and hung the lantern just behind its blade like a rigid fishing pole with an oversized bobber. "I feel like less of a target already," he said with a wink in Vera's direction.

The trio marched deeper into the catacombs, passing rows of non-descript doors. Gunny led the way, the lantern held low, to make sure the marks didn't diverge from the main passage. They passed two more sets of doors and came to a set of posts with an overhead timber inscribed in Japanese characters. Hanging on dowels mounted into the post were three more unlit lanterns. Gunny reached up and felt one. "It's still warm," he reported.

The posts marked the opening to a spur passage on the left side that led higher into the hill. Gunny stretched his lantern across the floor of the new passage to the far brick wall, while Alan and Vera waited behind him.

"Clog marks here," Gunny said.

He extended the lantern into the spur passage and peeked slowly around the corner. Then he swung the lantern back to set it on the pavers and patted Alan's shoulder. "Move to the other side of the entrance. We want to cover both sides. That will improve our field of fire—so you and Vera can shoot around me, not through me—when I go up to the door. Once you're in place, I'll use Little Windy to see what's at the top of the steps."

From behind him Vera touched Gunny's back. "You see steps?" she asked.

"Around the corner there's about a half-dozen stone steps carved out of the hill. Looks like they lead to an orange door."

"A painted door?" she asked.

"Yep. Orange and black, and there're incense sticks stuck into a bowl, mounted on a beam. Can you smell them?"

Vera inhaled deeply, sniffing the air. "Yes, indeed.

Markings of a temple, and the people inside probably hope the incense will drive away the rats." She nodded to herself and smiled. "This must be the Dragon's lair."

She slid up close behind Gunny and rested her hand on his back. "How long are the sticks?"

Gunny peeked around the corner again with the softer glow of his lighter. "Long," he said.

"Then they're fresh. Good. Which way is the smoke blowing?"

Gunny stole another look and then stepped back close to Vera. "Away from the door, toward us."

"Good omen." Vera patted his upper shoulder lightly. "When we make our entry, breathe in some of the smoke before going inside. It's supposed to drive away evil spirits."

Gunny gave her a sideways glance and grinned. "We use *their* magic for our advantage?"

"Sure. Why not trust their gods to decide who's right?"

Gunny touched his finger to the brim of his hat. "Good call," he said. Vera flashed Gunny her confident smile. Then she knelt next to him and squinted over at Alan who'd taken up a position on the other side of the entrance, barely six feet away.

After a few hushed whispers, Gunny darted across to Alan's position on the other side of the entrance. He tugged on Alan's coat, indicating he needed to get down. "Try to make yourself as small a target as possible."

Alan squatted next to him. "Roger that."

"Another thing: only one of us keeps an eye on the door at any given time. Gives them less to see and less of us to hide."

"You must have experience with this."

"After my plane was shot down in France, they had me teach—"

"Shot down? During a dog fight?"

"Hell no. It was ground fire, probably from some dim-witted Frenchman who was supposed to be on our side. That's why I worry about who's behind me. Right now I need you to cover me. The passage is too narrow for the both of us. Don't worry about pointing the muzzle up or down—just keep it away from me and your finger off the trigger until you have a clear target."

"Got it, but...one more thing?"

"Shoot."

"Were you an Ace?"

"Once an Ace, always an Ace. Four kills means, yes I am."

Alan grinned incredulously.

Gunny patted Alan's knee in an effort to refocus his attention. "We go in quiet, but once we're there, make all the noise you need. And one more thing—leave us a survivor. We need someone to tell us where the girl is, preferably the top dog—that Riki guy would do. You can't always rely on the working pups to know what's going on."

"Roger that."

Gunny crouched back on one of his heels. He balanced his .45 on his thigh and retrieved a whiskey flask from inside his coat with one hand. He unscrewed the cap and offered a taste to Alan, who shook him off. "I'm too nervous," Alan said. "It would burn right though me. How about after we're done?"

Gunny nodded, tipped the small bottle up for a sip and recapped it to put it back in his coat. "Watch for my signal and then come running. If I take a bullet and go down, you step over and blast away. We know Jennifer's not here, so leave nothing standing."

Without waiting for a response, Gunny darted into the side passage leading up to the temple doors. Alan stretched his leg out into the spur, bracing himself for the Thompson's powerful kick. For a right-hander he was on the wrong side to cover Gunny. He'd never fired the Thompson left handed.

It felt dead wrong. To provide the cover Gunny needed, he would have to slide out into the middle of the tunnel, exposing himself to danger.

Alan snuck a peek over at Vera, and she caught his eye. Watching his struggle to find a safe line of fire, she waved him over and pointed to a spot next to her. Alan quickly darted across and slid beside her, dropping to one knee. She leaned close to his ear and whispered, "I can shoot a pistol left handed. I'll switch sides."

"Is there anything you can't do?"

"Bake a soufflé. I've never been much with fancy desserts."

Before he could tell her he had never seen, smelled, or tasted a soufflé—or cared to, for that matter—Vera quick-stepped across to the other side of the passage, dropped into place, and took a ready position.

At the top of the carved steps, in the faint glow cast by the smoldering incense sticks, Gunny pressed his left ear against the temple door. After a long moment he snapped his lighter on and quickly waved at Alan and Vera to join him.

As Alan followed Vera up the steps, he brought the Thompson around but kept the barrel low. His instructions from his father, who had been the first to teach him how to fire the beast, echoed in his ears. *If you have to use it, lean into it...aim low at the knees and let the weapon work its way to the mid-section.* Instructions Alan knew all too well.

As Vera and Alan hit the top step, Gunny dropped his weight and rammed his left shoulder into the unlatched orange doors, which burst open towards the inner sanctum.

Compared to the darkness of the catacomb tunnels, the inside of the candlelit cavern was awash in light. The rapid opening of the door caused a breeze which made the candles flicker all at once. It was an eerie effect that made the large clay statues that filled the room appear even more menacing, like guardians to the gates of hell. Reflexively, Gunny dove to the ground while raising his pistol.

His pistol barked in his hand. BANG! BANG! He squeezed off two rounds at the eight-foot tall figure on his right, tearing into its mid-section and knocking out a large chunk of clay. As Gunny went down, Alan stepped forward and fired a short burst into the second figure, starting just above the armor protecting its knee. The Thompson roared. BANG! BANG! BANG! The machinegun's staccato was deafening in the tight confines of the brick and stone cavern.

Alan stepped over Gunny, and with a light push from Vera he pressed himself against the rough side of the large cave for a clear line of fire, scanning quickly for the next threat. His eyes washed over big Riki, who sat frozen on the far side of the room, his eyes bulging wide, but he displayed nothing that offered an immediate challenge.

Vera turned away from Alan toward the right side of the entrance, where a brood of living warriors groped clumsily for weapons. She swung out her .45 and targeted the tallest of the group, who cocked a revolver and brought it down to aim in her direction. Her gun spat fire. BANG! BANG! Her target shuddered spasmodically and fell backward, while Vera took aim again on a new target.

Across from her, Alan spun away from the wall and leaned forward to train the barrel of the Thompson on the same group Vera was dealing with. He exhaled, squeezed the stock of the weapon firmly against his hip, and softly tugged at the trigger with his index finger. The tommy-gun roared again. BANG! BANG! BANG! There was no escaping the maelstrom of deadly fire.

Alan glanced back over at Riki, who cautiously started to stand up but then plopped back down in his seat, raising his hands in surrender as best he could even though one of his arms was still in a sling. Alan covered Riki with the tommy-gun, ready to pepper him with a torrent of bullets at the first sign of danger, but Riki only sat there uselessly. Obviously his shoulder was still a major source of pain. Convinced that Riki wasn't playing possum, Alan turned to see if other Japanese operatives still posed a risk.

Gunny fired from his prone position into the tightly packed cadre of Japanese agents, and then quickly climbed into a kneeling position. One of the men leapt from behind a statue and darted for the sanctuary in the rear of the temple. Gunny fired just as the man passed the last two remaining clay guards. The bullet tore through the back of the man's coat at a shallow angle, catching him in the shoulder blade and spinning him awkwardly. At the last moment the operative regained his balance and lunged between the clay sentinels.

Alan also tried to draw a bead on the escapee, lifting the Thompson to eye level. As soon as he seated the butt of the stock into the crook of his shoulder, he squeezed off a short burst of rounds, knocking large wedges of clay from both of the large figures—but missing the agent.

Gunny sprang to his feet and dashed around the raised podium toward the back. "I'll get him," he shouted. "You stay with the prisoner!"

Alan lowered the chopper, swung it around to aim directly at Riki's face, and started walking toward the prisoner, before Vera interrupted. "Cover those on the floor," she called out. "Make sure none of them can use a weapon. I'll take Riki."

Alan glowered at the big man menacingly and then turned toward the other fallen men. Many of them were young and similarly attired. Except for all the blood, they could have been fresh recruits from a military academy. "What should I be looking for?" Alan asked, with his back to Vera.

"Movement, weapons, and running blood. If it's draining steadily, that's one thing, but if it's pumping in spurts, you've got a live one."

"And if I have a live one?"

"Your call, but I've seen enough death. Just make sure he can't hurt us while we're here."

"I get it. Like Vic would say, 'They can't fire—"

Suddenly Alan lurched forward and swung down viciously with the stock of the Thompson, smashing it into a hand that was crawling out from the pile towards a revolver lying on the floor. CRUNCH!

"—a gun with broken fingers."

"That would be my Victor. Still, while Riki and I have a chat you might want to collect their guns."

The candlelit backroom reminded Gunny of a sacristy in a Christian church, the formal dressing area where celebrants donned robes for official ceremonies. As Gunny scanned the room for the agent he was chasing, he passed a dressing table with makeup containers spread in front of a mirror. On top of a shelf beside the table were two shimada wigs mounted on carved heads. A number of silk samurai robes with puffy shoulders hung on satin covered hangers in an open Yoshida wardrobe. Displayed nearby on a mantle were the White Dragon's swords. Vera was right; this was the Dragon's lair. The only thing missing from the small room was the wounded agent, even though there was no sign of an exit.

Gunny readied his pistol and advanced through the room, searching for movement. The room was too small for someone to hide successfully, but he couldn't afford to be careless. While continuing to scan the room, Gunny backed up a step and called out. "I could use a hand in here; the little bugger seems to have disappeared."

Alan checked with Vera, and she nodded. "Leave the Thompson with me though," she added.

Alan scooped a .38 off the ground and stuffed it in his

belt. He walked over to Vera and handed her the chopper. She snuggled the butt of the Thompson against her side like an experienced pro who'd been properly trained, adjusting for the added weight of the big spool. With the weapon firmly in place, she sidled toward Riki, pointing the barrel squarely between his eyes to capture his attention.

Alan stepped around the podium and rushed to join Gunny, drawing his pistol. Gunny inclined his head toward the backroom. "See what I mean? There's barely enough room in here for oxygen. Did I just imagine winging some guy that ran back here?"

Alan surveyed the room, going over all the same things Gunny had. Then he dropped his gaze to the stone pavers on the floor, and after a second he squatted down and touched one. He dabbed his fingers into something dark and wet. He held his hand up close to the candlelight to catch the red glow. "You winged him, alright."

Alan stood and approached the open wardrobe that was full of the White Dragon's silk kimonos. He squatted down again, switched his pistol to his left hand, and reached back toward Gunny. "Let me borrow your lighter again, please?"

Gunny dug into his leather coat, smirked, and handed the lighter to Alan. "Her name's Windy, and you don't need to be so polite with me or her, Champ."

"Sorry, Ace. It's a habit."

"Of all the habits to have, being polite's a good one. Women find it charming. Especially ones with class, like Vera."

Alan glanced up to check Gunny's face for meaning, but all he caught was a friendly grin. Alan smiled to himself, feeling a burst of confidence that was quickly tinged by guilt. He was no Valentino and didn't know how to play games with affection. He flicked on the lighter and lowered it close to the floor, drawing it over the bottom of the wardrobe and between two of the robes, careful to keep the cloth far enough apart that he wouldn't light them on fire. Suddenly feeling moisture, he withdrew his hand and found a smear of fresh blood on his skin. Alan flicked the lighter closed and pushed the silk outfits further apart. "Bring one of those candles here, would you?"

"What've you got?"

While he waited for Gunny to bring a candle, Alan pushed the silk kimonos and clogs as far apart as he could to clear a space in the middle of the wardrobe. "He's not here now, but at some point he was," Alan said.

Gunny handed him a bronze Shokukai candleholder with a worn down candle that had created a tiny bowl of hot wax near its wick. Alan set the candle on the floor of the black-lacquered wardrobe and explored the interior of the cabinet. There had to be an opening somewhere, but he couldn't find anything out of the ordinary. He set his pistol down and worked both hands along the inside edges of the cabinet but still found nothing. Suddenly inspired, he grasped the metal catch where the cabinet's doors met when they were closed. He tugged on the catch and it instantly snapped forward. CLICK. Spring loaded, the mechanism released the rear panel, which drifted slightly open.

Alan leaned in to push gently on the doors, and they fell wide open. He reached for his gun and picked up the candle, catching a faint glimpse of pavers that lead to a wooden staircase behind the wardrobe. The stairs were better illuminated, as though someone had left a kerosene lamp burning.

Behind Alan, Gunny leaned in for a peek. "Champ, you're a genius at this. Detective magazines again, huh?"

Alan grinned apologetically.

Gunny stepped forward and moved in front of Alan to take the lead. "Same rules as before: cover me while I climb through. He's either lying in ambush, or he's high-tailing it down the middle of Main Street for re-enforcements."

"Not that I'm keeping count, but aren't they down about twenty men?"

"Near that, but there's no telling how many they have stashed away. It ain't any risk for them to sneak 'em through the tunnels we've seen, all the way from the waterfront to here. The police should assign a beat cop here to direct traffic."

Gunny slid backwards into the wardrobe and spun around to enter the tunnel feet first. He reached to take the candle from Alan and held it out in front, illuminating the roughly carved passage. "Nothing back here but wooden steps," he said over his shoulder. "We may as well find out where they lead."

Alan slid through the wardrobe the same way Gunny had and joined him on the other side. The small alcove was only partially finished. A trail of pavers led away from the wardrobe directly toward the wooden steps. The air in the confined area had the dank coolness of a mineshaft. Gunny set the candle down, planting it in a small mound of sand near a stack of unused pavers. "Won't need this now, and I want my hands free," he said.

Gunny led the way up the wooden steps, which crossed back and forth like the inside of a cathedral's steeple. The higher they went the easier it became to see ahead of them. For the first time Alan noticed that the walls to the shaft were lined with rough sawn cedar boards. An oaken handrail with blood smears marking every few steps seemed to be a more recent addition to the mineshaft, and the wet blood confirmed that the wounded agent had gone that way.

Two flights up the steps stopped at a closed door. Gunny paused for a moment and through the door they heard muffled mechanical sounds. Gunny took a deep breath, exhaled, and nodded to Alan. Then he grabbed hold of the bloodied doorknob and shoved his shoulder into the door—pushing it wide open. He burst into a sweatshop busy with workers, Alan hard on his heels.

The two men stood shoulder to shoulder and surveyed the Asian women with their heads stooped over yards of fabric being shoved into industrial sewing machines. The women were too preoccupied to glance up at the intruders. Just over the clacking noises of their sewing was the sound of a tabletop RCA playing Jo Stafford and the Pied Pipers.

Gathering their bearings, the men hurried between the machines and freshly made garments, following the trail of blood across the bare wooden floor toward the front of the building. Gunny lowered his pistol and shoved it inside his jacket for concealment, and Alan did likewise. They followed the trail through a swinging door into a front office. A woman clerk who was retrieving something from a file cabinet stopped what she was doing and dropped the file. She stepped back towards the wall and stared at the two foreigners without saying anything.

Alan followed Gunny through the front door and down the steps to the street. They didn't have to travel any farther. To their right the blood splatters jetted across the rust-colored brick pavers, leaving a staggering trail toward the Panama Hotel, which was just over a block away. Halfway to the hotel their wounded man reeled drunkenly and leaned on a youth in a similar outfit as his. The new agent did most of the work, half-dragging the escapee towards the hotel.

Gunny put up his hand and skidded to a stop as Alan joined him at the curb. While Alan followed the movement of the men he remembered the night his father was brought home to die by his union brothers. Suddenly what he'd been trying to suppress bubbled up and demanded to be dealt with. These men he'd been killing also had families—loved ones who'd miss and cry for them, like he had missed and cried for his dad. Alan shook his head, trying to shake any sympathy away so he could deal with the present. The memories would have to wait till later, after Jennifer *was* safe with her mother. It's what his dad would have wanted him to do: protect the family, and Jennifer was family—his family and his father's.

Gunny gently backhanded Alan's shoulder, snapping him out of his reverie. "This one's flown to the hive on a busted wing. We need to help Vera with the big fella. He's our best hope, and he's got some explaining to do."

Gunny and Alan retraced their steps back into the garment shop where the woman clerk was now huddled close to another man in the front office. The small man, dressed in an inexpensive suit and tie, wore wire-rimmed spectacles and an angry scowl. He stepped away from the woman and planted himself in the duo's path. "What is it that you want here?" he asked in heavily accented English.

Gunny stretched himself to his full height with his head tilted back slightly like an old time beat cop getting ready to clear the room in a bar brawl, and gazed intimidatingly at the smaller man. "We chased a man through your shop and—"

"I saw no man."

Gunny pointed to the wet drops of blood on the bare wooden floor. "He was leaking fluid when he ran—"

While Gunny spoke with the merchant, Alan glanced around the front office. The glass counter had several bolts of colored fabric stacked on top of a display case that featured Japanese figurines and carved treasures. Mounted behind the counter above a city business license was a picture of an Asian businesswoman in her mid-thirties. She was wearing a stiff suit and had a no-nonsense expression on her face. Her eyes were beautiful but different from any

196

of the others he had seen. They were more rounded, almost similar to his own.

The man arguing with Gunny shifted his weight, positioning himself so Gunny would not be able to pass uncontested. He showed no fear of the larger man, a fact not lost on Alan, but it didn't seem to register with Gunny.

"Alright, I'm done playing nice," Gunny snapped, an edge to his voice. "It's time you move out of the way."

Gunny lifted his left arm to shove the smaller man aside. Anticipating what was about to happen, Alan lunged between the two and knocked Gunny's hand away. At the same time, the businessman slid his back leg behind him, assuming a Martial Arts stance.

Alan grabbed his pistol from his coat and dropped his hand to the side, just as the smaller man kicked fiercely for Alan's head. Alan brought his left arm up swiftly and deflected the powerful blow, which partially knocked him off balance. The other man teetered backward, bounced on his toes, and prepared to come at the two intruders again. Thinking quickly Alan stuck his hand back in his coat and grasped the brass badge Vic had given him. He brought it up to eye level along with his .45. "We're detectives, and this is official business."

The Japanese man snapped his open hands into a defensive block, staring past them at the proffered badge and pistol which didn't seem to scare him. He huffed, glared at Gunny and Alan, and held his ground. "Are you police? I've never see you before."

Alan nodded and pushed the badge toward his opponent, fingers wrapped around the edges. "We're detectives and this is official business," he repeated. "Do we need to call the beat cops, Sullivan and McCarthy?"

The angry merchant glanced sideways at the apprehensive clerk. She closed her eyes and shook her head rapidly. The man finally relaxed his arms and eased out of his fighting stance to slowly step aside. "We do not want trouble with Sullivan," he said pronouncing the policeman's name correctly.

Without waiting for further permission, Alan and Gunny quickly strode through the doors to the work floor and passed between the women and their rapidly clicking sewing machines. As before, none of the workers looked up as the two men headed toward a door none of the women had ever used.

Gunny paused for a second at the bottom of the steps leading back through the wardrobe. "Who's this Sullivan?" he asked.

"I just picked a couple Irish names out of my hat, but if he's really out here—and they're afraid of him and not us— he's someone we don't want to mess with," Alan replied.

Gunny set the lantern down on the last step and extinguished the flame. "How'd you know that little shrimp was going to put up a fight?" Gunny asked.

"In boxing I learned to watch my opponent's eyes. I saw him sizing up your jaw, planning his strike, and one of his countrymen had already kicked me in the head. I knew to look for it."

"I've never been a bully, but I figured my size would make a difference. I didn't expect that. I owe you one, Champ."

"It all works out," Alan said with a smile. "I'm not keeping score."

🐉 ◉ 🐉

Back inside the temple chamber Vera paced back and forth behind Riki, who she had moved so that he faced his fallen comrades. His right arm still hung uselessly in the black silk sling, and he cradled it with his left hand.

Vera held the tommy-gun at the ready, like an angry sentry needing a skull to crack. On the raised platform behind her was a small cache of handguns, all .38 caliber Smith & Wessons with 4-inch barrels—police specials which Alan had retrieved from the floor earlier.

"I couldn't find anything to tie his hands with," she said when she saw Alan enter the room, "and I don't think in the least that he's not capable of inflicting harm."

She met Alan's eyes as he and Gunny approached, searching for an update on the man they'd chased. Alan shook his head and silently mouthed the words, *Panama Hotel.* Vera nodded.

Alan slid his pistol into his coat pocket and stepped in front of Riki. The gorilla's right eye was glowering red and his eyelid was swollen shut. Even though he knew he should have, Alan hadn't anticipated this from Vera.

When he glanced at her she roughly pressed the Thompson's muzzle against the back of Riki's head, pushing his skull forward. "He's not talking. Apparently he's more worried about what the White Dragon will do to him than what I'll do if he doesn't talk."

Riki grumbled something guttural in Japanese which sounded like a curse.

Vera spun the chopper around as if she was going to slam the stock into the back of Riki's head, but then stopped. "It's times like this when I miss Vic's skills," she said.

Alan nodded thoughtfully. "Vic's smile and...," Alan reached in his pocket and pulled out the tire iron he'd used to break into the baths, "...his power of persuasion."

Vera closed her eyes with a sense of relief and Alan squatted down so he was eye level with Riki, holding the wrench out in clear view. Riki's eye arched high and his mouth dropped open, but no words came out.

Alan spun the pointed end of the wrench around and

used it to scratch his temple, just above his ear. "Riki, is it?"

The big man turned his head to stare at Gunny. When he didn't find a sympathetic face there he tried to swivel far enough around to catch a glimpse of Vera again, as if hoping she would put a stop to this.

Alan swung the tire wrench with a fierce backhand, and it collided with Riki's kneecap. The big man snapped his head around and winced sharply in pain. Again he grumbled something in Japanese as he bent over to grab his wounded knee, cradling it with both hands. It was obvious he still favored his right shoulder, and his right hand was already swollen and discolored around an unset break that had come from Vera's baton strike during their first encounter.

"That was a warm up tap, Riki. I just want to get your attention. Your knee will swell up a little, but you should be able to walk—in a few days anyway. The next one's going to require a cast."

Riki closed his one good eye and bit down slowly on his lower lip, trying to internalize his pain.

"Now where's Jennifer?"

"I...do not...know," Riki said haltingly.

"I don't buy that. We saw you load her in the laundry truck before you ran in here to hide."

The big man opened his eye and glanced warily at Alan.

Alan patted the palm of his left hand with the beefy end of the lug wrench. "Vera, you might want to look away for a moment."

"Why? Because I'm a woman?"

It was Alan's turn to glance away for a second, embarrassed. "It's that I don't want you to see me like this," he said in a low tone.

Gunny stepped closer. "It's okay, Champ. I can take it from here if that's what concerns you. She already knows I'm a brute."

200

Alan shook him off. "I've got to see this through. Wouldn't be fair to let you fight my battles."

Gunny grinned and nodded, a hint of pride showing. He backed away.

Alan took the pointed end of the wrench and dragged it across the top of Riki's thigh, just above his knee. Then he glanced up to Vera and stared into her eyes, unsure of what he was searching for. She blinked softly and nodded. She was bracing for the worst and willing to accept what he'd do—at least he hoped she was. He didn't want her to see this side of him, the part that scared him. He worried about the monster he was becoming, but he also wanted her to know he'd do whatever it took to get Jennifer home safely.

Alan reared back and swung down hard with the force of Babe Ruth. Riki lurched forward to protect his knee but sacrificed his left hand in the effort. CRACK! The wrench landed squarely in the center of his hand, shattering the knuckles on both his middle and ring fingers. The force of the blow transferred through Riki's hand into his tender knee, pushing it to the side.

Riki went pale, his mouth dropped to form a scream, but all that came out were tight gasps of air. The big man curled into a ball, his eye rolled up into his head, and he tumbled off the bench to the stone floor.

Alan stood and shook his head, disgusted at what he'd done. He blinked a number of times rapidly, as if trying to make the scene disappear, and then he slid the wrench into his pocket. Afraid to look at Vera, he turned to Gunny and indicated he needed help picking Riki up and putting him back on the bench.

As the two men bent over and grabbed Riki under the arms, Vera leaned forward and placed the tommy-gun close to the man's head.

"A little caution never hurt," she said.

As dead weight Riki was a heavy load, but Gunny and Alan were determined. They hoisted him up and tossed him back onto his seat, but without support he began to roll forward again. Alan put his hand against Riki's right shoulder and held him upright. Under Alan's hand, Riki's suit felt wet. Alan pulled his hand away long enough to confirm his suspicion: blood. Riki's bullet wound from two nights before had either not been taken care of properly, or it had opened up again.

Alan pushed at Riki's shoulder like he was steadying the heavy bag in a boxing gym, measuring it for a blow. After a half-dozen pushes the big man stirred. He flapped his broken left wing like a wounded goose, slowly at first and then frantically, as if he were trying to shake the buzzing sting away. After a moment he opened his one eye wide. When he was finally able to form words his voice cracked. "What's wrong with you people? Are you barbarians?"

Alan frowned and his mouth sagged open. "Us?"

Vera poked the muzzle of the Thompson against Riki's right temple and pivoted so she was in his field of view. "What's wrong with us? Let me tell you. You've kidnapped my daughter—who has no part in any of this, and I want her back NOW!"

Alan reached out and clasped his hand around Vera's upper arm. She continued to glare at Riki a moment and then turned to Alan. He nodded confidently. "Let me finish this."

Vera exhaled heavily and stepped back.

Alan transferred the lug wrench to his left hand and jabbed it softly against the spot on Riki's shoulder where the blood was. Riki winced at the contact. "Stay focused, Riki. You're not getting the point. The point is at the end of this tire iron, which I'm going to bury in your shoulder if you don't tell me where my sister is."

Riki's eyebrows furrowed, even the one over his swollen

eye. "She's your sister?"

"That's besides the point."

"I do not understand."

"You don't need to. You just need to tell us where she's at—right goddamn now."

"I...can't."

Alan caught Gunny's eye and inclined his head toward Riki. Without having to be told what to do, Gunny slid behind the big man and grabbed the lapels of his coat to peel them back roughly. The coat fell away from Riki's shoulders to expose the blood-soaked area of the big man's injury. Gunny gave another tug and pulled the coat far enough down to pin Riki's arms back.

Alan took a deep breath and exhaled noisily. "I'm done being nice, I'm done begging, and I'm done waiting on you to change your mind." He reached up and tugged on the end of Riki's bowtie, pulling it loose. Once unfastened, he dug his fingers inside of the man's collar, grabbed hold of it tightly, and tore the collar free from his neck, sending buttons flying across the brick pavers. He gave the shirt another tug and pulled the vest open, exposing only a sleevelees undershirt over a heavily muscled chest.

With the wrench Alan lifted the strap of Riki's undershirt and found it stuck to the unhealed wound like a bandage that had been put on wet and left on too long. Using the tire iron as a lever, Alan ripped the shirt away from the seeping bullet hole, and as he did so he caught a faint whiff of decaying flesh. Gunny smelled it too and leaned over to take a closer look. "If that's gangrene setting in it's nothing to mess with."

Riki rolled his head on his thick neck, closed his eyes, and shook his head.

Alan took the wrench with both hands and probed the gaping hole with the tip of the iron.

"AAAHHHHRRRGGGHHH!" Riki screamed deeply, giving vent to his pain and revealing his terror. This time he was too scared to pass out. He glanced frantically at Alan, trying to read his eyes. Alan avoided looking directly at Riki's. Instead he furrowed his brow intently and focused on the man's shoulder, sending a message that more was coming.

"Like the dentist says, this is gonna hurt a little," Alan warned.

Riki's mouth started moving, as if he were trying to talk. Finally the words caught up with his moving lips. "Ah... ah...I...I...can't—"

Alan grasped the end of the wrench firmly, bracing his right hand behind the wrench's lug for leverage and smiled wolfishly at Riki. "Sure you can, and you will."

With both hands wrapped around the tire iron Alan took a practice poke at the wound, and then he reared back and cocked his arms like a Zulu warrior preparing to spear his first lion.

"NO!" Riki screamed loudly.

Alan stopped to glare into the big man's eyes. Riki's good eye blinked rapidly while the swollen one fluttered, unable to keep pace. "She will sail with the brass," he whispered at last.

Alan eased his grip on the tire iron. "Sail with the brass? On the ship?"

"Hai," Riki said with a slight nod.

Alan exchanged glances with Vera and Gunny, who both nodded.

"I believe him," Vera said.

Riki's head dropped low to his chest. Alan wasn't sure whether the gesture was in shame or because of the pain. He reached down, grabbed the man around the jowls of his neck, and lifted Riki's face higher.

"Where's the White Dragon now?" Alan demanded.

Riki shook his head slowly. "I have betrayed my country, that is enough. I am an unworthy servant and deserve to die. I will say no more. It is better you kill me now—please spare me that chore at least. I am a weakling."

Alan grabbed the tire iron once more and lifted it slightly. Before he swung the final blow, he again turned to Gunny and Vera to see if they were in agreement. This time they shook their heads together. They all sensed that no more information would be forthcoming despite whatever else they might do to this broken man. They had their lead, and that was all they could expect.

Alan and Gunny huddled with Vera a few paces from Riki. "We can't leave him here," she said. "Somehow, someway, he'll get word to the White Dragon that we're coming."

Gunny nodded in agreement and glanced at Alan. "It's like what Machiavelli said about good coming from evil deeds—isn't it? He didn't believe in leaving survivors that might return to fight another day."

Alan shook his head. "I'm sick of the violence, and I really can't justify it when the guy's already a prisoner. It's like a piece of the good in me dies whenever I hurt someone. I'm wondering how long it'll be before I've got nothing left—especially this time. There's just something wrong with abusing a beaten man. If it were left to me I couldn't pull the trigger."

Alan looked at Vera and then Gunny. After a moment's silence, they both shook their heads. They weren't up to it either. "Well one of us will have to stay with him, and I've got to be at the ship when we find my baby," Vera said.

Gunny gazed at Alan. "And she's your sister, huh? I missed that, by the way. I thought when we started out today, you said you'd only just met her."

Alan smiled sheepishly. "That's right, but if I remember, you said you saw the resemblance."

Vera tilted her head impatiently. "Can we talk about this later?" she snapped.

Gunny shifted his weight uncomfortably. "I'm sorry for prying, ma'am. I just like to know how things all fit together." He let out a sigh. "So then, it's got to be me. I'll stay."

Vera arched her eyebrows, pleading. "Would you?"

"Sure, but not in here. This place is like King Street Station. Soon enough somebody's going to come along, and I'll be fighting a whole new battle all by my lonesome. But I'm thinking I can fetch a wheelbarrow from the dig site back in the tunnel and run him down to Chinatown. I'll stash him in an opium den that'll dope him up for a week."

"How do you know you'll be safe down there?" Vera asked.

"I don't, but in the opium dens—"

"How will you find one?"

"It'll find me. If the dens here are anything like the ones in Kowloon, there'll be a boatload of shipping boxes and paraphernalia scattered outside their back door."

Vera shook her head. "I'll worry about you."

"I'll be fine. They catch a gander of Mr. Riki, and they won't want to mess with the one they think captured that big ape."

"We don't have time to argue, but promise me you won't take chances," Vera pleaded.

"If that's what you want. Cross my heart and hope to—"

Vera closed her eyes and waved her hand in front of her to silence him. "Don't finish that. It may just be a silly saying, but I'm superstitious about things like that. Times like this we don't want to press our luck."

Gunny chuckled and dashed off, only to return a few minutes later with a wheelbarrow. A skeptical Vera held the orange and black doors open when she heard him banging the wheel up the six steps to the temple.

"How're you going to get him down the steps in that?" she asked.

"One step at a time."

"He makes quite a load, and what if it gets away from you?" she asked, inclining her head toward the wheelbarrow.

"Well that wouldn't be so good for Mr. Riki. Would that bother you?"

Vera shook her head and twisted her lips into a wry smile. "Not so much."

Alan busied himself gathering up the pile of revolvers. Counting the one he carried in his waistband, there were eight. He unloaded the other seven and put their collected rounds in his coat pocket. Leaving the cylinders open, he threaded a silk belt from one of the White Dragon's robes through the open revolvers, sliding them together like a string of trout.

Alan hoisted the revolvers and plopped them on the podium next to the Thompson. He backed around and stood in front of Riki to help Gunny lift him into the wheelbarrow. Suddenly Alan hesitated, catching Gunny's attention. "Déjà vu," Alan said. "About a week ago a guy pulled a switch-blade from his sock and stuck it in a friend of mine. He tried to tear out his throat, but...ahh...point is I say we frisk him thoroughly before you run off with him by yourself."

Gunny nodded thoughtfully. "Your instincts are what got us here, Champ. You're absolutely right. A lesson learned the hard way is one to remember."

Bending over Riki, Alan couldn't help but evaluate his opponent. He leaned forward to grab hold of Riki's arms and tug him upright. "Thank God we've got Mr. Colt and his buddies on our team," he muttered. "I'd hate to have to take you on mano-a-mano."

Riki raised his head on his thick neck, and his eyebrows sagged in puzzlement. "I don't understand."

"Just stand up and don't try anything," Alan said.

With both men's assistance Riki stood and tottered on one leg. Gunny grasped Riki's lapels as he'd done earlier, yanking the coat down to pin Riki's massive arms behind his back and to keep him off balance. Alan stepped to the side and squeezed the agent's pockets between his hands, feeling for anything that could be used as a weapon. He ran one hand down Riki's back and felt around the bright obi he wore as a cummerbund. Just under Riki's left arm, which the big man tried to pin close to his side, Alan hit a hard, solid object tucked into the sash.

"I got something here," he called to Gunny.

Riki shook his shoulders contemptuously. "It is daisho," Riki said.

Gunny didn't understand, but he was having none of it. He tilted Riki off balance, forcing the big man to stumble and fall rear first into the wheelbarrow. Gunny pulled him backward and Riki's legs shot up in the air, leaving him helpless as a turtle on its back. Vera stepped forward with the Thompson and snuggled the muzzle up against Riki's good eye to discourage any lingering ideas he might have had of a struggle.

Alan pulled the obi loose, revealing the top edge of a knife's hilt. "What's this?" he asked.

Riki struggled spasmodically, but Gunny' grip on him was firm. "It is koto daisho, a sword for seppuku," Riki spat out.

Alan tugged vigorously on the sash, undoing it completely. The hilt of the short sword was more ornate than anything he'd seen before. "A sword for what?" he asked.

"Seppuku," Vera said. "We call it Hara-kiri, ritual suicide."

Riki growled gutterly. "Hara-kiri means 'to slice the belly.' It is a vulgar word that takes away from the meaning of honor, leaving only shame."

Alan shook his head and roughly removed the exquisite knife. The black enamel was embossed with a gold dragon that had sapphire eyes. "I don't understand. You carry a sword with you in case you have to kill yourself?"

"Maybe you first—then me, if I fail my master."

Alan grasped the handle, which was long enough to be held by two hands and withdrew the wakizashi from the tsuba. The blade was only five inches in length, which surprised everyone but Riki, who shook his head and snorted contemptuously. "It has been in my family for hundreds of years," he said.

Alan held up the fine blade as he tried to catch a glimpse of the exquisite craftsmanship in the faint light. "I guess that would mean you've served well and no one's had to put it to use." Alan spun the sword again. "It's a thing of beauty, but I can't let you keep it." He glanced to Vera to see if she had any ideas.

She frowned. "Find something we can tie him up with, while I think of what we'll do with his sword."

Gunny's eyebrows arched and he glanced hopefully at Vera. "Is keeping the little jewel out of the question? Spoils of war?"

"Wouldn't be right," she said. "If you took it during a fight, that's one thing. After a fight, it's like stealing. And his is a family heirloom."

"What if he'd died like he'd planned?"

"But he didn't. This is more about the symbolism of sacrifice than the actual usage. It's about loyalty and this just means he's put the White Dragon on a pedestal. She must possess qualities we don't see." Vera closed her eyes for a moment and then nodded. "Even if he'd used it on himself, I'd want to return it to his family."

Alan frowned quizzically. "How do you know so much about this?"

"You're not the only one who reads, Champ," Vera said. "I've been in this line of work a little while, and I keep my library card current."

Alan nodded thoughtfully and crossed the room to the pile of bodies. Within a moment he was tugging at a makiwara, pulling the long cotton belt free from one of the downed agents. Wet with blood that had soaked into its fabric, Alan held it for Gunny to consider. "Best I can come up with. It's a little thick, but we can slice it in two."

"With his sword?" Gunny asked.

"That's what I had in mind."

Alan set the tip of the blade on the podium, sharp end up. He stepped back to give Gunny room. Gunny carefully drew the belt over the blade splitting the fabric into equal pieces. "Look how clean that cut is," Gunny said.

They now had two lengths of belt to work with, and they began to tie Riki's hands together. First, Gunny made a small noose and slipped it over Riki's right hand, but when he and Alan tried to pull both of Riki's hands together behind his thick back, they couldn't make the wrists touch.

"This is as close as I can get these timbers together," said Gunny, indicating a ten-inch gap between Riki's wrists. "We'll have to tie the other hand the same way and try to cinch them together."

Alan glanced at Gunny, "I don't see how that would work. I learned to tie knots in Boy Scout, but I've seen a lot of them get pulled apart by guys not nearly as strong as our friend here. We don't have enough material."

Riki grimaced and shook his head angrily as Gunny tugged again on his right arm below his bullet wound. "Okay, I get your point," Gunny said. This just ain't going to work. It's against my better judgment, but I'll have to tie his hands in front."

Under Gunny's supervision, Alan tugged at the improvised tether, tying the knot in front as tightly as he could. "Hope you don't have far to go," he said.

"I reckon it's all downhill from here. We take a lantern—which he holds in those big mitts of his—and I should be able to keep an eye on them. Anything goes wrong and I'm going to inherit a genuine seppuku sword."

Alan checked the knots one more time and stepped back to admire his efforts. Gunny grabbed the handles of the wheelbarrow and gave them a playful shake, jostling Riki back in his seat.

"All aboard. Next stop: Chinatown," Gunny called cheerfully. He steered the wheelbarrow toward the orange and black doors, which Alan held open. "Once I get him down the steps. I'm good from there. Just wedge a lantern into his hands."

"What if he drops it along the way?"

"Good point," Gunny said, as he came to a stop on the top step.

Alan handed the kerosene lantern to Riki. Gunny raised his voice so there would be no confusion as to his meaning. "Riki, I want you to hold on tight to that lantern. Your life depends on it. If for some reason you get careless and drop it or the fuel leaks out—it's not just going to be lights out in the catacombs, it's going to be lights out permanently for Riki san. As soon as the lantern hits the pavers, but before the glass has time to break, I'll have put six bullets in your ten ring. Is there anything about that you don't understand?"

Riki sat in stony silence, not budging.

Gunny took the wheelbarrow to the edge of the top step and let it drop hard onto the one below it, causing pain to shoot through Riki's shoulder. "That required an answer," he said.

The big man shook his head in frustration. "Don't understand 'ten ring.'"

Gunny reached into the brick debris on the steps and picked up a soft shard to use as chalk. In the middle of Riki's broad back he drew an oval that was about six inches high and four inches across. Inside the oval he added a large X. "That's your ten ring, for those of us who like keeping score. Each shot inside is worth ten points, anything outside is worth five. A guy your size in a tunnel this small would be hard to miss. Even a lousy shooter would still score points with ricochets."

Gunny grinned at Alan and then turned back to address Riki with an even bigger smile. "Now do you understand?"

"You would shoot me in the back? That is not an honorable way to kill—or die."

"This is not about honor, it's about who survives this passage. Yes, I'd shoot you in your back, in your head, in your eyeball, in your knee, or whatever of yours I have a mind to aim at. But you've got nothing to worry about—as long as you don't drop the lantern."

Riki shifted the lantern to a secure spot on his middle, preparing for the bumpy ride that was ahead. Gunny edged the wheelbarrow toward the next step and then tightened his grip, leaning backward as he lowered the wheel slowly to the next step. As he slid by Alan he spoke just above a whisper. "Once we clear the last step we should be good, but you might want to hang back and cover me until we get into the Chinatown passage."

"Sure, but how will you get back to us?"

"I'll grab a cab and catch up somehow at your next port of call. Just in case you need an extra hand."

Alan smiled reassuringly. "An extra hand is always good. Just don't take any chances with him. I wouldn't be surprised if it was his sword that chopped up our friends in the rail yard. So if he were to have an unfortunate accident, I'm sure Machiavelli wouldn't mind."

"And...I'd get his sword," Gunny said with a wink.

Vera was waiting for Alan near the entrance to the dressing room, her mouth drawn tight, hinting at impatience. "We need to get a move on. The agent who got away could have sent reinforcements after us."

"You think there're many more of them at the Panama?"

"Given that these tunnels run down to the waterfront and through the seawalls, the Panama could be chock full of agents."

"Which way do we go then—through the catacombs or the wardrobe?" Alan asked, indicating each direction with the barrel of the tommy-gun.

"What's through the wardrobe?"

"A staircase to a sewing shop with a handful of workers— in fact, the exit door is right in the middle of the shop."

"Then it's the wardrobe. If we take the tunnel and surface through the theater, we can't be sure who we'd run into. My hunch is this is not their regular entrance. It's probably only for the White Dragon or emergencies. You lead the way, Champ."

Alan started toward the back room and then stopped. "What about Riki's sword?"

"All taken care of—I put it and the sling of revolvers

behind the Buddha. They should be safe there until archaeologists a thousand years from now dig up this place, and I hope by then the people will have no idea what those things were once used for."

"How will Riki know his sword is there?"

"I'm not worried about that. I just didn't think it would be right for any of us to steal it from him while he's helpless. The Chinese call it 'bad joss,' but I don't know what the Japanese term is. Either way I don't want to mess with it and tempt fate."

Alan pushed the robes aside in the wardrobe and shoved the rear panel open again. "I agree about the joss, but then I've always been superstitious—just like with the Lindbergh ransom. It was cursed money, and I really believe that. The sooner I got rid of it, the happier I was."

Vera stood close and watched Alan. "I don't like to make too big a fuss over fate and superstition," she said. "You've had pretty good luck with your detective skills today, even though this is Friday the 13th."

Alan stopped halfway through the wardrobe and stared back at her, shaking his head. "I completely missed that somehow," he said. "It snuck right up on me. There's no sense in letting it go to waste, so let's make it unlucky for them." He finished sliding through the cabinet and paused on the way out to offer Vera his hand. He knew she didn't need the help, but she squeezed his hand all the same, just enough to send sparks and a thrill through his entire frame. It was energizing, and he wanted more. As they climbed the wooden stairs to the shop his mind raced with reasons to touch her again—only he wanted it to appear necessary or accidental, not creepy and forced.

By the time they reached the closed door to the sewing shop, Alan had already begun chastising himself for having such thoughts about Vera. He forced himself to imagine

Alice as a distraction: images of her sitting on his lap and their kissing in her kitchen—memories he'd never forget. There had never been anything finer than that in his life. Even the sex he'd had in the brothel with the Chinese women didn't compare to the thrill Alice gave him with a tender kiss.

Vera stopped behind him, and Alan leaned back to whisper. "When we went through before the workers never bothered to look at us. We only had trouble when we came back. The manager stopped us and was ready to slug it out, but I told him we were police detectives and would sic the beat cops on 'em if he gave us any trouble."

"And that worked?" she asked, her lips brushing his ear. Despite what they had been through, she still had the soft smell of something powdery and feminine. He hated how she got him worked up, especially when he needed to focus all of his wits on the danger at hand. "Yeah, I threw out the name Sullivan and the manager didn't want any part of him."

"Officer Sullivan?"

"I don't actually know an Officer Sullivan. I just thought of John L. Sullivan, the boxing champion, so I used his name."

Vera patted Alan on the upper back, indicating for him to lead the way. "Seems like I've known two or three John Sullivans over the years, but they're probably all retired."

Alan lowered the tommy-gun and tucked it back under his jacket before he shouldered open the door. Together they stepped into the noisy room, which was just as busy as the last time he'd gone through it. The hands of the laborers moved rhythmically with purpose, pulling material for dress patterns through rapidly whirring machines. As before, none of the women took the time to glance up at them. This time Alan studied their facial features as best he could, and having had a second look, he was certain these women were Chinese.

He led Vera through the rows of sewing machines and pointed out the trail of blood on the bare wooden floor, which led toward the front. They walked quickly and emerged in the outer office. The woman clerk stopped what she was doing to stare, as did the manager who had been ready to fight earlier. Had his attitude changed during the interlude? Alan wondered.

While grasping the muzzle of the tommy-gun and forcing it up under his coat like a shoplifter, Alan tipped his hat politely. "Thank you for your cooperation. We got what we needed. I'll be sure to tell Officer Sullivan how helpful you were."

Without waiting for a reply, Alan and Vera continued out the door and turned left toward the theater. After they were fifty feet away, Alan glanced behind him to see the shop manager standing silently on the sidewalk with his arms crossed, as he watched them walk away.

After another forty feet, they were at the intersection kitty-corner from the theater. As they were about to cross the street Alan caught sight of two beat cops. They were standing below the theater by the tailor shop and just their shoulders and heads were visible at the street level. The officer with silver streaks encroaching on his red hair and a full, mostly white, mustache, was bent over as he talked to the little boy Alan had seen earlier on the same side of the street. A curly-haired officer stood nearby with one hand on his hip, gazing at the theater's entrance while he rubbed his jaw. Alan grabbed Vera's arm and steered her back to the sidewalk where he hoped they would be out of sight of the boy and the police.

Alan indicated the threat with a tilt of his head. "Two officers over there, and with one quick glance they'd figure out in a heartbeat what I've got under my jacket."

"Good eyes, Champ. Why don't we head up to the end of

the next block and drop down to Jackson?"

"Do you think they know what happened in there?" Alan asked.

"I don't hear sirens. Of course that could all change if they go inside the theater," Vera said.

🐦 ⊕ 🐦

Alan popped the trunk of the big Packard open, slid the Thompson inside, and re-positioned it next to the Garand. He breathed a sigh of relief and closed the trunk as he stepped to the curb to open the door for Vera. She took off the fedora she'd borrowed from Gunny and shook her hair out, just as the two beat officers came around the corner thirty feet behind them.

The eyes of the redheaded cop danced wide, and he headed straight toward the pair. "You're Tiger Lee," he said.

Alan snapped his head sharply toward the deep voice. The beatman's manner was gruff, so Alan tried to get a quick read on his intent. Was it an accusation or something else? He kept his back to the beatmen and tugged his coat open far enough so he could draw his Colt, should circumstances dictate the need. He had no grudge against these men and didn't want to tangle with them, but he would do whatever was necessary to protect Vera. Bile rose up from the pit of his stomach to the back of his tongue, forcing him to clear his throat to make the burning go away.

Vera squared up to the large beat officer. "Why yes, and you...you're Sully...Officer Sullivan."

The large man's cheeks glowed red. He touched the brim of his hat and beamed a ready smile from underneath a large mustache that overlapped his lip. "You remember me? I used to hang out backstage at your show." His accent was still flavored by the East Coast. Whether Philadelphia or New York, Alan wasn't sure.

219

"It's been a few years, but sure I do. You never missed a performance. We had the best police protection in town—without having to pay any extra. The other burlesque theaters were so jealous they complained to the Chief and the Mayor that there was no point in paying them off."

The second beat officer joined in, eager to bask in Vera's glow, and Alan let out the deep breath he'd been holding. Sully introduced Pat Moriarty to Vera, but neither of the beat officers showed any interest in Alan until Vera introduced him.

"Alan and I just came down for a bite to eat," she explained.

Sullivan stepped away from his partner and extended a hand, which Alan took, knowing the grip would be a firm and calculated measure of masculinity. The big redhead's blue eyes burnt right through him, but Alan met his gaze and held it, the same as he did the grip. Apparently he met the beat cop's approval by not wincing under the bone-crushing handshake. Sullivan returned his attention to Vera. "Your son looks an awful lot like his dad—that boxer you were seeing."

Vera's eyes pinched together as if she'd bit into something tart. "Alan's not...he's—"

Sullivan flushed and shook his head in self-disgust. There was no way to unsay what had been said. "My mistake. I stepped all over that with my big brogans. I'm sorry, Miss Tiger, but I'd heard you were pregnant back then and Alan here looks to be about the right age. I just filled in the blanks without asking anyone if I had the right answer or not."

Alan cut in, hoping to keep the conversation from leading to Jennifer and their real purpose for being down on Jackson. "I don't know if this helps any, but you had a lot of that right. Mackie Stewart—the boxer—he was my dad. I got his mug but not his nose; his was a boxer's nose. I'm

Alan Stewart."

The beat cop took a moment to nod politely in Alan's direction. "Was? You say?"

"He was killed two years ago—old union business. It was never solved."

"We had a lot of that a couple years back, particularly with the longshoremen and the shipyards. Usually guys went after strikebreakers disguised as special deputies, a lot of them Pinkerton men claiming to work for the Sheriff. In fact, I had one of those up at Third and Spring, back in '34. Strikers tipped over a Ford coupe, dragged the men out, and put the boots to all of 'em. They even shot one of the special deputies with his own gun, right in front of me. There were too many for me to stop them—or do anything about it for that matter. I couldn't even tell you which one did the shooting. That case has never been solved either. One of those things that haunts me."

"That wasn't how it was with dad. Seemed as if somebody he'd bested a long time before came back with a grudge and hired help. They jumped my dad outside a bar, caving in his head. He only made it home to die in my arms."

Sullivan's eyes lingered on Alan, appraising him. "Sorry to hear that, lad. It's amazing how long some people hold their grudges, but I'm surprised they never solved it. If they'd a put Lieutenant Harry Frantz on the case, he'd have solved it. He'd a worked a confession out of them, alright." In the same breath, Sullivan returned his gaze sheepishly to Vera.

Alan fought hard to maintain control and temper his anger. He had the sensation of fire burning up the back of his neck and across his scalp. As much as he hated Harry Frantz, all the working cops Alan met seemed to hold him in high regard. It wouldn't do any good to try to convince this old beatman it was Frantz and his personal crew who'd

221

bashed in his father's head.

Vera reached out and stroked Sullivan's arm, reassuring him she wasn't offended. His blue eyes flashed with electricity and he gushed a silly smile, happy as a puppy getting a good scratching behind the ears. Alan continued to fume but was relieved the beatmen favored Vera because he was sure that the grimace on his face, which he couldn't hide, would betray him.

As the adrenaline slowly ebbed, Alan watched Vera and the two policemen interact as though they were players on a movie screen who'd already forgotten he was in the audience. She has that effect on them too, Alan thought. Is she friendly with all the men she knows? But if so, why not? It gets her what she wants. Men are saps, and he admittedly was one of them.

Sullivan pulled off his leather glove, and clasped Vera's hand gently. "It's too bad burlesque is dying out, 'cause you still got the looks that could pack a house."

"You're sweet, Sully, but the theaters have all turned into movie houses. My days are gone, but I have no regrets. It was time to move on."

She let go of Sullivan's hand, and as he prepared to put his glove back on he accidentally dropped it to the sidewalk, where it landed with a soft thud. Seeing the puzzled expressions on Vera and Alan's faces, he grinned sheepishly and his eyes twinkled. "Shot gloves," he said as he bent over and picked up the weighted glove. "Each one has a few ounces of fine birdshot sewn in the palm."

Alan nodded and smiled as he thought of the advantage such gloves would give a boxer in a street fight—a lot like brass knuckles. The damage they'd do would be more jarring though, less likely to scar—and more likely to score a knockout. "Where could I get a pair?" Alan asked.

"You can't, because they're just like leather saps. Neither

are exactly street legal, but that Jewish tailor—the one that used to work up at Arctic Furs—made 'em for me."

Alan nodded thoughtfully. He knew that tailor and what had happened to him, but he thought better than to tell these cops the story—just like he couldn't exactly tell the truth about his dad's death. His father and Vic Morrison had been involved in the tailor's disappearance, but Vic had extracted a promise of secrecy when he told Alan years later. What had happened was on a need to know basis, and these cops didn't qualify for that.

Sully tugged on his gloves and tipped his hat to Vera. "We got to shove off, Miss Tiger, but I'm really glad I got to see you. I didn't mean any harm in what I said, I'm just not clever with words. If I'm thinking something at that very moment, that's just the way it's gonna pop out of my mouth. There're no surprises with me. My wife keeps saying I was never 'house broke' and never learned my manners. I suspect she's right, but I just wanted to say hi."

Vera slid into the car as the two beat cops crossed Jackson, heading toward the corner grocery. Alan plopped behind the wheel and let out a gush of air. "That was just too close. I don't know what I'd of done if they'd come a few seconds sooner."

"Don't worry, it's normal. We should've talked about this kind of thing happening, but there hasn't been time. Basically, we're all on the same team, but what we do and who we work for is our trump card—and we don't want to ever play it, unless it's the final trick in the game. Most of the time we cooperate with them, go along peacefully, and then I make the phone call to our people, who'll straighten things out."

"You know, I've got a lot hanging out on the line here. I'm working on blind faith alone, and it's all placed in you. I don't even know who 'our people' are. If something goes sideways or happens to you, how do I know 'our people' will ever admit to knowing me?"

"You're right. We'll take care of that as soon as I get Jenny back," Vera said.

"How about in the meantime we get something to eat? I'll buy."

"As long as it's fast."

"There's a place Vic used to take me to, about a block away."

"The brothel—where you two hid out?" Vera laughed at the expression of surprise on Alan's face. "Relax. He didn't tell me what you two did there. I just knew his girl was down there. When Alice and I dropped you off near here once, I put it together."

Alan took off his hat and scratched his head furiously. "That wasn't the way—"

"Don't worry. I won't tell your precious Alice."

"Anyway the place I had in mind is a Chinese restaurant. Serves Dim Sum. It's down a block. I say we lock the car up and walk."

"Sure, but let me buy. I insist," Vera said, as she rubbed his upper arm. "You were absolutely marvelous handling the part about Mackie's death. It must have been painful for you, and it would've been easy to lose your composure, get defensive about your dad, and...that would've ruined everything for Jenny and us. A good agent plays it cool, and you did just that."

As they started down the street Alan offered his arm to Vera, and she tugged it close to her side. "I've got to tell you," he said. "Spy work isn't anything like I'd imagined, but I'd say we make a pretty good team."

Vera squeezed his hand. "Hold that thought, it's a good one," she said.

"And you seemed comfortable handling the Thompson,"

Alan said. "Did my dad teach you that?"

Vera walked in silence for a few moments. "We shot a few rounds," she said finally. Her tone made it clear that there was nothing else to say on the subject.

After lunch, Vera grabbed Alan's arm and stopped him in front of the Bush Hotel on Jackson. "I need to call Marshal Dosch," she said, "and find out if there's a Japanese ship in port."

"If one's here to pick up the brass, do you think they'll allow it to tie up at a pier?" Alan asked.

"Most likely it would have cargo to unload, so yes I do, but there's another problem. The Port Authority will have embargoed the rail cars with the steel, but they won't know about the rest of the brass coming down from Fremont."

"Are you going to tell them?"

"This is tearing me up. I'm still worried about what the Japanese will do with it once it gets to their country, but what's best for my daughter is really what's in my heart. There's no toggle switch I can flip to shut off those feelings. I can't sacrifice her for something that may or may not happen."

"Which means?"

"They're going to have to trust me on this one. They owe me that much."

"I'm glad you feel that way." Alan closed his eyes and shook his head slowly. He pulled Vera close and wrapped one arm over her shoulder, hugging her tightly with a small sense of relief. "Thank, you," he continued. "I hardly know Jennifer, but I can't bear the thought of losing her."

Vera laid her head on his shoulder and nestled it under his chin. "Neither can I."

"While you make your call, I'll update Alice," he said, pulling away from her to open the hotel's front door. Her eyes met his and she smiled. It wasn't the confident one he was used to seeing but it was hauntingly beautiful all the same with a trace of sorrow the expression of joy couldn't hide.

To the right of the Bush Hotel lobby stood two wooden telephone booths with glass bi-fold doors shoved to the side. Vera stepped into one, and Alan slid into the other. He dropped his nickel and dialed the payphone at the Sorrento. On the third ring a young woman answered, her voice tentative and unsure.

"Alice?"

"Alan! How is everything?"

"Better for us, worse for them, but they've still got Jennifer."

"Are you okay? Why haven't you called? I've been worried, and the hotel people are starting to wonder what I'm doing here."

Her voice was a tonic for frayed nerves. Alan especially enjoyed her laughter, but this wasn't to be the kind of conversation in which that was likely to happen. "A lot's been going on, and I can't tell you all the details—especially over a telephone line. The person I'm with said to treat these phones like party lines, with all the neighbors listening."

"It's been two hours!"

"I'm really sorry about that, but it can't be helped. Have there been any calls from the other side?" Alan asked.

"Yours is the first."

"Are you okay there?"

"Sort of, but the hotel detective's taken notice of me. I got the feeling he's going to say something soon," Alice said.

"If it's what I think, he'll need a mechanic to unwire his jaw before he ever talks again."

"Alan! He'd just be doing his job. To him I look like an unescorted woman hanging out where a lady shouldn't. If—"

"Tell you what," Alan interrupted. "Go ahead and register for a room for the night. Ask for one of their more expensive ones with a view of the waterfront. Tell them Mr. B is expecting an important out of town client—and wife—from Boston. You've been waiting there to take care of their arrangements, but they must be running late. Bill it to the union. Vera will take care of it later. Then ask the concierge to alert you when the guests call the hotel. Make sure the house detective sees you talking to the concierge so he backs off."

"Alan! You sound like you've had experience with this kind of thing."

"It's not what you think, sweetheart. I've read a lot... and I picked up a few things listening to my dad," he said.

"I've been worried for you—imagining all kinds of horrible things. Do you have any idea how much longer you're going to be?" she asked.

Alan exhaled deeply and decided not to tell her how accurate her imagination might be. "I'm not sure, darling, because I'm in this until the end—until we get Jennifer back. I can't let her or Vera down."

"Promise me you'll be careful," Alice demanded.

"I will," Alan said. "I promise I will."

Alan drove west on Jackson toward the waterfront and Railroad Avenue. Vera retrieved the extra fedora from the rear seat, and pushed her hair under it, like she had before. "Drive till you find the Hiye Maru at Pier Six," she said. "It should be about half way up the waterfront. Marshal Dosch says they embargoed the gondola cars and the scrap based on the one shell you found, but the courts refused to go any further than that. They said they didn't have enough for the Coast Guard to keep the ship from unloading. The Port was going to have the ship dock up at Smith's Cove next to the Navy, but the captain didn't want anything to do with that. He wanted a pier farther away."

"What? I don't get it. Why wouldn't he want to be close to where the brass is stashed? It's not like the Navy's going to see them load it, recognize it as theirs, and ask for it back."

"It seems the skipper had some problems up there two years back. A couple of nutty Canadians tried to plant a time bomb under the ship's stern, but exposure got to the naked man in the water. He froze or drowned before he could finish."

"I remember reading that. I loved that case. The police arrested the dead guy's buddy for prowling the rail yards, even though he told them he was waiting for his friend who went swimming with a suitcase full of explosives. Naturally the cops thought he was nuts, because it was January in Seattle. They didn't bother to check until the ship reported a floater off their stern the next morning— buck naked except for a life jacket. Only reason the dynamite didn't go off was because the clock's face got wet and distorted it, stopping two minutes before it was supposed to explode! I'd completely forgotten the name of the ship."

"Same ship and same captain." Vera grinned at Alan

and then leaned forward to look down Railroad Avenue. "Now the skipper always insists that he gets a deep water pier, right in the middle of town, where he posts an armed guard. Pier Six is up around Spring or Seneca Street. Dosch says the ship's using its cranes and a couple gangs of longshoremen to unload it."

"So the three gondolas of brass are still your trump card?"

"I didn't bring them up, and he forgot to ask."

"I say we keep it that way. Gives you room to work."

🐉 ⊕ 🐉

Alan slid several nickels into a parking meter on Western Avenue, near Spring. "That should get us through the rest of the day," he said.

"Least of my worries is a parking ticket," Vera replied.

"Well, mine too, but it's Mr. B's car. No sense in creating bad blood between the traffic court and the union."

"You're a worrier, Champ, but that can be a good thing. You've got a keen eye for detail, and that's what's got us this far."

"Thank you, ma'am—Vera."

Vera rolled her eyes playfully, then reached around and flipped his hat forward, sliding it down the bridge of his nose.

"I was kidding," Alan said.

"I know," Vera said, "and I suppose that means you're not used to getting compliments. You don't know how to take them."

"I love my family, but receiving praise wasn't a part of our growing up. It's probably the Scottish way. We were tight with everything, but you're right, it makes me feel... weird—like everyone's looking at me."

"Look around you. There's no *everyone*—just you and me."

"But it means you've been thinking about me, making an evaluation."

"Yes, and you've been passing. With high marks."

"I understand now why dad couldn't let you go," Alan said as they moved to the back of the Packard.

"Alan...," Vera stopped what she was doing and stared into his eyes. "Okay, now I'm getting that self-conscious feeling you were talking about."

"It was you before my mother came along, wasn't it?"

Vera gazed across the waterfront's railroad tracks and exhaled, pushing out her lips. "Jennifer's older than you. So of course—"

"Besides that. It was you all the way, wasn't it?"

"Listen," Vera said, "there's still a sting inside me that's never going to go away."

"This isn't going in the direction I hoped," Alan said. "I wanted to let you know I'm not judging you, although I might have at first. But I'm well past that. I think I get what you two had now, and the last thing I want to do is to cause you more pain."

Vera stood silently for a moment watching the crews at work on the Hiye Maru. "It's just one of those bittersweet memories. If you don't have any of those yet, you will soon enough. And sometimes I enjoy wallowing in mine—with a bottle of expensive brandy and a box of chocolates—the dark ones with soft centers. I know you were thinking it'd be a compliment, but let's save it for another time shall we?"

"When we're done with this, we'll have dark chocolates and brandy," Alan said. "I'll wallow in it with you. My treat."

"Sharing?"

"Why sure."

"I eat those while soaking in a hot bath. Were you planning on joining me?"

The blood rose to his cheeks as he flushed with surprise.

At heart he was still a product of his mother's influence and proper upbringing, but before he could stop himself his mind flashed back to his first co-ed bath in the Chinese brothel, not even a month ago. The vivid memory of the two naked women, combined with his active imagination, substituted Vera into that same situation, and it was almost more than Alan could bear. Alan shook his head in embarrassment.

Vera beamed her confident smile. "Where'd you go, Champ? You must have been off chasing a fancy."

"Miss Deward, you can make a man blush, you know?"

"Yes, Mr. Stewart. I've made a very comfortable living for years doing just that."

Alan gazed at the red brick pavers for a moment as he gathered his thoughts, and then he glanced across to Pier Six and the Hiye Maru. "Do you think Jennifer's already on board?"

"They could be keeping her anywhere. We won't know until we look."

"And how are we going to do that? We can't just walk on the pier and start poking around. I hate to say it, but maybe we should call the police or the Port Authorities."

"We don't have enough evidence to get Ketchum involved, we just have suspicions. What would we tell Mike? That we just beat a confession out of a Japanese spy, after we machine-gunned-to-death twenty of his buddies, finally making him tell the truth, which only amounts to 'she sails with the brass?'"

"So what's your plan, Tiger Lee?"

Vera continued staring at the ship, watching stevedores as they systematically passed between the ship and the warehouse on the pier, while the ship's booms raised and lowered freight wrapped in heavy cargo nets. The men stacked loads onto hand trucks and dollies, and moved most of the off-loaded items inside the warehouse for temporary storage before they were shipped countrywide. "I don't think the brass is here yet. My guess is they'll work around the clock unloading the ship, and as soon as they've got the room, they'll bring up the gondola cars and push them onto the pier."

"There're a lot of men running around—but no women."

"And there'll be more men below decks. I bet they hired a bigger gang than normal, and there's probably a bonus if they finish early. That's how I'd run it."

"Voice of experience?"

"You might say, but this time I don't have a plan, and it makes me nervous when someone else controls what I have to do. The only idea coming to me now is that we're going to have to wait until dark. Other than that, I'm open to suggestions."

Alan joined Vera to stare across at the ship. "I hadn't realized it before, but every piece of cargo gets touched a number of times."

"What do you mean?"

"Let's say everything they're unloading is going to get sold in a store at some point. By the time it's gone from raw material to manufacturer, packager to docker, warehouse to ship, ship to dock, to another warehouse, and on and on, there are a lot of different sets of fingerprints on every piece."

"Spoken like a true detective."

"Sorry. It was the long way around, but what I'm thinking is we could get into the middle of this at any of the three stages in front of us. The pier, the warehouse, or the ship."

"And what do you recommend, Detective?"

Between where they'd parked and the longshoremen's hall, which was only four blocks north, there were several stores where Alan could get the stevedore attire they needed for their job. Vera had won that argument; it was more realistic for him to buy that kind of clothing than her. Besides, she pointed out, some of her former fan base from the days when she was a marquee's headliner came from the waterfront. It was more likely she'd be recognized than him.

Even in their casual attire, they were too overdressed to blend in on the piers. Dock workers didn't wear fedoras as a rule, only the foremen and gang bosses did. The stevedores wore knit caps, rag wool sweaters, and sturdy gloves. The chore for Alan was to find clothing that would disguise the fact Vera was every inch a woman. She would wait inside the car while he ran his errand.

Alan couldn't imagine how they'd pull it off, but when Vera gave him two C notes to cover the expenses, he dashed off to the nearest outfitter.

Inside the clothier Alan picked out a watch cap, sweater, and extra pants for him. Then he went down the list he had for Vera. The clerk helping him was efficient but short on salesmanship.

"What you got here ain't going to fit, mister," the man said to Alan. "You might want to try it on first."

"I'm getting these for my younger brother."

The clerk arched his eyebrow. "I haven't seen you in here before. You must be new to the docks."

"That's right. I'm following my uncle into the business."

"Well, having family is a help—but no guarantee. Suit yourself about their fit, but all sales are final."

A glass case behind the clerk featured an assortment of binoculars. "If you don't mind, mister, I'd like to get a pair of those for my uncle—a thank you gift for the job."

The clerk tilted his head back to get a better view of Alan. He nodded approvingly. "That's a dandy idea, son."

"Is there a pair you'd recommend?"

"Well, if it was me, I'd want this pair," the man said as he studied Alan. "They're what the Navy uses."

"Those are the ones. I'll take that pair."

"He probably already knows, but if he needs a reminder, cover the right lens while you sight in the left—and don't squint when you're doing it. Once you've got the left lens in focus, cover it and adjust the right. For changing distances, use the focus pull in the middle, and just roll the wheel back and forth. It moves both lenses so you don't have to re-adjust the lenses separately."

"I think I can remember that."

"Say, it ain't my business son, but I put my time in on the docks, and it's awful rough work—tough for a new guy to get on a crew. Unless his uncle's connections helped him get a ship already, a guy that size," he indicated the stack of smaller clothing with a nod, "might not get picked in the shape up unless he's willing to give his pay back to the gang boss his first time out or two."

"I don't think that's going to be a problem."

When Alan pulled out the large bills to pay for his

purchase, the clerk shook his head in wonderment. "Be careful with flash like this. Guys find out you're carrying that kind of dough, and you'll never get past the next alley."

"Sorry. I got a grubstake from my family. There won't be much left before long."

The clerk counted back the change carefully, laying out each bill in Alan's palm. He paused for a moment before handing him the last one. "If your brother's hands are as soft as yours, son, you'll both be sitting in the hall after the crew's picked. Don't let the foreman see your mitts until they've toughened up."

"We'll wear the gloves," Alan assured him.

Walking back to the Packard Alan couldn't help but feel insulted. The old clerk's intentions were probably good, but it didn't sit well to be told he might have trouble fitting in on the docks. Alan was sure he could do anything he set his mind to, but as he approached Vera, the humor of it all finally got to him. What if the clerk was watching out the store's window at this very moment and saw him waltz up to the union's Super Eight Packard, where a beautiful woman was waiting? He'd think Alan was just a rich kid wanting to see how the other half lived. Alan grinned to himself as he opened the door.

"What's so funny?" Vera asked.

Alan shared the experience he'd had with the clerk. Vera smiled broadly. "Let's hope he doesn't think the Communists are infiltrating his longshoremen with fraternity boys. He'd call the longshoreman's hall, they'd send down their muscle, and we'd have a fight on our hands. They're a tough bunch, and that's why Mr. B stays away from here."

"Now you're the worrier."

"Yeah, I am. We make a good team at that," Vera said.

Alan handed her the clothes and then ducked back outside to lean against the doors of the sedan, giving Vera privacy to change without him gawking. She hadn't said for him not to stare, but it didn't feel right to be watching her put on her clothes. She had a right to privacy and a right to choose when it was okay for someone to look. There was a principle in play that he didn't fully understand, but he decided to respect it all the same. They were a team, she'd agreed to that, and a teammate wouldn't cheat on a buddy. And if he didn't sneak a peek like he dearly wanted to do, he was going to make damn sure nobody else did either.

But just standing nearby while Vera was dressing sent Alan's mind racing about what he might be missing only a foot or so behind him. The more he was around her the more he fantasized, and idle times like this were the worst. One thing was sure, he resolved, if they ended up in a bathroom together again with her wearing only her bra and panties, he was going to stare until he had his fill—embarrassing erection sticking out of his underwear or not. He wouldn't apologize next time, nor would he push her away. Damn, he was supposed to be thinking about Alice not Vera. If only he could find a utility pole nearby, he'd ram his already aching head into it a couple of times to knock some sense into himself.

Alan slid his fingers up under his knit cap and ran them across the stitches Vera had sewn into his flesh. Between the raised knots and the fresh scabbing on his upper forehead, his skin felt like a baseball. He stared across at the Hiye Maru and wished Vera would hurry dressing so he could focus again on what was really important: rescuing her daughter, who also happened to be his sister.

Finally, Vera opened the car door and stepped out so he could see what they'd created. Before him stood a five-foot-something turtle in a dark shell of rag wool. She seemed to have used the broad leather belt to cinch her breasts down, because her shape was actually much more muted than before. There was still the problem, however, of her small feet. He'd brought back the tiniest pair of brogans in the store, men's shoes sized eight. They were between three and four sizes too large.

"As a savateuse, I fight with my feet, Alan. I need firm footing to plant a kick. Let's say I wanted to smack a boot against the White Dragon's head. A poorly fitting clunker like this would sail off and splash in the bay."

"I'll go back and get a couple more pair of socks."

"Try another store so the clerk won't get wise. You might also have better luck finding my size at another store and if you do, just buy them. Don't worry about the cost—I'll probably end up donating them to St. Vincent DePaul's when we're through."

Alan pinched the bridge of his nose and grimaced. "What I'd really like to find is a store that carries aspirin," he said. "How's your jaw feeling?"

Vera exhaled and rolled her head around gingerly. "It's sore, but I'm trying to ignore it," she said. "When you get back I'll rub your feet. There's a pressure point down there that if rubbed right can make the ache go away."

"You're serious?" Alan asked.

"Yes, Vic showed it to me," Vera said with an evil grin. "He learned it from his friends down at your Chinese brothel. I'm surprised they didn't teach it to you."

"When we were there my head wasn't hurting, so they taught me other useful things." Alan said, returning her grin. "And I taught them how to play pinochle."

🐉 ◉ 🐉

Alan crossed the street a block north of the first store and walked diagonally to the entrance of another outfitter. Midway down the block on his left a white Troy Laundry truck was parked at the curb. It appeared unoccupied but

Alan still slid his hand inside his coat and grasped the handle of his Colt. He worked his way down the sidewalk, checking the windows of neighboring businesses for any activity that might help alert him to danger. He slowed as he came parallel to the van and stepped into the shadows of a large hanging awning that covered the sidewalk. Even though he hadn't gotten the license number earlier, he knew it was the same van that had taken Jennifer—first from Kurtzer's and then from the Panama Hotel.

As he waited he exchanged friendly nods with a couple of dockworkers who passed by him on the sidewalk. Once they were gone he approached the van. He half chuckled to himself; at least these two men thought he fit on the docks. He leaned up near the closed driver's side door and peered at the ignition. The keys were still in it. He quietly moved around the back to check the truck's bay and found the back door ajar. With the edge of his thumb, he pushed it open far enough to scope out the inside. There were no carts, although the bay was big enough for two. Stacked in bins on the sides were small packages of laundry wrapped in brown paper and tied with string. It was just as cold inside the van as it was outside. Alan figured the van had been abandoned for a while.

In a hurry to report his find to Vera, Alan wasted no time in the maritime store. As he passed the section for shoes, he found a box of men's size six, marked for clearance. A good omen, he figured. Maybe their luck was changing. When he took the brogans to the clerk to pay, the man raised his eyes in surprise. Not wanting a repeat of the conversation he had with the clerk at the other store, Alan spoke first. "They're for my kid brother," he said.

The clerk chuckled and rang up the order. "These have been on the shelf for three years. We thought they'd never sell, unless it was to a midget."

"He needs them for his paper route."

"He'll get a lot of good wear out of them, but just remember: all sales are final."

Vera beamed at Alan as he approached the Packard carrying a shoebox. He slid in the driver's seat and handed the work shoes to her. "Guy thinks I bought these for a midget," he said, "and I've got some good news."

"What've you got?" Vera asked with a playful frown.

"The van they used to snatch Jennifer is stashed in the next block. It's been parked there awhile, and it was still there when I left."

Vera busied herself putting on her new shoes, and this time Alan watched her. Even performing a chore as simple as this was fascinating to him, although the smaller-sized shoes still took an extra pair of socks to make them fit.

"Thank you for these," Vera said. "Midget feet or not, I'm ready for battle."

"Do you want to check to see if I missed anything in the van?"

"No, I trust you."

"Good, because my instincts tell me to leave it the way we found it—as much as we can—just in case we need the police to go over it for fingerprints," Alan said. "I wouldn't want to smudge any prints that might be there."

"So if the van's here," Vera said, "then we know she's on the waterfront somewhere."

"Better than that. The laundry cart's missing, which means they probably used it to sneak her onto the ship, not just to stash her in a warehouse or some vacant room."

"You think so?" Vera asked hopefully.

"Well they either drove the van onto the pier and unloaded the cart there, or they parked it where it's at now and rolled her across the tracks. It would've been bumpy in the cart going over the rails, but from what I've seen, they wouldn't have cared. Either way, she's on the ship."

By 4:30 PM, the cloud-shrouded, steel-gray sky was already fading to darkness, a blessing for the kind of work Alan and Vera had in mind. Alan slumped down in the seat toward Vera as he focused the binoculars on the Hiye Maru. He adjusted the lenses as the clerk had told him to do and rolled the focus pull back and forth until he had a clear picture of the stevedores working the forward cargo hold. From what he could tell there was a crew boss, two deck men standing on the pier off-loading a cargo board, two sling men doing the rigging, and probably another four in the hold. The rear hold appeared to have about the same number of workers, and there were a half-dozen men running dollies and hand trucks in and out of the warehouse.

Alan lowered the binoculars to take in the bigger picture. "If our plans erupt on us, whose side do you think they'll be on?"

"The longshoremen?"

"Yeah."

"I'd rather keep them out of it, but it's hard to say. I haven't seen any recent intelligence reports on their union meetings."

"Intelligence reports?"

"Sure. Given the problems they've had on the docks with strikes, murders, and the communists trying to infiltrate the unions, the FBI pays a lot of attention to them."

"What about our people?" he asked and then chuckled. "I say 'our people,' but you and Gunny are the only 'our people' I've met."

"Our people would call that domestic counter-spying, and that's not what we do. Our interests lie in national security, not union squabbles."

Alan raised his binoculars and scanned the waterfront, working his way north as far as he could. "What the dock workers do doesn't affect national security?"

"Not as I see it. And not to duck your question, but these men look at this job as a way to put bread and butter on their tables and get a fair day's pay for their labor. Then again, they might also resent what Japan's doing in the Pacific."

Alan sat up higher in his seat and adjusted the focus pull on the binoculars, aiming them north along the waterfront. "Big light on the tracks ahead—train's coming."

Vera also sat up and cranked the window down a couple inches. "Lots of trains use this line," she said. "It could veer to its left a couple blocks up near Virginia Street to pass through the Great Northern Tunnel, which would take it under the city, or it might just head straight toward us, delivering the brass to the Hiye Maru."

"Who's the White Dragon paying off to get that here this quick?" asked Alan.

"We could snatch the engineer out of the cab and pin his ears back, but he's not likely to know. He probably hasn't even looked to see what's in the tubs. Like the dockworkers he's just doing whatever somebody's willing to pay him for."

Alan continued watching as the train passed the tunnel turnoff and approached the waterfront. "The engine's pulling gondola cars," Alan said. "I can't tell how many just yet, but bet me—they're hauling our brass."

Without warning there came a rapping at the passenger window, right beside Vera's head. Both Vera and Alan bolted upright and looked quickly in the direction of the noise. Vera was first to regain her composure and rolled the window down. "Gunny, you nearly scared the pants off me."

"Nearly? Then I need to work on my technique. Let me come back in a minute and try that again."

"You rascal! Get in the car."

Alan reached behind Vera and unlocked the door. Gunny slid across the backseat, pushing the extra shoebox aside. "I spotted your car and came up from the front. I thought you'd seen me."

"Sorry. We got distracted." Vera inclined her head toward the train that was nearly parallel to them. "We were busy watching the brass arrive."

Gunny eyed the loud diesel towing the three gondolas. The steel wheels screeched horribly in protest as the engineer brought the cars to a halt just past a switching plate. The train was now in position to change rails and back onto the pier. "That's it, then?" Gunny asked, referring to the Hiye Maru. "She's a big sucker, takes up the whole pier. Must be at least five-hundred feet long...passenger and cargo both."

Alan twisted in his seat so he could have a better view of Gunny. "So how'd it go with Mr. Riki and the opium den?"

Gunny impishly tilted his head nonchalantly from one shoulder to the other. "Not so well for Riki, but well enough," he said. "He went all wild-eyed when I wheeled him to the door of an herb shop—at least that's what they have going on upstairs at street level. He pitched a ruckus, so I pinched his shoulder. Pretty soon I had a lot of help eager to assist me with stopping his squealing. Uncle Sam's greenbacks are very persuasive down there. He was deep in La La Land when I left."

Gunny was eager to tell more, but Vera rested her hand on top of Alan's arm. "I'd like to hear the details, but they're best kept for later. Now's our opportunity to move in closer. We might not get another chance."

Vera opened her door, and the two men followed her lead, gathering behind the Packard for a final huddle. "Leave the Thompson here," Vera said. "As much as I'd love to have it for insurance, there're a whole lot of innocent people who could get in the way through no fault of their own. This isn't the crew or the passengers' battle—they might be protecting their ship, following orders, or just standing by. Our mission is to find Jennifer, remove her, and do as little damage as possible."

Gunny shrugged his shoulders dubiously. "But if we have to, then...."

Vera nodded her assent. "Of course, but it will be close quarters. I'd rather leave them sore and wounded. Besides, it takes more resources to tend the wounded than to bury the dead."

The effects of the chloroform slowly left Jennifer's system, and there was nothing dainty about their departure. She felt groggy, nauseous, and had a clinging headache as a kicker—just like the booze hangovers her mother had warned her to stay away from in college. It took her a few moments to gather her bearings, and all she could tell from her surroundings was that she was on a narrow bed in a small room with her hands tied in back. The walls were covered in gold-embossed wallpaper that was trimmed with varnished wooden posts. Everything, including the trim, was crisp, clean, and highly polished. For a minute she thought she was in a ritzy hotel room or a high-end apartment, but there was a smell in the air that didn't quite fit that scenario.

Jennifer strained at the ligature trussing her hands, but she couldn't get the knot to budge. She bent her head toward her chest so she could examine what was at the foot of her bed. Barely two feet away from her was a compact wooden chest of drawers with an ornate wood and brass railing on top, designed to keep items from rolling off and falling to the floor. Suddenly she realized the smell was coming from the waterfront and she was on a ship. She thought she should have a porthole on one of the walls, but she didn't see one. Did this mean she had an inside cabin?

She inhaled deeply and tried to force out more of the poisonous gas they'd used to sedate her. The first breath was invigorating, so she repeated the process, pushing her diaphragm outward and letting it fall back on its own. After five or six breaths she heard voices outside her cabin. Someone had just approached and was speaking Japanese—it was a woman's voice. A moment later there was a knock at the door before it opened. A strikingly beautiful woman poked her head in, and seeing Jenny was awake, she stepped inside the cabin to set a tray of tea on the dresser. While the woman was busy with that, an unseen hand closed the door behind her.

The well-tailored lady turned toward Jennifer and smiled. "How are you feeling, dear?"

Jennifer blinked trying to clear the last of the cobwebs caused by the forced sleep. "Who are you, and where am I?"

The woman held Jennifer's gaze, smiled serenely, and sat down on the bed next to her. "Let me help you out of your bindings," she said as she reached behind Jennifer. She pulled at the ropes but couldn't get them close enough to untie them without leaning across Jennifer's body.

Jennifer rolled onto her stomach to make it easier, and the woman began untying the soft fabric knotted at her wrists. "I am Mischa, and you and I are guests of some very dangerous people."

Jennifer arched her back, and worked her head to the side so she could see the other woman. "Guests?" she asked.

"As long as we do what they say and don't try to escape, we have limited freedom to move about their ship—at least on this deck, anyway."

Mischa finished untying Jennifer's bindings, but she continued to lean forward, propping herself on one arm.

After a moment Jennifer rolled onto her back, and since Mischa had made no attempt to get up, Jennifer slid away, sat up, and drew her legs under her. "Who's holding you here?"

"His name is Hideki, and he's from a noble Japanese family. Or maybe they're just rich—I don't really know the difference. He feels a woman of my ancestry should be returned to her country during these turbulent times—kicking and screaming if necessary. He's apparently used to getting his way, and you and I are what he wants right now."

"What about the White Dragon?"

"The who?"

"That woman—the White Dragon—the painted monster who abducted me?"

"As far as I can tell, you and I are the only women on this ship. All the passengers have disembarked."

"Then how'd I get here?"

"I don't know, dear. The Hideki man only told me you were in this cabin and asked me to check on you, make you comfortable." Mischa rested her hand on Jennifer's forearm and rubbed it reassuringly.

Jennifer swiveled her hips and adjusted her weight over her legs. "Are we at sea?"

"Not yet. Hideki is apparently waiting for something before we sail."

"The Navy brass?"

"Do you mean a captain?"

"No, spent munitions that belonged to the U.S. Navy—but that Japan now wants. The White Dragon kidnapped me so my mother wouldn't get in the way of its shipment. But she shouldn't worry about me, because the brass going to Japan is the bigger danger for America than losing me."

"Ohhh, I see," Mischa said with puzzled eyes.

"I'll be freed when the brass is delivered to a Japanese ship," Jennifer said.

247

"This is a Japanese ship, but who made that promise to you, dear?"

"I was there when the White Dragon said it to my mother."

Mischa nodded, contemplating. "I'm not sure that will be the same fate for me, but perhaps I can make your stay more comfortable. Would you like tea?"

"I'd love some, please."

Mischa drew her hand slowly across Jennifer's forearm, stood up, and began pouring them each a cup of green tea. "Upon my honor. I will protect you, but I don't understand why this White Dragon would be dealing with your mother. Is she someone powerful?"

32

Vera and Alan hurried with Gunny across the broad expanse of Railroad Avenue, drawing closer to the Hiye Maru. As they neared a train's stopped engine, it suddenly huffed and shot out a blast of smoke. Its wheels spun in reverse before catching on the rails, lurching, and loudly banging the gondola car's couplings against each other. Alan clasped Vera's arm and leaned in close. "I was just thinking that Gunny is biggest and probably should take the lead. You'd be better off in his shadow," he whispered.

Vera frowned.

"It's because—even when you're trying to look ugly, no make-up and all, like a man, it doesn't work. You still look great. If the guys here get a good look at your face, they'll figure us out."

Vera exhaled heavily. "Excuse me for not feeling flattered, but...."

"Just thought you should know," Alan said.

Without words Vera steered Gunny into the lead and edged behind him, staying abreast of Alan. They crept along in the shadow of the backing train, using it as a screen between them and the ship so they could approach the pier undetected. As the train bent around the tracks and straightened toward the pier, the threesome dashed across to the dock, stopping in front of the warehouse. Alan glanced down the pier over Vera's shoulder to the Hiye Maru's quarterdeck, which was abuzz with activity. It seemed as though the ship had brought its own compliment of Japanese workers, who now filled the topside railing. On command, the workers crowded onto the gangway and clamored down toward the pier. The longshoremen on the docks saw the gang of men coming and stopped working. Those who were in the warehouse poured out to join the other dockworkers.

Taking advantage of the distraction, Alan, Vera, and Gunny darted inside the warehouse unchallenged and made their way through the front room carefully, tip-toeing past cargo boards stacked high with wooden crates, shipping boxes, and large bags of rice with Chinese markings. They worked their way toward the next set of open doors that gave them a clear view of the ship.

Outside the warehouse, the train's engine idled and the wheels creaked to a stop. The trio slid behind the stacked cargo boards and climbed up on the bags of rice for a better view, while a band of Japanese workers stopped in front of the open doors on the pier, fifteen feet from a smaller group of dockworkers. A Japanese man who was dressed more formally than the others on the dock, stepped through the huddled group with a companion carrying a cash box. The dockworkers' foreman approached his counterpart and raised a hand. He punctuated his conversation with pointing and finger shaking.

"What's going on?" Alan whispered to Vera.

"I can't hear over the train, but it seems that the longshoremen aren't done unloading the ship and the Japanese want them to leave."

"So they're going to load the brass with their own men?" Alan asked.

"That's my guess. Apparently they don't think the American dockworkers will load it."

"Why's that?"

"There've been protests at docks up and down the west coast. In some ports, stevedores have refused to load steel and brass bound for Japan. Remember those two Canadians tried to blow up this very ship because it was transporting scrap iron. If they pay off the dockworkers and use their own crew, they cut down on the problems from the start."

"But why the hurry? Why not let the dockworkers finish unloading first?"

"Probably fear of another embargo if they wait around too long," Vera said. "The brass and scrap is the real reason they're here in Seattle. Everything else is just for appearances. I don't think they care if what's in their holds gets unloaded or not. They want brass, and they want it now. The sooner they get to sea, the better."

"So the lead foreman's going to press for payment, whether his men worked the full load or not?" Alan asked.

"You've got it. Full payment. That's what Mr. B would do, and notice that the purser isn't putting up much of an argument. He knows someone's watching from the bridge, so he can't just roll over and give away their money, but his heart isn't in the fight."

Alan cocked his head sideways and snuck another peek at her profile. Better than a painting or a sculpture, he could watch her for hours.

Without turning her head Vera glanced sideways at Alan. "You're staring, Champ. Like what you see?"

"That I do, ma'am."

She faked a scowl and then kicked his lower leg playfully. "Rascal."

He chuckled quietly. "Ouch."

"You're a romantic."

"Vic said that too. Is that a bad thing, like being simple?"

"Not really. It just means you see things the way you hope they'll always be, like chivalry and nostalgia, old movies, old songs, your first kiss—that kind of thing. But you've got to be careful with idealized notions of romance. That's feet off the ground and head in the clouds stuff."

"I thought that was what it was all about, what everyone wants at least once in life," Alan said.

"Real love is what your after; romanticized love leads to heartache and heart break."

"Do you really believe that?" Alan asked.

"Think of the great love stories," Vera said. "Romeo and Juliet, Laurence Olivier and Vivian Leigh, Joe Schmuck and Jill Schmoe. Tragedy comes after Romance in the dictionary, and it's that way in life too. You don't want to end up like star-crossed lovers, dead in each other's arms."

"Voice of experience?"

"You might say. At least that sounds better than 'the voice of bitterness,'" Vera said.

Vera's eyes had a misty sheen and Alan decided to leave her to her memories. Now who's the real romantic? He wondered. He ran his hand up her upper back and rubbed her shoulder reassuringly. He didn't want her to hurt—ever—and regretted that the conversation had gone in this direction.

After a moment of reverie, Vera rolled her eyes and sucked in her lower lip. "When it comes to settling down, you'll serve yourself well by picking the farm girl who'll bait a hook and clean fish, rather than the one who wants to go dancing and slosh cocktails every night."

"I'm not sure I follow you."

"You should figure out what real love is and go after it, not the illusion," she said.

Alan lay silent for a few moments, wondering what she'd

meant. After all of her earlier attempts at enticing him, was she trying to push him away? But she hadn't ruled herself out either; she had only suggested he go after what was real.

"Do you fish?" Alan asked finally.

Vera scrunched her eyebrows, and suppressed a chuckle. "When I can, but it's been awhile. I used to get out on Sundays for steelhead and trout, and after that a little target practicing."

Alan rolled to his side and stared at her a long moment. "But that stopped about the time he started taking me," he said.

Vera sniffed and tried to look him in the eye, but hers were misty again. She returned her focus to the dock and stared off in the distance. Alan patted her shoulder again. "I miss him too."

Vera raised her head for a better view of their surroundings. "Alright then, they're going to have to coax the last of the longshoremen out of the holds and off the ship. While they're all coming and going, we're going to sneak on board somehow. Once the Japanese take over this operation it'll be a lot more difficult to get on, because none of us is going to pass for one of them."

🐉 ⊕ 🐉

After the three had climbed down from their perch, Vera explained the updated plan to Gunny they hurried through the long warehouse toward the stern of the Hiye Maru, and the second gangway between the aft cargo hatches. The trio stopped near the opening to the last bay, and as they took new positions, Alan raised his hand to get Vera and Gunny's attention pointing to a collection of cigarette butts in front of a net-draped cargo board.

Vera sniffed the air for traces of smoke and nodded. Gunny smelled it too, and he cautiously approached the open doors, peeking around to get a view of the docks and the waterfront. He snapped his head back sharply and held up his left hand with two fingers extended.

Vera signaled for Alan to follow her to a spot near Gunny, where they would be out of view from the dock. She indicated for him to have his pistol ready, while she and Gunny both drew knives. They pressed their ears to the clapboard wall in between the stud frame and could hear voices in Japanese nearby.

Vera tapped on Gunny's shoulder. *How far?* she mouthed silently.

Gunny pointed to a spot on the wall past Alan's head. He held up one hand and extended his fingers four times. Twenty feet.

Vera pulled Alan into a huddle with Gunny. "We can't wait and hope they'll return sometime soon. We have to go now, quietly, and catch them off guard. Alan, you follow a few feet behind to cover us, but hold your fire—if you can. We don't want to draw attention to where we're at."

Vera and Alan squatted close to Gunny, who continued to sneak peeks at the armed sentries. The two men were loitering casually near a stout bollard that held the Hiye Maru's thick, draped lines, the butts of their rifle stocks resting casually on the pier's planking. The guard who was smoking was doing the majority of the talking, punctuating his conversation by waving the hand holding his cigarette.

Gunny glanced at Vera and waited for the signal that would indicate they were ready. Once she gave it Gunny checked the guards' positions one more time. A moment later he inhaled deeply and waved for Alan and Vera to follow him.

Vera sprang from her crouch with her knife drawn low at her side and followed Gunny through the opening. Alan trailed a half-dozen feet behind her. Just then, the smoker stepped away from his fellow sentry, who was casually sitting on the bollard. The standing guard leaned the muzzle of his rifle between his legs and steadied it with his other hand, as he gestured with his cigarette towards the train with the gondola cars.

Gunny suddenly pounced on the standing guard and grabbed him by his hair to snap his head back, ramming the point of his knife under the man's jaw and up into his skull.

As Gunny's victim slumped to the pier deck, Gunny took the man's rifle and kept it from dropping noisily after him. Stunned by the horror unfolding in front of him, the second guard froze, and his eyes bulged. Before he could regain his senses, Vera lunged and jabbed the fingers of her left hand into his eyes, pushing his head back and up. Before he could scream she thrust the blade of her knife through the man's neck and into his skull. Instead of pulling the blade out, she raked it through the outer side of the man's neck. His blood gushed down the front of his sweater like warm, dark oil spurting from a broken crankcase. The guard toppled backwards, sliding off the bollard onto the pier.

Gunny tossed Alan the sentry's rifle and then grabbed his kill by the arms, dragging him to the pier's edge. He swung the body out over the edge and dangled it like a perverse puppet master before he dropped the human carcass into the detritus of high tide.

Alan took the second sentry's rifle from Vera, and Gunny quickly dumped the other body in the same way. As soon as the second guard slid into the water the trio rushed back to the warehouse's opening and hid behind the wall next to the doorway. After they had caught their breaths, Alan stashed the two rifles behind a cargo board.

Gunny poked his head out and checked the surrounding area. The only action on the pier was at the far end, where the train's engine was noisily leaving. Vera joined Gunny at the opening and Alan slid in next to her, but she pressed her hand against his chest to keep his silhouette from sticking out too far.

"I think we're good," she said. "The ship's so long that anyone watching from her bridge would have to make a real effort to see what's going on back here. Grab something to carry so you look like a dock worker, and let's go before things settle down."

From the cargo board near the collection of cigarette butts, Alan pulled opened the thick netting and searched through the cache of medium-sized crates with both Asian and English markings. He tested one for weight and tossed it to Gunny. He repeated the process with another but was more careful handing it to Vera. He hoisted the last one on his shoulder.

"I hope the good bishop doesn't mind," Alan said with a grin.

Gunny glanced back, puzzled.

"On the label," Alan explained, "these boxes are from Bishop White, and they're on their way to—" Alan held his box out and took another look. "'M. OHARA: Seattle.'"

Gunny smiled. "Well then, we'll be sure to return these, just as soon as we're done. I wouldn't want to get on the wrong side of whichever church the good bishop or M. O'Hara are members."

The threesome quickly crossed the open pier to the gangway, Gunny again taking the lead, with Vera in the middle, and Alan in the rear. All carried their packages on their shoulders, situating the boxes between their faces and the bridge. The tide was still coming in, lifting the ship well above the pier, which forced them to grasp the gangway's railing as they made their way up the ramp.

At the top Gunny stepped off to drop below Alan's line of sight. Vera followed him, but the drop to the landing platform was steeper than she could reach safely with her shorter stride. Gunny tossed his package under a nearby lifeboat and came back for her, anticipating a problem, but he was a moment too late. Vera reeled as she dropped down to the platform, but recovered quickly, catching her balance on her own. Her little maneuver only came at the expense of the box she was carrying. The wooden crate popped free from her grip and fell to the unforgiving metal deck, splitting open.

Vera immediately went after the broken box, but it was cracked wide, with excelsior spilling out through the displaced slats. She knelt and hastily shoved the packing material back inside, but then she stopped abruptly. She put her index finger to her mouth and inclined her head toward the lifeboat. The other two followed her, hiding behind the small boat which was suspended by davits, just above the deck.

Vera went still as she listened, and then Alan heard it too. Footsteps. He hunkered low and stared out from underneath the lifeboat at a pair of boots that stopped in front of the gangway. Seconds later there were more footsteps, and then another set of legs appeared. Something was said between the two men in Japanese, and after a few moments they both walked toward the nearby cargo hold. Then they were gone.

Vera sat down on the cold deck and pulled the broken shipping crate into her lap. After she'd pulled several handfuls of the excelsior out, she reached into the box and carefully withdrew an ornate metal sculpture. The ambient lighting surrounding them was poor, but the threesome could still appreciate the splendid craftsmanship that went into creating the beautiful dragon figure. It stood coiled upright around a rock and held an orb of some kind high in the air in one of its talons. Alan couldn't tell whether the object was a skull, a pearl, or lotus bud—but it looked to him as if the dragon were evaluating the roundish sphere for its next meal.

"Is it gold?" Alan whispered.

"I'm not sure, but given the dull-green patina I'm thinking it's copper," Vera said. "Antique for sure, and I'm betting it's stolen."

Vera gently re-packed the treasure into the box and lifted the shipping label to examine it. The light was too poor to read the writing, but she could make out the bishop's name along with a fresher inking of "M. OHARA." Also on the box were two different kinds of Asian characters. Vera pursed her lips and nodded, affirming what she suspected. "Of course. The good bishop is—or was—sending this to Canada, probably to a museum that'll buy it from him. It's plunder from China, which he may have purchased on the black market."

Alan nodded. "But why are treasures this valuable being diverted here, not Japan?" he asked.

"I don't know. I'll have to kick that around awhile."

"Damn, they're nothing but grave robbers," Gunny said. He scowled, reached under the lifeboat and took out another one of the crates. He sat back on his foot to rest his weight on his heel, and removed his pocketknife. He snapped it open and wedged the tip into the edge of the wooden box, inserting it between the thin brads to pry them loose. In a matter of seconds he popped one board free and then the other. He reached inside and suddenly stopped. "It ain't tea, folks."

Silently Gunny withdrew a tall porcelain figure of a woman in flowing robes with a tiara on top of her head. She stood on a lotus flower with little cherubs perched around her feet. All of the smaller figures had their eyes closed and their hands clasped together as though they were praying. Gunny smiled knowingly. "This is Kuan Yin, the Compassionate Rebel, and she was in the box you tossed to me, Champ. Lucky it didn't break."

"Sorry, Gunny, I just figured it was tea."

"It could have meant a lot of bad joss for all of us, but now maybe it will be good. She represents China's acceptance of Buddhism—but that's about all I know of her. She's a wonder, and this is priceless."

Gunny handed the exquisite figurine to Vera and Alan to examine. It was similar in height to the coiled dragon Vera still held. Gunny reached behind and retrieved the third box. He popped the thin wood off the crate easily and pulled out another work of art. It was a different version of the same goddess, but this time she was in a seated position with her right arm raised slightly to drape over something unseen, as if she had once been part of another display. She also had strings of pearls inlaid across her outer clothing, and a raised mark in the middle of her forehead above her eyebrows.

"I think because of the bindi dot this one is Indian in origin, but I don't know for sure," Gunny said. "This is probably worth as much as the other two, maybe more, but whoever stole her has bitten off more than they'd want to chew. I'm not much into religion, but I do worry when you start talking about bad joss. Stealing something like this is exactly what's going to run up bad karma for the thieves. I wouldn't want to get in the thick of that. It could end up like Moses and the Egyptian plagues—eve of destruction for whoever's behind it, and maybe even for their whole country."

Alan nodded, agreeing with Gunny. "Call me superstitious if you like; I don't deny it. But I say we try to get this back to the rightful owners."

Vera shook her head slightly, thinking for a moment. "Precious art like this shouldn't have one owner. But we got a job to do first, before we can sort this out. Once we've got Jennifer back then we'll see what Customs has to say about all this. If they take a hands-off approach because their palms have been greased, or if they just don't want to meddle in the affairs of a country that's run amok, then we'll come up with our own plan. Agreed?"

Both Gunny and Alan gave their okay, and the three shook hands to seal the deal.

Mischa poured Jennifer another cup of tea, presented it gracefully, and sat next to her. "Almost adjoining your cabin is a larger stateroom assigned to me. Hideki is rarely so considerate, but this time he was kind enough to provide first-class accommodations. Would you like to freshen up in mine? I'll make sure you're not disturbed."

"Could I?"

"I don't see why not? I also have a full liquor bar, and I could order dinner delivered if you're hungry. Should I be concerned you're not old enough to drink, dear?"

"No liquor for me, thanks. My stomach's queasy. I guess it's because I'm so hungry."

"I apologize for calling you 'dear.' I'm being overly familiar, and I'm not nearly old enough to be your mother— an older sister perhaps, but not a mother."

"I don't mind."

"I understand your abductors used foul chemicals to sedate you. That could make your stomach queasy and give you a headache. Hot food and a bath would do you good, give you a chance to rinse away the chemicals."

Mischa stood up and gracefully raised her arm, indicating the door to the inside passageway. "Shall we?"

261

Jennifer gave her a small smile as Mischa extended a hand to help her up from the bunk. When her feet touched the floor Mischa wrapped one arm around Jennifer and squeezed her maternally. "We may as well make the most of this unfortunate disaster," Mischa said. "It seems like it's been forever since I've been a host to such a charming, young friend."

Mischa knocked on the passageway door and a young man with a severe military style haircut opened the door and bowed to her as he stepped inside. Slung over his shoulder was a rifle. As he raised his eyes from his bowed stance, he stole a peek at Jennifer, staring as she and her hostess walked past him. Mischa said something to him in his native tongue, and he bowed again, lowering his head farther. This time he kept he his eyes averted while the women walked down to Mischa's doorway.

"I told him we're going to my stateroom. I don't want to cause them any alarm and make trouble for us."

Mischa led the way past another sentry who opened her door and stepped aside, bowing as he did. Mischa's room was much more luxurious than the one they had just been in. It had red and gold colored drapes that covered windows, not portholes, and the twin beds were covered in gold-patterned bedspreads, separated by a small dining table that was set for two. There was also a wet bar, and near the entrance was a door to a full bathroom with a white tub. Stored neatly next to a wardrobe was a stack of suitcases in two different patterns.

Mischa opened the wardrobe and took out a bathrobe. "You can just drop your clothes on the bed, and if there is anything you'd like laundered I'll have that done while you're freshening up. You can wear something of mine in the meantime if you'd like."

Mischa sat at a small desk and picked up a telephone

handset. She spoke rapidly in Japanese, and then she held the phone away from her ear to face her companion. "The menu's in Japanese, and although I speak it passably, I can't read a word of it. Is there anything you'd like? Hideki told me they're quite well supplied."

"I'm not familiar with Japanese cuisine, but I hear it's uncooked, especially the fish."

"Just the Sushi and not all of that is raw. The meat would be cooked, if that's what concerns you."

"Then something with beef would be fine. I'm not feeling that adventurous right now."

"I'll ask for it."

With the phone still in her hand, Mischa inserted a cigarette into a holder and lit it with a heavy desktop lighter. Then she glanced at Jennifer who had just taken off her coat and was unbuttoning her blouse. Waving the cigarette holder casually, she asked, "You don't mind if I smoke do you?"

"Not really. I've just never seen anyone use a holder before—like in the movies."

Mischa finished her conversation with the kitchen and hung up the phone. "This?" she asked, waving the cigarette holder for emphasis. "I know it looks pretentious, but I hate handling tobacco more than I have to. It's a nasty habit, and I should never have started. But like other modern women I wanted to express my independence from everything traditional. That sounds trite now, but it wasn't a few years back. This is my way of keeping cigarettes as far from me as I possibly can, but I really should quit. I don't believe doctors who tell you smoking's good for you...but I'm running on and on, and you'd like a little privacy. I'll leave so you can finish undressing if you wish?"

"No, that's alright. I shared a room in my sorority with another girl. Modesty isn't a problem for me."

"I'm so glad you feel that way. Below the hotel where I live they have public baths, just like in Japan. I frequently go there to bathe even though I have my own. The public bath is so communal that it allows me to feel connected."

"That seems so risqué. Are there men there, too?"

"There's a partition between the baths, men on one side, women the other, which is actually the way I prefer it—although I'm no prude. I try to be progressive, but I'm not that comfortable with my body image. After all I'm growing older and am no longer in the flower of youth."

"How old are you?"

"Let's just say that in my country they'd call me an old maid."

"That's so old-fashioned. You look amazing."

Mischa's smile grew into a glow, warming her face, and an underlying iciness seemed to thaw. She sat back in her chair, crossed her legs, and made herself comfortable. "It will take at least thirty minutes for our food to arrive, maybe longer. The kitchen is short-staffed while they're in port. I think I may even have time to step in the bath right after you. Feel free to take your time though. Whatever it is they're loading should take awhile. There doesn't seem to be a hurry."

As soon as Jennifer stepped into the shower, Mischa opened the connecting door between her room and the one next to it. She mischievously eyed the man relaxing on the bed. "Care to meet our guest, Hideki?"

Mischa strode back into her stateroom and opened a dresser drawer. She selected silk undergarments and tossed them on the bed. Then she picked out a blouse and slacks and arranged them next to the other items, seeing how they went together. "She'll look delicious in these."

264

"You quite like her then?"

Mischa smiled at Hideki playfully. "Things have changed, and yes I do like her. Her mother's done a fine job raising her. They have similar qualities, but this one, however, hasn't angered me by trying to break my jaw. I'm almost hoping I won't have to give her back. She'd make a lovely cruise companion, don't you think?"

"But, then I'd never get to see you," Hideki said.

"I wouldn't be so sure about that. I have my own needs, too."

Hideki took out a cigarette case, withdrew one, and inserted it between his lips. He lit it and smiled dreamily at Mischa. "It is a long sail home, and it can get awfully lonely with nothing but men on board. Perhaps if your guest stays, you might allow me to entertain her?"

Mischa frowned dubiously. "How is the loading going?"

"The captain said he hoped to have it done in three hours, four at the most."

Mischa went to the window and pulled the drape back. "You know, Tiger Lee is out there. She's probably already watching us—plotting her next move."

"We have sentries out, and she can't possibly get down the pier without our seeing her approach. If she brings the Port Authority, then the captain will cut the lines and make for the open seas. We will take what we can carry and go."

Mischa pulled the curtain shut. "But if the Coast Guard catches us, they'll seize your ship," she said. "Won't your family be angry?"

"It's a risk I'm prepared to take."

"If something happens, remember our arrangement: I am your guest and not part of your shipping operation. I can't be tied up in this," Mischa said firmly. "And Jennifer is not to be hurt in any way," she added.

Hideki sighed and frowned. "Yes, I know, and your

payment is already in the warehouse," he said disapprovingly. "Once again your needs have been met first, leaving me with all the risk...."

Mischa scowled at Hideki. "That's only from this point onward. I've brought the precious metal this far, and it came at a very dear cost—that of many lives. Now you have an opportunity to share in the danger, which typically only involves money for you."

Hideki went over to the wet bar to prepare himself a drink. With a glass in hand he paused and glanced back at Mischa. "There have been very serious risks you are unaware of, but I'm not at liberty to discuss them with you. Perhaps when enough time has passed, you will allow me to boast of my accomplishments."

Mischa didn't respond but continued to stare at the hallway leading to the bathroom where the tub continued to fill.

Hideki took a sip of his drink and set it down. "If I were ever captured," he teased, "I could of course always tell them that it was you who tied me up, tortured me with lashes, and forced me to have insatiable sex with you until I could take no more."

He smiled devilishly but Mischa still didn't respond. "Would you like something?" he asked, holding his drink up.

"How about martinis all around? I'll tell our guest we have company, and while I'm there, I'll scrub her back with my nails. With you around I might just need to mark my territory."

Having hidden the treasures in a safe place, Vera,
Gunny and Alan climbed the ship's steps to the top level
carrying the empty shipping crates. They were playing a
hunch, but from Vera's experience she guessed whoever
was holding Jennifer would stash her close to the command
center in the area of the ship's bridge, and there would likely
be sentries stationed in front of her cabin. Vera reassured
Gunny and Alan that those watching would be more worried
about Jennifer's escape than a rescue, especially since no
one was aware they had boarded the ship.

The top deck had a large covered walking area on
each side with wooden lounge chairs stacked and pushed
up against the bulkheads of the first-class cabins. The trio
huddled together briefly at the top of the steps. Vera tugged
down the cowl neck on her sweater so she could speak more
clearly. "This is the high rent territory," she said. "It has
windows instead of portholes behind those chairs. I don't
see any outside sentries, but there're lights on in a couple
of the staterooms near the bridge. One of those could be
Jennifer's room, but let's check the other side first to be
sure. Then we'll take the middle passageway and see if we
can fake our way past the guards."

Crossing behind the doors to the central passageway they each snuck glances down the corridor and their suspicions were confirmed. Down near the end staterooms were two guards, each holding a rifle. They seemed to have wandered away from two separate cabins in order to strike up a conversation. The trio continued across to the opposite side and checked the starboard side, looking for lights coming from rooms near the quarterdeck. At the other end there was light shining from the cabin closest to the ship's bridge. Inside the bridge, there were a couple of men moving around, keeping watch over the pier and the forward part of the ship.

Alan leaned out for a quick glimpse of the pier. The gondola cars were already in the process of being unloaded. Japanese laborers were swarming about, hand-loading the brass shells into large metal tubs, one of which was shackled to the heavy rigging of the ships crane, ready to be hoisted onboard the ship.

Vera pulled Alan back, worried that he could be seen. Alan nodded in the direction of the pier. "They've already got half a car unloaded. At the rate their going, they'll be done in two hours at the most."

"Plus clean up and dogging down their hatches," said Gunny, "but they can finish much of that while they're underway, sailing up the Sound."

Vera closed her eyes thoughtfully and nodded. "So will we if we have to. If the guards are on the opposite side of the ship, then she'll be in one of those staterooms."

Alan nodded, agreeing with her logic.

"This'll be a little rougher than handling the sentries on the pier," Vera added.

"How so?" asked Alan.

"It'll be a direct, frontal attack, and you'll need to distract them so Gunny and I can get in close for the kill."

"Understood."

"You're okay with that?" Vera asked.

"They're obviously soldiers, and death is a risk that comes with serving their country. We'll just need to make sure it's them that die for theirs, not us for ours."

Vera sighed. "That's all true my little scholar, but right now those two are breathing their last breaths, they just don't know it yet. They're probably bitching about the boring assignment they've been stuck with. In a moment their days will be over and they'll get a chance to meet their Maker. I hope they're ready."

"You don't enjoy this either?" Alan asked.

"Not a bit."

Alan reached out and rubbed her forearm reassuringly. Behind her, Gunny shook his head with a frown. He wasn't looking forward to the violence either.

"I hate to sound like an old blood-and-guts soldier," Alan said, "but none of us chose this battle. They brought it to us. We're just going to make them wish they hadn't."

Gunny's eyes widened and his frown disappeared. "Machiavelli again?"

"No, Ulysses Grant or Robert E. Lee—I forget which one—but Machiavelli would approve."

Vera pulled out her knife, opened the blade and held it flat against the backside of the box out of view of the sentries. Gunny did the same and rested his box on his shoulder. Vera took a deep breath and exhaled. "Alright then," she said with a nod.

Alan banged through the door like a careless stevedore who'd lugged one too many crates for the pampered rich. He held the door with his shoulder long enough for Vera and Gunny to slide in behind him without taking their hands away from their crates. Down the passageway, the sentries spun in their direction and lifted their rifles slightly, but without urgency. Vera and Gunny fell in behind Alan, and they all moved with purpose toward the two soldiers.

As they neared the two guards, they huddled close together in front of the stateroom closest to the bridge. One of the guards stepped forward and pushed his rifle out in a blocking motion. "Teiryuu!" he said firmly.

Without understanding the guard's meaning, Alan lowered the crate in his hands and pointed to the damaged corner and the label on the topside of it. The sentry stared at the loose excelsior hanging out and gestured excitedly at the label. Alan nodded obsequiously. This was turning out to be easier than he'd thought.

The man lowered his rifle, and Gunny and Vera also approached to hold their broken boxes for inspection. While inching nearer to the two sentries, Gunny and Vera slid their open knives underneath the boxes. Just as the guards leaned closer to look at the empty boxes, the two assassins pushed the boxes into their faces, knocking them off balance. Before the men could respond, Gunny and Vera grabbed for the guards' rifles with their free hands, while savagely thrusting their knives into the necks of their prey. Blood gushed in a spray from both guards' necks as the sharp knives tore through their carotid arteries.

Their dead bodies flopped to the floor, limbs spread akwardly. As Alan already knew, there was no grace in death.

Vera shook her head in disgust and handed one of the seized rifles to Alan. "I only kill when I have to, but I'm getting tired of doing it to handsome young men. It would make it easier if we thought they really were evil demons, but the truth is we have no idea if they're deserving of death or not." Vera sighed heavily and closed her eyes a moment.

270

"Either way we shouldn't leave weapons lying around behind us," Gunny said. He checked the action on the rifle in his hand, releasing the safety and pulling back the bolt. He encouraged Alan to do the same with the other. "You'll need to know if it's loaded and ready to go. All too often soldiers aren't allowed to load their weapons in foreign ports. Loaded weapons are seen as a sign of aggression."

"And kidnapping and spying are not?" Alan asked sarcastically. He frowned and inspected the other rifle, as Gunny had done with his. "Locked and loaded," he reported.

Gunny nodded approvingly and then turned toward Vera. "You ready for this, gorgeous?"

"About as much as I'll ever be. I'll open the door and go in low. If I have to, I might even dive to the floor to draw their fire. I'd rather they shoot at me than hurt Jenny in anyway. Any shooting we do in there is as a last resort, and for God's sake, be careful."

Gunny smiled encouragement. "You've got it, darling."

Alan grabbed Vera's arm, pulling her so close their noses nearly touched. "I can't let you do that. I couldn't live with myself if something happened to you—either of you. Besides, you can do more to help her than I can. I'll go first, draw their fire."

Vera held his gaze, searching for strength or hesitation. He wasn't about to flinch. Finally she blinked, her eyes misty and accepting. "You be careful, sweetheart. I couldn't stand to lose another Stewart either."

It was Alan's turn to blink.

"You don't know this, and this might not be the best time to tell you," Vera said, "but I'm responsible for putting Mackie on the trail of the Lindbergh money—the case that got him killed. I ache all the time thinking of it. The target was supposed to be mine, not your dad's. I used Mackie because he wanted to help me; he liked doing favors for people, and he didn't expect anything in return. He never knew what Vic or I did, who else we worked for, or why. He just thought it would be fun to upstage Lieutenant Frantz again and help the Lindberghs while doing it. I played him— the man I loved—and I never got over it. I'm awful that way, and you should be careful around me. Because now you're here fighting another one of my battles, cleaning up another mess I've created. If I lost you, I'd die inside."

Alan pulled her even closer so that his cheek rubbed against hers. With his lips close to her ear he whispered, "Nobody made me come here. I'm right where I want to be—with you. You're not playing me—I'm here for you, I'm here for Jennifer, and I'm here to stop this damned brass from sailing to the wrong people."

Vera sighed and pulled back. "You be safe."

"I promise," Alan said. "Now let's move before their reinforcements show up."

Alan stepped over the sentry's body that was closest to the door. He lowered the rifle, gripping it with his right hand while he unlatched the door slowly and cracked it open. As soon as he cleared the doorframe he sprang into action, lunging into the stateroom. He ran past the unlit bathroom and darted across the open living quarters toward the two beds at the center of the room. He braced himself against the second bed and covered the area with his rifle. The room was empty, eerily quiet, and he hadn't taken a bullet for Vera yet. He exhaled a sigh of relief, and then he caught the scent of cigarette smoke still hanging heavily in the air.

Vera entered behind him and veered to her right, sliding along the interior gold-papered wall that separated the bathroom from the rest of the cabin. Gunny came in last and dropped to one knee next to the bathroom, bringing his rifle up to aim.

Alan shrugged and frowned, puzzled.

Gunny shut the hallway door behind him and glanced toward Vera, who motioned for him to check the bathroom. He leaned into the small room for a moment before he came back out and shook his head.

273

Alan mimicked holding a cigarette and Vera and Gunny both nodded agreement with him. Someone had just been in the room smoking. Vera pointed to the adjoining door between the two staterooms, and held her index finger up against her lips, indicating quiet. She crept along the wall and over to the door, stopping short of it and leaning close to the jamb.

As they got closer they could hear muffled voices coming from the other stateroom. With his rifle aimed level at the door, Alan crept across the carpet cautiously and stood opposite from Vera. She took a deep breath and sighed. Then she reached out to grab the door handle, while Alan leaned back and raised the barrel high enough to let the door swing out in front of him. Vera turned the knob slowly at first and then tugged the door open sharply as she stepped backward.

Alan dropped the barrel of the rifle to just below waist level and shouldered his way through the opening into the adjoining room, veering to his left.

BANG! The roar of a handgun rang throughout the two staterooms.

The hot lead from the automatic zipped under Alan's right ear, grazing the side of his neck and slamming into the wooden doorjamb behind his head. He dove into the room as he tried to reach cover behind the small table and chairs. The dining set wasn't big enough to hide his large frame, let alone provide protection from another shot if the marksman was skilled enough to hit a target on the move. The wound stung sharply, burning like a bully digging a sharp object through Alan's neck muscle, but he fought past the pain and brought the rifle up to eye level. He hastily scanned the room, searching for the source of danger. Over his sights, a Japanese woman in a red silk robe sat on the bed closest to the entry hall, her legs crossed elegantly, dangling a slipper

274

playfully off one foot. She inhaled from a cigarette in a long holder, unperturbed. Behind her stood a dapper Japanese man holding a black pistol in his extended hand.

Jennifer was pressed against the man's side. She wore a white terry cloth bathrobe, soft slippers, and her wet curls hung below a towel wrapped around her head like a turban. The man coiled his left arm under Jennifer's chin and tugged her closer to him. He held a cigarette in the same hand that clutched at the top of Jennifer's robe, and the trail of smoke lazily floated upwards in front of her face. With his right hand he swung the gun away from Alan and toward the empty doorframe.

Alan glanced past the opening to Vera, who was holding her pistol with both hands, waiting for his signal. Alan caught her eye and shook his head rapidly, then returned to his rifle, which was trained on the stylish fop's forehead.

The man flicked his wrist, as if improving his grip on the pistol, and then he brought it up and pointed it under Jennifer's chin. "You shoot me, and she dies too."

Vera leaned into the doorframe, then shouldered her way through it, quickly moving to the right side of the door, directly across from her daughter and the captor. She scanned the room, checking Alan, the woman on the bed, and finally settling on Jennifer and Hideki. "Are you okay, dear?" she called to Jennifer.

"Mother?"

"I said I'd come for you."

Hideki ducked his head behind Jennifer's turban and scowled wickedly at the woman on the bed. She exhaled and met his glare. "Be careful with your cigarette, Hideki, or you'll catch her on fire," Mischa said.

Hideki dropped his cigarette to the floor and pushed Jennifer forward so he could grind it into the carpet. Jennifer's robe draped loosely as she moved. She hurriedly

275

clutched the top with one hand and the bottom with the other. Still, the sudden movement revealed her bare, wet legs.

Alan started to glance away, embarrassed for her, but then he focused on Hideki's almond eyes. Alan wondered if he should risk a shot. Could he take Hideki out cleanly before the man had time to react? Alan quickly calculated the odds, but it was a risk he didn't want to take. Too much could go wrong. Too much was at stake.

Vera inched farther down the wall toward her daughter. Hideki started to lower the pistol to track her, but then he brought his pistol back up and pressed it against Jennifer's neck. He stepped backward toward the wall behind him, dragging his captive along. Vera held her pistol across her chest, the barrel pointing toward the ceiling. She glanced at the woman on the bed and then back to Hideki. "That's right," Vera said. "Point your pistol at me, and give the Champ a clean shot at your temple."

Hideki nervously twitched and spun toward Alan, but then Gunny distracted him as he stepped through the doorway, also bringing his rifle up to eye level. Hideki's eyes bulged wide, and he half-turned toward the passageway door. "GUARDS!" he yelled.

Mischa lowered her cigarette holder to the bed and slid her legs so they dangled over the floor as she prepared to stand. "Hideki, I'm afraid you'll have to let us both go," she said. "If your guards were still alive and up to the task, our rescuers wouldn't be here now."

Hideki glared at her, then he faced the other three. "Stay back or she dies!" he said, indicating Jennifer with his pistol.

Mischa half-smiled, while glancing one-by-one at the rescuers. Not sure why he was suspicious Alan continued to track her movements, particularly her hands. He glanced back toward Hideki. "What about her?" Alan asked, indicating Mischa with a tilt of his head.

"Miss Ohara's services are no longer required," Hideki spat out. "We have the brass we need. If you want her back, she's yours." Hideki backed into the hallway, pulling Jennifer with him. His left forearm squeezed tight under her chin, forcing her to back-peddle on her tiptoes so she provided a maximum shield for her captor. When he reached the passageway, Hideki stopped to unlatch the door. "Just be careful what you desire," he called back into the room.

Vera darted along the wall and knelt low, extending as little as possible of her head as she peaked around the corner. Alan crossed the room to come up alongside her, but Vera quickly put her left arm out to hold him back.

BANG! The small automatic barked again.

Hideki's shot slammed into the corner of the wall and tore through it, passing in front of Alan's face and just above Vera's head. The bullet tore through the stateroom's red curtains, making a small odd-shaped hole in the window.

Behind Vera, Mischa stifled a shriek, rolled across the bed, and landed unceremoniously on the floor between the matching beds, her bath robe falling open. "Son of a jackel!" she hissed angrily.

Alan stepped closer to the wall behind Vera, and plastered his back against it. "That nearly took my head off," he said.

Vera reached back and pressed her hand against his abdomen, keeping him out of harm's way. "Could have been my head too. He plays for keeps."

Alan reached up and probed the hole in the neck of his sweater with his finger. There was blood oozing out, but not too much. He blinked long and shook his head.

As the latch to the passageway clicked shut behind Hideki and Jennifer, Mischa crawled out from in between the beds. As she neared the dinette set she stood awkwardly, closed her robe, and covered her nakedness. She cinched the silk belt tight, pushed her hair back into shape, and recaptured her composure. Unlike seeing Jennifer's body, Mischa's full frontal display wasn't as disconcerting to Alan, even though it was also accidental. There was a difference between sister and stranger, even when the former was only a half-sister.

Suddenly Alan looked around. "Where's Gunny?" he asked.

As if in response, two shots echoed loudly from out in the passageway. Vera stood and faced Alan. "That's not good." She indicated toward Mischa with a tilt of her head. "Find out her story first, then follow me. If it comes to it, make sure you know who you're shooting at and what the backdrop is."

"Got it," Alan said.

After the door closed behind Vera, Alan lowered the rifle and held it in his left hand as he crossed the floor toward Mischa. "I need you to come with me, ma'am, while I look for my friend."

"Can't I just stay here?"

Alan stopped in front of her and frowned, puzzled. "Not if you want to get away from these people."

"Of course I do, but what about all my things?"

"We can come back for them later—"

From the passageway came a shout and more footsteps, which quickly faded toward the bridge.

He grabbed Mischa by her arm, feeling her well-toned bicep under her thin silk robe. He gazed squarely into her dark eyes. "I don't have time to argue or explain. Come with me!"

Alan tugged her along, firm but gentle, and led her through the connecting door to the adjoining stateroom. She didn't actively resist his aggression, but she didn't seem to go along easily either. They crossed the stateroom in hurried strides to the darkened hallway leading to the passageway. The outer door was ajar, letting in a crease of light and a breeze of cooler air. Alan pulled Mischa close so they could stand together in the confined area. The air wafted across her neck and cheeks, stealing some of her scent and sharing it with him. She smelled delicious, the essence of jasmine and roses. It was an expensive fragrance he'd smelled somewhere recently.

"You smell wonderful." As soon as he said it, he knew he shouldn't have. It wasn't the time or the place, and he didn't know her well enough to be familiar. He had a lot to learn, and he knew it.

She gazed at him, appraisingly and smiled. "Why thank you, kind sir."

Still holding her arm, he levered open the door with the tip of the rifle barrel. The passageway appeared empty other than the fallen guards, so Alan let go of Mischa's arm. His hand dropped down across an embossed pattern of a dragon on the back of her silk robe, and he encouraged her through the doorway. Once she saw the bodies on the floor, she balked and leaned into him. Alan squeezed her shoulders, pulling her close, and led her through.

Suddenly Alan stopped. There were three bodies on the floor where there should have been only two.

"Gunny! Are you all right?"

Covered in blood, much of it from the carpet and the two bodies next to him, Gunny rolled onto his back, and leaned against one of the corpses. "Of course not, Champ. I feel like I got a hot poker sticking all the way through me."

Alan let go of Mischa and squatted next to Gunny. "How bad is it? Can you tell?"

Gunny flapped his wounded upper arm and shoulder, winced, and closed his eyes with a sigh. "You mean am I going to die? Given that I'm able to talk at you now, I'm thinking my lungs and organs are good, but I don't know about the arteries and such."

Alan blinked and shook his head in disbelief.

"There's no doubt I'm bleeding," Gunny said, "but most of what you see is courtesy of these other two birds. Our gunman got me once. His second shot tore into this guy next to me. I'm lucky, and I think I'm okay—at least while I'm laying here."

Alan thought for a moment, processing the new information. "Okay then. I say we move you into the stateroom, where you'll be out of harm's way and can lay down properly."

Alan set his rifle on the carpet, reached under Gunny's good arm, and tugged his friend to his feet. He carefully draped Gunny's arm over his own shoulder and steered him toward the same doorway he and Mischa had just come through. After two lumbering steps, Alan stopped, remembering Mischa.

Behind him the Asian beauty held Alan's rifle loosely in one hand, allowing the stock's butt to sit on the floor. She stood silently and watched Alan and Gunny's progress, and then she squatted down to pick up Gunny's rifle with her other hand, trying to keep the pool of blood at her feet from getting on her exotic robe. Her beautiful legs shot out between the folds of silk, exposing their full length and a hint of the dark pubic bush between them. She quickly stood and stepped in line behind the two men, encouraging them to continue into the stateroom while she dragged the rifles, one in each hand, across the carpet.

Alan toted Gunny past the bathroom and across to the first bed, where he laid him on top of the covers. Mischa entered the room behind them, shut the door, and latched it. She stacked the rifles with their barrels up in the corner behind the door. Then she came over and stood next to Alan at the bed. "I suspect you'll want to join your other friend, Jennifer's mother—wasn't she? Go ahead. I'll run hot water and get towels. I'll take care of him."

"Would you, please?"

"Of course, darling. You're such a gentleman."

From his bed Gunny reached out and grabbed Alan's arm. He spoke in a slow, strained voice. "Hold on a second, Champ. Vera has more skills than you and I, and you don't know where she's at. You go running out of here without a plan, and you could end up dead or their next hostage."

"What do you think—" Alan started to ask.

Behind them, Mischa broke in. "While you two strategize—or whatever you call it, I'll slip into something more appropriate for guests."

There was a hitch in her voice as she paused to notice where Alan's eyes were focused. She'd obviously caught him ogling her, but what was a guy to do? Her thin robe clung like a layer of shimmering skin. It wasn't nearly thick enough to hide the shape of her breasts, especially her full-button nipples. A trace of a smile said she didn't mind at all. Maybe she even wanted him to stare, like Vera would—a blissful form of castration as he stood helpless in front of her. But he felt guilty all the same, afraid she'd pegged him for just another twenty-one year old with raging hormones.

Mischa retrieved her clothing lying on top of the second bed and loosened her robe. There was complete silence in the room as she held her panties out in front of her and stepped into them. She pulled them up across her thighs and over her pubic bush, pausing to gaze over at the men who were watching her, each with their mouth open slightly.

"Oh, I'm sorry, gentlemen," she purred. "I'm so used to public baths it didn't occur to me...I didn't mean to distract you from your conversation. Please go on."

With that she picked up her slacks and a sweater and draped them carelessly over her shoulder so that they hung down across the back of her robe. She casually walked around the bed toward the bathroom. Both men stared in silence as she passed, watching the shimmer of silk as it clung to her bottom, bouncing with each step.

Alan rubbed his brow and cleared his throat. "That's alright, ma'am," he called after her. "I apologize for staring."

She left the bathroom door open and he could still see her reflection in the full-length mirror in the hallway. "Please don't call me 'ma'am," she called in reply. "I'm not that old. You can call me Mischa."

She had taken off her robe and hung it out of view. Standing there in just her panties, she smiled at him through the mirror as she spoke. She slipped on her slacks, before pulling the sweater over her head, not taking the time to fit into a brassiere. He didn't miss a second of the show. It was one, wasn't it? As soon as she began to straighten her hair, Alan faced Gunny with a deep breath. "You doing okay?" he asked.

"I'm hanging in there," Gunny said. His voice cracked with the effort, but he attempted a smile.

Mischa slipped on a pair of Asian styled flats and walked out to join them. Alan glanced away for a second, embarrassed, and then met the eyes of the beautiful woman. "I'm sorry for staring," he said. "But I feel as if I know you. I'm sure I've seen you somewhere before, haven't I?"

Hideki hurriedly led Jennifer through the forward passage briefly pulling her out into the night air on the deck before bursting through the door to the bridge, which also served as the ship's quarterdeck. Although it was nearly empty of personnel, it was full of the sounds of the ship at work as the crew noisily loaded the brass. Winches screeched and whined, competing with the sharp metallic screams of brass clashing with iron, as a junior officer who was watching the loading from the starboard door turned toward the movement in the bridge. Hideki dragged Jennifer across the raised teak grid toward the helm, where he abruptly stopped, jerking her back by the collar.

"We have saboteurs on board," he declared firmly to the officer. "They do not wish us to sail with our cargo. Sound the alarm and make the ship ready to sail!"

The officer stared past Jennifer at Hideki and the gun in his hand. Then he looked at her for a short moment with a scowl of disapproval, before he addressed Hideki in English. "I'm sorry, sir, but only the captain can give that order."

"I am the owner of this entire line of ships. The captain works for me."

"But there is the chain-of-command sir, which I must

follow. I work for the captain first, the shipping line second. My orders come from the captain only."

"If you value your job, you'll do as I say."

"I do value my job—but not as much as I value honor: my family's and my own."

"Very well then, summon him. Where is he, anyway? Why isn't he here on the bridge where he belongs?"

"He is in the stern. We've had to reposition our cargo for proper ballast. We had been told there would be several rail cars of scrap steel for the stern holds, but now it appears they won't be coming, and we need to reposition the weight from the forward hold. All hands are on work details, and I don't have anyone to send after him."

"Then sound the whistle."

The ship's officer spread his weight over his feet. "I cannot do that, sir."

"Didn't you hear? I said we have saboteurs on board."

"I do not wish to be impudent sir, but the woman you have as a prisoner," the officer said as he glanced at Jennifer, "would be naked, except for her bathrobe. Where would she conceal explosives...or any weapons, for that matter?"

Hideki scowled. "Get the captain."

"As I said, sir, I have no one to send after him, and I cannot leave my watch unless relieved."

Hideki glared at the officer, whose weight was spread over his fixed stance, ready to hold his ground. The whistle's rope-pull hung just above the young officer's head. Hideki raised his pistol and indicated at the whistle and then the officer's chest. "Sound the whistle," he said.

The officer grabbed his dress coat with both hands and pulled the coat open, flexing his chest outward. "Here is your target, sir."

"You fool! You would risk a bullet and death before you would take an order from me?"

"If it must be, sir."

Hideki aimed his pistol squarely at the middle of the young officer's chest, but after a long moment, he lowered it to his side. Before Hideki spoke again he raised the pistol sharply and pointed past the officer. "What was that?" he asked, indicating a spot behind the officer.

Wary that it was a trick to catch him off guard, the officer stepped slowly to the side and glanced quickly at the starboard door opening before returning his gaze to Hideki. "What was...what?"

"Behind you. I saw a flash."

"It could be the yard lights reflecting off the brass we're loading. It happens all the time."

Hideki lowered his pistol again and sighed. "Japan will be a better country if you live. We might even win this cataclysmic war the soothsayers warn us is coming. To do so, we will need every man we have, especially gritty ones like you."

🐺 ✹ 🐺

Vera raced through the upper deck toward the bridge. It made sense that Hideki would seek reinforcements, so he'd head for the starboard side where those in command would likely be supervising the loading of the ship. She slowed as she came to the corner where the passageways met, pressed her back against the bulkhead and raised her pistol to shoulder height. She slid along the last few feet of the bulkhead to the starboard passage, while scanning the area that led to the portside sun deck, making sure there was no ambush waiting for her.

Vera leaned against the starboard door and glanced out its portal shaped window. She worked the door open a little at a time with her shoulder, listening for voices and scanning the ship for movement. When the opening was big enough, she slid through the door onto the darkened sundeck behind the bridge. Again she pressed her back against the bulkhead, slipping into the shadows as she scoured the deck for signs of danger. For the moment at least, all appeared quiet.

It didn't make sense that Hideki would have come this way only to double back and scramble down the outside deck. He and Jennifer would have ran the length of the top deck and descend three flights of stairs just to get to the stern. The only other option was that they had gone inside the bridge—or out through the other passageway to the opposite side of the ship. *That's it!* Vera thought. Whichever door he went through Hideki would want to get the ship to sea as soon as possible now—maybe even before she was fully loaded.

The starboard door to the bridge was open, and the red glow of the ship's night-lights shone onto the deck a few feet from where she stood, as if beckoning Vera inside. She edged closer to the door with her back against the bulkhead. Over the cacophony of the noises coming from the loading docks Vera could pick up snippets of a conversation inside the bridge house. It took her a moment to realize they were speaking English. Why not Japanese she wondered?

An angry male voice she recognized as Hideki's demanded that the ship's whistle be blown and the captain summoned. Vera shoved her hand into her coat pocket and retrieved her make-up compact. She snapped it open and extended the mirror just far enough around the corner to peek inside the bridge without giving away her position. It took only a second to lock in on the three people standing near the middle of the otherwise empty room.

A Japanese man in a ship's uniform had his feet set squarely next to the helm, and his back was to her. Beyond him were two figures, both obscured by the young officer's position. Vera tilted her mirror and Hideki came into view as he raised one arm to point a pistol at the officer. Suddenly Jennifer's face came into view. Under the ship's night-lights everything, especially the white bathrobe and towel Jennifer wore, was cast in an eerie, red glow.

Hideki gripped Jennifer by the collar just hard enough to keep her off balance. He lowered his pistol for a moment and then jerked it up again, pointing past the officer toward the doorway where Vera was positioned. Vera dropped her hand quickly and tucked the compact behind her, while quietly closing the case. She slipped it back into her pocket and braced for a confrontation.

Vera forced herself to take long, slow breaths as she anticipated her next move. She couldn't charge into the room because Hideki already had his pistol pointing in her general direction. If she attacked she'd run directly into his line of fire. And if she somehow managed to get the upper hand to fire a shot, it would only lead to another standoff because she wasn't about to fire at him with Jennifer in his clutches. Her best bet was to wait him out. She would eventually find her opportunity. Of that she was certain.

Hideki tugged hard on Jennifer's robe, pulling her backward and causing the towel on top of her head to unravel and fall to the deck. Her robe rose high on her bare legs and pulled apart at the top, exposing much of her body. Jennifer grabbed the lapels of the robe and grasped them together, hastily covering herself. She cinched the sash tight across her middle and tugged a hard new knot into it.

"Just tell me when you want me to move!" she complained angrily. "I'm not a puppet and don't need a strong hand. I can follow directions."

Hideki pushed Jennifer through the port door. "As you wish. Here are your instructions: We are heading for the

287

back of the ship, and you need to move. Quickly!"

"But I'm not dressed, and it's cold."

Hideki grabbed hold of her upper arm and forced her along at a rapid pace down the darkened sundeck. "Then we'll need to be fast to outrun the chill," he said. "If you hadn't noticed, I do not have a coat either, but I'm not complaining."

They ran past the captain's darkened stateroom, followed by more rooms that were all dark except two. Along the way, Jennifer alternated between keeping up and falling back, while Hideki tugged on her arm, trying to get her to match her pace with his.

She glared at him as they neared the first set of steps that would take them to the ship's lower levels. "What is it you want with me?" she asked. "You're getting your brass. Why don't you just let me go?"

"Because we're not safe with Tiger Lee on board. You are her cub, and as long as I have you, I have leverage. If she gets you back too soon she can have the authorities stop us and confiscate the valuables we've paid dearly for."

When they reached the second level down Hideki steered Jennifer across the outside deck, shifting from the port to the starboard side ladder, which brought them closer to the well-lit pier. Sensing the presence of a shadow above him, Hideki spun around and pointed his pistol up the ladder behind him. Was he just seeing things?

As Jennifer climbed down the narrow ladder, Hideki nudged her in the back, encouraging her to hurry along. For a moment she lost her balance, but she quickly regained it and made it down the rest of the steps. Hideki grimaced at his mistake, one created by impatience and fear, a misstep that could have been costly for him and his country. He would have to be more careful in his haste. Getting his cargo to sea depended on Jennifer's well being. The capture of

Tiger Lee would be an unexpected bonus. It looked like his fortune was turning after all.

From inside the stateroom Mischa suddenly glanced up and stared out the window. Alan followed her line of sight and caught a sudden movement darting past their window. He stepped quickly around the other bed and pressed his face against the glass. It was Hideki tugging Jennifer along on the darkened sundeck toward the rear of the ship. He was moving fast on the far side of her, cleverly keeping her as a shield between him and any threats that might leap out from the interior of the ship.

Alan stepped backward and bumped into Mischa, who'd silently joined him at the window. "Excuse me, ma'...Mischa. I didn't see you—"

"You're a quick study," she said with a smile. "It's quite alright. Who was that?' she asked, indicating outside the window with a nod.

"Hideki and Jennifer. He's taking her to the back of the ship."

"But not the mother?"

"I didn't see Vera, but I'm going after Jenny," he said, as he darted past Mischa.

"Vera? Yes." Mischa nodded thoughtfully. "Mind if I join you? I'm not completely helpless."

Alan paused to check on Gunny who appeared to be in and out of consciousness. His eyes were closed and he grimaced in pain, but he was breathing regularly. "I'll be back," Alan said, hoping Gunny was registering his voice. Alan blinked thoughtfully and half-heartedly returned Mischa's smile. "Sure. Why not? Grab your coat. We've got to hurry."

As they stepped into the passageway, Mischa pulled on an expensive fur coat that she held tightly over her chest. Alan led her over the dead soldiers and raced toward the rear doors of the deck. Alan was relieved that Mischa didn't seem to mind running at a fast clip, and that she could keep up with him. They hit the door, pushed it open, and raced to the railing that separated the two ladders, where they scanned the decks below them.

Two levels down Hideki hurried Jennifer along past the aft gangway and the lifeboat. They ran toward a large open hatch, while Jennifer's wet hair danced across the top of her robe, keeping time to her strides. As Alan pushed away from the railing to run for the starboard ladder, he spotted a dark specter gliding down the last ladder to the main deck. He knew instantly it was Vera. She moved effortlessly, gracefully, like a powerful feline. When she hit the main deck she veered to her right. She was on a course to flank Hideki, going around the far side of the large cargo hatch.

Mischa had also paused with Alan to see what was unfolding on the deck below, and she was first to the ladder but let Alan take the lead. They quickly descended to the second level where they paused again to evaluate what was taking place below them on the main deck. Although little time had passed since the three had bordered the ship, to Alan if felt as though everything had changed.

291

Hideki wasn't normally afraid of heights, but he found gazing into the ship's large hold disconcerting, like a black hole trying to suck him into oblivion. Because the lip to the hatch was so low to the deck there was nothing for him to catch onto should he lose his balance. He also faced the additional risk that his captive could catch him from behind and shove him into the ship's abyss, sending him headfirst to the unforgiving steel deck forty-five feet below. He knelt and pulled Jennifer down to his level, which still made him queasy.

A moment later Captain Nakauye appeared below on the lowest level of the ship where Hideki could see him giving orders to minions running back and forth with cargo. Hideki cupped the sides of his mouth with his hands, still griping the pistol. "Taii Nakauye!" he shouted.

Captain Nakauye waved up at Hideki, casually acknowledging his presence and then returned to giving directions in the hold.

"Taii Nakauye. Kikyuu!" Hideki yelled again.

Nakauye craned his neck so he could see Hideki again. He saluted perfunctorily and began to climb the long ladder that would lead him up and out of the deep hold.

The light emanating up from the hold highlighted Hideki's face, making him easy to locate. Aware of his sudden vulnerability, Hideki slipped back into the shadows of the lifeboats as Nakauye made his way closer.

Hideki tugged Jennifer by the arm, pulling her down to the deck near to him. She landed on loose excelsior and her feet slid out from under her, her bare legs protruding from her bathrobe. "I'm cold," she grumbled.

"Then cover yourself and be still," he barked in a strained voice. "It shouldn't be much longer."

Hideki rested his head against the lifeboat and inhaled the salt air deeply. He savored the darkness, which favored the nocturnal creatures who worked best in the night:

owls, jackals, jaguars, and spies who did black-bag jobs in service of their countries. As they waited for Nakauye in the shadows Hideki could also watch the two ladders on each side of the rear deck for pursuing intruders, if it were not already too late for that.

He needed time to think and sort this out. For now he was acting on instinct, which had served him well, but who did the White Dragon think she was? She believed her work was more important than his, even though she knew he was her assigned handler. She scarcely knew more than his code name. She had absolutely no idea what he and his other teams had accomplished in their homeland, much of it done quietly, like the burglary of the American Embassy. The U.S. State Department didn't even know yet that their embassy had been compromised and the keys to the codes photographed. The Americans were so naïve about spying—almost as bad as the French. They weren't anything like the British, who could be absolutely ruthless and took a back seat to no one—except him and his teams.

No, Mischa, it is not you who needs to get away to protect your fickle identity, he thought; it is Hideki who cannot be captured...alive. It is Hideki who holds the secrets that can change the fate of nations.

Alan led Mischa back into the ship through the rear doors to the second level, racing with her along the passageway to the inside staircase. She easily kept pace with him. They ran down the interior passage of the main deck toward the stern. "Won't they see us coming this way?" Mischa asked.

Alan slowed as they approached the rear doors and squatted on his haunches. Mischa did the same, positioning herself across the passageway from him. She eyed him thoughtfully, and he could feel it. It wasn't just a trick of his crazy hormones raging through his body. He knew she was sizing him up in some manner, and apparently she liked what she saw. Vic had often teased him about being a late bloomer—like the ugly duckling who'd finally got the attention he deserved. Alan was relieved that his awkward virginity days were over. He turned to face Mischa. "We'll know in a minute if he's set up an ambush," Alan said.

She frowned at him, but it was a friendly scowl. "That's reassuring," Mischa said.

Alan raised his .45 and rested his elbows on his knees. "Sorry. Did you want to wait here until this is over?"

"No. I'd like to see this through," Mischa said, "but since I don't have a pistol, I might hang back a bit. Will you be alright?"

"Now that I'm sitting here, I'm feeling a little dizzy," Alan said.

"You're wounded?"

Alan held his pistol with just his right hand, while he poked around at the wound on the side of his neck with his left thumb and forefinger. "Afraid so. It's a through-and-through, and at the moment it hurts like hell."

"Poor darling. I didn't know."

"This guy's a crack shot, but...I need to get moving. Distraction helps me forget the pain."

Mischa closed her eyes half way as if she were weighing a difficult problem. Then she nodded slowly, almost imperceptibly, and smiled. Alan returned the smile and shoved his shoulder into the door to push it open, before running through to the stern in a low crouch. He veered to his right, the last direction he had seen Vera heading in, and he skirted a small hatch in front of a bigger one, before ducking behind a deck-mounted capstan that the ship's crew used to move the big crane.

Like a knight on a chessboard given free rein to take

as many moves as he needed, Alan zigzagged across the deck in small spurts, using the various pieces of the ship's equipment to work his way around to the far end of the large cargo hatch. Next to the rear mast was a winch apparatus, and beside that was a figure that only could be Vera. Moving carefully, it took Alan a few seconds to cover the last twelve feet to where she was. When he reached her, he rolled into a sitting position and sat with his back next to her, leaning against the winch and its spool of wound wire rope.

Vera reached down and stroked Alan's cheek softly before kneeling next to him. "You're as subtle as a rutting Percheron in high season. You might as well have been shod in new horseshoes on a cobblestone street. We'll need to teach you proper approach techniques later. The only reason someone didn't find and shoot you is because there's so much other noise covering yours."

"Where's our shooter at now?"

"He's backed up against the lifeboat where we hid the antiques. He's waiting for the ship's captain."

"Perfect. There's a gap underneath the lifeboat, big enough that I could get my pistol under. I'll get behind and take a clear shot, point blank."

Vera leaned to the side and peered around the winch for a moment. Then she sat back and looked at Alan directly. "I want him alive," she said.

"Why? He's shot Gunny, and me, and he's holding Jennifer at gunpoint."

"How is Gunny?"

"Not so well. I put him on the bed in Mischa's stateroom. He's in a lot of pain, but he doesn't think anything vital's been hit. How's Jennifer?"

"She's doing fine," Vera said. "I'm proud of her, but there's something else you should know. Our shooter's worth more to this country than a convoy of ships loaded with brass."

"What—in ransom?" Alan asked.

"No. His code name is 'Jaguar,'" Vera said. "I can't tell you much more than that, at least not right now. But he's responsible for any number of black-bag jobs that Japan has successfully pulled off in every U.S. port city, and many overseas. In fact he might be the most successful team handler they've got. The White Dragon only takes directions from him. He's to be taken alive—at all costs."

"Even if the cost means Jennifer?"

Vera sighed and closed her eyes for a moment. "On paper yes, but...I'm not ready to make that kind of sacrifice."

"Neither am I," Alan said. "And speaking of the devil, where the hell is the White Dragon? Why haven't we seen her yet?"

"What makes you think we haven't?"

"Because she's not flying around in her samurai...wait. What do you mean?"

"Where's Mischa? She seemed rather too casual until the bullets started flying her way."

"It can't be her."

"Her English is good—very West Coast. If I heard more, I could tell you."

"She could've shot Gunny and me both and...shit! She followed me down here. I left her in the inside passageway." And she was flirting with me, and me with her, Alan thought—but he kept that to himself.

"I figured as much. You have such a soft spot for Asian beauty. You've got to keep your wits about you, Champ. Now be on your toes. Here comes the captain."

Close to the superstructure, the wheel on a watertight hatch finished spinning, and the hatch popped up and back, noisily flopping open. A head of salt and pepper hair poked through the opening, as the captain climbed out and stood at full height. Suddenly a woman spoke. "Taii Nakauye.

Hideki is over by the life boat."

Captain Nakauye climbed down from the raised hatch and moved to join the woman's dark silhouette. The woman stepped from the shadows to meet him on the harshly lit deck, the fine hairs of her brown fur coat trembled softly in the breeze. It was Mischa, but if she was the White Dragon, what was she doing? Alan wondered.

From beneath the lifeboat, Hideki called to Mischa. "Where is Tiger Lee?"

"I haven't seen her," Mischa said.

"Is it safe to come out?"

"As long as Jennifer is okay," Mischa replied. There was a trace of irritation in her voice.

Behind the winch Alan leaned close to Vera. "What's going on? She knows you're here. We both saw you from above."

"We'll know soon enough," Vera said without taking her eyes away from the scene in front of them.

🐉 ◈ 🐉

Hideki stood and tugged Jennifer up to stand alongside him as his shield. He surveyed the stern area around him, gazing over and past Alan and Vera, who had hunched back down behind the winch. "How can I be sure she isn't down here, now?" he asked.

"One can never be sure of anything, darling, now can they?" Mischa replied.

Hideki stepped from the shadow of the lifeboat. He jostled Jennifer with one hand while he held his pistol near her face with the other. He advanced toward Mischa and Captain Nakauye, who scowled his disapproval at Hideki's rough handling of Jennifer. "What is the meaning of this?" Nakauye barked.

Hideki glared back at Nakauye. "Don't forget who you

297

work for, Captain. The meaning of this is what I say it is, and right now I say this woman is with a group of saboteurs who plan to blow up the Hiye Maru just like the Smith Cove incident."

"Did you catch her swimming naked under the rudder like the Canadian?"

"No." Hideki closed his eyes, as if impatient with a slow child. "She and the others snuck on board, and they've killed two of my guards. Both are still lying on the floor outside my stateroom—along with one of theirs—if you'd like to see. The other saboteurs are aboard your ship running about—probably planting explosives."

"Lies!" Jennifer shouted, suddenly animated. She jerked her arm free from Hideki. "Your men kidnapped me, drugged me, and snuck me into your cabin, where you've also been holding Mischa. My mother has come looking for me—and that lunatic White Dragon said I could go free once you had the brass."

Hideki grabbed for Jennifer's arm but only managed to clasp hold of her sleeve before he addressed the captain. "Taii Nakauye, you know how important this brass is to our country's future. I implore you to set sail immediately. When we reach Canadian waters I'll set the girl free—if she still wants to leave."

Nakauye shook his head and ran his tongue across his lips. "And what about the others—her mother's on board, she says? What about her and those she brought with her? If we set sail with them on board, then we may have caged a dangerous animal without the good sense not to have locked ourselves inside the cage as well."

"Her mother is the notorious Tiger Lee, and if you help me deliver her to Japan I will reward you handsomely— let's say $250,000 American dollars if you can bring her in alive. Or $75,000 for her head."

298

Nakauye's mouth sagged open. "That is a staggering figure—a lifetime of pay—but these are spy games, and I'm not in that business. She," the captain gestured at Jennifer, "and her mother, I presume, are American citizens. How would I ever be able to return to this country if I participated in the kidnapping of its people?"

"Set sail now and I'll pay $300,000 U.S.—win, lose, or draw. Your family's families could live forever on that. You refuse and you'll never captain another ship of mine again."

"But I fear either choice dishonors me and my family."

"I disagree, Taii. Setting sail *and* trapping Tiger Lee on board will make you rich and a national hero."

Captain Nakauye canted his head slightly and glanced to Mischa, as if seeking a second opinion.

Despite the risk, Jennifer tried to pull her sleeve out of Hideki's clutches, but all her struggle did was open up the top of her robe again, exposing much of her chest. "You set sail with my mother and me on board, and she'll leave your ship a derelict. There'll be no survivors to spend all that money."

Hideki let go of her sleeve and dug his hands into Jennifer's hair, pulling her head back as he cocked his arm with the pistol in it, coiling it to backhand Jennifer across the mouth. Mischa suddenly sprang forward and caught Hideki's arm just as his blow was about to land. She easily twisted his hand across his body, pulling him off balance and releasing Jennifer. Mischa leaned in close to him. "I warned you not to hurt her—or to cross me.

38

Mischa slowly released Hideki's hand as Jennifer stepped back and adjusted her robe to re-tighten the sash. At the last second Hideki flicked Mischa's hand away from his with disdain.

"What do you think you're doing, Mischa?" Hideki asked. "My plan works only if everyone plays their part and stays in character—all the way to the end. Getting the brass to the pier and on the ship is only a job half done. You have collected your antiquities and your money, while I still need to get the brass to Japan." Hideki paused and slowly smiled. "And now we have an even greater opportunity, provided by the gracious gods. Surely it is a sign from above that they are with us. We have the chance to capture one of our country's worst enemies, yet you're hindering me, not helping."

Behind Hideki, Jennifer backed away a step and glanced quickly toward the gangway, which had been pushed to an extreme angle by the high tide. She focused on the ship's outer bulkheads, where a heavy hawser snaked its way from two large mooring bits through an opening in the gunwale to tie the ship to the bollard on the pier. Jennifer took another small step backward before she pivoted and dashed toward the ship's side, past the gangway to the gunwale just beyond it.

Catching the surprise on Mischa's face, Hideki jerked around to find Jennifer several steps away from him. He sprang after her and Mischa quickly fell in behind him, her graceful strides matching his powerful short ones.

Jennifer climbed up on the taut hawser and paused to look back at her pursuers. As they neared her daughter, Vera tensed in her hiding spot beside Alan.

"Don't jump, Jenny!" Vera shouted suddenly, unable to stop herself.

Both Mischa and Hideki stopped abruptly, less than ten feet from Jennifer, who had already slid one leg over the gunwale. Hideki spun back around and brought the pistol up to search for a target. Behind him Jennifer also looked for the source of her mother's voice. "With me out of the way, you can do what you need," Jennifer shouted.

The tide shifted and the large line slackened. Jennifer climbed over the rail and stood on top of the hawser. Almost as soon as she settled her weight on the thick rope the tide shifted again and the line sagged further, dropping Jennifer so that only her head and shoulders were visible from the ship's deck. She stumbled slightly toward the ship's railing, grasping for something to hold onto.

Vera's heart was racing, but she forced herself to keep calm and level-headed. "You're too high up. Even if you hit the water, the fall could kill you," she shouted.

Beside Vera, Alan stretched his pistol out at arm's length and lined up the sights on Hideki's upper torso. Vera put her hand on Alan's shoulder and shook her head. "He's lost his advantage. Let's see how this plays out," she cautioned him.

Hideki tracked Tiger Lee's voice and aimed his pistol close to where he thought she might raise her head. While he held his aim in Tiger Lee's general direction, the large ship caught a strong gust of a northerly breeze that swept

301

across Elliott Bay. The cold wind pushed against the ship's overly large broadside, shoving her away from the pier and forcing her to strain at her thick mooring lines, pulling the hawsers so tight that they groaned in pain. The upsurge in the line raised Jennifer waist high against the ship's railing, and then almost as quickly, the lines sagged again. Jennifer fought for traction with her slippers on the rough, wet line, but her feet couldn't find the toehold she needed. Simultaneously, her hands slid over the slick gunwale and she fell onto the thick rope that now sagged limply toward the pier. Jennifer screamed in fear as she rolled over and under the line, holding tightly to the five-inch thick rope with only her crossed legs and bare hands. Her bathrobe draped open and flapped below her, exposing her from the waist down as modesty was disregarded for the sake of survival.

Mischa moved quickly to the ship's railing, while Hideki backed cautiously toward the gunwale, still holding his pistol high. Mischa leaned over the gunwale and desperately tried to reach for one of Jennifer's hands. "Hold on, sweetheart! I'll help you," she cried.

Behind the winch, Vera grasped Alan behind the neck and pulled his face close to hers. "I go left, you go right. I'll draw the fire this time. If you have a clear shot, take it. Disabling them would be preferable. But if Jennifer breaks her neck or drowns, everyone dies—even the cook and the laundry attendants. I'll leave this a ghost ship. Machiavelli will have to write an addendum with my name on it." As she released her grip on his neck, she suddenly lurched forward and kissed him squarely on the mouth. The timing was all wrong, and the kiss wasn't nearly long enough. There was no chance to enjoy it. And damn it all, thought Alan. It better have been for luck, not as a goodbye.

Vera rolled to her left, sprinted and then dove to the deck like a base runner stealing second, landing behind the smaller hatch that the captain had emerged from.

BANG! A shot rang out from Hideki's pistol and slammed into the inside lip of the large hatch protecting Vera.

Savoring Vera's kiss, Alan spun and swung out his .45, catching a glimpse of Hideki hunched over as he tracked Vera with his small automatic. Alan drew his sights on Hideki's right shoulder imagining a hard disabling wound. Before he could squeeze down on the trigger, Mischa interrupted his plans. To Alan's surprise, she stepped away from the gunwale and appeared on Hideki's side, where she grabbed his extended arm and snapped it down fiercely on her knee.

BANG! Hideki's pistol cracked again, but this time the round slammed into the deck, ricocheting away harmlessly.

The pistol fell from Hideki's broken wrist with a clang to the iron deck. Mischa raised Hideki's fractured arm over his head and forced him to take several steps backward until he was leaning over the railing a few feet away from where Jennifer was hanging on for her life. Mischa glared into his bulging eyes. "I told you to leave her for me. Now see what a mess you've created!"

Mischa suddenly kicked her leg behind Hideki and swept his left leg against his right, causing him to fall back onto the railing as she released her grip on him. As Hideki's center of balance shifted, Mischa grabbed his leg and guided it skyward, sending him headfirst over the rail.

Hideki screamed and flailed at the air as he tried to right himself during the fall. Thirty-five feet below his body slapped flatly against the surface of the green foam in the middle of a triangle of frigid water between the ship and the pier. Alan heard the sound of Hideki's landing on the opposite side of the deck. He lowered his pistol and circled around the stern mast and across the deck.

Vera moved out of hiding as well and raced past the captain to pick up Hideki's pistol from the deck. Just as she slid it in her pocket, the ship's alarm blared over its public address system. "Man overboard, starboard side! Man overboard!" The message and alarm repeated itself over and over, first in English and then in Japanese, while those on the stern continued to work for positions that best suited their purposes.

Mischa leaned over the railing to offer encouragement to Jennifer, who was now kicking her bare legs at the thick but limp hawser, trying to hold on. "He's gone, darling," Mischa called. "Can you work your way closer to me?"

The lines continued to droop, and Jennifer reached desperately for Mischa's hand, but her fingers were just beyond Jennifer's grasp. As Jennifer tried to shinny up the hawser closer to the ship, she lost her grip on the thick line and screamed as she began to fall. Mischa pounded the gunwale and gripped it fearfully.

All eyes watched Jennifer's thirty-five foot fall, her arms flailing wildly before she slammed into the water at full force. But a moment later her body popped up to the surface. Her head flopped to the side, but her mouth and nose remained underwater.

Without hesitation, Mischa climbed onto the hawser as the ship shifted and pulled the thick rope taut again. Mischa gazed back at Vera. "Take the ramp!" she shouted.

Before Alan or Vera could reach her, Mischa clasped her hands together above her head and leapt off the thick rope. Alan got to the rail just in time to see Mischa enter the water between Hideki and Jennifer's limp bodies. The fur coat Mischa had been wearing bobbed to the surface. It seemed like several seconds before Mischa followed. When she did she swam toward Jennifer and grabbed her, wrapping her arm over the girl's limp shoulder and across her chest. With a few strong kicks Mischa edged Jennifer toward a mooring log that was tied to the pier supports.

Vera was already crossing the steep gangway to the pier before Alan hoisted himself up and started down the ramp. Halfway down he paused for a moment to watch Mischa and Jennifer below him. Mischa pulled Jennifer to the large log and draped her arms across it. Then Mischa disappeared under the water and heaved Jennifer higher up onto the log. She repeated the process until Jennifer's weight was centered well enough to hold her in place. As soon as it was, Mischa repositioned Jennifer's sopping wet bathrobe to cover her exposed legs and bare bottom.

Sirens wailed on Railroad Way, drawing closer to the pier. Dockworkers, crewmembers, and the curious all raced toward the Hiye Maru as the man overboard alert was repeated. Alan stepped off the gangplank and joined Vera on the pier, where she'd squatted next to a wooden ladder that had permanently been attached for small boats. It was twenty feet away from Jennifer's position on the mooring log.

"Are you alright?" Vera called to Mischa.

Mischa pushed away from the floating log and searched for the face that went with the voice. "I'm freezing, but... she's breathing. I can feel it," Mischa said, and then she rolled onto her stomach, lowering her face into the water, and breast-stroked back to Hideki, whose feet had sunk lower into the frigid water. She grabbed hold of his thick black hair and pulled him over backwards, raising his face out of the water. It was his first chance for fresh air in over a minute. Then she turned on her side and towed him to the same log that held Jennifer.

Alan clasped Vera's forearm. "I'm going down there."

Vera shifted and tightened her grip on Alan's upper arm. "Not you—me. You've got that bullet hole running through your neck, and I don't want this toilet bowl bilge running

305

through you. But thank you, all the same."

Vera stood, and Alan joined her. One of the longshoremen they'd seen earlier on the dock was the first to reach them. Vera met his eyes and addressed him authoritatively. "Would you call the U.S. Marshals and the Port Authorities for us, please?"

"Not the police?" he asked.

Vera shook her head. "Not this time. Tell the marshals they've got an illegal shipment of brass headed for Japan. They'll get in touch with the Coast Guard. We also have a badly wounded agent who needs medical help right away. You've got to do this before this ship sets sail and tosses everything and everyone overboard. Can I trust you?"

The dockworker's mouth went slack for a moment, and then he nodded enthusiastically and gave Vera a cheerful, military-like salute. "Yes, ma'am." He spun on his heels and started running the other way through the crowd that was fast arriving. Vera rolled her eyes and scowled at Alan. "Ma'am," she muttered. "I hate that."

Alan winked back at her. "I'm sure he meant to be polite, Tiger."

Vera half scowled and stepped close to him, handing over two pistols—hers and Hideki's. "Tuck these in your waistband before anyone sees them. Oh, and make sure the safeties are on. I wouldn't want you to shoot off your pecker."

Without waiting for his reply, she grabbed hold of the ladder, swung her leg onto a rung, and began lowering herself closer to the water. She stopped two steps above the mooring log. "As soon as you can, disappear into the crowd—back to the warehouse. Watch to see who I leave with when this is over, and then follow us in the Packard if you can. If for some reason we end up with the police, you stay away. I'll contact you...where?"

"The Sorrento. I had Alice take a room so we could call in."

"Perfect, Champ. You've got a talent for this."

Alan managed a quick smile, nodded his gratitude, and watched her disappear down the ladder. Then he leaned out and eyed the mooring log that was tucked against the pier. Jennifer was still on one end and Mischa continued to push Hideki onto the other end. Less than ten feet away, Mischa's fur coat continued to float on the surface, ignored by all but the small ripples that echoed off the ship's hull, which made the coat seem alive and playful like an otter.

Alan checked on Vera's progress as she let go of the last rung and slipped into the murky water. When the icy saltwater reached her neck, she kicked away from the pier to get a better angle to approach the floating log her daughter and Hideki were draped over. While watching Vera, Alan dropped to his knees and leaned farther out to check on Mischa. She had to be near exhaustion with the heat draining from her body into the icy cold water.

Alan looked carefully but he couldn't see her face. She was tucked in between the pilings and on the opposite side of the big log. The pilings obscured Alan's view, leaving just a glimpse of her arm. Before he could react, Mischa's delicate hand slipped out of sight.

Alan jumped to his feet and ran ten yards to the spot where he'd seen Mischa go down. He lowered himself prone to the deck and leaned out so he could see more clearly, but there was no light past the end of Hideki's hands. Mischa was gone! Alan focused on Vera, who had just reached her daughter. "Mischa's gone under!" he yelled. "She was holding Hideki on the log, but she hasn't come up."

As Vera changed direction, heading for Hideki's end of the log, Jennifer groggily lifted her head and then slid backward into the bitter cold water. Vera shifted her course again, and headed straight for her daughter. In a matter of seconds, she grabbed Jennifer around the waist and tugged her back up to the surface, kicking with strong legs to keep them both afloat. She tried to find something on the log to hold onto, but it was too slick. Like Mischa had done earlier, Vera slipped underneath the water, clasped Jennifer around her upper thighs, and then heaved her up on top of the log.

As Vera started to swim away, a small fireboat with twin engines came around the end of the pier and shone its spotlight down the side of the Hiye Maru to where Vera was treading water. The boat turned and the silhouettes on its small deck draped hand-held fenders over the boat's side as it wedged its way down the gap between the Hiye Maru and the pier.

Twenty minutes later the fireboat backed out from the shadow of the Hiye Maru and was motoring south toward the Washington Street Pier. On the stern, Vera cuddled Jennifer under two layers of wool blankets, each woman trying to warm the other. As soon as they had boarded the boat Vera told the fireboat crew about Mischa's disappearance under the mooring log. The crew scoured the area near where she went down with a searchlight, but there was nothing the firemen could do beyond that, not at night at least. They promised to report the incident to the Police Harbor Unit, who would send down a hardhat diver for a body recovery, most likely in the morning. If they were lucky, the tidal currents wouldn't draw the body too far from where Mischa was last seen.

Vera stroked Jennifer's forehead, pushing the salty hair away from her daughter's face as she tried to sort out the selfless act of courage that the White Dragon had displayed. Her enemy had risked it all to save Vera's daughter and that malicious mess of a master spy, the Jaguar. Unlike the White Dragon's fate, the firemen had been able to resuscitate Hideki, working on him until he spat out a shotglass worth of saltwater and then coughed. The firefighters nodded approvingly at each other and rolled Hideki over.

Vera addressed the boat's captain. "Have you got a pair of handcuffs?"

"No, ma'am."

Vera rolled her eyes and shook her head. "This is more than a water rescue, Captain. The man you have here is a dangerous murderer. Even now there is the very real possibility he'll try to kill you, kill us, escape, or drown himself. How do you propose to subdue him?"

"Are you serious?" the fire captain asked.

"Deadly serious."

"Look, lady, we're not the police. We—"

"Do you have a pistol?"

"Of course not...well, a flair pistol."

"Get it, please—and all the rope you have available. And have your men turn him onto his stomach again, would you?"

While the captain bent over to look through a storage locker, Hideki opened his eyes and blinked them several times. A moment later he shook his head, as if trying to cast out the confusion. He gazed around frantically and clambered to his feet, holding his broken wrist against his side awkwardly. One of the firemen tried to approach with a blanket, but Hideki threw a karate block with his left arm and the fireman backed away.

Hideki rocked unsteadily, like a drunken sailor trying to get his sea legs. He paused for a moment to stare at the stern of the Hiye Maru, which loomed high above them. His mouth fell open in puzzlement.

Jennifer sat erect, suddenly alert. "My turn, Mother," she said while exhaling and shaking her head angrily. She tugged her blanket close around her and stood up. She moved rapidly toward Hideki, and when he looked up, she let fly a powerful side-kick to his midsection. He bent over painfully, buckling at the knees. As his head came down, Jennifer tapped the deck with her toe for balance and brought her knee up sharply, smashing it into his nose and teeth. Hideki went down hard on his backside, banging his head on the steel plates. As he rolled his head in dazed pain, Jennifer plopped on his chest, gathered the blanket around her, and pinned his arms to his sides with her knees.

Two firemen stepped back farther, while their captain inched forward, the flare gun hanging limply at his side. "See here, miss, that's no way—"

Jennifer gazed up at him innocently, reached out, and removed the flare gun from his slack hand. Then she jabbed her left thumb down hard to push Hideki's nose up and back, forcing his mouth open. When it was wide enough, she jammed the flare gun in as far as it would go, initiating Hideki's gag reflex. While he coughed and sputtered, trying not to chew on the large barrel, Jennifer glanced at her mother and the firemen. She winked at the captain. "You think I'm dangerous? Try my mother when she's pissed. Now get me some rope before this thing goes off and you have a huge mess to clean up!"

Vera knelt next to Jennifer. "All right young lady," she whispered. "He had it coming, and now you've had your fun. We got the Jaguar and the White Dragon is gone. You did your part and can be proud. No more showing off though. No one should know what you can do, especially Alan."

"So this is really the Jaguar?" Jennifer asked, working the pistol inside Hideki's mouth as deep as it would go.

"It is, dear."

"He isn't so much. I could have taken him earlier, but I wanted to be sure. And since I didn't have an escape plan, I waited for you—I knew you'd come after all."

◇◇

Marshal Dosch and his partner Jack Quilliam met the fireboat at the once famous landing on Washington Street Pier, which had a lowered dock for small craft boats. Rather than tying up the boat, two firemen stood on the dock and held the lines taut at opposite ends, while the twin diesels idled noisily. The two marshals nodded to the captain, stepped onboard, and greeted Vera enthusiastically. She introduced them to Jennifer, who was curled up under her blankets, and then she pointed at Hideki, who they'd almost stepped on. He was face down on the deck with a blanket draped completely over his head and upper body, and the better part of a coil of rope wrapped around his middle, legs, and hands.

Dosch glanced down at Hideki and then grinned at Vera. "Who taught you how to tie a knot, sailor?"

Vera smiled back at him. "I wanted to make sure he wasn't going anywhere."

"Who—or what—is it you have there?"

Vera motioned for the marshals to lean in close, conspiratorially. "This is the one Naval Intelligence really wants. He doesn't get a potty break until they've had a chance to debrief him. And no one should know we have him, including the crew of this boat. In fact, there shouldn't even be a record that we were here."

Dosch nodded. "I think their trip log will say that they stood by to assist the Port Authorities with a possible water rescue," he said.

"Almost, but there's a Japanese woman who's still missing," Vera said. "She fell off the ship and made it as far as the mooring log before she went under. The police will be sending a diver for her body in the morning. The firemen can report that much and say that some unidentified citizens jumped in the water and tried to help her, but—leave it at that. Anyway, how long before the Port Authorities arrive for their brass?"

Dosch glanced skyward, as if praying for a better answer, and grinned. "Those old boys keep banker's hours... probably forty minutes at least."

"As soon as you got a big enough posse for a boarding party, one of my men needs medical aid—he's got a gunshot wound to his chest. He's up in a stateroom in First Class, port side. Two dead Japanese agents are outside his stateroom, but their bodies might be gone by the time you get there. If they are, the carpets should still be soaked with blood—there was a lot of that."

Dosch rolled his eyes. "Alright, we'll take your prisoner off your hands and square it with the fire boys," he said.

🐦 ◉ 🐦

While Marshals Dosch and Quilliam spoke with the fireboat crew, Vera helped Jennifer up the ramp to the pier. Alan flashed the Packard's headlights at Vera from across the street. She nodded back at him and pointed to a spot down from the dock's entrance. Alan put the car in gear and crept noisily across the long timbers laid between the railroad tracks. He parked as close as he could to shorten

312

their walk, and he held the door for Vera as she assisted her weary daughter into the car. Climbing in beside Jennifer, Vera propped her daughter's head softly against her shoulder.

Alan put the car in gear, heading south to Jackson, where he would turn toward First South. He had the choice of heading up the hill to the hospitals or east to Chinatown. He adjusted the mirror so he could see Vera and Jennifer. "Where to, ladies?" he asked.

"For your bullet wound, I'd say the hospital. We'll be all right, but I'm worried about you. Have you taken a look at it yet? You don't want to end up like Riki."

Taking his hand off the steering wheel, Alan cautiously probed his neck with his thumb and forefinger. Blood soaked the collar of his sweater around the hole, but more of it trailed down his back. He winced. "Vic told me hospitals have to report gunshot wounds. Do we want to risk that?"

Vera met his eyes in the mirror and shook her head. "I could do my best to sterilize it and put a field dressing on it," she said, "but you might be better off with your Chinese friend and his herbs."

Alan stopped at the light at First Avenue and stared at her in the mirror. "I'd trust you to do the mending on this. You know that."

Vera smiled. "I know Champ, but I'm going to be busy tending to Jenny," she motioned to her daughter who already seemed to be fast asleep. "You'll need to have somebody taking your temperature and checking it regularly—every two hours or so—for infection. At the first hint of anything, you'll need to get real medical help, and you won't be able to tell them where you got the quack-job patch. Don't risk it."

Alan nodded slowly, while he made another turn. "What I did to Vic's shoulder was a lot worse than this, and Papa San fixed him up just fine. 'Good as new!' Vic would say."

Alan turned the big Packard east and started up Madison

Street. He glanced at Vera's eyes in the mirror. "I need to give Alice an update, but it would take as long to find a payphone as it would to stop by. Do you mind?"

Vera met his eyes and then half closed hers for a moment. Was she just tired, or was she irritated with him he wondered? "No, not at all," Vera said finally. "She's part of the team now. Let's keep her updated."

Alan turned onto Terry Street and pulled into the hotel's circular drive, stopping just past the canopied entrance that circled around a tiered fountain. As he opened the car door, Vera stopped him. "Alan, I mean this in the nicest way, but you don't look...you're not at your best right now, and this is a very fine hotel. You go up to the door like that and the doorman will think you're a hobo riding the rails."

Alan let go of the door handle and twisted around, his eyebrows knitted in a frown. "What do you suggest?" he asked.

"Ditch the knit hat, put on your fedora, and cover that sweater with a coat...just for starters."

"What? I'm that ugly?"

"Ugly isn't a problem for you, honey, but looking like a rough-cut stevedore in the land of gentry is."

"I've been here before and never had a problem," Alan protested.

"Not looking like this you haven't," she said, frowning at his attire. "Do what you can with your clothes, and then I'll touch you up."

Alan put on his hat and then paused with his coat. "The blood that's soaked through my sweater will get on the liner."

"It'll dry clean out, and if it doesn't, I'll buy you a new one."

Alan chuckled and pushed his tongue across the inside of his cheeks, like he wanted to stick his tongue at her but didn't. He stepped around the back of the car and opened

Vera's door, presenting himself for inspection. She ran her eyes over him completely, smirked, and shook her head. "You have a trail of dried blood running across the back of your right hand, and your left hand is disgusting." Vera sighed. "I suppose you'll just need to wear gloves and avoid the hired help."

🐉 ⊕ 🐉

As Alan neared the Sorrento's main doors the dapper doormen in a beige ensemble stepped in front to grab the brass pull door handle. Was he blocking the door or preparing to open it? Alan wondered. The doorman twisted his head a few degrees and smiled thinly. "Will it be just the gentleman, or are there more in your party?" He asked, indicating the Packard with a tilt of his head.

Alan reached out a gloved hand, palming a twenty-dollar bill the same way Vic had taught him to do. "I'm Mr. Brinkman's driver, and he asked me to check on arrangements for an out-of-town guest of the union's."

The doorman shook Alan's gloved hand, accepted the tip, and opened the door. "Of course, for Mr. Brinkman. I do hope he's well." Without waiting for a response, he continued, "Then perhaps the gentleman would like to use the house phones to the right of the door?"

Alan read the doorman's nameplate and met his eyes. "Yes, that would be sufficient."

Passing through the double doors, Alan stopped at the house phone, directly across the entrance from the concierge's unoccupied desk, and glanced back at the doorman. As he surreptitiously snuck a peek at the contents in his cupped hand, and slid the tip into his pocket. Alan hope'd he hadn't smeared blood on the man's soft gloves during the exchange.

It was still early in the evening and guests filled the

315

lobby, a cozy extension of the Hunt Club's cocktail lounge. Alan rang the front desk, which was only thirty feet across the wood-paneled lobby. This was doubtless the less intrusive approach, and there was no sense in upsetting their sensibilities. "This is Mr. Brinkman's driver," Alan said. "Would you ring up the room he reserved? I believe his assistant is waiting for the guests from Boston."

"Would that be Miss Mahoney?"

"I believe so."

"One moment please."

On the third ring, Alice picked up the phone. "Hello?"

"Miss Mahoney, this is Mr. Brinkman's driver, Alan Stewart."

There was a slight hesitation on Alice's end. "Oh, Mr. Stewart, yes. I'm still waiting for our guests, and I'm not sure why the delay."

There was a metallic click as the operator rang off. Alan craned his neck to see if he could locate the operator behind the registration desk, but he couldn't. The operator at a nice hotel like this wouldn't keep her job long if she were a snoop like the one in Alice's apartment, but there was no sense in taking chances. "Alice, I've got to keep this brief."

"I understand."

"Everyone on our team's fine—at least they'll be okay."

"What do you mean okay?"

"I mean we're fine, but I've got to make another delivery first."

"I see, and what should I do about this wonderful room, Mr. Stewart?" Alice asked.

"It'd be a shame to let it got to waste, don't you think?" Alan replied.

"Why Mr. Stewart, I'm shocked you'd think...that the view here is better than from my apartment."

"Is it?"

"Alan, it's gorgeous! I have us a luxury suite, right under the penthouse on the west side, and I don't have neighbors that I'll have to see on a daily basis. When can you come up, Silly Goose?"

"Maybe a couple more hours. After I deliver two guests to their home, I'm in need of a little equipment repair—"

"Alan Stewart, are you injured?"

Alan paused a moment, trying to think of a diversion, but it didn't come. He was glad to hear her voice, gratified she cared enough to worry about him. "I need a couple more stitches, and then I'll be good as new."

"Couple more?"

"Yes and it's not a problem. What room are you in?

Alan stopped the Packard in front of Vera's apartment building, but neither Vera nor Jennifer stirred. Alan checked in the mirror, and Vera's eyes were closed, her head tilted back and her mouth slightly open. Jennifer's head was in Vera's lap, and she was asleep as well.

Alan walked around to Vera's side of the car and opened the door quietly. He leaned inside to wake the two sleeping beauties but then decided it was a shame to disturb their slumber. Lord knows they need their rest, he thought. His face was less than twelve inches from Vera's, and he stared at her full lips, craving them again. The kiss earlier had only hinted at what could still come. He leaned closer and hesitated, wondering if a stolen kiss would be a sin. Would she mind? Would she get angry?

Vera's hand was suddenly behind his neck, pulling him forward, firm but gentle. The easy movement almost made him lose his balance, but he grabbed the doorframe to keep from falling inside and landing on top of her. Her lips reached up and brushed against his, rubbing back and forth, teasing. After a moment she nibbled softly on his lips with her teeth, and then she relaxed her grip on him. "That's what you wanted, wasn't it, Champ?"

318

Alan brushed his cheek against hers. "No it's not; I want more," he said and then pulled back to stare into her eyes.

Vera shifted Jennifer's head slightly off her lap and drew Alan closer. "Be careful of tigers. You never know when they're going to bite," she said. She tugged on his neck again and kissed him with her lips separated so their tongues met. He kissed her back, just as hard as she'd kissed him, savoring the taste of her. His right hand caressed her neck and chin, gently stroking back and forth. He loved that feature on women: long necks and smooth jaw lines that craved kisses.

Alan put his hand on Vera's shoulder and slowly pushed himself away. He tried to read her face for cues, to see if he was playing into a fantasy, a feud, or the real thing. She was his dream woman, but he wasn't about to be played for a fool. After all, tigers were beautiful but dangerous, and she was like having a full-grown man-eater as a pet—one that could never be completely domesticated.

Vera smiled at him through hooded eyes. "You naughty boy. It's been a long time since I've had a kiss like that."

Alan returned the smile and tugged at the brim of his hat, a casual salute. "We better get you both inside."

Alan went around the car to the opposite side and opened Jennifer's door. He slid her across the seat and hoisted her into his arms. Vera met him on the curb and made sure the blanket was tucked around Jennifer to cover her decently. As they took a few steps up the brick walkway, Jennifer opened her eyes and smiled at Alan. "Put me down, please," she said. "I'm not a baby and your neck's injured."

Alan paused at the front steps and did as she requested. Vera opened the door to her building and Jennifer led the way up to the apartment. Once they were all inside, Jennifer slumped against a wall in the hallway while Vera pointed Alan to the bathroom he'd used before. "Strip down to your waist and wash around your wound as much as you can

319

with soap and warm water—the warmer the better, but try not to get any into the wound. If it's stopped bleeding, and I can stitch you up, then you'll need to keep it dry for a few days. If it's still leaking, you'll need your Chinese friends to patch you up. I'll put on a kettle of hot water and be back in a few minutes."

🐉 ◉ 🐉

Vera took Jennifer to her end of the converted apartment, where she had her own bath, complete with a claw-footed tub. Jennifer slouched on the tub's edge, while Vera turned the taps up full blast. "You should rinse off the saltwater before you fill the tub. Then you can settle for a soak in clean water. After I've stitched Alan up, I'll come back and help you wash your hair."

Jennifer rocked forward and leaned her head against her mother's side while Vera tested the water temperature. "What are your plans for him, Mother?"

"You saw us kissing?" Vera asked.

"The electricity from that lightning bolt curled my toes, and I wasn't even involved," Jennifer said.

"It was something, wasn't it?" Vera said dreamily. "But are you asking about now or in the future?"

"Either one."

Vera took a step back and motioned for Jennifer to stand. She removed the blanket wrapped around her and helped her step into the tub. "I haven't decided yet," Vera said.

"Is that fair to him? I quite like him and don't want to see him hurt."

Vera draped the blanket over her arm, while Jennifer knelt down in the tub and ran warm water through her hair. Vera set the blanket aside to help untangle a clump of hair. "Hurting him is not in my plans."

"This is an awful lot like *Tristan and Isolde*. Remember?

You two have been slipped a magic potion meant for someone else that you drank by mistake. This has courtly love written all over it—and all the trappings that go with it."

Vera frowned at Jennifer but didn't respond.

"He worships you, not loves you, and you do exactly the same with him. I don't think anybody really knows what love is at my age—his age—but you do...at least in theory."

Vera shook her head, frowning. "When you've got something on your mind you spout *Tristan and Isolde*," she said. "He does the same, only with him it's Machiavelli or the like. There's a common thread between you two."

"He reads?" asked Jennifer.

"It appears so—from the classics to detective magazines, I never know which one he'll quote next."

"Then I like him even more. But I'm serious, Mother. This could be heated passion—maybe even for the both of you, but neither of you'll have anything when it's burnt out. I say you stay on your pedestal and keep him on his. Save your friendship—for all our sakes."

"When'd you get so old on me?"

"It's not that I'm thinking old, Mother, I'm thinking smart. You've taught me that. Don't hurt him. He's not going to replace my father, no matter how much he—"

"Stop that, would you please? That hurts."

"Alright, I'm sorry, but I'm looking out for your own good."

Jennifer finished rinsing and slowed the water taps, so the tub would drain. Once it did she put the plug in place and turned the taps on again. She pulled her knees up to her chest while the bath filled. "I love you, Mom, and I don't want you getting hurt either. At twenty-one he's likely to change his mind several times before he settles down."

Vera leaned into the tub and swirled the water with one hand, blending it so that the hot water wouldn't burn Jennifer's legs. She gave her a half-hearted smile and sighed deeply. "He's beautiful, isn't he?" Vera asked.

"He's not a fragile fop, Mother, he's handsome—meaning that he's virile, brave, clever, strong, and fierce."

"Like his father," Vera said.

"But he *could* work on his confidence some," Jennifer added.

Vera smiled thoughtfully. "I'm not making you any promises. I have my own desires, and I don't think I even understand them all. I certainly can't rationalize them."

"I'm just saying...." Jennifer smirked and shook her head, apparently deciding her warning had been enough. "Another thing, Mother?"

"Yes, darling?"

"If Mischa was the White Dragon, why'd she turn on the Jaguar to save me?" Jennifer asked.

"I don't know that I can answer that," Vera said. "Maybe she didn't even know why when she did it. She might have acted on some primal or maternal instinct she felt toward you, though I didn't see that quality in her. It will take me awhile to sort it all out." Vera paused for a moment to collect her thoughts. "You know how disappointed you get when you find out someone you once admired can't be trusted? It's almost the same as finding out someone you despised and feared is actually quite human. It changes everything you once thought about them, makes it a lie somehow. Then you have to come up with a new way to define them."

"I felt something with her—it was like we clicked and would have been good friends if the world were different. Were you worried, Mother?"

"When I saw her on stage in the theater staring at you, there was something there—"

"Not sexually—" Jennifer interrupted.

"I thought that at first, but now I'm not so sure. It was more as if she wanted you to be hers—as a possession of some sort. It might have been that she wanted you as her daughter, or maybe it was another form of your chivalrous love. And maybe it was a mixture of all of that."

"She might have been a great friend, if...." Jennifer let her words trail off and shook her head silently.

<<<<<<<<<<<<<<<<<<<<<<<<<<<<<<<<<<<<<<<<<<<<<<<<<<<<<<<<

After hoisting Hideki up onto the mooring boom,
Mischa took a deep breath and slid under the saltwater to
a point where the light no longer penetrated. Sinking lower
and rapidly losing body heat, she finally kicked explosively,
like a manta ray that had been playing possum on the ocean
floor until its prey drew within striking distance. She came
back to the surface and gulped in air, her lungs screaming
for oxygen. With very little light filtering through under the
pier, she was forced to feel her way through the maze of
pilings that were heavily encrusted with jagged barnacles
all the way up to the high tide mark. The sharp edges tore
hungrily at her skin and clothing, but her biggest concern
continued to be the freezing cold water. If she didn't get out
of it soon she would die.

Mischa prayed the stories she heard were true about
the catacomb's entrance being under this pier. Rumors were
that as the seven seawalls moved incrementally outward
into the harbor, the city engineers repeatedly sealed the
catacomb entrances they discovered—only to have the next
wave of immigrants excavate them again, restoring the lost
entrance. Seven was Mischa's lucky number.

Mischa felt hopeful that the entrance would be there

because she had smelled the salt breezes so often while inside the catacombs, wafting all the way up to Japan Town and the Panama Hotel. She cursed herself for having never explored the tunnels and darkness this far to the west. It was so inky black under the pier, nearly impossible to see, and there were no clues to help her. She both feared and hated the dark. That was why she preferred to stay up late, working the night away with the lights on. When she finally went to bed she left a night-light on in her room, an indulgence for her nerves that she never spoke of to anyone.

As she floated through the pilings, working her way toward the seawall, she found a rhythm and pattern to the positioning of the posts. She stole glances to her left at the Hiye Maru, gauging her progress. Her eyes began to adapt to the darkness, and the silhouettes of the pilings gradually became clearer, as long as she stayed fairly close to the edge of the pier.

Her plans didn't change as the twin-diesel boat rumbled closer to her, working its way to the survivors she had left on the log. She had gone too far to turn back and be rescued along with them. Now that her identity had been compromised it would be better if they believed she'd drowned.

After what seemed like an eternity, she worked her way to the front of the ship, not far from the seawall. It was easier now to find her way, but the terrible chill was taking its toll, draining the energy from her. She knew the stories of sailors falling overboard and dying from the cold well before they came close to drowning.

She had to keep moving, gambling that the portal would even be there. If it wasn't, she wouldn't have enough energy to pursue any other option, and that's where they would find her remains some day. There was also the chance that she would finally get to the entrance and find it closed and covered with a grating—like a portcullis draped over a castle entrance. She shivered. She couldn't think about that now.

Finally her foot touched the seawall. It felt more like a pile of debris made from boulders, broken slabs of concrete, and dirt. The rocks were slimy with algae, intermixed with sharp barnacles. She was grateful she still had slippers on her feet. She found a steady perch and began pulling herself up toward the cement wall that extended down into the rubble. She worked her way along it and went deeper under the pier into the blackness she abhorred. She climbed to the top of the rubble and felt the stinging cold breeze knife its way through her wet clothing, sharply taking her breath away.

She steeled herself to the pain and forged onward until she found a lowered platform—the planks to the catwalk under the pier, only an arm's length away. She patted it with her hand to be sure it was what she hoped and exhaled a noisy sigh of relief. She reached with her other hand to grab the cross boards and pull herself up. The air here was slightly warmer, and she could almost smell Japan Town's aromas.

Within reach there was an opening right above her wrist. It was brick lined, but there were no steps to climb and nothing to grab onto to hoist herself. Mischa felt along the dank opening, hoping to find something useful that would help or inspire her, but still there was nothing.

Mischa stepped back along the wall and gazed desperately back toward the Hiye Maru. From her vantage point she could see the broken slabs of concrete she had been walking on. They were discarded pieces of building foundations from long ago, and some of the chunks were small enough that she thought she could move them. She would have to stack several of them, but there was no other choice. She didn't have the strength remaining to pull herself up onto to the catwalk unaided.

She quickly set about the task, because the clock and the cold were working against her. She had to make the most of what energy remained. The pile of rubble steadily grew, piece by piece. Finally she stood on the pile, grabbed the end post and kicked her leg up, catching a toehold on the wall. She slapped her other hand around the post and worked her way up the timber until she was in a position to launch herself into the tunnel.

At last she stood erect in the walkway to the catacombs, the underground arteries to Japan Town. She paused for a moment to catch her breath and savor the small victory. Would there be more, or was this her last hurrah? Near the end of the catwalk, she probed with the tip of her toe until she found the edge of the plank. There was no portcullis to block her. It was time to step off and plunge into the darkness of the tunnel. She shook her head, resigning herself to what she felt was her only option.

Mischa took a deep breath of cold air and stepped onto firm brick pavers. With her hand straight out she touched the wall to her right. The only strategy she could think of was to use the wall as a guide and hope there weren't divergent tunnels that led into the mazes under Pioneer Square, where the derelicts had found their own entrances and made unsanitary encampments. She was determined to follow her nose, hoping it would guide her east, up the hill to her home.

Ten feet into the tunnel, Mischa's hand bumped against a wall timber. She frantically patted around the timber and found a clutch of lanterns—not just one, but several. Thank the gods! She took one from its peg and shook it briskly, listening to the wondrous sound of kerosene oil sloshing back and forth inside. Now if only she could find a match. Surely there'd be some here. Mischa rolled her lower lip back and sucked on it for a moment. Think high up. Earlier travelers would have made sure that matches were stashed above in case of flash flooding in the tunnels or other mishaps. Mischa patted along the wall, hoping for a shelf of some kind, but there weren't any. She set the lantern down at her feet, and as she did, her foot bumped solidly against a kerosene can that was so full it didn't budge—another good omen. She used both hands to search her way up the sides of the large timbers, but there were no notches or shelves. Then it occurred to her to check the top of the timbers, maybe at the corners where there might be a crevice. Just as she guessed there was a wedged crevice where the timber braced the beam. Something slid away from her fingers. With her other hand she reached around the timber and felt the firm edges of a large matchbox. "Thank the heavens and all that is in them!" she cried with relief.

Mischa brought the matches down and shook them, grateful that it had the heft of a mostly full box. She squatted next to the lantern, dragging it a few feet away from the kerosene can. She carefully slid open the box of matches, feeling first to see if the opening was on the top or the bottom. She had guessed right; it was facing up—maybe another positive sign. She took out a match and scraped it along the strike pad. It sprung to life, illuminating the beautiful brick walls, which looked like they had been made of recycled brick pavers. She adjusted the wick on the lantern, slid the glass up, and lit the lamp. Then she lowered the glass and held the lantern out in front of her. The way ahead of her was clear, and it promised to be warmer than where she was now.

It was near 9:00 p.m. when Alan returned to the Sorrento Hotel, parking the union's big Packard on the street. Clean and in his own clothes, he touched his hand to his fedora as he passed the doorman and smiled. "Evening," he called cheerfully.

"Good evening, sir."

The stitches Vera had put in both sides of Alan's neck tugged uncomfortably at the sinew and taut skin around them. She had given him aspirin and suggested that a few shots of scotch would help him forget his pain, but after bringing the subject up, she didn't offer him the drink she had once suggested.

Unlike the frisky Vera from earlier in the car, she remained aloof while patching up his wounds. Adding to Alan's disappointment, this time she didn't strip to her underwear and parade her assets in front of him. Now that he wanted this to happen and was ready for it, he was a little miffed that it didn't. Was it because her daughter—his half-sister—was somewhere in the apartment? Is that what changed things? As soon as he had the thought, he was ashamed that he did. Alice was his girl after all, and he had a fresh invitation to see her tonight...in a luxury hotel room.

Alan couldn't sort it through in the time he was in Vera's apartment. She hadn't given him any clues so he tried to convince himself it was for the best, but it wasn't working—he still wanted her. There were probably other empty platitudes he could recite in an attempt to make himself feel better about forgetting her, but nothing came to mind. He ached for her. And he also wondered what he might have done to anger her.

Alan nodded at the receptionist working the front desk and passed by the lobby to the elevators. As soon as he stepped into an open elevator his mood changed. On his way to the fourth floor, he became almost giddy with anticipation—or maybe it was delirium caused by exhaustion and hunger. There was a lot tumbling through his head that he had trouble sorting into proper categories—too much coming in at one time.

Alan stared at the elevator floor and tried to shake Vera out of his mind, but it just wasn't happening. As far as memories go, the ones of her had a pleasant, lingering, aftertaste. He hoped they would always be there for him, because it was the kind of misery one could still enjoy, wallow in, and get drunk over.

As the elevator slowed, Alan's stomach growled, protesting his body's lack of sustenance—but even this was a form of relief from the visions haunting him. He hoped Alice was as starved as he was. He'd heard the food in The Hunt Club was fabulous, but oddly at that moment he had a craving for Papa San's chow mein. For an instant he entertained the thought of leaving this uncertainty with Vera and Alice and racing down to Chinatown, where life was safe, predictable, and free of emotional entanglements.

But that's not what he really wanted, was it? As the elevator door opened, Alan inhaled and set his brow low with determination. Alice was the one he really wanted.

330

Vera had the innate ability to draw him in with her powerful sexual allure, and their one great kiss had been more than spectacular, but it was Alice's snuggling he wanted. She shared his sense of wonderment, and it was her affection that satisfied him.

Walking down the hallway Alan slowed as he approached the room. He wanted to say the right thing, and for Alice to know that he respected her no matter what. He inhaled deeply and knocked softly on the door, hoping not to attract the attention of the neighbors. It took a few seconds for Alice to reach the door, and when she did she opened it calmly, like she was expecting room service. When she saw Alan her green eyes flashed wide and sparkled more than he had ever seen them do before.

Without saying a word, Alice's bare arm stuck out from a bathrobe sleeve and grabbed him, tugging him inside. As soon as Alan cleared the threshold she shoved the door shut and pushed him against the wall. She held him at arm's length and checked him up and down, from head to toe. Satisfied that all of his necessary body parts were in place, she grabbed his lapels, pulled him close, and stood high on her tiptoes to kiss him.

Alan removed his hat, leaned into her and met her waiting lips, glad she was eager for him. He wrapped his arms around her and hugged her closely, almost squeezing the air out of her lungs. She was the third woman he'd seen in a bathrobe in the past few hours, but this time he wasn't embarrassed at what charms might spill out. In fact he hoped something would, and that it would very soon.

After a long moment, Alice pushed Alan away to examine his face thoroughly, and then she drew close again and kissed him tenderly. He dampened his own fire and relaxed enough to enjoy the moment, his hands running up and down the back of her robe. He found there were no lines where undergarments should be. He ran his hand farther down her back and across her bottom, and still there were no belts or seams to betray underclothing. This time she didn't object to his tactile explorations, as she had the last time he tried it in her apartment. He reached up and guided her head next to his chin for a snuggle. "Alice Mahoney, it would appear you're naked under this robe."

"Of course silly, I took a bubble bath while I was waiting for you," she said. "I had to have something to do, and I got tired of listening to the radio."

"So if I were to tug on this sash, you might fall out of it?" Alan asked.

Alice smiled playfully. "You should see the bathroom they have. I filled the tub to the top and just soaked. I was trying not to think about what you'd done to yourself." Her smile sparkled with little girl excitement. That was what he wanted to see—that imperfect innocence he loved and missed, the country girl with big city smarts, who enjoyed all of her discoveries and could thrill him in the process. But then she could entertain him just by turning the pages of a book, like the time she read passages from Faulkner out loud to him. He leaned down and sniffed near her ear. "You smell...delicious."

Alice pushed him away to take another look at Alan's face. Her eyes circled until they latched onto the knot above his eye and then the injury above it—the seam of stitches on his forehead. Her mouth fell open, as if the pain of his injury wounded her inside. "Alan Stewart! What have you done there?" she asked.

"I ran into a wall the other night."

"The other night? Then what was it you were having done tonight? Did you get more stitches from that same fumble-handed quack?"

He grinned sheepishly. "Ah...yes, but there's a story to

this you should hear first," he said.

Alice grabbed him by his coat sleeve and led him over to the sofa. "Show me where they are." It was a clear, unwavering order.

Alan chuckled, not at all upset with her bossiness. "It's above the collar bone. They call it a trapezes muscle...I'll have to take my shirt off."

Alice pushed him onto the sofa and climbed up into his lap, straddling him, with her knees on the cushions. She began working at his buttons. "I'll help you then."

Alan arched his back to pull his shirt out from his pants, while Alice slowly undid button number two. Her bathrobe scooped open wide and deep, exposing her chest down to her navel. Her breasts were full and well shaped, begging to be squeezed, but he held back, forcing himself to be patient. He didn't want to scare her away. He leaned back farther and gazed down the outside of her robe to where her strong legs stuck out from underneath the fabric, pinning him to the sofa. This was a battle he hoped would never end.

Alan relaxed and let his hands drop to her sides, sliding them over her hips and onto her smooth legs. Alice paused for just a second and glanced up at him. She smiled wryly, grabbed the top of her robe, and pinched it back together, clutching it between her breasts with feigned contempt. "You're not seeing any more of these until I've seen yours."

Alan grinned wolfishly, let go of her legs, and began tugging clumsily at a button. He played to the pain in his shoulder. "I'm having trouble concentrating. It's the bullet hole."

"Bullet hole?" she asked with her eyes flaring wide. "Alan Stewart!"

"Yeah but it could have been worse...much worse."

Alice shook her head with mock disgust and took over for him, working on button number three. When she started on the fourth he reached over the top of her arms and flicked her robe open again. She slapped at his hand, playfully. "Would you behave, Alan?"

Alan laughed, almost in a cackle. She started on button number five, and he reached over her arms and pulled gently at the top of her robe, pulling it back softly so that it draped loosely from her shoulders, exposing her upper body and breasts completely. His eyes widened dreamily and his nostrils flared.

Alice gazed up at his face, and Alan somehow managed to take his eyes off her torso long enough to meet her green eyes, which flashed brightly. He felt a little guilty but was still grateful for what she allowed him to see. By God she was beautiful—one of the Almighty's finest creations.

Alice smiled impishly. "Honestly, Alan!" She shook her shoulders and let the robe slide down her back and over her arms. Then she pulled her hands out of the sleeves and slowly returned to work on his buttons. "There, you happy now?"

And for the moment at least, Alan had to say that he was.

❧ THE END ❧

Neil Low is a captain with the Seattle Police Department and the agency's first commander of its new Ethics and Professional Responsibility Section. Other areas he has commanded include: Homicide and Violent Crimes, Internal Affairs, Domestic Violence and Sexual Assault. He is a Vietnam veteran and a cum laude graduate of the University of Washington's Bothell campus, where he also wrote for the school's weekly newspaper, *The UW Bothell Commons*. A Seattle native, he now lives in Everett with his wife and three daughters.

Also by Neil Low

THICK AS THIEVES

from Tigress Publishing

337

ACKNOWLEDGEMENTS

Although writing is often a lonely pursuit in which authors, such as me, spend our lives pecking away at computers, the end product would not have been as polished as it should without the help of several people along this journey. In my case I am eternally grateful and wish to acknowledge the many who made this dream come true. First and foremost is my wife Lesley and our three daughters, Amanda, Michelle and Meghan, whom I thank for their patience and acceptance of my passion. The longer that I am away from school the more I appreciate the help and encouragement I received while I was there. I continue to be immensely grateful to my University of Washington instructors, such as Rebecca Brown and Carole Glickfeld, both wonderful writers in their own right, and of course I cannot forget the wonderful professors from the Bothell campus who generously gave of their office hours, answering hundreds of questions and offering encouragement.

In alphabetical order they are: Constantine Boehler, Michael Goldberg, David Goldstein, Gen McCoy and William Seaburg. Obvious to anyone picking up this book is the wonderful artwork. Special thanks goes to Steve Montiglio for the original cover art and interior design. I also wish to acknowledge the first draft readers who eagerly read this creation in its early stages and offered critical advice and the occasional challenge. They include: Terrie Johnston, Carole Jordan, Mary and David Tilbury, and Dawn Todd. Then there are special fans like John Fowler, Myrle Carner, Larry Quilliam, and Jack Dosch who have been steadfast. Special thanks again to my chiropractor, Dr. Jeffrey Abrams, whose wonderful stories of South Philadelphia inspired some of my characters' traits. And of course none of this would have been possible without the expert help and guidance of my publisher, the very wonderful Kristen Morris and her chief editor Amelia Boldaji. Again, to all of you, thank you.